Is the human race approaching the final days?

Is the world beyond healing?

Will we be given one last chance
to save ourselves?

VIRGIN

Author Mary Elizabeth Murphy has created a thought-provoking thriller with a unique and startling premise. As the millennium's end draws near, the newspapers report countless stories of spiritual sightings. Murphy takes this phenomenon one step further—by imagining an event of apocalyptic proportions. A priest and a nun discover the remains of the Virgin Mary. And into our modern world of pain and suffering comes the light of hope. The wonder of healing. The return of miracles. And something more . . .

A dark omen that could mean a new beginning
—or the final battle.

**"A gripping page-turner . . . I couldn't
put it down."**
—F. Paul Wilson

VIRGIN

MARY ELIZABETH MURPHY

BERKLEY BOOKS, NEW YORK

VIRGIN

A Berkley Book / published by arrangement with
the author

PRINTING HISTORY
Berkley edition / January 1996

All rights reserved.
Copyright © 1996 by Mary Elizabeth Murphy.
This book may not be reproduced in whole or in part,
by mimeograph or any other means, without permission.
For information address: The Berkley Publishing Group,
200 Madison Avenue, New York, New York 10016.

ISBN: 0-425-15124-7

BERKLEY®
Berkley Books are published by The Berkley Publishing Group,
200 Madison Avenue, New York, New York 10016.
BERKLEY and the "B" design
are trademarks belonging to Berkley Publishing Corporation.

PRINTED IN THE UNITED STATES OF AMERICA

10 9 8 7 6 5 4 3 2 1

To my husband,

without whom this book would not have been possible

CONTENTS

VIRGIN

Part I

Scrolls

After they banished me from Jerusalem, I wandered south, leaving my position and my inheritance behind. What need had I of money? I wished to be dead.

I tore my blue robe with the three-striped sleeve and cast it from me. I traded it to a beggar for the filthy, louse-infested rags on his back. But the lice have not bitten me. They deserted the rags as soon as I donned them.

Even the vermin will have nothing to do with me!

FROM THE GLASS SCROLL
ROCKEFELLER MUSEUM TRANSLATION

1991
Winter

1

Israel
The Judean Wilderness

"Don't spare that switch, Achmed," Nabil called back from the lead position where he played the flashlight along the slope ahead of them. "Getting there second is as good as not getting there at all."

Achmed swatted the donkey's flanks with greater vigor as he and his brother pulled and drove the reluctant beast up the incline into the craggy foothills of the Judean Wilderness. Behind him the parched land sloped away to the Dead Sea; ahead lay the mountains, forbidding during the day, terrifying at night. Countless stars twinkled madly in the ebon dome of the sky, and the near-full moon on high etched the sere landscape with bleached light and Stygian shadow. The beam from Nabil's flashlight was barely distinguishable in the moonglow.

An empty sky now, but not long ago a dark object had screamed through the night, trailing fire and smoke. Achmed and Nabil had leapt from their camel-hair blankets and stumbled out of their tent into the cool night air in time to see the bright flare of its explosive collision with the nearby hills.

Achmed remembered his initial awe and terror. "It is the hand of Allah!"

He also remembered Nabil's none-too-gentle shove against his shoulder.

"Goat! It's a missile. You heard the talk around the fire

last night. The hero Saddam is sending missiles against the Jews. Thousands of missiles. And he's killing them by the *millions*. Already he has sent the Americans howling with their tails between their legs. Soon there will be no more Israel and our herds will graze among our enemies' bones in the ruins of Tel Aviv. Let's go!"

"Go where?" Achmed cried as his older brother began pushing through the huddled goats toward their tethered ass.

"Into the hills!"

"Why?" He wasn't challenging his older brother—a good Bedouin boy did not question the eldest son of his father—he simply wanted to know.

Nabil turned and pointed toward the jagged sawblade of rock that cut the western sky. His face was shadowed but Achmed knew from the impatience in his voice that his brother was wearing his habitual you're-so-stupid scowl.

"That was a missile that just passed, a giant bullet. And what are bullets made of?" Achmed opened his mouth to answer but Nabil wasn't waiting. "Metal! And what do we do with any scrap metal we find?"

"We sell it," Achmed said quickly, and suddenly he saw the reason for Nabil's haste. "There will be *lots* of metal!" he said.

Nabil nodded. "*Tons* of it. So move those feet, camel face!"

Once again he realized why their father placed so much trust in Nabil, and why he was glad Nabil had been born first. Achmed doubted he could handle the responsibility of being the eldest son—the only thing he did better than Nabil was play the *rababah*, hardly a useful skill. He hoped he was as muscular as Nabil when he reached seventeen in three years, and prayed he'd be able to sport such a respectable start at a beard. At times he despaired of outgrowing this reedy, ungainly body.

And tonight was but further proof of his unsuitability for leadership. Never would he have thought of making profit for the family from the remnants of a spent and exploded missile. But he could lend his back to gathering the scrap so that his *abu* could be proud of both of his sons.

And now, as they clambered up a slope that seemed ever steeper, a thought struck him. The goats! Father had entrusted them with one of the family herds, to take it north in search of better grazing. That herd now stood untended and unguarded on the plain below, ready to be driven off unchallenged by any passer-by with a larcenous heart.

Achmed turned and gazed back down the slope. The Dead Sea gleamed in the moonlight like a strip of hammered silver, shadowed on the far side by the mountains of Jordan and outlined on the near by the black, shore-hugging ribbon of Highway 90. No lights moved on the highway. Their herd was safely huddled in a dry basin kilometers from the road. He realized his fears were groundless. Who would be wandering about the Judean Wilderness in the dead of night? The only thing moving here was *Hamsin*, the desert wind.

As he returned to the climb, a question popped into his mind.

"Nabil," he called. "Why has this missile landed here instead of in Tel Aviv?"

"Probably one of the Israelis hit it with a lucky shot and knocked it off course."

Of course, Achmed thought. Why didn't I think of that? Nabil always had an answer.

Achmed followed his brother up the steepening incline of the dry wadi, so steep at times that he had to heave his shoulder against the donkey's hindquarters to assist the beast up the slope. Eventually they came to a ribbed outcrop of stone that towered over them. In the daytime this rock would have looked sandy red and yellow. Now in the moonlight it glowed goatsmilk white, streaked with the stark shadows of its crevices.

"What do we do now?" Achmed said.

Nabil looked around, then up, then ranged left and right along the face of the rock as if he expected to find a path into the cliffside.

"I don't know. There must be a way around this. The missile crashed atop it. We must find a way up."

"Maybe it crashed on the other side," Achmed said. "I couldn't tell from where we stood. Could you?"

Achmed saw his brother shake his shadowed head. "I'm sure it crashed atop this cliff. *Almost* sure. Maybe if we travel around it we'll find a way up."

To the left looked no more promising than the right, but something in Achmed drew him leftward.

"That way," he said, surprised by the certainty in his voice as he pointed south.

Nabil stared at him a moment, then shrugged and turned south.

"As good a way to start as any."

The going got rougher. No path here, no sign that man or beast had ever traveled this route. Their sandals and the donkey's hooves slipped on the loose shale that littered their way. The jagged edges angled up, cutting Achmed's feet and ankles.

After struggling along for a few hundred feet, Nabil turned and stopped the donkey.

"This isn't going anywhere," he said. "We'll turn back and try the other way."

"We've come so far already," Achmed said. "Just a little farther. Let's see what's around that bend before we turn back."

"All right," Nabil said. "To the bend and no more."

They struggled farther along the narrow path, and as they were slithering past a jagged rib in the cliff wall, Nabil called back from the lead.

"You were right! It ends here. We can get past it here!"

As Achmed followed the donkey around the rib, he saw that the far side was just as steep as the near, with no gully or ravine to allow them passage to the top. And worse, the landing edge of the outcrop was topped by an overhang of stone that would have daunted them even had there been a way to climb the face.

Achmed saw that they had entered the mouth of a deep canyon. Beyond the outcrop a broad dry wadi swept down from the upper reaches of the range; half a dozen feet above that, a small, raised field. And beyond the field stood another sheer-faced cliff even more forbidding than the one they had just skirted.

Nabil stood in the moonlight, head back, hands on hips, staring at the cliff face.

"There's no way up," he said.

Achmed's voice choked on his disappointment. He could only nod. He'd been so sure . . .

Something stung his nostrils. He blinked his suddenly watery eyes. He couldn't see it but he could smell it. Smoke . . . riding the breeze that wafted down the wadi.

"Nabil . . . ?"

But his brother had smelled it too.

"Achmed! Follow! Quickly!"

They drove the donkey up the gentler slope of the dry riverbed. As they neared the small field the smoke became thicker. Another hundred feet and Achmed spotted the flames.

"It's here!" Nabil cried. "It crashed here!"

They dragged and pushed the donkey up the far bank of the wadi and stopped at the top to stare at the tiny field that ran across the base of the canyon mouth. Stunted fig trees reached their twisted branches heavenward at regular intervals across its narrow span. A few of them were burning. Dozens of tiny grass fires crawled along the field's smooth surface.

"Let's get to work!" Nabil said.

As his older brother tethered the donkey to the nearest tree, Achmed spotted a dark lump in the sand to his right. He knelt and touched it, gingerly. Hard, with sharp, twisted edges. And warm. Still warm.

"I've found a piece!" he cried aloud. The *first* piece! he boasted silently.

"Drop it here," Nabil said, pointing to a spot near the donkey's feet. "We'll collect as much as we can and pile it here. When we've got as much as we can carry, we'll load up and head back to the herd. And hurry, Achmed. As sure as you breathe, we're going to have company soon."

Company? Did he mean other Bedouin, or Israelis? Not

that it mattered. Either way, they stood to lose whatever metal they gathered.

Over Beit Shemesh

Chaim Kesev set his jaw to keep his teeth from chattering. He wasn't cold—far from it in this bulky flack jacket. No, the incessant vibrations from the engine coursing throughout the helicopter's fuselage were penetrating the padding of his seat, jittering up his spine, piercing his skull, and running to his teeth. He was sure a couple of them would rattle loose if he had to take much more of this.

Man was not meant to fly.

Kesev hated flying, and he hated flying in helicopters most of all. But after he'd watched the computer plot the course of the errant SCUD on the map, and seen the area encircled for maximum probability of impact—120 kilometers southeast of Tel Aviv—he knew he couldn't wait in the city for the report from the crash site. Everyone else in the tracking center had been relieved that the SCUD had landed in an unpopulated area of the Southern District wilderness. Not Kesev. Not when it was that particular area.

As soon as the all-clear had sounded, he'd pushed his way aboard the reconnaissance helicopter. His presence had raised eyebrows among the crew. Who was this pushy little man, this swarthy, slight, five-eight, middle-aged, bearded wonder to elbow his way onto their craft? But when he'd flashed them his Shin Bet identification they'd sealed their lips. None of them had the nerve to challenge the wishes of a Domestic Intelligence operative when the country was under attack.

Kesev stared down at the mountainous terrain below and wondered where they were.

"How much farther?" he asked the copilot lounging in the seat directly ahead of his.

"Not much longer now, sir," the airman said, then laughed.

"What's so funny?" Kesev said.

"Sorry, sir. It's just that whenever my family used to take

a trip, I'd drive my father crazy saying, 'Are we there yet? Are we there yet?' And that's the answer he'd always give me: 'Not much longer now.' And here I am, saying it to you."

"I was not aware," Kesev said icily, "that a question concerning our arrival at the crash site of a weapon hurled at us by one of our most vicious enemies, a weapon that might contain chemical or biological toxins, could be construed as childish."

"Oh, sir," the copilot said, straightening in his seat and half turning toward him. "I meant nothing like that. I—"

He knew he was being unfair, but he was edgy and irritable and wanted to lay off some of that burden on this youngster.

"Nor was I aware that I was driving you crazy."

"Sir, I was just—"

"Just keep us on course."

"Yes, sir."

On course. The SCUD in question had been anything but. They had a reputation for being about as accurate as a fireworks rocket, but this particular missile's course had added a new dimension to the concept of erratic. It had turned so far south that it never came within range of the Patriots the Army had borrowed from the Americans. For a while it looked as if it might crash into the Dead Sea, but its trajectory had flattened momentarily, carrying it into the Wilderness.

Near the Resting Place.

Kesev had no doubt that it had missed the Resting Place. A direct hit was inconceivable. But anything focusing attention on that area posed a threat to the secret. He wanted to see the crash site himself, and he wanted to be there when the inspection team arrived. He'd be there to deal with any other intelligence service that might try to tag along. Domestic intelligence was Shin Bet's domain and Kesev was here to claim it for them. He feared that if he didn't stake out his territory now, Mossad and Aman would be horning in and might wander into areas they shouldn't.

One area—the Resting Place—was not to be disturbed.

Never disturbed. He shuddered to think of the consequences. . . .

Kesev tried to shake off the unease that had encircled his
throat since he'd seen the computer MPI printout.

"I'm still waiting for the answer to my question," he said
to no one in particular.

"ETA twenty minutes, sir," the copilot said without
looking at him.

That's better, Kesev thought. *That's* the way to treat one
of Shin Bet's top operatives.

Then he reconsidered. Perhaps he was being too hard on
the youth. He'd been a young upstart once.

Dear Lord, how long ago had that been?

Never mind.

"Who do you think aimed this missile?" Kesev said,
trying to lighten the leaden mood that had settled on the
cabin. "A blind man?"

"Yeah," the pilot said. "Ayatollah Stevie Wonder."

The copilot laughed and Kesev forced a smile, all the
while wanting to ask, Who's Stevie Wonder? But he feared
sounding out of touch. He was ever on guard against
sounding out of touch.

"Yeah," the copilot said. "Someone put a mean hook on
that SCUD."

"Hook?" Kesev said.

"You ever play golf, sir?"

Kesev had tried it once or twice but had been unable to
comprehend the fascination the game held for so many of
his countrymen.

"Of course."

"Well, you aim a SCUD at Tel Aviv and it just misses the
Dead Sea. I'd say that's one hell of a hook."

Missed Tel Aviv by 120 miles. That was indeed far off
course. Too far off. Almost . . .

Don't think crazy thoughts, he told himself. It's an
accident. Another one of those crazy things that just seem to
happen.

But he'd long known from personal experience that some
things which seemed to "just happen," didn't.

And he trembled at the possibility that this errant SCUD incident might be one of those.

The Judean Wilderness

Achmed darted about the field, collecting metal scraps of assorted sizes until both arms were full, then he scampered back and dumped his finds on the steadily growing pile by the donkey. The clang of metal on metal echoed like cracked bells through the still air.

On his next run he ranged farther from the donkey, searching for the crater where the missile had exploded. He figured he might find the most metal there. Then again, he might not—the blast might have hurled it in all directions, leaving metal everywhere *but* the crater. But either way, he wanted to see it, be near it, wanted to stand in the heart of its power.

He thought he saw a depression in the sand on the far side of the field, at the base of the opposite wall of the canyon. He ran for it.

As he neared he noticed that the otherwise smooth sand of the field was increasingly littered with shards of stone and streaks of darker earth, and how the trees surrounding the depression were broken or knocked flat. The sparse grass smoked from fires that had already burned out.

This was it. The missile must have exploded here.

When he arrived at the crater he saw that the blast had shattered part of the cliff wall, causing a minor landslide into the crater. A deep cavity there in the wall. Almost as if . . .

He picked up a stone and hurled it at the hollow. It flew into the blackness but did not bounce back. It disappeared, as if it had been swallowed. Then Achmed heard it strike. Not with the solid impact of rock upon rock—with more of a *clink*. And then a clatter. As if it had struck something hard and thin and hollow . . . and broken it.

Achmed stood on the crumbling rim of the crater and stared into the blackness in the wall. No mere blast cavity here. This was a cave. He shivered with anticipation as thoughts of Muhammad adh-Dhib raced through his mind. Every Bedouin knew the story of the ten-year-old boy who discovered the first Dead Sea scrolls in Qumran, not too many miles north of here; the tale had been told around the fires for nearly half a century. And had there been a Bedouin boy since who did not dream of finding similar treasure?

"Nabil!" he called. "Nabil come quickly! And bring the light!"

Nabil came running up. "What is it?"

"I think I've found a cave!" Achmed said, pointing to the dark splotch in the wall.

Nabil snorted. "There are caves all over these hills."

"No. A *secret* cave."

Nabil froze an instant, then flicked on the flashlight and aimed the beam into the darkness. Achmed's heart picked up its rhythm when he saw the smooth edges of the opening and the deep blackness beyond.

"You're right, little brother," Nabil said, keeping the beam trained on the opening as he moved around the rim of the crater. "It *is* a cave."

Achmed followed him to the mouth. Together they peered in. The floor of the cave was littered with small rock fragments, a thick layer of dust, and . . . something else.

The beam picked out an object with four short straight legs and what appeared to be a seat.

Achmed said, "Is that—?

"A bench or a chair of some sort," Nabil said.

Achmed was shaking with excitement. He grabbed Nabil's shoulder and found that his brother too was shaking.

"Let's go in," Nabil said.

Achmed's dry mouth would not allow him to speak. He followed his brother's lead, climbing over the pile of broken and fallen-away stone. They entered the cave in silence.

Dry, musty air within, laden with dust. Achmed coughed and rubbed his nose. They approached the little bench, covered with a thick coat of dust like everything else. Achmed reached out to brush the dust away, to see what sort of wood it was made of. He touched it lightly.

The bench gave way, falling in on itself, crumbling, disintegrating into a lumpy pile of rotted flakes.

"Oaf!" Nabil hissed.

"May Allah be my witness, I barely touched it!"

Apparently Nabil believed him. "Then this cave must have been sealed for a *long* time. This place is *old.*"

He flashed the beam around. To the right—another bench and what looked like a low table; to the left—

Nabil's gasp echoed Achmed's.

Urns. Two of them: one lying on its side, broken; the other upright, intact, its domed lid securely in place.

"That's what my stone must have hit!" Achmed said.

Nabil was already moving forward. He angled the beam into the broken urn.

"Achmed!" His older brother's voice was hushed. "A scroll! There's a scroll in this one! It's torn and crumbling . . . it's *ancient!*"

Achmed dropped quivering to his knees in the dust.

"Allah be praised! He has led us here!"

Nabil lifted the lid of the second urn and beamed the light into its mouth.

"More scrolls! Achmed, they will be singing our names around the night fires for generations!"

"Allah be praised!" Achmed was too overcome to think of anything else too say.

Nabil replaced the lid and swung the flashlight beam back to the broken urn.

"You take that one. It's already broken but *be careful!* We don't want to do any more damage to that scroll. I'll take the unbroken one."

Achmed bent, slipped his sweating, trembling palms under the broken urn, and gently lifted it into his arms as if it were a cranky infant brother who had finally fallen asleep. He rose to his feet and edged toward the mouth of the cave. He didn't need the flashlight beam to light his exit—after the deep night of this tiny cave, the moonlit canyon outside seemed noon bright. He stepped carefully over the jumbled rocks outside the mouth, then waited on level ground for Nabil.

This is wonderful, he thought. Our family will be rich, and Nabil and I will be famous.

He saw the hand of Allah in this, rewarding him for his daily prayers, his fasting, and his strict observance of Holy Days. He turned and faced south, toward Mecca, and said a silent prayer of thanksgiving. Then he looked at the moon, thanking Allah for making it full tonight.

But the prayer choked in his throat and he nearly dropped the treasure in his arms when he noticed a figure standing atop the far cliff they had skirted to reach this canyon. Silhouetted against the moonlit sky, it seemed to be watching him. For a moment he was transfixed with fear, then he heard Nabil behind him. He turned to see his brother stepping over the rubble before the cave mouth.

"Nabil!"

His brother looked up and stumbled, but caught himself before he fell.

"What *is* it?" he said between his teeth.

"Up on the cliff . . ." Achmed turned to look and saw that the upper edge of the cliff was now empty. The sentinel figure had vanished.

"What?" Nabil said, the irritation mounting in his tone. "Finish what you begin!"

"Nothing."

"Then why are you standing there like a blind camel? Move! We'll take these back to the donkey then search the cave for more."

They had just reached the donkey and were laying their treasures in the sand when Achmed heard something. He lifted his head and listened. A low hum. No . . . a pulsating *thrum*.

"*Tayya'ra!*" he cried.

Nabil leapt into motion.

"Quickly! The scrolls! Bundle them up!"

They pulled the blankets they had brought, wrapped the urns in them, then slung them over the donkey's back.

"Let's go!"

"What about the metal?" Achmed cried.

"Forget the metal! We have a far greater treasure! But if the Israelis find us, they'll steal it! Hurry!"

With Nabil pulling from the front and Achmed again switching from behind, they drove the donkey down the bank and across the wadi. As they slipped around the leading edge of the outcrop, the sound of the helicopter grew louder.

"It could be anywhere down there," the copilot said.

Kesev stared below, watching the bright beam of the searchlight lance the darkness and dance along the peaks, plateaus, and crevasses that dominated this area of the Wilderness. They had been running a crisscrossing search pattern for thirty minutes now.

"Keep going," he said.

"I think we can be pretty sure no one was hurt by this thing," the pilot said after a few more minutes of searching. "Maybe we'd better put this off, come back when it's light and—"

"Keep going," Kesev said. He was getting the lay of the land now. "Follow this canyon south."

Out of the corner of his eye he saw the pilot and copilot exchange glances and discreet shrugs, but neither challenged his authority.

The canyon widened below them, and then the search beam picked up white wisps trailing through the air.

"Smoke!" the copilot cried.

"Turn off the search beam," Kesev said.

As soon as the beam died, tiny flickers of light became visible on the canyon floor.

"Down there," Kesev said. "It exploded on the canyon floor."

He released a soft sigh of relief. A glance to his left at the top of the east wall of the canyon reassured him that the Resting Place was untouched.

Close, he thought. Too close.

And then he remembered that the canyon floor had its own secrets.

"Let's have the light again," he said. "See if we can find the point of impact."

It took less than a minute.

"There!" the copilot said. "At two o'clock. Looks like it took out part of the cliff wall too."

Kesev went rigid in the seat. The SCUD crater was right where the cave had been—still was. Had the explosion—?

"Take us down."

"Sir, we've accomplished our objective," the pilot said. "We've found the impact sight and determined that there's been no personal injury or property damage, so—"

"Land this thing now," Kesev said softly, just loud enough to be heard over the engine noise, "or you'll spend the rest of your career working a broomhandle instead of that joystick."

The pilot turned. For a heartbeat or two he stared at Kesev from within the confines of his flight helmet, then took the copter down.

As soon as the wheels touched earth, Kesev was out of his harness. He pulled off his flack jacket—he didn't need it, had only worn it because of regulations—and reached for the hatch handle.

"Stay here and train the search beam on the crater," Kesev said. "This will only take a minute."

He opened the hatch and ran in a crouch through the hurricane from the whirling blades, following the path of the search beam. He cursed as he neared the crater for he saw that the cave had been exposed by the blast. What abysmal luck!

On the other hand, how fortunate that he'd obeyed his instincts and come along to check this out personally. As a result, he was first on the scene. He could prevent this minor mishap from escalating into a catastrophe. He skirted the edge of the crater and stepped over the rocks tumbled before the cave mouth. Whoever was working the search beam back in the copter was doing a good job keeping it trained on him. The cave lit up before him.

That was when he noticed the footprints.

Panic clamped his heart in an icy fist as his gaze ranged wildly about the cave.

Empty. But in the dust on the floor . . . sandal-prints . . . two sets . . . one larger than the other . . . the old chair—reduced to dust . . . the urns . . .

The urns! Gone! No, not completely. Fragments from one of the urns lay scattered in the dust.

How could this be? How could a pair of thieves have come and gone so soon? So swiftly? It wasn't possible!

And yet the fresh footprints and the missing urns reminded him that it was indeed possible.

The urns . . . what had been in them? It had been so long, he could barely remember. Had there been anything of value? Old shekels? He didn't care about losing little bits of gold or silver. What he did mind was word of the find getting out and causing archeological interest to center on this place. That could be extremely dangerous.

But *what* had he put in those urns? He prayed it was nothing that might reveal the secret of this place. He racked his brain for the memory. It was there, just out of reach. It—

The scroll!

Dear Lord, he'd left the scroll in one of those urns!

Kesev staggered in a circle, his breath rasping, his heart beating wildly against the inner surface of his sternum as his vision blurred and lights danced in his vision.

He had to get it back! If it fell into the hands of someone who could translate it—

He leapt from the cave and ran back to the helicopter.

"Give me a flashlight! A canteen too." When the copilot handed them out, Kesev jerked a thumb skyward. "Return to base. I'm staying here."

"That's not necessary, sir," the pilot said. "The inspection team will be here at first light and—"

"Someone's already beat us here. Probably picking up scrap metal. I'll stay on and make sure they don't come back and disturb anything else."

Kesev was back outside, stepping clear of the blades and waving them off. He couldn't see them inside the cabin, but he was sure the two airmen were shrugging and saying, If the crazy little man from Shin Bet wants to stay in the middle of nowhere until morning, let him.

Kesev watched the copter rise, bank, and roar away into the night. As the swirling dust settled on and about him, Kesev stood statue still among the stunted olive trees and listened . . . for anything. For any hint of movement that might lead him toward the thieves. But all he heard was the ringing aftermath of the helicopter's roar. His hearing would be of little value for the next quarter hour or so.

He walked back to the cave. He had to look again, had to be sure he'd seen those footprints, be absolutely certain the urns were gone.

He searched the cave inch by inch, poking the flashbeam into every nook, corner, crack, and crevice. And as he searched he pounded the remaining furniture to rotted splinters; the same with the remnants of bedding against the rear wall; he systematically shattered anything that might hint that the cave had ever been inhabited by a human being. He took the crumbled remnants of the furniture and pulverized them under his heels, then he kicked and scattered the resultant powder, mixing it with the fine dust that layered the floor.

Satisfied that he'd made the cave as uninteresting as possible, he pocketed the broken fragments of urn, then went outside and cried silently to the sinking eye of the moon.

Why? Why has this happened?

Kesev did not wait for an answer. Instead he headed across the field toward the east wall of the canyon.

One more place left to check.

He knew the way. He hadn't been up to the ledge in a long, long while, but his feet had trod the hidden path so many times over the years of his life that they carried him along now with no conscious effort.

He reached the top of the cliff and stood on the broad ledge, breathing hard. He'd grown soft in many ways., He coughed and sipped from the canteen. So dry out here. The membranes inside of his nostrils felt as if they were ready to crack and peel like old paint. In the old days he wouldn't have noticed, but he'd grown soft living so near the sea all these years in Tel Aviv.

He hurried to the mound of rocks that covered the entrance to the Resting Place. They remained undisturbed, as he'd expected. Still, relief flooded through him.

This was holy ground. Kesev had vowed to protect it. He would gladly die—more than gladly—to preserve its secret.

But his relief was short lived. The secret of the Resting Place lay within the coils of the stolen scroll. Its theft could have disastrous consequences.

He drifted to the edge of the ledge and stared down the sheer three-hundred-foot drop to the canyon's shadowed floor. In the old days, at least for someone who didn't know the torturous little path to the top, this sort of climb would daunt all but the most foolhardy adventurer. Nowadays, with modern climbing techniques—or helicopters, for those with deeper pockets—such a precipice offered but a momentary obstacle.

He turned and stared east, across the lengthening shadows behind the foothills that sloped down to the mirror surface of the Dead Sea. He hurled the urn fragments into the air and knew he'd never hear the clatter of their impact with the rocks so far below. The Resting Place was safe up here, hidden from the casual observer as well as the determined searcher . . .

Unless . . .

Unless a searcher had something to guide him.

Where are you? he thought as he searched the craggy Wilderness spread out below. Where have you thieving bastards hidden yourselves? You can't stay hidden forever. I'd be searching for you now if I weren't afraid to leave this place unattended. But I'll find you eventually. Sooner or later you'll have to show yourselves. Eventually you have to slither out from under your rock to sell what you've stolen from me. And then I'll have you. Then you'll wish you'd never laid eyes on that scroll.

The scroll . . . how much did it tell? How detailed were its descriptions of the area? If only he could remember. So long since he'd last read it. Kesev squeezed his eyes shut and rubbed his temples, trying to massage the hidden information from the reluctant crevices of his brain.

Was the scroll even legible any longer?

That was his single best hope: that the scroll had been in the urn the thieves had broken, that it had been damaged to the point where its remnants were little more than an incoherent jumble of disjointed sentences.

Kesev turned and was so startled by the sight of her that he nearly tumbled backward off the ledge.

Robed and wimpled exactly as she had been in life, she stood near the rubble that blocked the entrance to the Resting Place and stared at him. Kesev waited for her to speak, as she had spoken to him many times in the past, but she said nothing, merely stared at him a moment, then faded from view.

So many years, so *many* years since she had shown herself here. Kesev had heard reports from all over the world of her appearances, but so long since she had graced this spot with her presence.

Why now, just after the scroll had been pilfered? What did this mean?

Kesev stood on the precipice and trembled. Something was happening. A wheel had been set in motion tonight. He could almost feel it turning. Where was it taking him?

Where was it taking the world?

I approached the Essenes at Qumran but they
tried to stone me. I fled farther south,
wandering the west shore of the sea of Lot.
Perhaps Massada would have me. Surely they
would welcome one of my station. Or perhaps I
would have to push farther south to Zohar.

   I do not know where to go. And I am alone in
Creation.

FROM THE GLASS SCROLL
ROCKEFELLER MUSEUM TRANSLATION

1995
Fall

2

Jerusalem

The poor man looked as if he were going to cry.

"You . . . you're sure?"

Harold Gold watched Professor Pearlman nod sagely as they sat in the professor's office in the manuscript department of the Rockefeller Archeological Museum and gave Mr. Glass the bad news.

Richard Glass was American, balding, and very fat—a good hundred pounds overweight. He described himself as a tourist—a frequent visitor to Israel who owned a condo in Tel Aviv. Last month he'd brought in a scroll he said he'd purchased at a street bazaar in the Arab Quarter and asked if its antiquity could be verified.

"I'm afraid so, Mr. Glass." Pearlman stroked his graying goatee. "A gloriously skillful fake, but a fake nevertheless."

"But you said—"

"The parchment itself is first century—we stand by that. No question about it. And the ink contains the dyes and minerals in the exact proportions used by first century scribes."

The first thing the department had done was date the parchment. Once that was ballparked in the two-thousand-year-old mark, they'd translated it. That was when people had begun to get excited. *Very* excited.

"Then what—?"

"The writing itself, Mr. Glass. Our carbon dating tests—and believe me, we've repeated the dating numerous times—

all yield the same result: The words were placed on the parchment within the past two or three years."

Mr. Glass's eyes bulged. "*Two three*—*!* My God, what an idiot I am!"

"Not at all, not at all," Professor Pearlman said. "It had us fooled too. It's a *very* skillful job. And I assure you, Mr. Glass, you cannot be more disappointed than we by these findings."

Amen to that, Harold thought. He'd been in a state of euphoria for the past month, thanking God for his luck. Imagine, being here on sabbatical from N.Y.U. when the manuscript department receives an item that could make the Dead Sea scrolls look like lists of old matzoh recipes. When he'd read the translation he'd suspected it might be too explosive to be true, but he'd gone on hoping . . . hoping . . .

Until the dating on the ink had come in.

Harold leaned forward. "That's why we're very interested in where you got it. Whoever forged this scroll really knows his stuff."

He watched Glass drum his fingers on his thigh, carefully weighing the decision. No one in the department believed for a moment that Richard Glass had picked up something like this at a street stall. Harold knew the type: a wealthy collector, buying objects here and sneaking them back to the states to a mini-museum in his home. He also knew if Glass named his true source he might precipitate an investigation of other purchases he'd made on the antiquities black market, and his shipments home would be subject to close scrutiny from here on in. No serious collector could risk that.

"We're not interested in legalities here, Mr. Glass," Professor Pearlman assured him. "We'd simply like to interview your source, learn *his* sources."

Harold grinned. "I think most of us would like to shake his hand."

No lie there. Undoubtedly the forger possessed some sort of native genius. The scroll Glass had presented was written on two-thousand-year-old parchment in ink identical to the type used in those days. The forger had used an Aramaic form of Hebrew enriched with Greek and Latin influences—much like the *Mishna*, the earlier part of the Talmud—and had created a narrative that alternated between first and third person, supposedly written by a desert outcast, a hermit but obviously a well-educated one, living in the hills somewhere west of the Dead Sea. But the events he described . . . if they'd been true and verifiable, what a storm they would have caused.

Perhaps that was the forger's whole purpose: controversy. The money from the sale to someone like Glass was a lagniappe. The real motive was the turmoil that would have arisen had they not been able to disprove the scroll's authenticity. The forger could have sat back and watched and smiled and said, *I caused all this.*

After a seemingly interminable wait, Glass shook his head.

"I don't know the forger. I can't even find the stall where I bought it—and believe me, I've searched high and low for it. So I can't help you find the creator of this piece of junk."

"It's not junk," Pearlman said. He slid the wooden box containing the scroll across the desktop toward Glass. "In its own way, it's a work of art."

Glass made a face and lumbered to his feet.

"Then hang it on *your* wall. I want nothing further to do with it. It only reminds me of all the money I wasted." He took the box and looked around. "Where's your trash."

"You can't be serious!" Harold said.

Glass turned to him. "You want it?"

"Well, I—"

He shoved the box into Harold's hands. "Here. It's yours."

With that he turned and waddled from the office.

Professor Pearlman looked at Harold over the tops of his glasses. "Well, Harold. Looks like you're the proud owner of a genuine fake first century scroll. It'll make a nice curiosity back at N.Y.U."

Harold gazed down at the box in his hands. "Or a unique gift for an old friend."

"A colleague?"

"Believe it or not, a Catholic priest. He's something of an authority on the early Christians. He's read just about everything ever written on the Jerusalem Church."

Pearlman's brown eyes sparkled. "I'll bet he's never read anything like that."

"That's for sure." Harold almost laughed aloud in anticipation of Father Dan Fitzpatrick's reaction to this little gift. "I know he'll get a real kick out of this."

I despaired.

The Lord oppressed me, my fellow men oppressed me, the very air oppressed me. Perhaps the only fitting place for me was in Sodom or Gomorrah, cities of the dead, hidden beneath the lifeless waves. I threw myself into the salty water but I could not drown.

Even the sea will not have me!

FROM THE GLASS SCROLL
ROCKEFELLER MUSEUM TRANSLATION

1996
Spring

3

Manhattan

Father Daniel Fitzpatrick stopped in front of the Bank of New York Building, turned to the ragged army that had followed him up from the Lower East Side, and raised his hands.

"All right, everybody," he called to the group. "Let's stop here for a sec and organize ourselves."

Most of them stopped on command, but some of the less alert—and there were more than a few of those—kept right on walking and had to be pulled back by their neighbors.

Father Dan stepped up on the marble base of a sculpture that looked like a pair of six-foot charcoal bagels locked in a passionate embrace and inspected the ranks of his troops.

Even if we turn back now, he thought, even if we don't do another thing tonight, we'll have made a point.

Already they'd garnered more than their share of attention. During the course of their long trek uptown from Tompkins Square Park they'd earned themselves a police escort, a slew of reporters and photographers, and even an *Eyewitness News* van complete with minicam and blow-dried news personality.

Why not? This was news, a mild spring evening, and a fabulous photo op to boot. A small army of chanting, sign-carrying homeless marching up Park Avenue, around and through the Met Life and Helmsley Buildings, to the Waldorf—the contrast of their unkempt hair, shambling gaits, and dirty clothes against the backdrop of luxury hotels and pristine office buildings was irresistible.

As Dan raised his hands again and waited for his followers' attention, he noticed all the camera lenses coming to bear on him like the merciless eyes of a pack of hungry wolves. He was well aware of the media's love of radical priests, so he'd made sure he was in uniform tonight: cassock, Roman collar, oversize crucifix slung around his neck. The works. He was well aware too of how his own appearance—clean-cut sandy hair, slim, athletic build, younger looking than his thirty-two years—jibed with that of his followers, and he played that up to maximum effect. He looked decent, intelligent, dedicated—all true, he hoped— and most of all, *accessible*. The reporters would be fighting to interview him during and after the demonstration.

And as far as Dan was concerned, that was what this little jaunt to the Waldorf was all about: communication. He hated the spotlight. He much preferred to keep a low profile and let others have center stage. But no one else was interested in this little drama, so Dan had found himself pushed into a leading role. Media-grabbing was not his thing, but somebody had to get across the message that these people needed help, that they couldn't be swept under the rug by the presidential wannabe appearing at the Waldorf tonight.

That wannabe was Senator Arthur Crenshaw from California, and this high-profile fund raiser was a golden opportunity to confront the senator on his radical proposal to solve the homeless problem. Normally Dan wouldn't have given a second thought to a crazy plan like Crenshaw's, but the way it had taken hold with the public was frightening.

Camps.

Of course Crenshaw didn't call them camps. The word might elicit visions of concentration camps. He called them "domiciles." Why have a hundred programs scattered all over the country? Senator Crenshaw said. All that duplication of effort and expense could be eliminated by gathering

up the homeless and putting them in special facilities to be
built on government lands. Once there, families would be
fed and sheltered together, with the children attending
schools set up just for them; all adults would receive free
training for gainful employment; and those who were sick
or addicted or mentally ill would receive the care they
needed to make them productive citizens again.

The public—especially the urban-dwelling public—
seemed to be going for the Domicile Plan in a big way, and
as a result the concept was gaining support from both
parties. Dan could understand the attraction of getting the
homeless out of sight while balming one's conscience with
the knowledge they were being cared for as they were
retooled for productivity, but he found the whole idea
unsettling. The domiciles *did* sound like concentration
camps, or detention camps, or at the very least, gilt-edged
prisons, and he found that frightening. So would many of
the homeless folks he knew—and Dan knew plenty.

But how many homeless did Senator Arthur Crenshaw
know?

These were people. It was easy to forget that. Yes, they
were on the bottom rung of the socioeconomic ladder—hell,
most of them had fallen *off* the ladder—and they sure as
hell didn't look like much. They tended to be dirty and smell
bad and dress in clothing that wasn't fit for the rag pile.
They offered nothing that society wanted, and some of them
undoubtedly had AIDS and wouldn't be around much
longer anyway. But each had a name and a personality, and
they'd hoped and dreamed about the future before they'd
forgotten how. Truth was, they could all vanish into smoke
and the world would not be appreciably poorer, and only a
few would mark their passing, and even fewer would mourn
them.

But they were *people*, dammit!

People.

Not a cause.

People.

Dan hated that the homeless had become such a trendy
cause, with big-name comedians and such doing benefits for

them. But after the stars took their bows, after they were limoed back to their Bel Aire estates, Dan stayed downtown and rubbed elbows with those homeless. Every day.

And sometimes at the end of a particularly discouraging day of elbow-rubbing with the folks who wandered in and out of the kitchen he ran in the basement of St. Joseph's church, even Dan found a certain guilty attraction in Crenshaw's Domicile Plan. Sometimes he wondered if maybe Crenshaw could indeed do more for them than he ever could. But at least with Dan they had a choice, and that was important.

And that was why they had come here tonight.

They stood quietly now, waiting for their last-minute instructions. They numbered about thirty, mostly males. Dan had hoped for more. Forty or fifty had promised to make the march but he was well satisfied with a two-thirds showing. You quickly learned to lower your expectations when working with these people. It came with the territory. After all, if they had enough control over their lives to act responsibly, if they knew how to follow through with a plan—even as simple a plan as gathering in Tompkins Square at six o'clock—they probably wouldn't be home-less. About half of the ones who were here carried signs, most of which Dan had hand-printed himself during the week. Among them:

SAY *NO!*
TO CONCENTRATION CAMPS
FOR THE HOMELESS!

and:

WHAT ABOUT *US?*
WHERE DO *WE* FIT IN?

and Dan's favorite:

ARE WE OUR
BROTHER'S KEEPERS?

OR DO WE TELL
BIG BROTHER TO KEEP HIM?

"All right!" he said, shouting so he could be heard in the back. "Let us say this once more in case some of you have forgotten: We're not here to cause trouble. We're here to draw attention to a problem that cannot be solved by putting you folks in camps. We're here for informational purposes. To communicate, not to confront. Stay in line, don't block traffic, don't enter the hotel, don't fight, don't panhandle. Got that?"

Most of them nodded. He had been pounding this into them all week. Those who could get the message had already got it. This last harangue was for the benefit of the press microphones and the police within earshot, to get it on the record that this was intended as a strictly peaceful demonstration.

"Where's Sister Carrie?" one of them asked.

That had to be One-Thumb George, but Dan couldn't place him in the crowd. George had asked the question at least a dozen times since they'd left Tompkins.

"Sister Carrie is in her room at the convent, praying for us. Her order doesn't allow her to march in demonstrations."

"I wish she was here," the voice said, and now Dan was sure it was One-Thumb George.

Dan too wished Carrie were here. She'd done as much as he to organize this march, maybe more. He missed her.

"And I'm sure she wishes she could be here with us!" Dan shouted. "So let's make her proud! Waldorf, *ho!*"

Pointing his arm uptown like an officer leading a charge, he jumped off the sculpture base and marched his troops the remaining blocks to the Waldorf. He was just starting to position the group when Senator Crenshaw's limousine pulled up before the entrance. Dan had a brief glimpse of the senator's head—the famous tanned face, dazzling smile, and longish, salt-and-pepper hair—towering over his entourage as he zipped across the sidewalk, and then he was through the front doors and gone.

Damn! He'd shown up early.

He heard groans from the demonstrators but he shushed them.

"It's okay. We'll be all set up for him when he comes out. And we're not leaving until he does."

They spent the interval marching in an oval within the area reserved for their demonstration, demarcated by light blue horses stenciled in white with POLICE LINE - DO NOT CROSS. Dan led them in chants updated from the sixties, like: "Hey, hey, Arthur C., why you wanna imprison me?" and "Hell, no! We won't go!" And of course there were the endless repetitions of "We Shall Overcome."

The choices were calculated. Dan wanted to bring to mind the civil rights marches and antiwar protests of the sixties to anyone who saw this particular demonstration on TV. Many of the movers and shakers in the country today—the President included—had participated in those demonstrations in their youth; many of them still carried a residue of nostalgia for those days. He hoped enough of them would realize that but for luck and the grace of God they might be marching on this line tonight.

As he marched and led the chants and singing, Dan felt *alive*. More truly alive than he had felt in years. His priestly routines had become just that—routine. Hearing confession, saying Mass, giving sermons—it seemed little more than preaching to the converted. The souls who truly needed saving didn't go to Mass, didn't take the sacraments. His priestly duties around the altar at St. Joseph's had become . . . empty. But when he left the main floor and went downstairs to the soup kitchen in the basement—the place he'd dubbed Loaves and Fishes—*then* he felt he was truly doing God's work.

God's work . . . Dan had to smile at the phrase. Wasn't God's work for God to do? Why was it left to mere mortals like him and Carrie to do God's work?

And lately, in his darkest moments, Dan had begun wondering if God was doing *anything*. The world—at least the part of it in which he spent his days—was, to put it bluntly, a fucking mess. Everywhere he looked people were sick, hurt, or dying—from AIDS, from racism, from drugs, from child abuse, from stabbings, shootings, or just plain old kick-ass muggings. And the violence was escalating. Every time Dan told himself it can't get any worse than this, sure enough, it did.

And every year there seemed to be more homeless—more lost souls.

Tighten up on the misery spigot, will you, God? We're up to our lower lips down here.

Yeah. Where *was* the hand of God in all of this? Why wasn't *it* doing God's work? A long, continuous howl of agony was rising from this city, this world. Was Anybody listening? Why didn't He respond? Dan could do only so much.

Like tonight. This was doing something—or at least Dan hoped it was. Who knew if it would accomplish anything? All you could do was try.

And then word came out that the thousand-dollar-a-plate dinner was over. The doorman started signaling the hovering limos forward. Taxis nosed in like koi at feeding time. Dan pulled Dirty Harry out of the line and set him in the middle of the circle.

"All right, everybody! He's coming. Chant as loud as you can. Harry's going to lead you."

"Me?" Harry said. He had long greasy hair, a thick beard matted with the remains of his last three meals, and probably hadn't changed his four or five layers of clothing since the winter. "I dunno what to—"

"Just keep leading them in the same stuff we've been doing all night," Dan told him. "And give me your posters. I want to get up close."

Harry lifted the sandwich-board placards over his head and surrendered them with obvious reluctance. Dan grabbed them, waved, and hurried off. He didn't dare slip them over his own head—not after Dirty Harry had been wearing them.

He headed for the Waldorf entrance. As he squeezed between two of the barricade horses, one of the cops moved to block his way but let him pass when he saw the collar.

Ah, the perks of the Roman collar.

Celebrity gawkers, political groupies, and the just plain

curious had formed a gauntlet along the path from the Waldorf entrance. Dan pushed, squirmed, wheedled, and elbowed his way to the front row where anyone exiting the hotel would have an unobstructed view of the sandwichboard's message:

CONCENTRATION
CAMPS ARE
UNAMERICAN!

Finally he saw his man. Senator Crenshaw appeared at the door. He stopped inside the glass, shaking hands and smiling at some of the hundreds of people who'd plunked down a grand for a chicken dinner. Dan ground his teeth as he calculated how many people he could feed at St. Joe's for the cost of just one of those dinners.

He watched him through the glass and reviewed what he knew about Senator Arthur Crenshaw, the Silicon Valley giant. In the mid-seventies, at age thirty, he'd started CrenSoft on a shoestring. His software innovations earned him huge profits, which he plowed back into the company, which in turn yielded even larger profits. When Microsoft bought him out for an ungodly sum, he traded the corporate rat race for politics. He didn't start small. He challenged an incumbent for one of his native California's U.S. Senate seats and won. Now he had his eye on the Presidency. He hadn't declared himself yet, but no one seemed to have any doubt that he'd be stumping in New Hampshire when the next round of Presidential primaries rolled around.

A widower now—his wife had died five years ago—with one grown son, he was a formidable candidate. The Born-Again line of moral righteousness and family values he spouted guaranteed him a built-in core constituency. But he needed a broader base if he was aiming for national office, and he was steadily building that with his speech-making and his strong-featured good looks. Especially his speech-making. Crenshaw was a mesmerizing orator, whether from prepared text or off the cuff. In unguarded moments even

Dan had found himself nodding in agreement with much of his rhetoric.

But when he listened carefully, Dan tapped into an undercurrent that told him this was a man who had quickly become extremely powerful in his own little world and had grown used to having things his own way, a man of monstrous self-esteem who knew—*knew*—he had the answers, who believed there could be only one way of doing things—the Arthur Crenshaw way.

But Father Daniel Fitzpatrick was here tonight to let him know that there were a few folks around who didn't think Senator Arthur Crenshaw had *all* the answers, and that he was downright wrong when it came to the Domicile Plan.

Here he comes, Dan thought as the glass door was held open for Crenshaw by a broad-shouldered Hispanic with dark glasses and "security" written all over him.

A cheer went up from the onlookers as the senator stepped outside. Lots of normally liberal Manhattanites seemed enthralled with the man. Dan put it down to his resemblance to Pat Riley, the Knicks' former coach, but knew it went deeper than that. The man was magnetic.

And as the cheer rose, so did the chanting from Dan's homeless. Good for you, Harry, he thought.

Crenshaw walked the gauntlet, shaking hands and smiling that smile. When he came within half a dozen feet, Dan held up his placard and thrust it toward the senator to make sure he didn't miss it. The dark-skinned security man moved to push Dan back but Crenshaw stopped him. He stared at the message, then looked Dan in the eye.

"Is that directed at me?" he said.

Dan was momentarily taken aback by the man's directness. He'd expected to be ignored. But he met the senator's steely blue gaze with his own.

"Yes, Senator. And at your out-of-sight-out-of-mind Domicile Plan. You can't lock the homeless up in camps and think that will solve the problem."

"I resent that," Crenshaw said, his eyes flashing, his voice soft but forceful.

The crowd around the entrance had stopped cheering;

they were listening instead. Only the chanting of the homeless from behind the barricades disturbed the sudden silence.

Dan was not prepared for this. His mouth went dry; his voice was hoarse when he replied.

"And I think the homeless will resent being carted off to camps in the middle of nowhere."

"What's your connection with the homeless, Father?" he said.

"I run a kitchen for them downtown."

Crenshaw nodded. "That's very admirable. My hat's off to you. But how many of their lives have you changed?"

"I don't under—"

"How many have you gotten off the street and into some sort of self-supporting activity?"

Dan had a feeling he was being maneuvered into a corner, but he had to answer—and truthfully.

"I couldn't say. We barely have enough money to keep them fed."

"Exactly! They need funds and there aren't enough funds to go around. That's why we have to centralize our efforts to help them." He gestured to the crowd. "Look around you, Father. See these people? They support the Domicile Plan. They're all willing to put their money where their mouths are, because they're going to pay for the plan with their tax dollars. But they want to see those dollars well spent. Soup kitchens only perpetuate the problem—like giving a transfusion to a bleeding patient without sewing up the wound."

God, he's good, Dan thought. And he means every word. He truly wants to help. That's what makes him so convincing. But he's still *wrong!*

"I couldn't agree more," Dan said, "but concentration camps aren't a moral alternative."

Senator Crenshaw's eyes flashed with sudden anger.

"You're handy with the loaded terms, aren't you, Father. And I'm sure you have a real talent for dishing out the soup on the breadline at your kitchen, but have you ever actually gone into a factory and worked to earn a single dime to pay for their shelter? Or your own, for that matter? Have you ever labored to grow a single grain of wheat or a single kernel of rice to feed them? Or yourself? Have you ever woven or cut or sewn a single stitch for their clothing? Or for your own? If you want to be a man of God, then limit your concerns to Godly things; but if you want to be a man of the people, then get out and sweat with them, Father. Until you do, you're nothing but a middleman, trafficking in their troubles. A hand-wringing monger of misery, hoisting yourself up on their crosses to allow yourself to be better seen from afar. Which is fine, if that's the way you want to spend your life. This is still a free country. But don't block the way of those who really want to help."

Dan was stunned by the quiet tirade. Before he could frame a reply, Crenshaw turned away and stepped into his waiting limo. His security man closed the door, glanced at Dan with a smirk on his dark face, then slipped around to the other side.

Someone patted him gently on the shoulder. Dan looked around and saw an elderly stranger standing next to him.

"Don't take it too hard, Father. We all know you mean well. But you just ain't getting it done."

Still mute, Dan turned back to the street and watched Senator Crenshaw's limo pull away. On the surface he knew he appeared unscathed, but he was bleeding inside. Hemorrhaging. Crenshaw's words had cut deep, right to the heart of his deepest doubts.

And the elderly stranger had twisted the knife.

. . . *you just ain't getting it done* . . .

Knowing I was not fit for the company of other men, I turned from my southward course and searched the wilderness for a place in which to spend the rest of my allotted days alone.

I wandered the deserted hills, searching for a sign. Finally, as I climbed a steep incline, I looked up and beheld a bellied cliff with an overhanging ledge. The letter tav leaped into my mind. Tav . . . the letter to which the Kabbalah grants a numerical value of 400 . . . highest of all the letters.

This was the sign I had sought. This is where I would stay. The lowest huddling in the shadow of the highest.

FROM THE GLASS SCROLL
ROCKEFELLER MUSEUM TRANSLATION

4

Emilio Sanchez regarded his employer with awe as the limo whisked them uptown.

If only I could use words like that, he thought. I would not have to be a guard dog. I could be anything . . . even a *senador*.

But Emilio had come to terms long ago with who he was . . . and *what* he was. He was a guard dog. He would always be a guard dog. And with those facts in mind, he had become the best damn guard dog in the world.

"You sliced up that *padre* like a master chef, *Senador*. One would almost think your words were planned."

"In a sense, Emilio, they were. I spotted the priest and his group on the way in but I didn't know what they were up to."

"And you asked me to find out."

"Right. And when you told me they were homeless types, I spent the time before my speech preparing a few remarks in case they cornered me on the way out."

Imagine . . . to be able to come up with word-razors while listening and responding to tabletalk.

"But they didn't corner you," Emilio said.

"No matter. I liked what I came up with. Too good to waste. So I let the priest have it."

"With both barrels."

The *senador* smiled and nudged Emilio with an elbow. "You of all people should understand that."

Emilio nodded. He understood. One of his rules had

always been: Don't aim a gun if you have no intention of pulling the trigger. And if you do pull the trigger, shoot to kill.

Emilio's cellular phone trilled softly in his breast pocket. He pulled it out and tapped the SEND button.

"Sanchez."

"We've found him."

Emilio recognized Decker's voice.

"Good work. Where is he?"

The *senador* stiffened beside him. "Charlie? They've located him?"

Emilio nodded as he listened to Decker's reply.

"The West Village. Where else?"

"Public or private?"

"A dive called The Dog Collar, believe it or not. On West Street. Want me to bring him in?"

"No. Wait for me outside. And make sure he doesn't leave before I get there."

"Will do. I called Mol. He's coming over. We'll meet you here."

"Good."

Emilio stared straight ahead as he punched the END button.

"Charlie is in a bar in Greenwich Village. Want me to bring him back to the hotel?"

The *senador* sighed and rubbed his eyes for a long moment. Then: "No. Who knows what shape he's in? I don't want a scene. Use the jet to take him home, then send it back for me. I won't be leaving until tomorrow night anyway."

"Very well. I should be back by early afternoon."

"No. Not you. I want you to stay with Charlie. Do not let him off the grounds. Do not let him out of your sight until I get back."

"If that is your wish, then that is the way it will be."

The *senador* laughed softly. "Wouldn't it be wonderful if that were true with everything. I'd have wished Charlie to be a different sort than he is. Let us pray that he'll cooperate this time."

He took Emilio's hand in his and bowed his head. Emilio

set his jaw. The very thought of holding another man's hand, even in prayer, even if it was the *senador*, made him queasy. He bowed his head but he did not pray. That was for women. Old women. This incessant praying was the only part of the *senador*'s character he did not respect. It was unmanly.

But in all other matters he revered him.

That did not mean that he understood him. Why track down Charlie and bring him back to Paraiso? He had done a good job of hiding himself away. Why ferret him out? Let him stay hidden. Let sleeping dogs lie. . . .

If you're going to do anything, Emilio thought as the *senador* prayed, do something permanent. As much as I like Charlie, just say the word and he will *really* disappear. Without a trace. Forever.

But he knew the *senador* would never order the death of his *maricon* son.

After dropping the *senador* at the Plaza and seeing him safely to his suite, Emilio returned to the limousine, but this time he took the front passenger seat.

"You'll probably be more comfortable in the back," the driver said.

"I will not argue with that, Frederick," Emilio said. He knew the man's name, home address, and driving record. He'd checked all that out before letting the *senador* into the limo. "But I wish to speak to you as we drive."

"Okay," the driver said. Emilio detected wariness in his tone. That was good. "But you can call me Fred. Where to?"

"Downtown?"

"Any particular—?"

"Just drive, Fred."

As Fred turned onto Fifth Avenue, Emilio said, "Have you chauffeured many famous people around?"

Fred grinned. "You kidding? You name 'em, and if they've been to the Apple, I've driven them around. Madonna, Redford, Luke Perry, Winona Ryder, Cher, Axl Rose . . . the list goes on and on. Too many to mention."

"I'll bet you can write a book about what's gone on in the rear section of this car."

"*A* book?" He laughed. "Try *ten* books—all of them X-rated!"

"Tell me some of the stories. The juiciest ones."

"Uh-uh. No way. My lips are sealed. Why y'think all those folks hire me? Why y'think they always ask for Fred? Because Fred gets Alzheimer's when people come sniffing around about his clients?"

Emilio nodded. That jibed with what he'd heard about Fred.

He pulled a switchblade from the side pocket of his coat and pressed the button on the handle. The gleaming narrow blade *snick*ed out and flashed in the glow of the passing street lamps.

"Wh-what's that all about?" Fred said, his voice half an octave higher now.

"I've caught some dirt under one of my fingernails."

"B-better keep that out of sight. They're illegal here."

"So I've heard." Emilio used the point to scrape under a nail. "Listen, Fred. We're going to be stopping at a place called The Dog Collar."

"Oh, boy. On West Street. I know the joint."

"Some of your famous clients have been there?"

He nodded. "Yeah. And you wouldn't believe me if I told you who—which I'm not."

"I admire your discretion, Fred. Which brings me to the heart of our little talk. You will receive a generous tip tonight, Fred. An extravagant tip. It is meant to not only seal your lips tighter than usual, but to erase from your memory everything that occurs from this moment until you drop me off at LaGuardia."

"You're not going to mess up my passenger area, are you?"

"I'm not planning to. But on the subject of 'messing up,' I feel obliged to give you a warning: In my homeland we have a way of dealing with someone who has seen too much and talks about it. We cure him of his affliction by removing his tongue and eyes. Unless we're feeling particularly merciful, in which case we leave the eyes and take only the eyelids. And the tongue, of course. The tongue always goes. Do you understand what I am saying, Fred?"

Emilio hoped the driver would not take this as an empty threat. He knew of no such tradition in Mexico, but that didn't matter. He meant every word, and would personally do the cutting. And enjoy it.

Fred gulped. "Yeah. Loud and clear. No problem."

"Excellent. Then you can look forward to being hired whenever Senator Crenshaw comes to town."

Fred's expression did not exactly reflect unbridled joy at the prospect. He said, "You want to hit The Dog Collar now?"

Emilio folded the stiletto blade and put it away.

"Yes. Immediately."

As they drove on in silence, Emilio hoped the *senador* had some plan for Charlie, some solution for the threat he posed. For he was indeed a threat. In order to be President, the *senador* first had to be nominated by his party. And in order to secure that nomination, he had to run in primary elections in various states. Emilio had studied all this in his civics lessons for his citizenship test, and he'd heard the *senador* discuss it numerous times, but none of it made much sense. However, one thing that did make sense was that many of those primary states were in regions of the country where the right kind of rumor could tilt a close race the wrong way. And if the primaries were going to be as hotly contested as the experts were predicting, having a *maricon* son might be the kiss of political death.

But there seemed to be more to it than that. The *senador* seemed obsessed with finding Charlie and keeping him under wraps. Emilio didn't understand.

What he did understand was that whatever kept the *senador* from the White House also kept Emilio from the White House.

The White House. It had become Emilio's dream.

Not to become President. That was to laugh. But for

Emilio Sanchez to accompany the *senador* to the world's center of power, that was the ultimate spit in the eye to the many throughout his life who had said he'd go nowhere, be nothing unless he changed his ways.

But *I* never changed, Emilio thought. And look at me now. I am the most trusted aide of United States Senator Arthur Crenshaw. I am riding in a stretch limo through New York City. I have my pick of the women in the Senate Building in Washington. I own my own Coupe de Ville. And I'm still moving up. *Up!*

Even now he loved to drive his shiny Cadillac back to his native Tijuana and park in front of the old haunts. Pay some street *tonto* to guard the car while he went inside and watched their eyes go wide and round as he flashed his money and rings and bought a round for the house.

In the span of a few heartbeats the word would get around: *Emilio's back! Emilio's back!* So that when he strolled the narrow streets the children would follow and call his name like a deity and beg for his attention. And not far behind them would be their mothers and older sisters, doing the same.

He loved to drive by the St. Ignatio School where the priests and sisters had tried to beat some religion into him and make him like all the other sheep they imprisoned in their classrooms. He loved to stop in front of the adobe chapel and blow the horn until one of those black-robed fools came out, then give them the dirty-digit salute and screech away.

He knew where his mother was living—still in the same old shack down in the Camino Verde settlement where he'd been born—but he never visited her. They'd be ice-skating in hell before he gave that *puta* the time of day. Always putting him down, always saying he was a good-for-nothing *puerco* just like his father. Emilio had never known his father, and he'd spent years hating him for deserting his family. But after Emilio's last blowup with his mother, he no longer blamed his old man for leaving.

That blowup had come when Emilio turned twenty and

took the bouncer job at The Cockscomb, the toughest, meanest, low-rent whorehouse in Tijuana. His mother had kicked him out of the trailer, telling him he was going to hell, that he was going to die before he was twenty-one. Emilio had sauntered off and never looked back.

He proved himself at The Cockscomb. He'd been fighting since he was a kid and he'd learned every cheap, dirty, back-alley brawling trick there ever was, usually the hard way. He had the scars to prove it. He was good with a knife—very good. He'd stabbed his share and had been stabbed a few times in return. One of his opponents had died, writhing on the floor at his feet. Emilio had felt nothing.

He started working out, popping steroids and bulking up until his shoulders were too wide for most doorways. He had a short fuse to begin with, and the juice trimmed it down to the nub.

But not to where he was out of control. Never out of control. He always eased the belligerent drunken *Americanos* out to the street, but heaven help the locals who got out of line. Emilio would beat them to a pulp and love every bloody minute of it. Another man died from one of those beatings, but he'd deserved it. Over the succeeding years he caused the death of three more men—two with a blade, and one with a bullet.

He moved up quickly through the Tijuana sex world, from whorehouses, to brothels, to chief enforcer at the renowned Blue Señorita, a high-ticket bordello and tavern that catered almost exclusively to *Americanos*. Orosco, the owner, liked to brag that the Blue Señorita was a "full-service whorehouse," catering to all tastes—strip shows, live sex shows, donkey sex shows; where a man could have a woman, or another man, or a young girl, or a young boy, or—if he had the energy and a fat enough wallet—all four.

For his first few years at the Blue Señorita Emilio had been proud of his position—inordinately so, he now thought—but the sameness of its nightly routine, along with the realization that he had risen as far as he could go and that somewhere along the corridor of his years, when he'd aged and softened and slowed, he'd be replaced by someone younger and stronger and hungrier. Then he'd find himself out on the street with no income, no savings, no pension. And he'd wind up one of those useless old men who hung around the square in their cigarette-burned shirts and their pee-stained pants, sipping from bottles of cheap wine and yammering to anybody who'd listen about their younger days when they'd had all the money they could spend, and any women they wanted. When they'd been *somebody* instead of nobody.

He could see no future in Tijuana. Nowhere in all of Mexico. Perhaps America was the place. But maybe it was too late for him in America. He would be turning thirty soon. And how would he get in? Damned if he'd be a wetback. Not after practically managing The Blue Señorita.

The featureless corridor of his future seemed to stretch on ahead, with no exits or side passages. Just a single door at the far end. Emilio promised himself to keep an eye peeled for a way out of that corridor.

Charlie Crenshaw turned out to be that way.

Emilio hadn't realized that at first. The pudgy, brown-haired, blue-eyed boy had looked terribly young when he stumbled into the Blue Señorita that night ten years ago. He'd been roaring drunk and obviously under age, but he'd flashed his money and spread it generously, and everyone had nudged each other when he bought doe-eyed José for an hour.

When the *maricon*'s time was up, Emilio had let him out a side door and stood watching to make sure he got good and far away from The Blue Señorita before he forgot about him. But at the mouth of the alley the kid was jumped by three young *malos*. Emilio hesitated. Served the little *maricon* right to be beat up and robbed, but not on The Blue Señorita's doorstep. The local *policia* wouldn't care— Orosco paid them plenty not to—but if the brat got killed there could be a shitstorm from the States and that might lead to trouble from the capital.

Cursing under his breath, Emilio had pulled on his weighted leather gloves and charged up the alley. By the time he waded into the fight, the kid was already down and being used as a soccer ball. Emilio let loose on the *malos*. He crushed noses, crunched ribs, cracked jaws, shattered teeth, and broke at least one arm. He smashed them up and left them in a bleeding, crying, gagging, choking pile because it was his job to look out for The Blue Señorita's interests, because he wanted to make sure these *malos* never prowled The Blue Señorita's neighborhood again.

Because he *liked* it.

He dragged the unconscious kid back to the side door and checked out his wallet. He learned his name was Charles Crenshaw and that he was only fifteen. Fifteen! Hell to pay if he'd been kicked to death out here. He shuffled through pictures of the boy with his parents, posed at different ages before different homes. As the boy grew, so did the houses. The most recent was a palace.

The little *maricon* was *rich*.

And then Emilio came to a photo of the boy and his father standing before a building with a shiny CRENSOFT sign over the reflecting pool set in the front lawn. CrenSoft . . . Crenshaw . . . the rich boy's father owned a company.

As he stared at the wallet, thoughts of blackmail, and even ransom tickled Emilio's mind. But those were just quick fixes. They would change nothing. Perhaps there was another way. . . .

And somewhere down the long, featureless corridor of his future, he saw a red EXIT sign begin to glow.

Emilio threw Charlie over his shoulder and carried him back to his apartment. He placed a call to the family, told the father where Charlie was, and said to come get him. Then he sat back and waited.

The father arrived at dawn. He was taller than Emilio, and about ten years older. Every move, every glance was wary and full of suspicion. He had another man with him; Emilio later learned he was the father's pilot. When Emilio showed him Charlie's battered, unconscious form, the father's face went white. He rushed to the bed and shook the boy's shoulder. When Charlie groaned and turned over, the father seemed satisfied that he was only sleeping it off. Emilio noticed him checking to make sure his son's watch and ring were still where they belonged.

When the father spoke, his voice was tight and harsh.

"Who did this?"

"*Tres malos*," Emilio said. His English was not very good then.

"Where are they?" the father said in fluent Spanish.

Emilio ground a fist into his palm. "Worse off than your son."

The father looked at him. "You helped him? Why?"

Emilio shrugged. He'd been practicing that shrug all night. "They would have killed him."

"Why would they do that?"

"He's an *Americano* who looks rich. Plus he's a boy who likes boys. They figure sure, he's easy to kick over."

The father's eyes turned to ice. "And are you a man who likes boys?"

Emilio laughed. "Oh, no, señor. I like the women. If I want to play with a boy"—he patted his crotch—"I got one right here."

The father didn't smile. He continued to stare at Emilio. Finally he nodded, slowly. "Thank you."

Emilio helped him and the pilot carry Charlie to the car outside, then handed Charlie's wallet to the father. The father checked the credit cards and the bills.

"I see they didn't rob him."

"And neither did Emilio Sanchez. Good-bye, señor."

Emilio played his riskiest card then: He turned and walked back into his apartment building.

The father hurried after him. "Wait. You deserve a reward of some kind. Let me write you a check."

"Not necessary. No money."

"Come on. I owe you. There's got to be something I can do for you, something you need that I can get you."

Emilio took a deep breath and turned to face him. This was the big moment.

"Can you get me a job in America, señor?"

The father looked confused. As Emilio had figured, the rich *Americano* hadn't counted on anything like this. He was dumbfounded. Emilio could almost read his thoughts: *You save my son's life and all you want in return is a job?*

"I'd think that'd be the least I could do," the father said. "How do you make your living now?"

Another of those rehearsed shrugs. "I'm a bouncer at the whorehouse where your son spent much of his money last night."

The father sighed and shook his head in dismay. "Charlie, Charlie, Charlie," he whispered to the floor. Then he looked back at Emilio. "That's not much of a résumé."

"I know the value of silence."

The father considered this. "Okay. I'll give you a shot. Apply for a work visa and I'll fit you into plant security. We'll see how you work out."

"I will work out, señor. I promise."

The father kept his word, and within a matter of weeks Emilio was patrolling CrenSoft's Silicon Valley plant, dressed in the gray uniform of a security guard. It was deadly dull, but it was a start.

Charlie came by one day to thank him. He said he remembered being attacked by the three punks, but little else. Emilio found the boy very shy—he must have needed a tankful of tequila to work up the courage to walk into The Blue Señorita—and completely normal in most ways. As the years went on, Emilio actually grew fond of Charlie. Strange, because Emilio had always hated *maricones*. In truth, Charlie was the only one Emilio had ever really known. But he liked the boy. Maybe because there was nothing swishy about him. In fact, no one in security, or anywhere else in CrenSoft, seemed to have the vaguest notion that Charlie was a *maricon*.

Which was probably why the father called on Emilio to find Charlie the next time he ran off. Each time Emilio brought the boy back, the father offered him a bonus, and each time he refused. Emilio was waiting for a bigger payoff.

That came when the father sold his company. The entire staff, including security, went with the deal. All except Emilio. Mr. Crenshaw took Emilio with him when he built his mansion into a cliff overlooking the Pacific between Carmel and Big Sur. He put Emilio in charge of security during the construction, and when it was finished, he kept him on as head of security for the entire estate. The *senador* called the place Paraiso. The papers, the architectural magazines, and the TV reporters compared Paraiso to San Simeon, and people from all over the world came to gawk at it. It was Emilio's job to keep them out. He was aided in the task by the fact that access was limited to a single road which wound through rough terrain and across a narrow, one-car bridge spanning a deep ravine with a swift-flowing stream at its base.

After Mr. Crenshaw became Senator Crenshaw, Emilio often shuttled between Washington and California on the Crenshaw jet. And now he was shuttling down the West Side of Manhattan in a stretch limo.

Life was good on the fast track.

Emilio hadn't wasted his spare time during the past ten years. He'd gone to night school to improve his English and his reading. And he'd kept in shape. He'd sworn off the steroids but kept working out. The result was a slimmer, meaner frame, with smaller but denser muscles. At forty-one he was faster and stronger than he'd been in his halcyon days at The Blue Señorita. And this Dog Collar place might be a little like his old stomping grounds . . . and he did mean *stomping*.

He popped his knuckles. He almost hoped somebody got in his way when he picked up Charlie.

"It's up here on the left," Fred said.

But Emilio was watching to the right. On the near side of West Street, near the water, a group of young men dressed in everything from leather pants to off-the-shoulder blouses were drinking beer and prancing around. Every so often a car would stop and one of them would swish over and speak to the driver. Sometimes the car would pull away as it had arrived, and sometimes the young man would get in and be whisked off for a rolling quicky.

Fred did a U-turn and pulled up in front of The Dog Collar. As Emilio stepped out, Decker and Molinari appeared from the shadows. Decker was fair, Molinari was almost as dark as Emilio. They were his two best men from the Paraiso security force.

"He's still there. Want us to—?"

"I'll get him," Emilio said. "You two watch my back." He pulled out a pair of plain, black leather gloves. "And be sure to wear your gloves. You don't want to split a knuckle in this place."

They smiled warily and pulled on their gloves as they followed Emilio inside.

"He's wearing a red parka," Decker said as he and Mol flanked the door.

Crowded inside, and dark. So dark Emilio had to remove his shades. He scanned the bar that stretched along the wall to his right. No women—not that he'd expected any—and no red parka. He met some frank, inviting stares, but no sign of Charlie. He checked out the floor—crowded with cocktail tables, a row of booths along the far wall, and an empty stage at the rear. Slim waiters with boyish haircuts and neat little mustaches slipped back and forth among the tables with drinks and bar food. Emilio spotted two women—together, of course—but where was Charlie?

He edged his way through the tables, searching the faces. No red parka. Maybe he'd taken it off. Who knew what Charlie might look like these days—the color of his hair, what he'd be wearing? One thing Emilio had to say for the boy, he was discreet. He wasn't deliberately trying to ruin his father's political chances. He usually rented a place under an assumed name, never told any of his rotating lovers who he was, and generally kept a low profile. But nonetheless he remained a monster political liability.

Maybe that was why the *senador* had decided it was time to reel Charlie in. He'd been gone for almost two years now. Emilio had tracked him to New York through the transfers from his trust fund. He'd traced him across the country but now he couldn't spot him across this single room. Had he made Decker and slipped out the back?

Emilio was about to return to the door to quiz Decker when he saw a flash of red in the rearmost booth and homed in on it like a beacon. Two guys in the booth—the one holding the parka had his back to him. Emilio repressed a gasp when he saw his face. It was Charlie. The curly brown hair was the same, as were the blue eyes, but he looked so thin. Emilio barely recognized the boy.

Why do I still think of him as a boy? he wondered. He's twenty-five.

Perhaps it was because part of his brain would always associate Charlie with the pudgy teenager he'd carried out of that Tijuana alley.

Charlie looked up at Emilio with wide blue eyes that widened further when he recognized him.

"Oh, shit," Charlie said. "You found me."

"Time to go home, Charlie."

"Let me be, Emilio. I'm settled in here. I'm not bothering anybody. I'm actually *happy* here. Just tell Dad you couldn't find me."

"That would be lying, Charlie. And I never lie . . . to your dad."

He grabbed the boy under his right arm and began to pull him from his seat. Charlie tried to wriggle free but it was like a Chihuahua resisting a pit bull.

The guy in the other half of the booth stood up and gave Emilio a two-handed shove.

"Get your mitts off him, fucker!"

He was beefier than Charlie, with decent pects and a good set of shoulders under the T-shirt and leather vest he wore, but he was out of his league. Way out.

"No me jodas!" Emilio said and smashed a right uppercut to his jaw that slammed him back into the inner corner of the booth. He slumped there and stared up at Emilio with a look of dazed pain.

Emilio turned and started dragging Charlie toward the

door, knocking over tables in his way. He didn't want a full-scale brawl but he wouldn't have minded another *maricon* or two trying to block his way. But most of them seemed too surprised and off guard to react. Too bad. He was in the mood to kick some ass. He saw the bartender come out from behind the bar hefting an aluminum baseball bat. Decker and Mol intercepted him, and after a brief struggle Mol was holding the bat and the bartender was back behind the bar.

Once he was free of the tables, Emilio swung the stumbling Charlie around in front of him and propelled him toward the door. Decker and Mol closed in behind them as they exited. Emilio heard the bat clank on the floor as the doors swung closed. Half a dozen steps across the sidewalk and then they were all inside the limo, heading uptown.

Charlie opened the door on the other side but Emilio pulled him back before he could jump out.

"You'll get killed that way, kid."

"I don't care!" Charlie said. "Dammit, Emilio, you can't do this! It's kidnapping!"

"Just following orders. Your father misses you."

"Yeah. Sure."

Charlie folded his arms and legs and withdrew into himself. He spent the rest of the trip staring at the floor.

Emilio kept a close eye on him. He didn't want him trying to jump out of the car again—although that might be a blessing for all concerned.

He sighed. Why did the *senador* want this miserable creature around? He seemed to love the boy despite the threat posed by his twisted nature. Was that parenthood? Was that what fathering a child did to you? Made you lose your perspective? Emilio was glad he'd spared himself the affliction. But if he'd had a child, a boy, he'd never have let him grow up to be a *maricon*. He would have beaten that out of him at an early age.

What if Charlie did die by leaping from a moving vehicle? Or what if he fell prey to a hit-and-run driver? A major stumbling block on the *senador*'s road to the White House would be removed.

Emilio decided to start keeping a mental file of "accidental" ways for Charlie to die should the need suddenly arise. The *senador* would never order it, but if the need ever arose, Emilio might decide to act on his own.

I was two decades and a half in the desert when they came to me. How they found me, I do not know. Perhaps the Lord guided them. Perhaps they followed the reek of my corruption.

They too were in flight, hiding from the Romans and their lackeys in the Temple. The brother of He whose name I deserve not to speak led them. They were awed by my appearance, and I by theirs. Barely did I recognize them, so exhausted were they by their trek.

I was astounded to learn that they had brought the Mother with them.

FROM THE GLASS SCROLL
ROCKEFELLER MUSEUM TRANSLATION

5

Father Dan Fitzpatrick strolled the narrow streets of his Lower East Side parish and drank in the colors flowing around him. Sure there was squalor here, and poverty and crime, all awash in litter and graffiti, but there was *color* here. Not like the high-rise midtown he'd visited last night, with its sterile concrete-and-marble plazas, its faceless glass-and-granite office towers.

A mere forty blocks from the Waldorf, the Lower East Side might as well be another country. No skyscrapers here. Except for aberrations like the Con-Ed station's quartet of stacks and the dreary housing projects, the Lower East Side skyline rises to a uniform six stories. Window-studded facades of cracked and patched brick crowd together cheek by jowl for block after block, separated occasionally by a garbage-choked alley. They're all brick of varying shades of red, sometimes brown or gray, and every so often a daring pink or yellow or blue. With no room behind or to either side, a mazework of mandatory fire escapes hangs over the sidewalks, clinging to the brick facades like spidery steel parasites, ready-made perches for the city's winged rat, the pigeon.

Everywhere Dan looked, everything was old, with no attempt to recapture youth. Graffiti formed the decorative motif, layer upon layer until the intertwined snake squiggles and balloon letters were indecipherable even to their perpe-trators. The store signs he could read advertised old bed-ding, fresh vegetables, used furniture, and the morning paper, offered food, candy, magazines, cashed checks, and booze, booze, booze. And some signs he couldn't read—Koreans and Vietnamese were moving in. He passed pawn-shops, bodegas, boys' clubs, schools, churches, and playgrounds. Children still played, even here.

He looked up at the passing windows. Behind them lived young, hopeful immigrants on their way up, middle-aged has-beens on their way down, and too many running like hell just to stay in place. And out here on the streets dwelt the never-weres and the never-will-bes, going nowhere, barely even sure of where they were at any given moment.

He wore his civvies this morning—faded jeans, flannel shirt, sneakers. He wasn't here on Church business and it was easier to get around without the Roman collar. Especially in Tompkins Square. The collar drew the panhandlers like moths to a flame. And can you believe it—every single one of them a former altar boy? Simply amazing how many altar boys had become homeless.

Tompkins Square Park was big, three blocks long and running the full width between Avenues A and B. Black wrought-iron fencing guarded the perimeter. Oaks, pale green with new life, stood inside the fences but spread their branches protectively over the surrounding sidewalks. Homeless shantytowns used to spring up here every so often, and just as often the police would raze them, but closing the park between midnight and six A.M. every night had sent the cardboard box brigade elsewhere.

Dan walked past the stately statue of Samuel S. Cox, its gray-green drabness accentuated by the orange, red, and yellow of the swings and slides in the nearby playground, and strolled the bench-lined walks, searching for the gleaming white of Harold Gold's bald head. They'd met years ago when Dan had audited Hal's course on the Dead Sea scrolls. They'd got to talking after class, found they shared an abiding interest in the Jerusalem Church—Hal from the Jewish perspective, Dan from the Christian—and became fast friends. Whenever one dug up a tasty little tidbit of lore, he shared it immediately with the other. Dan was sure Hal had picked up some real goodies during his sabbatical in Israel. He was looking forward to this meeting.

He didn't see Hal. Lunch hour was still a while off but already seats were becoming scarce around the square. Then Dan spotted someone waving from a long bench in the sunny section on the Avenue A side.

No wonder I couldn't spot him, Dan thought as he approached Hal's bench. He's got a tan.

As usual, Hal was nattily dressed in a dark blue blazer, gray slacks, a pale blue Oxford button-down shirt, and a red-and-blue paisley tie. But his customary academician's pallor had been toasted to a golden brown. His nude scalp gleamed with a richer color. He looked healthier and better rested than Dan had ever seen him.

"The Middle East seems to agree with you," Dan said, laughing as they shook hands. He sat down next to him. "I can't remember ever seeing you looking so fit."

"Believe me, Fitz," Hal said, "getting away for a year and recharging the batteries does wonders for the mind and body. I heartily recommend it." He looked around. "You came alone?"

"Of course. Who else would I bring?" Dan said, knowing perfectly well who Hal was looking for.

"I don't know. I thought, well, maybe Sister Carrie might come along."

"No. She's back at St. Joe's, working. You'll have to come by if you want to see her."

"Maybe I will. Been a long time since I stopped in."

Dan knew Hal had a crush on Carrie. A strictly hands-off, love-from-afar thing that reduced him to a stumbling, stammering twelve-year-old around her. But he wasn't alone. Everybody loved Sister Carrie.

"Do that. And bring some food. A long time since you made a contribution."

Just then an eighth of a ton of black woman in a frayed yellow dress lumbered up and spread a large green garbage bag on the bench. She seated herself so close to Dan that one of her massive thighs rubbed against his. He smiled at her and inched away to give her some room as she settled herself.

Hal clapped Dan on the shoulder. "Saw you on TV last night, Fitz."

"Did you. How was I?"

"You sounded good. I thought you came off very well."

You wouldn't think so if you'd been there, Dan thought. *. . . you just ain't getting it done . . .*

His herd at his heels, he'd slunk back to St. Joe's with his tail between his legs. At least that was the way it had felt. The on-camera interview Hal had seen had been taped during the fund-raising dinner, while he and the demonstrators were all waiting for Senator Crenshaw to come out. After the senator's exit—after he'd been sliced and diced—Dan had fielded a few questions from reporters but his answers weren't as sharp as they might have been. They'd seemed almost . . . empty.

But perhaps that was just his own perception. Everyone he'd seen so far today had told him he and the protesters had come across extremely well on the tube. Dan would have to take their word for it. He'd lacked the nerve to tune in last night.

Luckily, no one seemed to have caught Senator Crenshaw's little diatribe on tape. Dan knew the wounded part of him within would shrivel up and die if he had listen to that again.

"What the—?"

Hal's voice jolted Dan back to the here and now. He glanced up and saw Hal staring past him in horrified fascination at the fat black woman. She'd removed the mirrored half of a compact and a pair of tweezers from her huge purse and was now plucking at her face. Dan couldn't see anything to pluck at but that didn't seem to deter the woman. She was completely engrossed in the task.

Hal shook himself. "Anyway, seeing you reminded me that I had a present for you."

He picked up a football-sized box from the bag between his feet and placed it in Dan's hands.

"What's this?"

"A gift. From the past . . . sort of."

Dan hadn't expected a gift, though God knew his spirits needed lifting after last night.

"Well, don't just stare at it. Open it."

No ribbon or wrapping to remove, just a plain, oblong wooden box. Dan lifted the lid and stared.

"What . . . ?"

"Your own Dead Sea scroll," Harold said.

Dan glanced at his friend. He knew Harold was kidding, but this thing looked so damned . . . real.

"No, really. What is it?"

Harold launched into the explanation. A fascinating story, during which a pair of thin, dark-haired, mustached men seated themselves on the far side of the black woman; each began drinking his lunch from a brown paper bag. Dan listened to Hal and sensed the mixture of excitement and disappointment in his voice. When he finished, Dan looked down at the loosely rolled parchment in the box on his lap.

"So, you're giving me a first-century parchment filled with twentieth century scribbles."

"Damn near twenty-*first* century scribbles. An oddity. A collector's item in its own right."

Dan continued to stare at the ancient roll of sheepskin. He was moved.

"I . . . I don't know what to say, Hal. I'll treasure this."

"Don't get carried away—"

"No, I mean it. If nothing else, the parchment was made in the early days of the Church. It's a link of sorts. And I'm touched that you thought of me."

"Who else do I know who's so nuts about the first century?"

"You must have been crushed when you found out."

Harold sighed. "*Crushed* isn't the word. We were all devastated. But I tell you, Fitz, I wouldn't trade the high of the first few days with that scroll for anything. It was the greatest!"

Just then a woman dressed in satin work-out pants and a red sleeveless shell top walked over to the bench and stood on the other side of Hal. She was middle-aged with a bulging abdomen. Dan noticed that she wore red slipper-socks over red lace knee-highs. She'd finished off the ensemble by wrapping Christmas paper around her ankles.

Hal looked down at her feet and said, "Good Lord."

She smiled down at him. "Ain't blockin' yer sun, am I?"

Hal shook his head. "No. That's quite all right."

She then pulled a bottle of Ban deodorant from her pocket and began to apply it to her right underarm—and only to her right underarm. Dan and Hal watched her do this for what seemed like five minutes but was probably only one. During the process she also managed to coat half of her shoulder blade as well.

She was still at it when Dan turned back to his gift and spotted a legal-size envelope tucked in next to the scroll. He pulled it out.

"What's this?"

Hal dragged his eyes away from the woman with the deodorant. "The translation. I know you're pretty good at old Hebrew, but this will save you from risking damage to the scroll by unrolling it. And as jumbled, paranoid, and crazy as it may read, you can rely on the accuracy of the translation. The folks who did it are tops."

"Great, Hal. You've thought of everything."

An elderly man in a shabby blue suit slipped past the Ban lady and seated himself next to Hal. Immediately he began untying his shoes.

"You don't mind, do you?" he said in an accented voice as he slipped the first one off. "They're really sweaty. I need to air my feet something awful."

"Be my guest," Hal said, rolling his eyes at Dan as the odor from the exposed feet and empty shoes began to rise. "We were just leaving. Weren't we, Fitz."

"Gee, I kind of like it here, Hal," Dan said in his most guileless tone. "Why don't you save our seats while I run up to the corner and buy us a couple of hot dogs. We can eat them right here. You like sauerkraut?"

"I've lost my appetite," Hal said through a tight, fierce grin. "Let's. Go. For. A. Little. Walk. Shall. We?"

Dan hadn't the heart to play this out any longer. After all, Hal had just given him a first-century scroll.

"Sure."

As they left, the Ban lady took their spots and switched to her left underarm.

When they reached the sidewalk on Avenue A, Hal said, "I think I preferred living under the threat of a PLO attack."

Just then a very pale woman with very black hair, black blouse, and black stretch pants walked by balancing a loaded green plastic laundry basket on her head.

"And sometimes I wonder if I've truly left the middle East."

Dan smiled. Poor, fastidious Hal. "You should be at Princeton or Yale."

"Yeah. I could have been. But I thought I'd like New York. Don't they get to you?"

Dan shrugged. "Those folks are like most of the people I hang out with every day, but considerably more functional."

"How do you do it? You all but live with them. And you don't have to."

"Jesus hung with the down-and-outs. Why shouldn't I?"

He noticed Hal looking at him closely. "You don't think you're Jesus, do you?"

"Hardly." Dan laughed. "But that's what being a priest is all about—modeling your life on the J-man, as he's known around here. Truth is, we don't know much about His life. He might even have been married."

"We don't look into the New Testament much where I come from, but I don't remember ever hearing that he was."

"True. But nowhere is it said that he wasn't."

"Well, we do know that he rubbed the higher-ups the wrong way."

"I've done my share of that," Dan said, thinking of his long-running battle with Father Brennan, St. Joseph's pastor, over his soup kitchen in the church basement.

"It got him killed."

Dan laughed again. "Not to worry. I'm not looking to get my palms and soles ventilated."

"You can't be too careful, Fitz," Hal said, glancing back

toward the plaza. "A lot of these folks are more than a few bricks shy of a full load."

Dan nodded. "I'm aware of that." He thought of the couple of occasions when some of Loaves and Fishes' "guests" got violent, mostly screaming and shouting and pushing, but one went so far as to pull a knife during an argument over who would sit by a window. "And I'm careful."

"Good. I'm sure there's a place in heaven for you, but I don't want you taking it just yet."

"Heaven's not guaranteed for anybody, Hal. Sometimes I wonder if there is such a place."

Hal was looking at him strangely. "You?"

He didn't want to get into anything heavy with Hal so he grinned. "Just kidding. But how about lunch? It's the least I can do." He pointed to Nino's on the corner of St. Mark's Place. "Slice of Sicilian?"

"I'll take a raincheck," Hal said, extending his hand. "Got to run. But I want to get together with you again after you've read the translation. See if you can make any sense of it."

"I'll do my best. And thanks again. Thanks a million. Nice to own something this old—and know it's one of a kind."

"Not one of a kind, I'm afraid," Hal said, frowning. "Shortly before I left, an Israeli collector came in with another scroll identical to this one. The parchment and the writing carbon dated the same as yours—about two thousand years apart."

Dan shrugged. "Okay. So it's not one of a kind. It's still a great gift, and I'll treasure it. But right now I've got to get back to the shelter for the lunch line."

Hal waved and started down the sidewalk. "See you next week, okay? For lunch. I should have my appetite back by then."

Dan waved and headed back to St. Joe's, wondering how many of these weird scrolls were floating around the Middle East?

She had been dead for two years and more, yet her body showed no trace of corruption. The brother had kept her death a secret. He and the others feared that Ananus or Herod Agrippa or even the Hellenists might make use of her remains to further their various ends.

FROM THE GLASS SCROLL
ROCKEFELLER MUSEUM TRANSLATION

6

Chaim Kesev stared westward from the picture window in the living room of Tulla Szobel's sprawling hilltop home. He could see the lights of Tel Aviv—the IBM tower, the waterfront hotels—and the darkness of the Mediterranean beyond. The glass reflected the room behind him. A pale room, a small pale world—beige rug, beige walls, beige drapes, pale abstract paintings, low beige furniture that seemed designed for something other than human comfort, chrome and glass tables and lamps.

Kesev wrinkled his nose. With all the money lavished on this room, he thought, the least you'd think she could do was find a way to remove the cigarette stink. The place smelled like a tavern at cleanup time.

He had arrived here unannounced tonight, shown Miss Szobel his Shin Bet identification, and all but pushed his way in. Now he waited while she procured the scroll from a room in some other quarter of the house.

The scroll . . . he'd begun a low-key search for it immediately after its theft four years ago. A subtle search. Not *I'm looking for a scroll recently stolen from a cave in the Judean Wilderness. Have you seen or heard of such a thing?* That kind of search would close doors rather than open them. Instead, Kesev had extended feelers into the antiquities market—legitimate and underground—saying he was a collector interested in purchasing first-century manuscripts, and that money was no object.

Perhaps his feelers hadn't been subtle enough. Perhaps the seller he sought preferred more tried-and-true channels of commerce. Whatever the reason, he was offered many items but none were what he sought.

Then, just last year, his feelers caught ripples of excitement from the manuscript department at the Rockefeller Museum in Jerusalem. A unique first-century scroll had been brought in for verification. As he homed in on the scent, word came that the scroll turned out to be a fake. So he'd veered off and continued his search elsewhere.

And then, just last month, whispers of another fake, identical to the first—the same disjointed story, written in the same Aramaic form of Hebrew, on an ancient parchment.

Something in those whispers teased Kesev. The scant details he could glean about the fakes tantalized him. He investigated and learned that the first scroll had been brought in by an American who had since returned home. But the second . . . a wealthy woman from a Tel Aviv suburb had brought that in, and taken it home in a huff when informed that she'd been duped.

Kesev was standing in her living room now.

He heard her footsteps behind him.

"Here, Mr. Kesev," said a throaty voice behind him. Her Ivrit carried a barely noticeable Eastern European accent. "I believe this is what you want."

He turned slowly, hiding his anticipation. Tulla Szobel was in her mid-fifties, blond hair, reed thin, prematurely wrinkled, and dressed in a beige knit dress the color of her walls. A cigarette dangled from her lips. She held a Lucite case between her hands.

Kesev took the case from her and carried it to the glass-and-chrome coffee table. Without asking permission, he lifted the lid and removed the scroll.

"Careful!" she said, hovering over him.

He ignored her. He uncoiled a foot or so of the scroll and began reading—

Then stopped. This wasn't the scroll. This looked like the

scroll, and some of it read like the scroll, but the writing, the penmanship was all wrong.

"They were right," he said, nodding slowly. "This is a fake. A clumsy fake."

Miss Szobel sniffed. "I don't need you to tell me that. The Rockefeller Museum—"

"Where did you get this?" Kesev said, rerolling the scroll.

She puffed furiously on her cigarette. "Why . . . I . . . picked it up in a street bazaar."

"Really?" They all said that. Amazing. Israel seemed full of lucky collectors who were forever happening on price-less—or potentially priceless—artifacts in street stalls, and purchasing them for next to nothing from vendors who had no idea of their true worth. "You must take me to him."

"I wish I could," she said. "I've been looking for him myself, trying to get my money back. But he seems to have vanished into thin air."

"You are lying," Kesev said evenly, replacing the Lucite lid and looking up at her.

She stepped back as if he'd spit at her. "How dare you!" She pointed a shaking finger toward her front door. "I want you out of—"

"If I leave without the name that I seek I will return within the hour with a search warrant and a search team, and we will comb this house inch by inch until we turn up more forgeries from this mysterious source."

Kesev couldn't back up a word of that threat, but he knew the specter of a search of the premises would strike terror into the heart of any serious antiquities collector. There wasn't one who didn't dip into the black market now and then. Some bought there almost exclusively. If Miss Szobel followed true to form, a search might result in the seizure of half her collection; maybe more.

Miss Szobel's pointing arm faltered and fell to her side.

"Wh-why? On what grounds? Why does Domestic Intel-ligence care—?"

"Oh, it's not just the Shin Bet. The Mossad is involved too."

She paled further. "The Mossad?"

"Yes. We have reason to believe that these scrolls are merely the latest in an ongoing scheme to sell worthless fakes to wealthy collectors and funnel the money to Hamas and other terrorist organizations."

Amazing how facile a liar he'd become. It hadn't always been this way. As a younger man he'd insisted on speaking nothing but the truth. But that youth, like truth, was long gone, swallowed up by time and tragedy.

He sighed and rose to his feet. "Please do not leave the house, Miss Szobel. I will return in—"

"Wait!" she cried, motioning him back toward the couch. "I had no idea terrorists were involved. Of course I'll tell you where I bought it."

"Excellent." Kesev removed a pen and a note pad from his breast pocket. "Go ahead."

"His name is Salah Mahmoud. He has a shop in Jerusalem—the old town. In the Moslem quarter, off Qadasiya."

Kesev nodded. He knew the area, if not the shop.

"Thank you for your cooperation." He bent and lifted the scroll and its Lucite box from the table. "I'll need to take this back to Shin Bet headquarters for analysis."

"Of course," she said, following him to the door. "But I will get it back, won't I?"

"Of course. As soon as we are finished with it."

He waved good-bye and headed for his car. Another lie. Miss Tulla Szobel had seen the last of her forged scroll. He'd take it with him to Jerusalem for his visit to a certain Salah Mahmoud. The dealer couldn't plead ignorance if Kesev held the scroll under his nose. Threats probably wouldn't suffice to loosen Mahmoud's tongue. Kesev might have to get rough. He almost relished the thought.

I asked the brother why he had come to me with this miracle.

He said to me, Because it has been told to us that you are to guard her, and protect her as if she were your own mother and still alive.

I told him, Yes. Yes, I will guard her with my life. I will do anything you ask.

FROM THE GLASS SCROLL
ROCKEFELLER MUSEUM TRANSLATION

7

Manhattan

The Gothic, granite-block bulk of St. Joseph's Church sits amid the brick tenements like a down-on-her-luck dowager who's held on to her finer clothes from the old days but hasn't the will or the means to keep them in good repair. Her twin spires are alternately caked black with city grime and streaked white with the droppings of the pigeons who find perches on the spires' remaining crockets. The colors of the large central rose window over the double doors are barely discernible through the grime. She's flanked on her left by the rectory and on her right by the Convent of the Blessed Virgin.

From his room in the rectory Father Dan saw the hungry homeless lining up next to the worn stone steps in front of St. Joe's, waiting to get into the Loaves and Fishes for lunch. He dearly would have loved to sit here and read the translation of the scroll Hal had given him, but duty called.

He left the wooden box on his bed and hurried down to the rectory basement. From there it was a quick trip through the dank, narrow tunnel that ran beneath the alley between the church and the rectory to the basement of St. Joe's. As he approached the door at the far end, the smell of fresh bread and hot soup drew him forward.

The tunnel ended in the kitchen area of Loaves and Fishes. He stepped inside. Heat thickened the air. All the ovens were going—donated by a retired baker—heating loaves of Carrie's special bread: multiple grains mixed with high-protein flour, enriched with eggs and gluten. A meal in itself. Add a bowl of Carrie's soup and you had a feast.

Dan sniffed the air as he headed for the huge stove and the cluster of aproned volunteers stirring the brimming pots.

"Smells great. What's the *soup du jour?*"

"Split pea," Augusta said.

"Split pea?" Dan said. "I ordered *boeuf bourguignon!*"

A slim brunette at the center of the cluster turned and gave him a withering, scornful stare.

"Don't you be starting that again," she said, pointing a dripping spoon at him.

"Oh, that's right," he said. "I forgot. This is a *vegetarian* soup kitchen."

The volunteers glanced over their shoulders and giggled. This argument had become a litany, recited almost daily.

"Hush up or we'll be making a beef stew of *you!*"

Now they were laughing aloud. The brunette tried to hold her scowl but finally a smile broke through and its brilliance lit the room.

"Good morning, Sister," Dan said.

"Good morning, Father," she said.

Sister Carolyn Ferris fixed him a moment with her wide, guileless blue eyes. Her normally pale cheeks were flushed from the heat of the stove. The rising steam had curled her straight dark hair, cut in a bob, into loose ringlets around her face. She was in her late twenties dressed in the shapeless, oversized work shirt and baggy pants she favored when working at the shelter. Her lips were on the thin side, and her teeth probably could have done with a little orthodontic work in her teens, but she'd joined the convent at fourteen so they remained *au naturel*. The way her smile lit up her face erased all memory of those minor imperfections.

As often as he'd seen it, Dan never tired of that smile. He'd enjoyed it in all its permutations, and sometimes he'd catch a hint of sadness there, a deeply hidden hurt that clouded her eyes in unguarded moments. But only for a moment.

Sister Carrie was the sun and the Lower East Side her world; she shone on it daily.

But for all her gentle, giving girlish exterior, she was tough inside. Especially when it came to her beliefs, whether religious or dietary. No meat was served at the shelter—"We won't be killing one of God's creatures to feed another, at least not as long as I'm in the kitchen"—which was just as well because the food dollars stretched considerably further with the Sister Carrie menu.

And Dan, who'd always been pretty much of a beer-and-a-burger man himself, had to admit that he'd got out of the meat habit under her tutelage and no longer missed it. At least not too much.

"Sorry I'm late," he said. "What needs to be done?"

"Our guests should be getting low on bread by now."

She always called them "our guests," and Dan never failed to be charmed by it.

"Consider it done."

She smiled that smile and turned back to the stove. Shaking off the lingering aftereffect, Dan gathered up half a dozen loaves and carried them out to the shelter area.

A different mix of odors greeted him in the Big Room. Split-pea and fresh-baked bread aromas layered the air, spiced with the sting of cigarette smoke and the pungency of unwashed bodies swathed in unwashed clothes.

Dan squeezed past Hilda Larsen's doubly ample middle-aged rump and dumped the loaves on one of the long tables lined up against the inner wall as the serving area.

"Good afternoon, Father," she said, smiling as she stirred the soup with her long, curved ladle.

"Hello, Hilda. You look ravishing as usual today."

"Oh, Father Dan," she said, blushing.

Thank God for volunteers like Hilda, Dan thought as he picked up the bread knife and began cutting the loaves into inch-thick slices.

A small army of good-hearted folks donated enough hours here at the shelter to qualify as part-time employees. Most of them were women with working husbands and empty nests who'd transferred the nurturing drive from their now grown and independent children to the habitués of Loaves and Fishes. Dan realized that the kitchen filled a void in their lives and that they probably got as much as they gave, but that didn't make him any less appreciative. Loaves and Fishes would never have got off the ground without them.

"Could youse hand me wunna dose, Fadda?"

Dan looked up. A thin, bearded man in his forties with red-rimmed eyes and a withered right arm held a bowl of soup in his good hand. His breath stank of cheap wine.

"Sure thing, Lefty."

Dan perched a good thick slice on the edge of the bowl.

"Tanks a lot, Fadda. Yer a prince."

Looked as if Lefty had got into the Mad Dog early today. Dan watched him weave toward one of the tables, praying he wouldn't drop the bowl. He didn't.

"Hey, Pilot," said the next man in line.

Rider in his suede jacket. At least it had been suede in the sixties; now the small sections visible through the decades of accumulated grime were as smooth and shiny as dressed leather. Probably an expensive jacket in its day, with short fringes on the pockets and a long fringe on each sleeve; only a couple of sleeve fringes left now, gone with the lining and the original buttons. But no way would Rider give up that coat. He'd tell anyone who'd listen about the days he'd worn it back and forth cross country on his Harley, tripping on acid the whole way. But Rider had taken a few too many trips. His Harley was long gone and most of his mind along with it.

"How's it going, Rider?" Dan said, dropping a heavy slice on his tray.

Rider always called him Pilot. Because Rider slurred his words as much as anyone else, Dan had asked him once if that was Pilot with an *o* or an *a-t-e*. Rider hadn't the vaguest idea what Dan was talking about.

"Good, Pilot. Got a new lead on my Harley. Should have it back by the end of the week."

"Great."

"Yep. Then it's so long."

Rider's quest for his last bike, stolen sometime during the

early eighties, lent a trace structure to his otherwise aimless day-to-day existence. Rider was the shelter's Galahad.

The rest of the regulars filed by with a few newer faces sprinkled in; a couple of those new faces might become regulars, the rest would drift on. The locals, the never-miss-a-meal regulars were all there, some in their twenties, some in their sixties, most of indeterminate age somewhere between. Some called themselves John and Jim and Marta and Thelma, but many had street names: Stoney, Indian, Preacher, Pilgrim, Lefty, Dandy, Poppy, Bigfoot, One-Thumb George, and the inimitable Dirty Harry.

They all got one bowl of soup and one thick slice of Sister Carrie's famous bread. After they finished they could have seconds if there was anything left over after everyone had firsts. Off to his left, Dan heard scuffling and a shout as the seconds line formed.

"Oh, Father," Hilda said, leaning over the counter to look. "I think it's Dandy and Indian again."

"I'll take care of it."

Dan ducked under the table and got to the trouble spot just as Dandy was picking himself up off the floor and crouching to charge Indian. Dan grabbed him by the back of his jacket collar.

"Whoa, Dandy! Hang on a sec."

Dandy whirled, snarling. The fire in his eyes cooled immediately when he saw who he faced. He shrugged to settle his jacket back on his shoulders and straightened his tie. Dandy had earned his name from his taste in fourth-hand attire. He always managed to pick the brightest colors from the donated clothing. His latest get-up consisted of an orange shirt, a green-and-white striped tie, a plaid sports jacket, and lime-green golf pants. All frayed, all dirty, but worn with the air of someone who considered his life a fashion statement.

"Lucky for Indian you came along."

"What happened?"

"He pushed me out of my place in line."

Dan glanced at Indian, who faced straight ahead, ignoring the two of them. Dan knew he'd get nothing out of Indian, who wasn't Indian at all—unless that kinky hair and ebony skin were *West* Indian. Indian never spoke, never smiled, never frowned. Apparently someone had called him a cigar-store Indian years ago and the name had stuck.

"You were cutting into the line, weren't you, Dandy."

"No way."

"Dandy." Dan knew Dandy didn't like to wait in line, especially with those he considered his sartorial inferiors. "This wouldn't be the first time."

"I didn't cut. I axed. I axed him if he minded if I got ahead of him. He didn't say no so I—"

Dan jerked his thumb over his shoulder. "End of the line, Dandy."

"Hey, Father—"

"We've got plenty today. You won't miss out."

"But I got places to go."

Dan said nothing further. He stared Dandy down until he shrugged and headed for the end of the line.

Like dealing with eight-year-olds, he thought as he headed back to the serving area.

But juvenile behavior was only one side of them, and that was the least of their problems. A fair number of them were mentally ill—paranoids, borderline personalities, and out-right schizophrenics—and many had drug and alcohol problems. Multiple substance abuse was common. Some combined the problems: chronic brain syndromes from long-term drug and/or alcohol abuse, or mental illness compounded by substance abuse.

For most of them it was a no-win situation. And Senator Crenshaw's concentration camps would do nothing for them.

Dan had finished slicing the bread and the ones who wanted seconds had passed through when he heard a chorus of voices saying, "Hello, Sister Carrie," and "Good after-noon, Sister Carrie," and "Thanks for the great meal, Sister Carrie."

He glanced up and there she was, wiping her hands as she surveyed the diners.

"Did everyone have enough?" she said.

They answered almost as a group: "Oh, yes, Sister Carrie."

Dan watched her walk out through the Big Room and slip among her guests, an almost ethereal presence, speaking to them, touching them: a hand on a shoulder here, a pat on a head there, a whispered word for old friends, a handshake and a smile for the new faces. He envied her ability to make everyone of them feel special, to know they mattered.

"Was it good?" she said when she reached the far end of the Big Room. They cheered and applauded, and that made her smile. And the light she shed on the room made the applause double in volume.

Hilda was tsking and shaking her head. "Look at them! They're ga-ga over her." But there was wonder rather than disapproval in her voice. "What a politician she'd have made."

Dan could only nod, eternally amazed at Carrie's talent for making people love her.

Still smiling, she curtsied and returned to the kitchen. As the room's illumination seemed to dim by half, the guests began to clear their places and shuffle out to the street or line up for the bathroom.

Dan was wiping away the bread crumbs when he heard cries of, "Word up, Doc" and "How's it go, Doctor Joe?" He looked up and saw a short, white-coated Hispanic strolling toward him.

"Things slow at the clinic?" Dan said.

"I wish."

Dr. Joe Martinez's dark eyes twinkled as he picked up a leftover piece of bread, tore it, and shoved the right-hand half into his mouth. He had mocha skin, dark curly hair, and a body-builder's frame.

"Want some soup?" Dan asked.

"Carrie make it?"

"Of course."

"Then that's my answer."

"What?"

"Of course."

"Right." Dan got him a bowl and a spoon and slid them across the table.

Joe stared down at the steaming green but didn't reach for the spoon.

"Something wrong?" Dan said.

Joe continued staring at the soup. "Three new HIV conversions this morning."

"Jesus!"

"Jesus had nothing to do with it."

"I know, but . . . anybody we know?"

Finally Joe looked up from the soup. "You know I can't tell you that."

"Sure, sure, and I appreciate that, but we've got close quarters here. Know what I'm saying?"

"Sure I do. But you can't catch AIDS sitting next to someone. It doesn't jump plate to plate."

"No kidding. But it does jump vein to needle and needle to vein, and not a few of our guests have been known to shoot up when mood and opportunity permit."

Joe shook his head. "Can't tell you, Fitz."

"I don't want names. Don't tell me *who*, just tell me *how many* HIV positives in and out of here."

Dan wasn't looking to ostracize anyone, but it certainly would be useful to know who was positive. A lot of St. Joe's guests regularly fell or got into fights. It was a common occurrence for one of them to stagger in hurt and bleeding—amazing how much blood could pour out of a minor scalp cut—and either he or Carrie would clean them up. He wasn't so worried about himself, but Carrie . . .

"I don't have to look at any faces to tell you that you've got HIV positives here. The homeless population is loaded with them."

Dan knew that. He just wished he knew *who*.

"So when do I put on the rubber gloves?"

"Whenever you see red." Joe took the other half of his bread slice and dipped it into his soup. "By the way, how's Sister Carrie?"

"You just missed her."

"Oh."

"She's in the back. Want me to get her?"

"No. Don't bother her. Just wanted to say hello if she happened to wander through."

Is that the only reason people come here? Dan thought. To see Carrie?

First Hal asking about her, now Joe. They were like puppies, panting for a glimpse of her. No lascivious ogling here—no curves in those asexual, baggy clothes she wore— just a simple desire to bask in her glow. He knew their love for her was the worship-from-afar kind, but still it bothered him. He should be used to it by now, but he wasn't.

After all, Dan loved her too.

I knew a place for her, a small cave set far back on the ledge above the tav rock. Together we prepared a bier for her and placed her upon it.

And then we sealed her in, carrying rocks that one man could not lift alone, and choking the mouth of the cave with them.

It will take many men to reopen her Resting Place. But they shall not touch these stones. They shall have to deal with me first.

FROM THE GLASS SCROLL
ROCKEFELLER MUSEUM TRANSLATION

8

Paraiso

As Emilio wheeled the black Bentley limo through the iron gates on the rim of his estate, Arthur Crenshaw sat alone in the backseat and closed his eyes, praying for guidance in the coming confrontation with his son.

Charlie, Charlie, what are we going to do about you?

He'd been up all night praying over the problem. And during the six hours alone in the passenger compartment of his *Gulfstream II*, four-and-a-half miles over the country he prayed would elect him its president, he'd continued praying for an answer.

Thank the Lord for prayer. He only wished he'd discovered it sooner in his life. He'd never been much of a one for prayer in his younger days. In fact he remembered secret sneers at the breast-beaters, the bead-pushers, the doe-eyed heaven-gazers who couldn't solve their problems on their own and had to beseech some Santa Claus in the sky to bail them out. He'd always considered them fools and losers.

Until he ran up against a problem neither he nor anyone else could solve: Olivia's cancer.

The tumor started in her left ovary, growing, insidiously, worming its way out into her pelvis. By the time the first symptoms appeared—subtle even then—it was seeded throughout her abdominal cavity.

What a vicious, ruthless, perfidious disease, a spreading army of militant cells causing no pain, no visible lumps, no blockages, covertly infiltrating the abdomen until it had gained a foothold upon every organ within reach.

Even now Arthur suppressed a moan as he remembered the moment in the hospital room when they got the news. Too late, the doctors said. They'd give it their best shot but the prognosis was bleak.

Still fresh in his mind was the look on Olivia's face—the panic and terror that raced across her features before she controlled them and donned the brave mask she wore to her grave. For the timeless instant between the devastating realization that her lifespan was numbered in months, and the determination that she would not surrender to the tumor, her innermost fears had lain naked before him.

Olivia, God bless her, never gave up. Together they tried everything. When traditional therapies failed, she volunteered for experimental protocols. When the cancer resisted those, Arthur took her around the world, to the sincere quacks and out-and-out charlatans who offered hope to the hopeless. Arthur spent a fortune—perhaps two fortunes—but it was only money. What was money? He could always make more of it. But there was only one Olivia.

And brave Olivia, she withstood the endless array of tests and scans and pills and needles and baths and rubs until she could stand no more.

Because none of it was working.

And then, for the first time in his adult life, Arthur Crenshaw began to pray. Not for himself—he swore he'd never stoop to praying for himself—but for Olivia. He resented the need to pray. He knew now it was pride. He'd always been the problem solver, always the one who managed to find the needed answer. But he'd already done everything humanly possible; now the only place left to seek help was beyond the human.

He went to a church and spoke to a young minister who told him to put Olivia's problem in God's hands and pray to Him to save her.

Arthur did just that. He prayed and he forced himself to let go, to step back and trust in the Lord. To his dismay, despite his prayers, his agonized cries to heaven, Olivia continued her downward course.

Only one person appeared to benefit from his prayers: Arthur Crenshaw. It left him feeling buoyed, lighter than air, filled with an inner glow that could only be the Peace of the Lord.

He could imagine the facile rationalizations the unbelievers in his circle would offer to explain his sudden inner tranquility: Giving over responsibility for Olivia to God had relieved him of an awesome psychological burden. What he interpreted as Divine Grace was merely his psyche rebounding after being released from the crushing weight of accountability for Olivia's cure.

Nonsense. God had willed him to be tranquil so he could fully concentrate on being with Olivia. Which was exactly what he did.

And when Olivia died in his arms in their bedroom in Paraiso, they were both at peace.

But Arthur hadn't stopped praying then. Prayer had become a habit during Olivia's illness and so he'd continued a ritual of starting and finishing each day by talking with the Lord. And when he'd been troubled by problems with the company, when a solution eluded him, he'd pray. And, praise the Lord, not long after he prayed the answer would come to him.

He was well aware of the nonbeliever's rational explanation for that, as well: When you gave a problem over to God you stopped gnawing at it; you relaxed your stranglehold on the elements of the problem, allowing them to reassemble into new and different configurations. The fresh perspectives afforded by those new configurations, the different light in which you saw the problem, allowed you to arrive at a solution. Nothing divine about it. The same thing happened with Transcendental Meditation. With self-hypnosis. With standard mental relaxation techniques.

Again, nonsense. Arthur came to realize that the Lord had become an integral part of his life and was working through him. To bind himself closer to Him, he went to Bible study groups, prayer meetings, healing sessions, immersing him-

self in the new Christian Fundamentalism and becoming
one of its more visible members. And when he sold his
company and decided to run for the Senate, he discovered
that his new beliefs guaranteed him a huge, ready-made
constituency eager to work for him and propel him to the
Capitol.

Surely anyone with half a brain could see the hand of God
at work in all this.

He opened his eyes as he heard the rattle of the bridge
timbers under the wheels. He leaned against the window and
stared down over the edge of the narrow, one-car span.
Afternoon sunlight dazzled and danced on the cascading
surface of the brook one hundred feet below.

Emilio guided the Bentley from the bridge onto a path
that wound through the pines for half a mile, then they broke
from the shade into the light. Before them stretched a lush
garden of flowering fruit trees surrounded by sprays of
forsythia and rhododendrons and azaleas. Wild flowers
bloomed in the interstices. No grass. Just ground cover and
natural mulch. Arthur spent tens of thousands of dollars a
year to keep the garden looking wild and untended and yet
perfect. Beyond the garden stretched the western sky. And
two hundred feet straight down—the Pacific Ocean.

Emilio pulled into the bower that served as a carport.
Arthur opened his own door—he disliked being waited
upon—and stepped out. The fresh, salt tang of the on-shore
breeze felt marvelous after the fumes of New York.

Every time he returned from a trip he appreciated anew
Olivia's wisdom in naming their home Paraiso.

Then he thought of his son and his mood darkened. Yes,
their home looked like a paradise. If only it could *be* a
paradise.

"Where's Charlie?"

"He was still asleep when I left," Emilio said.

Arthur nodded. Time for the showdown. He didn't want
this. And when he'd left New York he hadn't known what to
do. But during the flight he'd prayed and placed the problem
in God's hands.

And praise the Lord, by the time the *Gulfstream* had landed he had the solution.

He strode toward the low dome that was the only part of the house visible from the garden. He tapped the entry code into the keypad and the door swung inward. He passed the door of the waiting elevator, preferring the extra time the spiral staircase would afford him. As he descended to the top floor, the endless grandeur of the Pacific opened before him.

Arthur had built the house downward instead of up, carving it into the rocky face of the oceanfront cliffs. It hadn't been easy. When he finally found a suitable coastal cliff south of Carmel that was an extrusion of bedrock instead of the soft clay that dominated the area, strong enough to support his dream house, he ran up against the California Coastal Commission. Many were the times during his epic battles with those arrogant bureaucrats that he'd wished he'd never started the project. But he was determined to see it through. After all, he'd promised Olivia. It took threats, bribes, and in one case, plain, old-fashioned blackmail to get all the permits. It was during that period that he learned the power of the government, and decided that the only way to protect himself from it was to join the club and wield some of that power himself.

But Paraiso was finally built, exactly to his own specs. The entire front was a dazzling array of floor-to-ceiling windows, enticing the sky and the sea indoors, making them part of the interior. From the sea, Paraiso appeared as a massive mosaic of steel and crystal—a three-story bay window. At night it glowed like a jewel set into the cliff side. On sunny weekends the waves below were acrawl with a bobbing horde of boats, private and chartered, filled with sightseers pointing and gazing up in open-mouthed awe.

Within, the ceilings were high, the rooms open and airy. The dining room, the kitchen, Arthur's office, and the bedrooms made up the two lower levels.

Arthur paused on the first landing and surveyed the sprawling expanse of his favorite place in the world, the pride of Paraiso—the great room that occupied the entire top floor.

The afternoon sun beat through the glass ceiling; he adjusted a switch on the wall to his left, rotating the fine louvers above to reduce the glare. He gazed outward through the convex expanse of glass before him and watched the whitecaps flecking the surface of the Pacific. Carved into the living rock of the room's rear wall was a huge fireplace, dark and cold. He and Olivia had planned to spend the rest of their days entertaining friends and family in this room. Since her death he'd converted it to a chapel of sorts. No pews or crosses or stained-glass windows, just a quiet place to pray and contemplate the wonder of this majestic corner of Creation. It was here that he felt closest to God.

Be with me, Lord, he thought as he tore himself away from the view and continued toward the lower levels.

He found Charlie in his bedroom, its walls still decked with the Berkeley pennants and paraphernalia left over from his undergraduate days. He was sipping coffee from the lunch tray Juanita had prepared for him. He looked up and slammed his cup on the tray. His eyes blazed.

"Damn you," he said softly. "Damn you to hell."

Arthur stood in the doorway, unable to move, unable to speak, staring at the son he hadn't seen in nearly two years.

Charlie looked awful. The old gray sweatsuit he'd worn to bed hung around him in loose folds. He looked a decade older than his twenty-five years. So thin. Cheeks sunken, face pale, his black, sleep-tangled hair, usually so thick and shiny, now thin and brittle looking. His eyes were bright in their deep sockets. The dark stubble on his cheeks accentuated his pallor.

"Charlie," he said when he finally found his voice. "What's happened?"

"What's happened is I've become the Prisoner of Zenda."

Charlie had never been a sturdy sort, but now he looked positively gaunt. Arthur wanted to throw his arms around him and tell him how much he'd missed him, but the look in Charlie's eyes stopped him cold.

He sat on the foot of the bed, carefully, so as not to upset the tray.

"You know better than that. This is your home."

"Not with turnkey Sanchez around."

"Charlie, I brought you back for your own good. That's not the kind of life for you. For anybody. It's an abomination in the eyes of God."

"It's *my* life." Charlie's eyes flashed. Arthur had never seen him so defiant.

"It's a sinful life."

"Life, liberty, and the pursuit of happiness—isn't that what a United States senator is supposed to protect?"

"Don't be flip. I want to help you turn your life around."

"By when? For the primaries in a few years?"

If only it were that simple, Arthur thought. If that was all there was to it . . .

He shuddered as old memories surged to the fore. Violently he thrust them back down into the mire where they belonged.

No. This was not only for himself. Charlie's sodomite urges were a test. If Arthur could help his son out of this moral quagmire, he would prove himself, he would . . . *redeem* himself. And God would know what a weapon he had in Arthur Crenshaw.

"Do you like the life you're living, Charlie?"

"It's the only one I've got."

"That doesn't answer the question."

"It has its moments."

"In the wee small hours, Charlie . . . when it's just you and God and the dark outside the window . . . how do you feel?"

Charlie's gaze faltered for the first time. He fiddled with a slice of toast on his breakfast tray.

"I wake up at three or four in the morning, shaking and sweaty. And I sit there thinking about how I've failed you. I remember how Mom never put me down, but every so often I'd catch her watching me and there'd be this unreadable look in her eyes. I didn't know what she was thinking, but I have to assume I disgusted her. And I know what *you* think, Dad—you've always been up front about how you felt. So I sit there in the dark thinking about how

repulsive I am to the two most important people in my life."
His voice fell to a whisper. "And I feel like such a loser."

Arthur felt his throat tighten. He had to help this boy. He
reached out and put a hand on Charlie's arm. Dear Lord, it
was so *thin*.

"You can't be judged a loser until you've given up trying,
Charlie. And that's why I brought you home. I want you to
try."

Charlie looked up at him again. "Try what?"

"To change."

He shook his head. "That's not possible."

"It is, Charlie," he said, gently squeezing his arm. "With
God's help and the right doctors, you can do it."

Charlie's laugh rang hollow against the walls. "I think
God must have lots of concerns more pressing than my
sexual orientation. And really, Dad, if it's the election
you're worried about, relax. No one will connect me with
you. And even if they did, it could actually work to your
advantage. We're a pretty cohesive voting block now. We
proved that in the last election."

We . . . Arthur shuddered at Charlie's casual alignment
of himself with the likes of Act Up and Queer Nation and
the pathetic human mutants and aberrations that marched
in those Gay Pride parades. If getting elected depended on
their votes, he'd rather not run.

But public knowledge of Charlie's homosexuality was
only part of the real threat.

"I won't deny the election is important to me," he told
Charlie. "You know that. There's so much good I can do for
this country if they'll only let me. I have plans. I can make
us great again." He didn't just believe that—he *knew* it.
"But if I can't help my own son back on the right path, how
can I expect to do it for an entire nation?"

"Dad—"

"Give me a year, Charlie. One year of prayer and therapy.
That's all I ask. You're young. One year out of the rest of
your life is not too much for your father to ask, is it? If
there's been no change at the end of that time, and if I see

you've made a sincere effort, then I'll accept your . . . the way you are and never bother you again about it."

Charlie was staring at him. "Accept me? I don't think you can."

"If you can try, I can try. One year." He thrust out his hand. "What do you say?"

"One year . . . that's too long."

"*Half* a year then. Six months. *Please!*"

Charlie hesitated and Arthur sent up a prayer: *Please make him accept, Lord. Between the two of us I know we can make him normal.*

Tentatively Charlie reached out and grasped his father's hand.

"All right. Six months. As long as you understand that I'm not promising you results, just to give it the old college try."

Arthur blinked back the tears that surged into his eyes. He pulled Charlie close and embraced him.

"That's all I ask, son. That's all a father can ask."

Thank you, Lord, he said in silent prayer. I know this is going to work. If I can teach my boy to pray, if he can learn as I have learned, if he can find for himself just one tenth of the peace I find in you, he will be saved. I trust in you, Lord, and I know that you will help me in this.

But as he held his son, Arthur was alarmed at how frail he seemed. He could feel the corduroy ridges of ribs through Charlie's sweatshirt. Weight loss, night sweats . . . Charlie couldn't possibly have . . .

No. That was impossible. God wouldn't do that to him. Arthur didn't know if he could handle that. Not after Olivia. He was strong, but he had his limits. He wasn't cut out to be a modern-day Job.

He cast the thought from his mind and held his son tighter.

"Everything's going to be all right, Charlie. God will make it so."

I swore to all present that I would guard her until my last breath. I told the brother, I will kill to keep her safe.

But he said to me, No, you must not kill.

And then I swore I would die to keep her safe. But within I promised that if the need arose I would gladly kill to keep her secret. It is the least I can do.

I do not fear killing. I have killed before, slipping through the crowds in Jerusalem, stabbing with my knife. And I fear not damnation. Indeed, I am already thrice-damned.

FROM THE GLASS SCROLL
ROCKEFELLER MUSEUM TRANSLATION

9

As Sister Caroline Ferris reached behind the scratched
and dented dresser in her room at the Convent of St. Ann,
she caught sight of herself in the mirror on the wall behind
it.

You're twenty-eight, she thought, and you still look like
a child. When are you going to get wrinkled so men won't
stare at you?

Maybe if she'd spent her teenage years worshiping the
sun instead of God, she'd have at least a few wrinkles to
show. But she'd entered the convent at fourteen, and as a
result her skin was pale and flawlessly smooth. She kept her
thick, dark, hair cut in a bob—straight, functional, easy to
care for. She wore no makeup—never a trace of mascara or
shadow for her large blue eyes, never even a touch of color
to her thin lips, and when out in public she tried to look as
serious as possible. Yet despite her shapeless clothing and
carefully cultured Plain Jane look, men still approached her.
Even in habit!

Maybe I should put on forty or fifty pounds. That would
stop them.

But no matter how much she ate, her body burned it off.
She seemed doomed to remain 120 pounds forever.

She removed the compact-like case from under the rear
lip of the bureau top and opened it. Inside was a foil and
plastic card with twenty-one clear bubbles, one for each of
the contraceptive pills the pack contained. The label inside

the lid read Ortho-Novum 7-7-7 and gave the patient's name as Margaret Jones. Half the pills were gone. Quickly Carrie pushed the next light-peach tablet in line through the foil and popped it into her mouth, dry swallowing it as she shut the case and returned it to its hiding place.

Good. The daily risk of taking her pill was out of the way. With no locks on the doors within the Convent of the Blessed Virgin, someone could pop in at any time.

Carrie had noted she had two refills left on her pills. After that, the fictitious Margaret Jones would need another appointment at the West Side Planned Parenthood clinic. She shuddered at the thought. She hated pelvic exams and lived in fear of the chance that someone in the waiting room might recognize her as Sister Carrie. But she put up with the indignities and the fear to avoid the greater terror of pregnancy.

Since she'd be traveling alone, she'd leave her habit behind. She adjusted the collar of her starched white blouse and straightened the jacket of her black gabardine suit. "Sensible" shoes—black pumps with one-inch heels—completed the picture.

She checked the rest of her room to make sure it was neat. A bed, a nightstand with a handpainted statue of the Blessed Virgin, a reading lamp, a dresser, a crucifix, and a closet—not much to take care of. Everything was in place. One last thing to do . . .

She knelt by her nightstand and gazed at her Virgin Mary statuette. She repeated the same prayer she said every time she was about to sin:

Forgive me, Mary. I wish I could have been like you, but I was never given the choice. And though I sin with full knowledge and forethought, please know that I am devoted to you and always shall be. Yet despite all my devotion, I know I'm still a sinner. But in just this one thing. In everything else I gladly deny myself to do your work, do your bidding. Yet a small part of my heart remains unruly. I hope, I trust, I pray that in your own heart you will find room to forgive this sinner.

Sister Carrie crossed herself, rose, and headed for the first floor.

On the way out she checked in with Mother Superior to let her know she was leaving and told her when to expect her back.

The older woman smiled and looked up at her over the tops of her reading glasses. "Tell your father our prayers are with him."

"Thank you, Sister. I'm sure that will give him comfort."

If you knew that monster as I do, Carrie thought, you'd withhold your prayers. Or perhaps you wouldn't. She stared a moment at Mother Superior's kindly face. Perhaps you'd pray for even the most ungodly sinner.

Not me, Carrie thought, turning and heading for the street. Not for that man. Not even an "Amen."

Supposedly she was visiting him at the nursing home. Usually the sisters traveled in pairs or more if shopping or making house calls to the sick or shut-ins, but since this was a parental nursing home visit, Carrie was allowed to travel alone.

She'd never been to the nursing home. Not once. The very thought of being in the same room with that man sickened her.

Brad took care of the visits. Her brother saw to all that man's needs. The cost of keeping him in the Concordia, which its director had described as "the Mercedes Benz of nursing homes," was no burden for Brad. Her investment banker brother's Christmas bonus alone last year had come to over a million dollars.

Brad traveled a lot to earn that kind of money. Many of his clients were headquartered on the West Coast and he spent almost as much time in California as he did here in Manhattan. So whenever he headed west he'd call and leave word that he'd be out of town. That meant his condo was hers to use whenever she wanted a change from the convent. Carrie availed herself of that offer by saying that her brother's absence made it necessary for her to attend to her father more often at the nursing home.

And when she visited the condo, she did not visit it alone.

Poverty, chastity, and obedience, she thought as a cab pulled up outside the convent. This afternoon I'm breaking all my vows at once.

A wave of self-loathing rose from her belly into her chest, reaching for her throat, momentarily suffocating her. But it receded as quickly as it had come. She had hated herself for so long that she barely noticed those waves anymore. They felt like ripples now.

She descended the convent steps and slipped into the cab.

As the cab rounded Columbus Circle and headed up Central Park West, Carrie gazed through the side window at the newborn leaves erupting from the trees in the park, pale, pale green in the fading light. Spring. The city's charms became most apparent in spring. Nice to live up here, far from the squalor of downtown.

She spotted a homeless man, trudging uptown on the park side, wheeling all his worldly possessions ahead of him in a shopping cart.

Well, not too far. You couldn't escape the homeless in New York. They were everywhere.

You can run but you can't hide.

Brad had run to the Upper West Side, to Yuppy-ville. Or Dinc-ville, as some folks were calling it these days. But Brad wasn't a dinc. Wasn't married, lived alone. Carrie guessed that made him a sinc: single income, no children. He could have lived anywhere—Westchester, the Gold Coast, Greenwich, anywhere—but he seemed to like the ambience of the newly gentrified neighborhoods, and he often spoke of the friends he'd made in the building.

The cabbie hung a mid-block U-turn on Central Park West and let her off in front of Brad's building. Carrie counted up five floors and saw a light in one of Brad's windows. Had to be one of Brad's windows—his condo took up the entire fifth floor. She smiled as desire began to spark within her. She was the latecomer this time. Usually it was the other way around.

Good. She wouldn't have to wait.

The doorman tipped his cap as he ushered her through to the lobby. "Beautiful evening, isn't it, Sister."

"Yes, it is, Riccardo. A wonderful evening."

Carrie had to use her key to make the elevator stop on the fifth floor. The sparks from groundlevel had ignited a flame of desire by the time she stepped out into a small atrium and unlocked the condo door. Slowly she swung it open and slipped through as silently as possible. Light leaked down the hall from the dining room. She removed her shoes and padded toward it in her stockinged feet.

On an angle to her right she spotted him, hunched at Brad's long dining room table, his back to her, his sandy-haired head bowed over half a sheaf of typewritten sheets, so engrossed in them she had no trouble entering the room unnoticed.

Desire grew to a molten heat as she crept up behind him.

Closer now, she noticed the waves in his hair as it edged over his collar and ears, the broad set of the shoulders under his shirt. She loved this man, loved the scent of him, the feel of him, the sound of his voice, the touch of his fingers and palms on her. She wanted him. Now. Every day. Forever. The times they could sneak away to be together were too, too few. So she made these times count, every minute, every second, every racing, pounding heartbeat they were together.

She laid her hands on his shoulders and gently squeezed. "Hi there."

He jumped. Through the fabric of his shirt she felt his shoulder muscles harden to rock then relax under her hands. He turned in the chair and looked up at her.

"God, don't *do* that! My heart almost stopped."

Carrie tilted his head back and kissed him on the lips. His skin carried a trace of Old Spice. She nodded toward the papers on the table.

"What's so interesting?"

"The translation of an old scroll. It's—"

"More interesting than me?"

She kissed the tip of his nose, then each eye in turn.

"Are you kidding?" Father Daniel Fitzpatrick rose, lifted

her in his arms, and carried her toward the guest bedroom.
"Not even close."

Dan was dozing. He often nodded off as they snuggled
after their lovemaking. Carrie rose up on an elbow and
stared at his peaceful features.

I love you, Danny boy.

They first met about five years ago when he stepped in as
the new associate pastor at St. Joe's, ran into each other
occasionally at parish affairs, and for the past three years or
so had been working side by side at Loaves and Fishes.
They'd come to know each other well during those years,
discovering that they shared the ecclesiastically incorrect
notion that the Church should expend at least as much effort
in nurturing minds and bodies as saving souls, that the
well-being of the last was dependent to a large extent on the
health of the first two.

Last year they became lovers.

Precipitously.

A strange courtship—long, slow, and tentative, never
kissing or even holding hands. An occasional bump of the
shoulders, a brush of a hand against an arm, long looks,
slow smiles, growing warmth. Carrie doubted it would have
progressed beyond that stage if she hadn't take the initiative
last summer.

Up to that time she had used Brad's condo as a vacation
spa—her private retreat from the soup kitchen, from the
convent, from the world in general. She'd soak for hours in
his whirlpool bath while watching old movies from his
laserdisk library. She'd return to the convent physically and
mentally refreshed. But last summer she asked Dan to drop
her off on his way to the Museum of Natural History to see
a new exhibit. When he pulled up in front, she asked him to
come inside and see how the other half lived.

An hour later one of them was no longer a virgin.

It wasn't me. Oh, no . . . not by a long shot.

After the first time they both went through a period of
terrible guilt—Dan's much deeper and more racking than
hers—and for a while Carrie feared he might never speak to

her again. Then their paths crossed in a deserted hallway and he took her hand and said they had to talk. The only place to do that was Brad's apartment. So they met there on the condition that they would talk and nothing more.

And talk they did. Dan poured out his feelings for her, his doubts about his calling, about the priorities of the priesthood and the Church itself. Carrie told him that she had none of those doubts: Sister Caroline Ferris was all she ever wanted to be, all she ever would be. But she knew she loved him and she couldn't change that.

Despite their good intentions, they wound up in the guest room bed again. And when they were together like that, neither could find any wrong in it.

They made love here as often as timing and circumstance permitted, which wasn't nearly often enough. And after they loved they talked. Dan opened up to her as she was sure he opened to no one else.

And finally, Carrie opened to Dan. She hadn't intended to, but one afternoon the story burst from her in a rush and she told Dan about that man . . . her father . . . and how he'd started sneaking into her bedroom at night when she was twelve. . . .

Mom had been sick for a while, almost helpless. Her multiple sclerosis had accelerated to the point where the only time she spent out of bed was in her wheelchair. That man had said his dear Carrie had to do what Mom couldn't, that it was her duty as a good daughter. And when it was over, and she'd cry, he'd tell her it was her fault for tempting him and making him want to do what he'd done, and if she told Mom he'd tell everyone what she'd done . . . *everyone*.

For two years it went on, Mom becoming increasingly disoriented, growing weaker and weaker, fading into the sheets of her bed, and that man sneaking into Carrie's room with increasing boldness and frequency until Mom died. She'd been so terrified of what would happen with Mom gone that she ran away immediately after her funeral.

Ran to the Convent of the Blessed Virgin. Virgin . . . something young Carrie Ferris was not. But the sisters had accepted her and she'd been there ever since. She'd devoted her life to God, and to Mary, but she'd never felt worthy of her calling.

Dan had been stiff and silent as she'd wept on his shoulder. She'd never told anyone—*anyone*—until then, and it felt so good to get it out. Yet she was so afraid, as she'd been afraid all her life, that anyone who knew the truth would hate her and shun her. But Dan had held her close and absorbed her racking sobs, and the secret became a bond that welded them even closer.

Carrie kissed Dan's cheek and slipped from his side. She found a terrycloth robe in the bathroom and wrapped it around her as she wandered through the silence of the huge apartment.

She almost wished she smoked. As much as she hated the smell, a cigarette would have given her something to do with her hands. She liked to keep busy and she always felt at loose ends here in Brad's. She couldn't do any cleaning because his housekeeper kept the place immaculate; she couldn't rearrange things because none of it was hers. So she stuck her idle hands—those Devil's workshops—into the pockets of the robe and continued to wander aimlessly.

As she meandered through the dining room she spotted the typed sheets Dan had been so intent on when she'd entered. She sifted through until she found the face sheet. The title caught her interest.

Translation: the Glass scroll

The Glass scroll. What was that?

She glanced at the first paragraph and her interest was piqued. She scanned the second, then the third. Captured, she sat down and began to read.

I have left this place only once. I traveled north
to Qumran one night and stole upon the
sleeping Essenes. I moved among them like a
shadow, taking two jars of scrolls and some
ink. I loaded them on the back of three goats
and returned to the Resting Place, where I
feasted upon one goat and kept the other two
for breeding.

And then I began to write my story.

FROM THE GLASS SCROLL
ROCKEFELLER MUSEUM TRANSLATION

10

Jerusalem—The Old City

Kesev followed Qadasiya north from the Via Dolorosa. His footsteps echoed on the street stones. Well after midnight and all was quiet in the Moslem quarter.

Suddenly the sound of a car engine echoed off the surrounding stone walls and bouncing lights cast long, jittering shadows up ahead. Had to be a Jeep. A military patrol most likely. Things had been quiet in the Moslem quarter for a while now, but the patrols stayed on schedule. That was the way to make sure things remained quiet.

Kesev had donned Arab dress for the night—a frayed jellaba and a striped keffiyeh held in place around his head with a worn akal. He knew he looked more Arab than many natives of the quarter, and if the patrol spotted him they'd stop and ID him. He ducked into an alley and crouched behind some debris, waiting for them to pass.

One look at the Shin Bet ID in his wallet and the patrol would wish him well and continue on its way. But Kesev didn't want to be stopped at all—the supposedly sleeping walls were full of eyes. He didn't want *anyone* to know he was here, especially his superiors.

This business had nothing to do with the Shin Bet.

Kesev stepped out of the alley after the patrol had passed. He scanned the street to see if anyone else might emerge in its wake. Nothing moved. Rising above the silent Old City, the Dome of the Rock gleamed in the starlight. A brilliant gold in daylight, it looked more silver now.

Continuing along Qadasiya, Kesev shoved three sticks of gum into his mouth. He chewed steadily, savoring the peppermint sweetness as he turned into the narrow side street that led to Salah Mahmoud's antique shop. The dealer lived above his place of work, the better to keep watch over his inventory, Kesev supposed.

Kesev had been watching the shop for three days and nights now, and had finally paid it a visit this afternoon. Most of the statuettes and carvings on Mahmoud's dusty shelves were junk, some outright fakes, waiting to hook some well-heeled European or American tourist with a craving to take home a piece of the Holy Land.

Mahmoud himself was obviously playing to the foreigners with his waxed mustache and red fez perched atop his balding head. With his jowls and rumpled suit, he looked like a transplant from Hollywood.

But the portly dealer's manner had changed abruptly when one particular customer arrived. Mahmoud greeted the German-speaking man warmly, ushered him to a secluded corner where they spoke in whispers, then led him up a flight of stairs at the rear of the store. That would be where the items of real value were stored, Kesev decided.

During an apparently casual perusal of the artifacts and rickety third-hand furniture that passed for antiques, Kesev had surreptitiously surveyed the premises and found no security device more sophisticated than a bell attached to the inside of the front door.

Now, in the shadowed recess of that front door, Kesev used a slim piece of plastic to slip the latch on the rickety, post-World War II lock. Gently he eased the door open a few inches, spit the gum into his palm, reached inside and used it to fix the clapper to the side of the bell.

Once inside, he pulled a penlight from the folds of his jellaba and wound his way among the dealer's wares to the stairs at the rear. He had spent most of the evening mulling the best way to proceed from here. He'd heard the squeaks and groans from the old wooden staircase as Mahmoud and his customer had ascended this afternoon, so sneaking up was out. That left a more direct approach.

Kesev switched the penlight to his left hand and pulled a silenced Tokarev 9mm from his robe. Then he took a backward step and charged up the stairs, taking them three at a time. He threw his shoulder against the upper door and smashed through to the second floor. Days of watching had told him that Mahmoud lived alone and slept in the room overlooking the street. Kesev barreled straight ahead, burst into the room in time to find a very startled and frightened Salah Mahmoud sitting up in bed, reaching into the top drawer of his night table. Kesev kicked the drawer closed on the dealer's wrist and jabbed the business end of the Tokarev against his throat as he began to cry out.

"Not a sound, Mr. Mahmoud," Kesev said softly in Arabic. "I have come to rob you, not to kill you. But I am not adverse to doing both. Understand?"

Mahmoud nodded vigorously, his jowls bulging and quivering under his chin, his eyes threatening to jump from their sockets. He looked like a toad that had just come face to face with the biggest snake it had ever seen.

"Wh-whatever it is you want," Mahmoud said, "take it. Take it and go!"

"That's a very good start."

Kesev allowed him to remove his hand from the drawer. As the dealer cradled his injured wrist in his lap, Kesev switched on the bedside lamp. He removed Mahmoud's snub-nose .38 from the drawer and tossed it under the bed. Then he produced the scroll he'd coerced from Tulla Szobel and dropped it on the sheet.

"I want the original," Kesev said.

Mahmoud stared at the scroll, then looked up. "I don't know what you are talking about."

Kesev felt his anger flare but controlled it. He forced himself to smile. It must have been a disturbing grimace because Mahmoud flinched.

"Before I came here," Kesev said evenly, "I decided I would allow you one lie. That was it. Now that it's out of the way, you may answer truthfully. Where is the original?"

"I swear I don't know what you are talking about."

He struck the dealer a backhanded blow with the Tokarev.

Mahmoud fell on his side, a mass of quaking blubber, moaning, clutching his cheek. Blood seeped between his fingers.

Kesev's arm rose to deliver another blow but he reined his fury and lowered the pistol. Instead he grabbed the front of Mahmoud's nightshirt and pulled him close. He turned the broad face so that they were nose to nose. He wanted the dealer to look into his eyes, to see the fury there to feel the truth of what Kesev was going to say.

"Listen to me, Salah Mahmoud, and listen well. The original of that scroll was stolen from me. I intend to retrieve what is mine, and for the past four years I have been searching for it. You are merely the latest phase of that search. Now, you can be a stepping stone or you can be a stumbling block. The choice is entirely yours."

Mahmoud opened his mouth to speak but Kesev pressed the barrel of the Tokarev's silencer against his lips.

"But let me warn you. I will not tolerate lies. This is extremely important to me and I have already expended enormous time and effort in my search. I am out of patience."

He pressed the silencer more firmly against Mahmoud's mouth.

"This pistol has a seven-shot clip loaded with 9mm hollowpoint bullets. Do you know what a hollowpoint does after it enters the body? It breaks up into a thousand tiny fragments. Each of those fragments continues forward, tearing through the flesh in an expanding cone of destruction. The bullet enters through a little hole and exits through a gaping maw. It is not a pretty thing, Salah Mahmoud."

Sweat beaded the dealer's forehead, dripping into his eyes.

"So . . . here are the ground rules: I will ask questions and you will answer truthfully. The first time I think you are lying I will shoot you in the left knee." The dealer stiffened and shuddered. "The second lie will earn you a bullet in the right knee. The third in your right elbow, the fourth in your left. The fifth bullet I will use on your manhood. By that time I will have decided that you are either a pathological liar, or you really don't know anything. I will then leave you. Alive. And you will spend the rest of your days unable to walk, unable to use crutches or a wheelchair, unable to feed yourself or wipe yourself, your urine running through a tube into bag strapped to your leg. Is that what you want?"

Mahmoud shook his head violently, spraying drops of perspiration in all directions.

"Good," Kesev said.

He straightened and stepped back from the bed. He had no particular desire to shoot this man, but he would do so. He had to retrieve that scroll.

He pointed to the forged scroll on the bed.

"Now tell me: When did you get this scroll?"

Mahmoud hesitated. His nightshirt was soaked with sweat. His eyes darted about the room, like a rabbit looking for a hole to run to.

Kesev worked the slide to chamber a round.

"No!" Mahmoud cried, trying to curl into a ball.

Kesev pulled the trigger once. The Tokarev jerked and gave out a *phut!* as a bullet tore into the mattress near the dealer's face.

Mahmoud thrust out his hands amid the flying feathers and began to whimper. "Please don't shoot me! I'll tell you! I'll tell you everything!"

Kesev lowered the pistol a few degrees. "I'm waiting."

"I made that scroll," Mahmoud said.

Kesev raised the pistol again.

"It's true!" the dealer cried. "I copied it myself from a crumbling original!"

"Really. And where did you find the original?"

"I-I didn't. Two nephews of my father's uncle's brother discovered it in a cave in the Wilderness. I don't know if it's true, but they claimed one of Saddam's missiles uncovered it."

Now we're getting somewhere.

Kesev felt relief begin to seep through him, but he

resisted it just as he'd resisted the rage. He could not let down his guard, not until the scroll was safely back in his hands.

Mahmoud was still talking, babbling, flooding the room with rapid-fire Egyptian-flavored Arabic.

"Their father brought their find to me: a written scroll that was heavily damaged—the boys had been in a hurry and did not know how to care for it—and a sealed jar with two unused scrolls within. I laid out the written scroll as best I could and copied what was left of it onto the blank parchments." He shrugged, almost apologetically. "I . . . I've done this before. I have formulae for all the ancient inks. I was especially careful with the copying because I knew the parchments would pass the dating test." His attempt at a smile was a miserable failure. "I figured, why sell one scroll when I could sell three?"

"Did you read it? Did you understand it?" Kesev held his breath as he waited for the answer.

"I tried. But my Aramaic is rudimentary at best; there were words I could not translate. And besides, the scroll was incomplete. Fragments were out of place and some were missing completely. I reassembled them the best I could but—"

"Where is that original now?"

"It . . ." His voice shrank to a whisper. "It's gone."

Sudden rage crackled through Kesev's brain. He leaned forward and jammed the muzzle of the silencer against Mahmoud's thigh.

"You *sold* it?"

"No-no! Please! It's gone! Whisked away into the air!"

"I warned you about lying!"

"Please! I swear by Allah! The wind took it! It happened in the back room, not ten meters from here, just as I was finishing the first copy. Suddenly all the windows in the building crashed inward and a blast of icy wind tore through the halls and rooms. The winds seemed to gather in my workroom. They rattled my walls, knocked me to the floor, and upset my worktable. The scroll fragments swirled into the air in a whirling column, then they blew out the window and were gone."

Kesev's rage cooled rapidly, chilled by the dealer's words. A wind . . . filling the halls and rooms . . . stealing the fragments in a miniature whirlwind . . .

"You must believe me!" Mahmoud wailed. "Every word is true!"

Kesev nodded slowly, almost absently. The fat forger wasn't lying. He wouldn't make up something so fantastic and try to pass it off as the truth.

And that meant that the original scroll had been destroyed, reduced to scattered, indecipherable bits of parchment . . . but not before it had been copied.

"How many copies did you make?" Kesev asked finally.

"Two," Mahmoud said. "There were only two blank scrolls. I forged the second copy from the first."

How many scrolls had been in the sealed jar? Two sounded right but he couldn't be sure. He didn't remember.

Two copies: one here in Kesev's possession, and the other in America. That thought would have panicked him if he hadn't known it had been branded a forgery.

He had a sense that events were spinning out of control. An odd progression of incidents—the errant SCUD, the theft of the scroll, the copies, the destruction of the original. Especially unsettling was the last incident. An unnatural wind had whirled the scroll fragments into oblivion, but only after they had been copied. *After.* Unfortunate happenstance, or design? He sensed a power at work, a deft hand moving behind the scenes. But what power? And to what end?

He had to stay on guard. The scroll in America was probably rolled up and sealed in a glass case, just like Tulla Szobel's. A curio. Something to be looked at but not touched. And besides, how many Americans knew Aramaic? Highly unlikely that anyone would realize what it was about.

But something was happening. Once again he was overwhelmed by the sensation of giant wheels turning, ready to crush him if he stepped the wrong way.

Increased vigilance was the key. He'd have to find a way to keep a closer watch on the Resting Place. And be ready to deal swiftly and surely with any curious Americans he found wandering in the area.

So here sit I, alone, a filthy cave for a home and only locusts, wild honey, a few goats, and figs for sustenance. I who once dwelt in luxury, who once wore the striped blue sleeve and had free access to the Temple.

I am alone and mad. And sometimes I imagine I am not alone. Sometimes I see her walking. Sometimes she speaks to me. But it isn't her. Only a fever-dream of my madness.

I pray that each day is the Last Day, but each day ends like the one before it. When will it end? Dear Lord, when will you allow it to end for me?

FROM THE GLASS SCROLL
ROCKEFELLER MUSEUM TRANSLATION

11

Dan awoke with a start—bright light in his eyes and an excited voice in his ear.

"Dan! Wake up! Wake *up!*"

He blinked. Carrie . . . leaning over him . . . dark hair falling about her face . . . bright eyes wide with excitement. God, she was beautiful. She made him want to sing though he knew damn well he couldn't carry a tune. How had he spent his whole life without this woman—not any woman . . . *this* woman? Celibacy was an unnatural state for a human being. He didn't care what the Church said, he was a better person—a more compassionate, more understanding, more fully rounded man—and therefore a better priest, because of Carrie.

He'd never been in love before. Grade school and high school puppy loves, sure. But this went beyond physical attraction, beyond infatuation. If Carrie were a lay person he'd leave the Church for her—if she'd have him. But Carrie had no intention of leaving her order. Ever. So he'd have to settle for things the way they were.

Of course, if she'd been laity, the relationship never would have begun. He wouldn't have let her within arm's reach. His guard would have been up, his defenses primed at all times when he was around her. But Carrie, being a nun, being a member of the club, so to speak, had slipped past his guard without even trying.

That first afternoon in her brother's condo had awakened

a long-dormant hunger in him. Along the course of his years
as a priest he'd learned to structure his life without regard to
sex. Excruciatingly difficult at first. He'd found it went
beyond avoiding thoughts of sex. It meant avoiding thinking
about avoiding thoughts of sex. You did that by cramming
your days full of activity, by hurling yourself headlong into
the neverending hustle and bustle of a downtown urban
parish, by sublimating your own needs to those of your
parishioners. After all, that was what it was all about, wasn't
it? That was why you joined the priesthood. And if you did
your job right, at the end of the day you collapsed into bed
and slept like the dead until dawn when it was up and out for
early Mass and back again into the parish whirl.

After a while you got pretty good at it. After a while, the
lusty parts of the brain atrophied and became too weak to
bother you with much more than an occasional, feeble
nudge.

Unless something kick-started them with a steroid charge
and pumped them up to strength again.

Something like making love to Sister Carrie.

Now he was like a randy teenager. He wondered where
the guilt had gone. Overwhelmingly awful at first, especially when she'd told him about her father and what he'd
done to her. Dan had almost despaired then, wondering if he
might be aiding and abetting some dark, self-sabotaging
compulsion within Carrie. She'd run to the convent to
escape a sexually molesting father; she'd become a model
nun, a paradigm of virtue and saintliness except for the fact
that she was having a sexual relationship with her parish
priest . . . a man everyone called "Father."

Dan had always been skeptical of facile parlor psychoanalysis, but the doubts nagged at him when he was apart
from Carrie. When he was with her, however, they melted in
the warmth of her smile, the glow of her presence. Carrie
seemed perfectly comfortable with their relationship; it took
him a while, but now he was just as comfortable.

And Dan loved her as he had never loved another human
being, and that love let him see the world in a whole new

light, brought him closer to the rest of humanity. How could that be wrong.

He loved Carrie completely, and he wanted her—*all* the time. Every moment they were together at Loaves and Fishes was a struggle, a biting agony to keep his hands off her. He'd learned to freeze his emotions at those times, confine his thoughts to the instant, force his brain to regard her as no more than a pleasant co-worker and to leave her clothes on whenever he looked at her.

But God, it was hard.

But more than wanting Carrie physically, he wanted her emotionally. Just being near her was a thrill. But being near her in bed was heaven. Like now . . .

He noticed her bathrobe hanging open, exposing the rose-tipped globe of her left breast. He reached for it but she brushed his hand away with a sheaf of papers.

"What *is* this?" she said, shaking them in his face.

"Wha—?" Dan propped himself up on his elbows and stared at the papers in her hand.

"Where did you get this, Dan?"

He couldn't remember ever seeing Carrie this excited.

"Oh, that. Harold's back from Jerusalem. It's the translation of a scroll that somebody turned in to the Rockefeller Museum over there. He gave it to me as part of a little gift."

She laughed. "A gift? He gave this to you as a *gift?* But this is fabulous! Why hasn't the world been told?"

"There's nothing to tell, Carrie. The scroll is a fake."

She stared at him in silence, the glow of excitement slowly fading from her eyes. She shook her head.

"No." Her voice was a whisper. "That can't be."

"It's true. Hal said the carbon dating showed the ink is only two or three years old."

Carrie was still shaking her head. "No. There's got to be a mistake."

Dan leaned forward and kissed her throat. "What's so important about it? It's paranoid, jumbled, and seems deliberately obscure. The forger was probably some nut who—"

"It's about Mary," she said.

Now it was Dan's turn to stare. "Mary? Mary who?"

"The Blessed Virgin Mary."

Dan knew from Carrie's expression that he'd better not laugh, but he couldn't repress a smile.

"Where on earth did you get an idea like that?"

"From this." She held up the translation. "The dead woman he's talking about, the body he's supposed to guard—it's Mary's."

"I guess that means we're tossing out the Glorious Mystery of the Assumption."

"Don't be flip, Dan."

"Sorry," he said.

And he meant it. He knew of Carrie's devotion to the Blessed Virgin and didn't want to tread on any of her vital beliefs. But even though he was a priest, Dan had never been able to buy the Assumption. The thought of Mary's soul reentering her body after her funeral, then reviving and being carried aloft to heaven by a host of angels was pretty hokey.

That sort of fairy-tale stuff was all through the Bible, Old Testament and New, and had nothing to do with Dan's idea of what the Church was all about. Nifty little stories to wow the kids and get their attention, but sometimes fairy tales only served to distract from the real message in the Gospels: the brotherhood of man.

"But you've got to admit," he said cautiously, "that the Assumption is a bit hard to buy." Carrie didn't react; she simply stared down at the papers in her hands. So he pressed on. "I mean, we can agree, can't we, that heaven isn't a *place*. It's a state of being. So how could Mary be 'assumed' into Heaven body and soul when heaven is a spiritual state? Her body was a physical object. It couldn't go to heaven. It had to go somewhere else. And I doubt it's in orbit."

A vision of the space shuttle passing the floating body of the Virgin Mary popped into his head. He shook if off.

Carrie looked up at him, her eyes bright again.

"Exactly! And that's what this is all about. This tells us *where* she really is!"

Uh-oh. He'd backed himself into that one. "Now wait just a minute, Carrie. Don't get—"

"Listen to me, Dan! Whoever wrote this was assigned the task of guarding the body of a woman, a very important woman. 'Twenty years and five after his death they found me.' Tradition holds that Mary died twenty-two years after her son's crucifixion. The timing is almost perfect."

"But, Carrie, the guy never says *whose* death. In all the Gospels and letters and other texts, Jesus was called by name or referred to as the Master, the Lord, the Son of Man, or the like, and the Dead Sea scrolls referred to the Messiah as the 'Branch of David' or a 'shoot from the stump of Jesse' or as the 'Prince of the Congregation.' I'd expect the writer to use one of those terms at least once if he was referring to Jesus."

"Maybe he wrote the scrolls for himself. Maybe he feared mentioning Jesus by name—there were all sorts of persecutions back then."

"That's possible, of course, but—"

"But I get the feeling from this that he didn't feel worthy to speak Jesus's name."

A rather melodramatic interpretation, Dan thought, but he said nothing. Carrie's intensity impressed him. The translation had really got to her. She was inspired, afire with curiosity and . . . something else . . . something he couldn't put his finger on.

"And here," she said, tapping one of the pages, "this part where he refers to 'his brother.' Who else can that be but St. James the Apostle, the brother of Jesus."

"His brother or his cousin," Dan said, "depending on which authority you believe."

But he sat up straighter in the bed and took the page from her. As he scanned the passage Carrie had mentioned it occurred to him that she had a point. The recent publication of some obscure Dead Sea scroll fragments suggested a link between the Essenes of Qumran and the Jerusalem wing of the early Christian church, or "Nazarean movement," as it was called. The Jerusalem Church had been led by St. James. King Herod Agrippa martyred his share of early

Christians, and even the High Priest Ananus was after them.
So they were periodically fleeing into the desert.

"You know," he said softly, "I never saw it before. I
mean, the writing was so disjointed and cryptic, but the
timing fits. If we assume that 'his death' refers to the
crucifixion, and that 'his brother' arrived 'two decades and
a half' later, that would date the Glass scroll somewhere
around fifty-eight A.D." Dan felt a tingle of excitement in his
gut. "James was still alive in fifty-eight. Ananus didn't have
him killed until sixty-two A.D."

Carrie clutched his arm. "And tradition says Mary died
twenty-two years after Jesus's death, which is pretty darn
close to two decades and a half."

Dan could tell Carrie was getting pumped again. It
seemed to be contagious. His own heart had picked up its
tempo.

"But who wrote this? If we can trust the little he says
about himself, I would guess he was a scribe or a Pharisee,
or both."

"How can you tell that?"

"Well, he's educated. Hal told me the scroll was written
in the Aramaic of the time with Greek and Latin words and
expressions thrown in. The striped blue sleeve he mentions,
and his former free access to the Temple—he's got to be a
Pharisee."

"He talks about the inheritance he left behind."

"Right. A rich Pharisee."

"But weren't the Pharisees proud? This guy's wearing
rags and he says even the lice won't bite him. And he tried
to drown himself."

"In the Dead Sea, apparently—it was called the Sea of
Lot back in those days. Okay. So he's a severely depressed
Pharisee who's fallen on hard times and suffers from a
heavy-duty lack of self-esteem."

Carrie smiled. God, he loved that smile. "Sounds like
he'd fit right in at Loaves and Fishes," she said. "But what's
this about Hellenists?"

Dan reread the passage. The pieces began falling into
place. "You know . . . he could be referring to St. Paul's

wing of the early church. The two groups had a falling out."

"I knew there were disagreements, but—"

"More than disagreements. A complete split. James and his followers remained in Jerusalem as observant Jews, sticking to all the dietary laws and customs while they awaited the Second Coming of the Messiah, which they assumed would happen any day. St. Paul, on the other hand, was out in the hinterlands, working the crowds, converting Jews and Gentiles alike to his own brand of Christianity. His father was a Roman and so Paul had a different slant on Jesus's teachings, one that sacked the dietary laws and most Jewish traditions. It mentions here 'the brother's fear of the Hellenists using the mother's remains for their own purposes'—the scroll has *got* to be referring to St. James's rivalry with St. Paul's movement."

Dan stared at Carrie, his heart pounding, his spirits soaring. Good God, it all fit! The scroll described an encounter with St. James and the remnant of the Jerusalem church shortly before James was martyred.

"Carrie, this is incredible! Why hasn't anybody else—?" Then he slammed on the brakes as he remembered. "Wait. Just wait." He shook his head to clear away the adrenalin buzz. "What am I doing?"

"What's wrong?"

"*Everything's* wrong. The scroll is a fake, Carrie. The ink is two or three years old. We've got to remember that. A damn skillful job, but a proven forgery. Almost had me going there, wondering why nobody else had put these pieces together. Then I realized why: nobody bothered to try. Why waste time interpreting a fake?"

"No," Carrie said, shaking her head defiantly. "This is true."

"Carrie," he said, stroking her arm. "Somebody tried to pull a fast one on the world."

"Why? Why would someone want to do such a thing?"

"Maliciousness. Like calling in a bomb scare to a concert and watching everybody scramble out. Malicious mischief on an international scale. If the scroll had been released to the world as authentic, someone would have come to the same conclusion as we. The liberal and fundamentalist sects of the Christian world would be up in arms, the Vatican would be releasing encyclicals, the Judean Desert would be filled with expeditions in search of the remains of the Mother of God. There'd be years of chaos. And all the while, our forger would be sitting back, giggling, knowing he caused it all."

"But to what end? I don't get it."

Dan looked at her. No, Carrie wouldn't get it. This sort of maliciousness was beyond her comprehension. That was why he loved her.

"A power trip, Carrie. Pure ego. The Christian world is in chaos, all because of your clever forgery. All I can say is it's a damn good thing the Rockefeller Museum did a thorough testing job."

"I don't care what the tests say," she said, tapping the sheets on her lap. "This is true."

"Carrie, the ink—"

"I don't care! I don't care if the ink's still *wet*! This man speaks the truth. Can't you feel it? There's real pain here, Dan. Whoever wrote these words is isolated—from his friends, from his family, from his God. The loneliness, the anguish . . . it seeps through in every sentence."

"Then how do you explain the carbon dating?"

"I can't. And I'm not going to try. But I am going to prove the truth of these words. And you're going to help."

Dan had a sudden bad feeling about what was coming.

"I am?"

"Yes, dear. Somehow, some way, you and I are going to Israel and we're going to find the earthly remains of the Virgin Mary."

Dan smiled, humoring her. She was just a little crazy now. She'd get over it. Besides, there was no way they'd be able to get away to Israel together.

Part II

Journeys

Summer

12

The Judean Wilderness

"Let's find a shady spot and take a break," Dan said, wiping his face on his sleeve as they drove through the barren sandy hills.

"There is no shade," Carrie said. "But I'll drive if you want."

Dan peered through the Explorer's dusty windshield at the undulating landscape shimmering before them. They'd been wandering through the desert mountains most of the morning, following one wadi, then another, turning this way and that. Still Dan was unable get a handle on his surroundings. He'd never seen anything like it. So barren, so desolate, so close to the sky, so *alone*. No wonder the prophets went to the desert to find and talk to their God—this was a place devoid of earthly distractions.

Except, perhaps, survival.

"No. Better if I drive and you navigate."

"Okay. But we're going to find it soon. It's somewhere up ahead, I just know it."

"How can you possibly know it?"

She looked at him. Her face was flushed, just like it got in the shelter kitchen, but her eyes were brighter and more exited than he could remember.

"I can feel it. Can't you?"

Dan shrugged. The only thing he felt was hot.

The air conditioner had given out somewhere around

Enot Qane and they'd been sweltering ever since. At least Dan had. Not Carrie. The heat didn't seem to affect her. Or perhaps she was too excited to notice.

Carrie had changed. She'd always been driven, and her boundless energies had been focused keeping St. Joe's homeless kitchen operating at peak efficiency, doing as much as possible for as many as possible. But her focus had shifted since that evening when she discovered the translation of the forged scroll. She'd become obsessed with finding this so-called Resting Place.

Nothing would turn her from the quest. Dan had argued with her, pleaded with her, tried to reason with her that she was falling victim to an elaborate hoax. He threatened to make her go alone, even threatened to expose to Mother Superior the true reason for the leave of absence she'd requested this summer.

Carrie had only smiled. "I'm going, Dan. With you or without you, whether Mother Superior knows or not, I'm going to Israel this summer."

For a while he'd hoped that money, or rather the lack of it, would keep her home. Neither of them had any savings—their vows of poverty saw to that—and this pipe-dream trip of Carrie's was going to be costly. But money turned out to be no problem at all. Her brother Brad had seen to that years ago when he'd presented her with an American Express card in her name but drawn on his account. Keep it handy in case of an emergency, he'd told her. Or use it to buy whatever you need whenever you need it.

Carrie had filed it away, literally forgetting about it until she decided that she needed two tickets to Israel. She said Brad wouldn't mind. He had deep pockets and was always trying to buy her things . . . trying to assuage his guilt, she'd said, although she wouldn't say what kind of guilt he was assuaging.

And so it came to pass that a certain Ms. Carolyn Ferris and a male companion arrived in Tel Aviv at the height of the summer, hopped a tour bus to Jerusalem where they spent two nights in the Hilton, toured the Old Town for a day, then rented a four-wheel-drive, off-road vehicle, stocked it with a couple of flashlights, a cooler filled with sandwiches and soft drinks, and headed south.

And now here they were, trekking through the Judean Wilderness—the *Midbar Yehuda* of yore—in a Ford Explorer on a wild-goose chase.

But it was Carrie's wild-goose chase. And that was why Dan was along.

But weren't you supposed to protect the one you loved from harm, from the pain of dashed hopes at the end of wild-goose chases?

Well, even though Dan knew this quest of hers was a hoax, the trip wasn't a total loss. They'd seen the Holy Land. During their day in Jerusalem they'd walked the Via Dolorosa—the original Stations of the Cross—and visited the Church of the Holy Sepulcher, the Garden of Gesthemane, and the Pater Noster Church on the Mount of Olives.

Through it all, Carrie had been so excited, like a child on her first trip to Disney World. "We're really here!" she'd kept saying. "I can't believe we're really here!"

And all along the Via Dolorosa: "Can you believe it, Dan? We're actually walking in Jesus's footsteps!"

That look on her face was worth anything. Anything except . . .

He glanced over at her, sitting in the passenger seat, scanning the cliffs ahead as the Explorer bounced up the dry drainage channel. A yellow sheet of paper sat in her lap. Dan had drawn a large ת on it—a *tav*, the Hebrew equivalent of the letter T, or Th. Carrie was hunting for a cliff or butte in the shape of that *tav*. Dan doubted very much they'd find one, but even if they did, there'd be no Virgin Mary hidden in a cave there.

And that worried him. He didn't want to see Carrie hurt. She'd invested so much of herself in this quest, allowed it to so consume her for months that there was no telling what the painful truth might do to her. Let them spend their entire time here driving in endless circles, finding nothing, then heading home disappointed and frustrated that the desert had kept its secret, but leaving still alive the hope that somewhere in this seared nothingness there remained the find of the millennium, guarded by time and place, and perhaps even God Himself. Better than that to see her crushed by the realization that she'd been duped.

Ahead of him, the wadi forked into two narrower channels, one running northwest, the other southwest. The trailing cloud of dust swirled around them as Dan braked to a halt. He coughed as some of it billowed through the open windows.

"Where to now?"

"I'm not sure," Carrie said.

Without waiting for the dust to settle, she stepped out of the Explorer and stared at the cliffs rising ahead of them. Dan got out, too, as much to stretch his legs as to look around. A breeze drifted by, taking some of his perspiration with it.

"You know," he said, "I do believe it's gotten cooler."

"We're finally above sea level," Carrie said, still staring ahead as if expecting to find a road sign to the *tav* cliff. The light blue short-sleeve shirt she wore had dark rings of perspiration around her armpits and across her shoulder blades where they'd rested against the seat back. Her loose, lightweight slacks fluttered around her legs. She stood defiantly in the sun, unbowed by the heat.

Dan looked back the way they'd come. Rolling hills, dry, sandy brown, almost yellow, falling away to the Dead Sea, the lowest spot on earth—the world's navel, someone had called it. The hazy air had been unbearably thick down there, chokingly laden with moisture from the evaporating sea; leaden air, too heavy to escape the fifty-mile trench in which it was trapped. Maybe it wasn't cooler up here, but it was drier. He could breathe.

Above, the sky was a flawless turquoise. The land ahead was as dry and yellow-brown and barren as behind, but steeper here, angling up sharply toward a phalanx of steep cliffs. Looked like a dead end up there.

He plucked a rag from the floor by the front seat and began wiping the dust from the windshield.

"When's the next rain?" he said.

"November, most likely."

Dan had to smile. Carrie had done her homework. She'd spent months preparing for this trip, studying the scroll translation and correlating its scant geographical details with present day topographical maps of the area. He bet she knew more about the region than most Israelis, but that probably wasn't saying much. They hadn't seen another soul since turning off the highway. They were completely alone up here. The realization gave Dan a twinge of uneasiness. They hadn't thought to get a car phone—not that there'd be a cell out here anyway—and if they broke down, they'd have to start walking. And if they got lost . . .

"We're not lost, are we?" Dan said.

"I don't think so. I'm sure he came this way."

How could she be certain? Sure, she'd put a lot of research into this trip, but there hadn't been much to go on to begin with. All they knew was that the fictional author of the scroll—*fictional* was an adjective Dan used privately when referring to the character who had supposedly written the scroll; never within Carrie's hearing; she *believed*—had turned west from his southward trek and left the shore of what he called the Sea of Lot to journey into the Wilderness.

But where had he turned?

"I don't know, Carrie . . ."

"This has to be the way," she said. She seemed utterly convinced. Didn't she have even a shade of a doubt? "Look: He mentioned being driven out of Qumran—that's at the northern end of the sea. He says he headed south toward Masada and Zohar but he never mentions getting there. He doesn't even mention passing En Gedi which was a major oasis even then. So he must have turned into the wilderness somewhere between Qumran and En Gedi."

"No argument there," Dan said. "But that stretch is more

than thirty miles long. There were hundreds of places we could have turned off the road. Why did you pick that particular spot back there?"

Carrie looked at him and her clear blue eyes clouded momentarily. For the first time since their arrival she seemed unsure of herself.

"I don't know," she said slowly. "It just *seemed* like the right place to turn. I've read the translation so many times I feel as if I know him. I could almost see him wandering south, alone, depressed, suddenly feeling it was no use trying to find other people to take him in, that he was unfit for human company, and turning and heading into the hills."

Dan was struck by the thought that she might be describing her own feelings as a fourteen-year old entering the Convent of the Blessed Virgin.

That moment back on the highway had been kind of spooky. They'd been cruising south on Route 90 along the Dead Sea shore when Carrie had suddenly clutched his arm and pointed to a rubble-strewn path, little more than a goat trail, breaking through the roadside brush and winding up into the hills.

"There!" she'd cried. "Follow that!"

So Dan had pressed the *4x4* button on the Explorer's dash and followed the trail here.

"Which way does it *seem* we should go now?" he said and knew right away from her expression that it hadn't come out the way he'd meant it.

"Look, Dan," she said, eyes flashing. "I know you think I've gone off the deep end on this, but it's important to me. And if—"

"What's important to me is *you*, Carrie. That's all. Just you. And I'm worried about you getting hurt. You've pumped your expectations so high . . ."

Her eyes softened as she challenged the sun with that smile. "You don't have to worry about me, Dan, because she *is* up here. And we're going to find her."

"Carrie—"

"And now that I think about it, it *seems* we should take

the south fork." She swung back into her seat and closed her door. "Come on, Driver Dan. Let's go! Time's a-wastin'!"

Dan sighed. Nothing to do but humor her. And it wasn't so bad, really. At least they were together.

It was getting near four o'clock. Dan was thinking about calling it a day and heading back to the highway while there was still plenty of light left. Wouldn't be easy finding his way back down in the light. No way in the dark. He was just about to suggest it when Carrie suddenly lurched forward in her seat.

"Oh, my God!" she cried, her eyes darting between the windshield and the sheet of paper in her lap. "Jesus, Mary and Joseph, could that be *it*?"

Dan skidded to a halt and craned his neck over the steering wheel for a look. As before, the trailing dust cloud caught up to them and he could see nothing while they were engulfed. But as it cleared . . .

"I'll be damned," Dan muttered.

No, he thought. It's got to be a mistake. The sun is directly ahead, it's glaring off the dirt on the windshield. A trick of the light. Got to be.

Hoping, praying that his eyes were suffering from too much glare, Dan opened the door and stepped out for a better look. He shielded his eyes against the sun which was sitting on the flat ledge atop a huge outcropping of stone ahead of them, and blinked into the light. He still couldn't tell if it—

And then the sun dipped below the ledge, silhouetting the outcropping in brilliant light. Suddenly Dan could see that the ledge ran rightward to merge with the wall of the mountain of which the outcropping was a part, and leftward to a rocky lip which overhung a sheer precipice that bellied gently outward about halfway down its fall.

Damned if it didn't look just like . . . a *tav*.

"Do you see it, Dan?"

He glanced right and there was Carrie, out of the cab, holding the yellow sheet of paper at arms length before her and jumping up and down like a preschooler who'd just spotted Barney.

He hesitated, unsure of what to say. As much as he wanted to avoid reinforcing her fantasies, he could not deny the resemblance of the cliff face to the Hebrew letter he'd drawn for her.

"Well, I see something that might remotely—"

"Remotely, shlemotely! That cliff looks exactly like what you drew here, which is exactly the way it was described in the scroll!"

"The *forged* scroll, Carrie. Don't forget that the source of all these factoids is a confirmed hoax."

"How could I possibly forget when you keep reminding me every ten minutes?"

He hated to sound like a broken record, but he felt he had to keep the facts before her. The scroll and everything in it was bogus. And truthfully, right now he needed a little reminder himself. Because finding the *tav* rock had shaken him up more than he wished to admit.

"Sorry, Carrie. I just—"

"I know," she said. "But you've got to *believe*, Dan. There's truth in that scroll." She pointed at the *tav* rock looming before them. "Look. We're not imagining that. It's there."

Dan wanted to say, Yes, but if you want to perpetrate a hoax, you salt the lies with neutral truths, and the most easily verifiable neutral truths are simple geological formations. But he held his tongue. This was Carrie's show.

"What are we waiting for?" she said.

Dan shrugged and got back in behind the wheel. The incline ahead was extra steep so he pressed the LOW RANGE button on the dashboard.

"Can you believe it?" Carrie said, bubbling with excitement as they started the final climb. "We're traveling the same route as St. James and the members of the Jerusalem Church when they carried Mary's body here."

"No, Carrie," he said softly. "I can't believe it. I want to believe it. I'd give almost anything to have it be true. But I can't believe it."

"You will, Danny, me boy-o," she said, smiling that smile. "Before the day is out, you will."

The closer they got to the rock, the less and less it resembled a *tav* . . . and the more formidable it looked. Fifty feet high at the very least, with sheer walls that would have challenged an experienced rock climber even if they were straight; but the outward bulge and the sharp overhang at the crest made ascent all but impossible.

As they rounded the outcropping, Dan realized they'd entered the mouth of a canyon. The deep passage narrowed and curved off to the left about a quarter of a mile north. He stopped the Explorer in the middle of the dry wadi running along the eastern wall. Cooler here. The canyon floor had been resting in the shadow of its western wall for a while. To his left he spotted a cluster of stunted trees.

"Aren't those fig trees?" Carrie said.

"Not sure," Dan said. "Could be. Whatever they are, they don't look too healthy."

"They look old. Old fig trees . . . didn't the scroll writer said he was subsisting on locusts, honey, and wild figs?"

"Yeah, but those trees don't look wild. Looks like somebody planted them there."

"Exactly!" Carrie said, grinning.

Dan had to admit—to himself only—that she had a point. It looked as if someone had moved a bunch of wild fig trees to this spot and started a makeshift grove . . . out here . . . in the middle of nowhere.

But that only meant the forger of the scroll had to have been here in order to describe it; it didn't mean St. James had been here, or that the Virgin Mary was hidden away atop the *tav* rock.

But a big question still remained: Who had planted those fig trees?

He turned to Carrie but her seat was empty. She was walking across the wadi toward the *tav* rock. Dan turned off the motor and ran around to catch up to her.

"Where do you think you're going?"

"Looking for a way up," she said, studying the cliff face as she walked. "The scroll says there's a path."

Dan scanned the steep wall looming before them.

"Good luck."

"Well, this isn't nearly as smooth as the far side. There could be a way up. There has to be. We simply have to find it."

Dan saw countless jagged cracks and mini-ledges protruding randomly from the surface, but nothing that even vaguely resembled a path. This looked hopeless, but the scroll had been accurate on so many other points already, there just might be a path to the top.

He veered off to the left.

"Giving up so soon?" Carrie said.

"If there *is* a path," he said, "you won't spot it from straight on. It'll only be visible from a sharp angle. You didn't spot one as we rounded the front of the cliff, so let's see what things look like from the back end."

She nodded, smiling. "Smart. I knew I loved you for some reason."

Dan figured he'd done enough nay-saying. The only way to get this over with was to find a path to the top—if there was one—and convince Carrie once and for all that there was no cave up there and that the Virgin Mary was not lying on a bier inside waiting to be discovered. Then maybe they could get their lives back to normal—that is, as normal as life could be for a priest and a nun who were lovers.

He reached the northern end of the outcropping and wound his way through the brush clustered around its base. When he was within arm's reach of the base itself, he looked south along the cliff wall.

"I'll be damned . . ."

Carrie hurried to his side. "What? Did you find it? Is it there?"

He guided her in front of him and pointed ahead. Starting a dozen feet behind them and running up the face of the cliff at a thirty-degree angle was a narrow, broken, jagged ledge. It averaged only two feet or so in width.

Carrie whirled and hugged him. "That's it! You found it! See? All you need is a little faith!" She grabbed his hand and began dragging him from the brush. "Let's go!"

He followed her at a walk as she ran back to where the ledge slanted into the floor of the canyon floor. By the time he reached it she was already on her way, scrabbling upward along the narrow ledge like a lithe, graceful cat.

"Slow down, Carrie."

"Speed up, slowpoke!" She laughed.

She's going to kill herself, he thought as he began his own upward course along the ledge. He glanced down at the jagged rubble on the hard floor of the wadi below and quickly pulled his gaze away. Maybe we're both going to get killed.

He wasn't good with heights—not phobic about them, but not the least bit fond of them. He concentrated on staying on the ledge. Shale, sand, and gravel littered the narrow, uneven surface before him, tilting toward the cliff wall for half a dozen feet or so, then a crack or a narrow gap, or a step up or down, then it continued upward, now sloping away from the wall. These away sections were the worse. Dan's sneakers tended to slip on the sand and he had visions of himself sliding off into—

"Dan!"

A high-pitched squeal of terror from up ahead. He looked up and saw Carrie down on one knee, her right leg dangling over the edge, her fingers clawing at the cliff wall for purchase. She'd climbed back into the sunlight and it looked as if her sharp-edged shadow was trying to push her off.

Oh my God! "Carrie! Hang on!"

He hurried toward her as quickly as he dared but she was back on the ledge and on her feet again by the time he reached her.

"What happened?"

Pale, panting, she leaned against the cliff wall, hugging it. "I slipped, but I'm okay."

Suddenly he was angry. His heart was pounding, his hands were trembling . . .

"You almost killed yourself, dammit!"

"Sorry," she said softly. "That wasn't my intention, I assure you."

"Just slow down, will you? I don't want to lose you."

That smile. "That's nice to hear."

"Here. Let me slide past you and I'll lead the way."

"Not a chance. I'll take my time from here on up." She held up two fingers. "Promise."

Carrie kept her word, taking it slow, watching her footing, with Dan close behind. They reached the summit without another mishap. He glanced around—no one else here, and no place to hide.

"Oh, Lord," Carrie said, wandering across the top of the *tav* toward the far edge. "Look at this!"

Dan caught up to her and put an arm around her shoulders, as much for a need to touch her as to stop her from getting too close to the edge. The sun cooked their backs while the desert wind dried the sweat from the climb, and before them stretched the eastern expanse of the *Midbar Yehuda*, all hills and mounds and shadowed crags, looking like a rumpled yellow-brown blanket after a night of passion, sloping down to the lowest point on earth where a sliver of the Dead Sea was visible, sparkling in the late afternoon sun.

Breathtaking, Dan thought. This almost makes the whole wild-goose chase worthwhile.

Together they turned from the vista and scanned the mini-plateau atop the *tav*. It ran two hundred feet from the front lip to the rear wall, and was perhaps a hundred and fifty feet wide. And against that rear wall, to the left of center, was a pile of rocks.

Carrie grabbed his upper arm. He felt her fingers sink into his biceps as she pointed to the rocks.

"Oh, God, Dan! There it is!"

"Just some rocks, Carrie. Doesn't mean—"

"She's there, Dan. We've found her! We've *found* her!"

She broke from him and dashed across the plateau. Dan hurried after her.

Here it comes, he thought. Here's where the roof falls in on Carrie's quest.

By the time he reached the pile, Carrie was on it, scrambling to the top. The pile was about eight feet high and she was already at work pulling at the uppermost rocks to dislodge them.

"Easy, Carrie," Dan said as he climbed to her side and joined her atop the pile. "The last thing we need is for you to slip and sprain an ankle. I have no idea how I'd get you back down."

"Help me," Carrie said, breathless with excitement. "She's just a few feet away. We're almost there! I can *feel* it!"

Dan joined her in dislodging the uppermost rocks and letting them roll to the base. The first were on the small side, cantaloupe-sized and easy to move. But they quickly graduated to watermelons.

Carrie groaned as she strained against one of the larger stones. "I can't budge this. Give me a hand, will you?"

Dan got a grip on the edge of the rock and put his back into it and together they got it overbalanced to the point where it tumbled down the pile.

Dan saw even bigger stones below.

"We're going to need help," he said, panting and straightening up. The sun was still actively baking the top of the *tav* rock and he was drenched. "A lever of some sort. We'll never move those lower rocks by ourselves. Maybe I can find a tree limb or something we can use to—"

"We've *got* to get in!" Carrie said. Tears of frustration welled in her eyes as she looked up at him. "We can't stop now. Not when we're this close. We can't let a bunch of lousy rocks keep us out when we're so *close*!"

With the last word she kicked at one of the larger stones directly below her—and cried out in alarm as it gave way beneath her. Dan grabbed her outflung hand and almost lost his own footing as the entire pile shuddered and settled under them with a rumble and a gush of dust.

"You all right?" Dan said, pulling Carrie closer.

She coughed. "I think so. What happened?"

"I'm not sure." The dust was settling, layering their skin,

mixing with their sweat. Even with mud on her face Carrie was beautiful. Over her shoulder, down by Carrie's feet, Dan saw a dark crescent in the mountain wall. "Oh, Jesus."

Carrie turned and gasped. "The cave!"

Maybe, Dan thought. Maybe not. The only sure thing about it is it's a hole in the wall.

But he knew it was the upper rim of a cave mouth. Had to be. Everything else in this elaborate scam had followed true to the forged scroll. Why not the cave too?

But what sort of ugly surprise waited within?

Before he could stop her, Carrie had dropped prone and pushed her face into the opening.

"We left the flashlights in the car," she was saying. "And I can't see a thing."

Quickly he pulled her back. "Are you nuts?"

"What's the matter?"

"You don't know what's in there."

"What could be in there?"

"How about snakes or scorpions? Or how about bats? It's a cave, you know."

"I know that, but—"

"But nothing," he said, pulling her to her feet. "You keep your nose out of there while I go get the flashlights."

"All right," she said reluctantly as she allowed him to guide her down to the bottom of the pile. "Can't see anything anyway."

"Precisely. So you just wait here while I go back to the Explorer."

"Okay, but hurry." She squeezed his hand. "Don't hurry so much you fall, but hurry."

Dan made the round trip as quickly as he could, hugging the cliff wall all the way down, concentrating on the path and not looking down. He did spot another cave in the far wall of the canyon—probably where the fictional author of the scrolls supposedly had lived. He reminded himself to check it out before they left.

The sun had continued its slide and the shadow of the canyon's western wall had crawled three-quarters of the way up the *tav* by the time he returned to the top with the two flashlights.

He stood there a moment, panting, sweating from the climb, before he realized he was alone on the plateau.

"Carrie?" He dashed toward the rock pile, shouting as he ran. *"Carrie!"*

"What?"

Her head popped up atop the rock pile, smiling at him, and as he clambered up the boulders he saw her lying on her belly with her legs and pelvis inside the opening. She looked like someone half-swallowed by a stony mouth.

"My God, Carrie, couldn't you wait? Get out of there!"

"I'm fine." She reached a hand out to him. "Flashlight please."

"I'll go first."

"No way. You didn't even want to come."

Dan was tempted to withhold the flashlight, make her climb out of there and let him flash a light around inside that hole before she crawled in. But the excitement, the childlike eagerness in her eyes weakened him. And after all, this was her show.

He flicked one on to make sure it worked, then slapped the handle into her waiting palm.

"Be careful. And wait right there. Don't go anywhere without me."

"Okay." Another smile, so confident looking, but Dan noticed the flashlight shaking in her hand. She pushed herself backward and slipped the rest of the way inside.

A chill of foreboding ran through Dan as he saw Carrie disappear into that hole, swallowed by the darkness. God knew what could be in there.

"Carrie? You there? You okay?"

Her face floated back into the light. "Of course I'm okay. Kind of cool in here, and dusty, and it looks . . . empty."

I could have told you that, Dan thought, but kept it to himself. He'd give anything to make this right for her, but that was impossible. So the least he could do was be there when the hurt hit.

"Stand back a little. I'm coming in."

Dan slid down onto his back and entered the opening feet first. A tight squeeze but he managed to wriggle through with only a few minor scrapes and scratches.

Carrie stood a few feet away, her back to him, playing her flashlight beam along the walls.

"You're right," he said, coughing as he brushed himself off. "A lot cooler in here. Almost cold."

Quickly he flashed his own beam around. Not a cave so much as a rocky alcove, maybe a dozen feet deep and fifteen wide, with rough, pocked walls. And no doubt about its being empty. Not even a spider. Just dust—dry, powdered rock—layering the floor. Only Carrie's footprints and his own marred the silky surface.

What do I say? he wondered. Do I say *anything*—or let Carrie say it first?

As he stepped toward her, Carrie suddenly moved away to the left.

"Look, Dan. I think there's a tunnel here."

Dan caught up to her, joined his flash beam to hers, and realized that what he had thought to be a pocket recess near the floor of the cave was actually an opening into another chamber.

Carrie dropped to her hands and knees and shone her light through.

"See anything?" Dan said, hovering over her.

"Looks like more of the same. Tunnels only a couple of feet long. I'm going in for a look."

Dan squatted behind her and gently patted her buttocks. "Right behind you."

Carrie began to crawl through, then stopped, freezing like a deer who's heard a twig break, then quickly scrambled the rest of the way through.

"Oh, Dan," he heard her say in a hoarse, quavering voice just above a whisper. "Oh-Dan-oh-Dan-oh-Dan-oh-*Dan!*"

He belly-crawled through as fast as his elbows and knees could propel him and bumped his head on the ceiling as he regained his feet on the other side.

But he instantly forgot the pain when he saw what lay in the wavering beam of Carrie's flashlight.

A woman.

An elderly woman lying supine in an oblong niche in the wall of the chamber.

"It's . . ." Carrie's voice choked off and she cleared her throat. "It's her, Dan. It's really her."

"Well, it's somebody."

A jumble of emotions tumbled through Dan. He was numb, he was exhausted, and he was angry. He'd been preparing himself to comfort Carrie when she discovered she'd been played for a fool. Entering the cave was supposed to be the last step in this trek. Now he had one more thing to explain.

The scroll, the careful and clever descriptions of this area of the Wilderness were one thing, but this was going too far. This was . . . *ghoulish* was the most appropriate word that came to mind.

"Look at her, Dan," Carrie said. "It's *her*."

Dan was doing just that. The woman's robe was blue, its cowl up and around her head; short, medium build, with thick strands of gray hair poking out from under the cowl. Her wrinkled skin had a sallow, almost waxy look to it. Her eyes and lips were closed, her cheeks slightly sunken, her nose generous without being large. Even in the wavering light of the flash beams, she appeared to be a handsome, elderly woman who might have been beautiful in her youth. She looked so peaceful lying there. He noticed her hands were folded between her breasts. Something about those hands . . .

"Look at her fingernails," Carrie said, her voice hushed like someone whispering during Benediction. Obviously she shared his feeling that they were trespassing. "They're so long."

"I hear they continue to grow . . . the nails and the hair . . . after you're dead."

Carrie stepped closer but Dan gripped her arm and held her back.

"Don't. It might be booby-trapped."

Carrie shook off his hand and whirled to face him. He couldn't see her face but the anger in her whisper told him all he needed to know about her expression.

"Stop it, Dan! Haven't you gone far enough with this Doubting Thomas act?"

"It's not an act, and I wish there was more light."

"So do it, but there isn't. I wish we'd brought some sort of lantern but we didn't. This is all we've got."

"All right," he said. "But be careful."

Dan fought a sick, anxious dread that coiled through his gut as he watched her approach the body. And it *was* a body. Had to be. Too much detail for it to be anything other than the real thing.

But whose body? What sort of mind would go to such elaborate extremes to pull off a hoax. A sicko mind like that would be capable of anything, even a booby trap.

Of course, there was the possibility that these actually were the earthly remains of the mother of Jesus Christ.

Dan wanted to believe that. He dearly would have loved to believe that. And probably would be fervently believing that right now if not for the fact that the scroll that had led them here had been proven beyond a doubt to have been written two years ago.

So if this wasn't the Virgin Mary, who was she? And who had hidden her here?

Carrie was standing over her now, staring down at the woman's lifeless face.

"Dan?" she said. "Do you notice something strange about her?"

"Besides her fingernails?"

"There's no dust on her. There's dust layered everywhere, but not a speck of it on her."

Dan stepped closer and sniffed. No odor. And Carrie was right about the dust: not a speck. He smiled. The forger had finally made a mistake.

"Doesn't that indicate to you that she was placed here recently?"

"No. It indicates to me that dirt—and dust is dirt—has no place on the Mother of God."

As he watched, Carrie sank to her knees, made the sign of the cross, and bowed her head in prayer with the flashlight clasped between her hands.

This isn't real, Dan thought. All we need is a ray of light from the ceiling and a hallelujah chorus from the Mormon Tabernacle Choir to make this a Cecil B. DeMille epic. This can't be happening. Not to me. Not to Carrie. We're two sane people.

Impulsively, gingerly, he reached out and touched the woman's cheek. The wrinkled flesh didn't give. Not hard like stone or wood or plastic. More like wax. Cool and smooth . . . like wax. But it wasn't wax, at least not like any wax Dan had ever seen.

He heard a sob and snatched his hand away . . . but the sound had come from Carrie. He flashed his beam toward her face. Tears glistened on her cheeks. He crouched beside her.

"Carrie, what's wrong?"

"I don't know. I feel so strange. All this time I thought I believed, and I prayed to her, and I asked her to help me, to intercede for me, but now I get the feeling that all that time I didn't believe. Not really. And now here she is in front of me, not two feet away, and I don't know what I feel or what I think." She looked up at him. "I don't have to believe anymore, do I, Dan? I *know*. I don't have to believe, and that feels so strange."

One thing Dan knew was that he didn't believe this was the Virgin Mary. But it was somebody. He played his flashlight beam over her body.

Lady, who are you?

Another thing he knew was that Carrie was heading for some sort of breakdown. She was teetering on the edge now. He had to get her out of here before she went over. But how?

"What do we do now?" he said, straightening up.

He felt her grip his arm as she rose to her feet beside him.

"What do you mean?"

"I mean we've found her . . . or someone . . . or something. Now what do we do?"

"We protect her, Dan."

"And how do we do that?"

Carrie's voice was very calm, almost matter of fact. "We take her back with us."

13

"What's the matter, baby?" Devorah said from behind him, casually raking her sharp nails down the center of his back.

Kesev sat on the edge of the bed in Devorah's apartment. They always wound up at Devorah's place, never his. They both preferred it that way. Kesev because he never allowed anyone in his apartment, and Devorah because when she was home she had access to her . . . props.

He'd met her last year. An El Al stewardess. She could have been Irish with her billowing red hair, pale freckled skin, and blue eyes, but she was pure Israeli. Young—mid-twenties—with such an innocent, girlish face, almost childlike. But Devorah was a cruel, mischievous child who liked to play rough. And when it came to rough she preferred to give rather than receive. Which was fine with Kesev.

Their little arrangement had lasted longer than any other in recent memory. Probably because her job took her away so much, she'd yet to grow tired of his black moods and long silences. And probably because Devorah had been unable to find a way to really hurt him. Kesev absorbed whatever she could dish out. She considered him a challenge, her perfect whipping boy.

So Devorah seemed happy with him, while he was . . . what? Happy? Satisfied? Content?

Hardly. He couldn't remember the last time he'd felt something approaching any of those.

The situation was . . . tolerable. Just barely tolerable. Which was more than he'd learned to hope for.

"You weren't really into it tonight," she said.

"Sorry. I . . . I'm distracted."

"You're always distracted. Tonight you're barely here."

Probably true. A vague uneasiness had stalked him all day, disturbing his concentration at the Shin Bet office, stealing his appetite, and finally settling on him like a shroud late this afternoon.

More than uneasiness now. A feeling of impending doom.

Could it have something to do with the Resting Place? He followed the wire services meticulously and there'd been no word of a new Dead Sea scroll or startling revelations regarding the Mother of Christ. Not even a ripple.

But that was hardly proof that all was well, that all was safe and secure.

"I'm afraid I'm going to have to cancel our date for tomorrow," he said, turning to face her.

She lay sprawled among the sheets, her generous breasts and their pink nipples exposed. Even her breasts were freckled. But she didn't lay still long. She levered up and slapped him across the face.

"I don't like broken promises!" she hissed between clenched teeth.

The blow stung but Kesev didn't flinch. Nor was he angry. One deserved whatever one got when a promise was betrayed.

"There is a hierarchy of promises," he said softly. "Some promises take precedence over others."

"And this promise," she said. "Is this what distracts you?"

"Yes."

"Does it involve another woman?"

"Not at all." *At least not in the sense you mean.*

"Good." She smiled as she clicked a handcuff over his right wrist. "Come. Let Devorah see if she can make you forget all your mysterious distractions."

The Judean Wilderness

It had taken some heavy persuasion, but Dan managed to convince Carrie to leave the cave so they could talk outside . . . in the light . . . in the air . . . away from that . . . thing.

He felt instantly better outside. It had seemed like night in there. Even though the entire *tav* rock was in shadow now, he squinted in the relative brightness.

And he was still staggering from Carrie's words. He'd never thought they'd find anything on this trip, so he'd never even dreamed that Carrie might want to . . .

"Take her back? To the U.S.? Are you serious?"

"We have to," she said. "If we don't, other people might decipher that other scroll you mentioned and find her. The wrong kind of people. People who'd . . . misuse her."

"Then why don't we just move her from here and bury her where no one will find her?"

She wheeled on him. "This is the Mother of *God*, Dan! You don't just stick her in the dirt!"

"All right, all right." He could see she wasn't rational on this. "But even if we could get her back home—and believe me, that's a big *if*—what'll we do with her? Give her to a museum? To the Vatican?"

"Oh, no. Oh, Lord, no," she said, vigorously shaking her head. "We've got to keep her secret. She was hidden away for a reason. We have to respect that. Imagine if the wrong religion got hold of her, or some sort of satanic cult. Think how they might desecrate her. Now that we've found her, we have a very clear duty: We have to take her back with us and hide her where no one else can find her."

"You're not thinking, Carrie. We'll never get her past customs."

"There's got to be a way. Your friend Hal says people are smuggling archeological artifacts out of the Mideast all the time. Call him. He can tell you how."

"Call Hal? Sure. Hand me the phone."

"This is not a joking matter, Dan."

He saw her tight features and the look in her eyes and realized how serious she was. But she wasn't thinking straight. Finding that strange body in there, whoever it was, had jumbled up her rational processes. He had to get her away from here, get her calmed down so she could get some perspective on this whole situation. . . .

And calling Hal might be just the excuse he needed.

"All right. We'll call Hal and see what he says."

Her expression relaxed. "You mean that?"

"Of course. We'll drive back to the highway, maybe go to En Gedi . . ." He glanced at his watch. "It's seven hours earlier in New York so we can still catch him in his office. And we'll ask his advice."

"You go," she said. "I'm staying here."

"No way, Carrie," he said. "No way I'm leaving you sitting up here at night in the middle of nowhere."

"I'll be all right. Now that I've found her, you can't expect me to leave her."

"If she is who you think she is, she's been fine here for two thousand years. One more night isn't going to matter."

"I'm staying," she said.

Dan had humored her as far as he could. He wasn't backing down on this point.

"Here's the deal, Carrie," he said, fighting to keep from shouting. "Either we go down to En Gedi together or we stay up here and starve together. But under no circumstances am I leaving you alone. So it's up to you. You decide. And make it quick. Because when night falls, we're stuck here—I won't be able to find my way back to the highway in the dark."

They went round and round until she finally agreed to accompany him to En Gedi in return for a promise to come straight back to the *tav* at first light.

The downhill trip going was shorter by hours than the uphill trip coming, but it seemed much longer. Carrie hardly spoke a word the whole way.

En Gedi

They lay side by side in their double bed in the local guesthouse. Dan's arms and legs were leaden with fatigue as he floated in a fog of exhaustion. Here they were, in bed together in one of the world's most ancient resorts, a green oasis of grasses, vineyards, palm trees, and even a waterfall in the midst of the barren wastelands. A beauty spot, a lowers' rendezvous, mentioned even in the ancient *Song of Solomon*, and all he could think of was sleep.

Not that Carrie would have been receptive to any romantic advances anyway. She'd seemed more than a bit aloof since they'd left the *tav*.

That and the knowledge that they'd be returning to the Wilderness tomorrow only heightened Dan's fatigue.

Hal had been no help. As soon as they had arrived in En Gedi, Dan called him and explained that they needed a way to get a five-foot-high artifact out of the country.

"Quietly, if you know what I mean."

Hal had known exactly what he meant and gave him a name and a telephone number in Tel Aviv. He'd said he was very interested and wanted to see this artifact when it reached the states. Dan had thanked him and hung up.

Yeah. Thanks a lot, Hal.

Nothing was working out the way he'd hoped. He'd expected Hal to tell him to forget it—no way to get something that size past the inspectors. Instead of no way, it was no problem.

Damn!

Carrie had remained in a sort of semidream state. What little conversation she'd initiated had been whispers of "Can you believe it? Can you believe we've actually found her?" as they stocked up on twine, blankets, work gloves, a pry bar, a lantern, and hundreds of feet of rope.

And now, beside him in bed, after a long silence . . .

"I've been thinking . . ."

"Great," Dan said, dragging himself back from the

borderlands of sleep. "Does that mean you're giving up this ca-ca idea of bringing that corpse home?"

"Please don't refer to her so coarsely. Please?"

"Okay. Just for your sake. Not because I believe it."

"Thank you. Now tell me: Who do you think wrote the scroll?"

"A clever, phony bastard," Dan said.

"All right," she said with exaggerated patience. "Let's humor Sister Carrie and assume that the scroll is genuine. Who wrote it?"

"We've been over this already. A Pharisee. An educated man."

"But what of the passage where he says 'I do not fear killing. I have killed before, slipping through the crowds in Jerusalem, stabbing with my knife. And I fear not damnation. Indeed, I am already thrice-damned.' That doesn't sound like a Pharisee."

"What'd you do, memorize that translation?"

"No. But I've read it a few times."

More than a few, Dan bet.

"Some of the upper-class Israelites, a few Pharisees among them, got involved with the anti-Roman rebels, some with the zealots. These were a rough bunch of guys, sort of the Israelite equivalent of the IRA. They mounted guerrilla attacks, they murdered collaborators and informants and generally did whatever they could to incite revolt. These were the guys who gathered at Masada after the fall of Jerusalem. They held out for three years, then all 950 of them chose to die rather than surrender to the Roman siege. This scroll writer—*fictional* scroll writer—is patterned after that sort of zealot."

"He was a pretty tough cookie then."

"Extremely. Not the kind you'd want to cross."

"I wonder what happened to him?"

"He's probably hanging around, laughing up his three-striped sleeve, waiting for someone to chase the wild goose he created."

He regretted the words immediately, but he was *tired*, dammit.

Carrie yanked the sheet angrily and turned onto her side, her back to him. "Good *night*, Dan. Get some sleep. We're out of here at dawn."

"Good night, Carrie."

But exhausted as he was, thoughts of the forger kept sleep at bay. And the more Dan thought about how this slimy bastard had sucked Carrie in, making her believe all this nonsense, the more he wanted to get back at him.

And removing that corpse or whatever it was from its cave was the perfect way.

Then it wouldn't matter who came searching for the secret atop the *tav* rock—*The New York Times*, the *Star*, or even a mission from the Vatican itself—all they'd find was an empty cave. *The tomb is empty!* There'd be no turmoil, no orthodox confusion, no Catechismal chaos. And the forger would be left scratching his head, wondering where his clever little prop had disappeared to.

Dan smiled into the darkness. *Two can play this game, Mr. Forger.*

Tomorrow Carrie would have enthusiastic help in her efforts to smuggle the forger's prop out of Israel.

After that, Dan would have plenty of time to coax her back to her senses. If he could. He was more than a little worried about Carrie's mental state. She seemed to be drifting into some religious fantasy realm. He sensed some strange chemistry between her and that body that he could not begin to comprehend. A switch had been thrown inside her, but what circuits had been opened?

Maybe it all went back to her childhood. Maybe it was all tied up in the abuse by her father. Little Carrie had been a virgin and no one had protected her; now here she was with what she believed to be the Virgin Mary and the grown-up Carrie was going to become the protector.

More parlor psychoanalysis. But perhaps it gave some clue as to why this artifact was so important to Carrie.

Too important, perhaps.

And that frightened him. How would she react when it finally became clear—as it must eventually—that the body she thought belonged to the Blessed Virgin was a hoax? What if she cracked?

Whatever happened, he'd be there for her.

But what if he couldn't bring her back?

He stared into the darkness and wished Hal had brought him another sort of gift from the Holy Land. Anything but that damned scroll.

Tel Aviv

Kesev watched the morning news on TV while he sipped his coffee and considered the journey ahead of him. Oppressed by some nameless sense of urgency, he'd left Devorah's in the early morning hours, fighting the urge to jump into his car and drive into the Wilderness.

Instead he'd driven home and attempted to sleep. Wasted hours. He'd had not a minute of slumber. He should have driven to the Resting Place. He'd have been there by now and all these vague fears would be allayed.

He'd called into Shin Bet with an excuse about a family emergency that would keep him from the office all day, but he wondered if this trip was necessary. He'd be on the road all day, probably for nothing. Only eighty air miles, but three times that by car. And for what? To satisfy a nameless uneasiness?

Idly he wondered if he could get a helicopter and do a quick fly-by, but immediately discarded the idea. He'd made a spectacle of himself back there in '91 during the Gulf War when he'd refused to leave the SCUD impact site until all the investigations had been completed. He'd actually camped out there until the last missile fragment had been removed and the final investigator had returned home. There'd been too many questions about his undue interest in that particular piece of nowhere. If he requested a copter now . . .

He sighed and finished his coffee. Better get moving. He had a long drive ahead of him, and he'd know no peace until he'd assured himself that no one had disturbed the Resting Place in his absence.

Absence . . . guilt twisted inside of him. He wasn't supposed to be away from the Resting Place. Ever. He'd promised to stay there and guard it.

He shook off the guilt. How long could you sit around guarding a place that no one even knew existed?

The Resting Place was as safe as it ever was, protected by the greatest, most steadfast guardian of all—the *Midbar Jehuda*.

The Judean Wilderness

Carrie held her breath going through the little passage to the second chamber. But then the beam flashed against the Blessed Mother and she let it out.

"She's still here! Oh, thank God, Dan! She's still here!"

"What did you expect?" Dan muttered as he crawled in behind her with the electric lantern. "Not as if we left her on a subway."

She knew Dan was tired and irritable. Anyone seeing him stumbling around the guesthouse this morning would have thought he'd been drinking all night. Her own back ached and her eyes burned, but true to her word, Carrie had awakened him at first light this morning and had them on the road by the time the sun peeked over the Jordanian highlands on the far side of the Dead Sea. It glowed deep red in the rearview mirror as it crept up the flawless sky, stretching the Explorer's shadow far before them as they bounced and rolled into the hills.

And now as she stood in the chamber, staring down once more at the woman she knew—*knew*—was the Mother of God, she felt as if her heart would burst inside her. She loved this woman—for all her quiet courage, for all the pain she must have suffered in silence. But the Virgin didn't look quite like what she'd expected. In her mind's eye she'd imagined finding a rosy-cheeked teenager, or at the very least a tall, beautiful woman in her early twenties, because that was the way Carrie had always seen her pictured. But when she thought about it, the Virgin probably had been average height for a Palestinian woman of two thousand years ago, and must have been pushing seventy when she died.

Dizziness swept over Carrie as she was struck again by the full impact of what—*whom*—she had found. God had touched this woman as He touched no other human being. She'd carried the incarnation of His Son. And now she lay here, not two feet in front of Carrie.

This is really her. This is the Mother of God.

Until yesterday, the Blessed Virgin had been a statue, a painting, words in books. Now, looking at her aged face, her glossy, uncorrupted flesh, Carrie appreciated her as a woman. A human being. All those years, all those countless Hail Marys, and never once had Carrie realized that this Mary she'd prayed to as an intercessor had once been a flesh-and-blood human being. And that made all the suffering in Mary's life so much more real.

And rising with the love was a fierce protective urge, almost frightening in its intensity.

No one must touch her. No one must desecrate or defile her in any way. No one must use her for anything. *Anything!* The Church itself couldn't be trusted. Who knew what even the Vatican might do? She'd dreamed during the night of the Blessed Mother's remains on display in St. Peter's in Rome and it had sickened her.

Mary had given enough already, and Carrie knew it was up to her to see to it that no one demanded any more of her.

Dear Mother, whoever was left to guard you is long since dead and gone. I'll take care of you. I'll be your protector from now on.

She unfolded the dark blue flannel blankets she had brought. Dan set the lantern down and helped her spread them out on the floor. The bright light cast their distorted shadows against the wall where the Virgin lay in her stony niche.

"All right," she said when the blankets were right. "Help me move her out."

She didn't want anyone else touching the Virgin, not even

Everything okay down there?"

he waved without looking up. Her eyes were fixed on blanket-wrapped bundle lying before her. She still didn't w what she'd do with the Virgin once she got her to New k; she simply knew she had to keep her near.

he spoke softly. "Perfect."

Heads up!" Dan called from above.

he glanced up and saw the remaining length of the rope tched out in the air, coiling like a collapsing spring as it to earth.

I'm on my way," he said.

'ifteen minutes later he arrived, lugging the lamp and the hlights. He quickly unloaded them into the back of the lorer.

Carrie said, "What about the rope?"

We'll leave it. Can't fly it back to the States anyway."

How about that other cave? Didn't you say you wanted ake a look in it before we leave?"

le stared across the canyon a moment, then shook his d.

Maybe some other time."

Other time? When will there be another time?"

Probably never. But I think I've had enough of this place now. I'd like to be out of here."

Carrie nodded. She had the same feeling. She didn't know , but she had an urge to put this place behind them as kly as possible.

s Kesev cruised down Route 90 he saw a black, klike vehicle pull onto the highway about half a mile ad and accelerate toward him in the northbound lane. No ds around here, at least nothing paved. Whoever was ing must have been roaming the hills and desert. hing unusual about that. Off-road exploring was popular tourists these days, which was why the rental compa- in the Central and South districts did such a brisk ness in four-wheel-drive vehicles. But what bothered ev was *where* the truck had come onto the highway.

Dan, but she couldn't risk lifting her out of that niche on her own. God forbid she slipped from her grasp and tumbled to the floor.

As Dan approached the Virgin's upper torso, Carrie waved him back.

"I'll take this end. You take her feet."

Her hands shook as she approached the Virgin. What was this going to be like, touching her? She hesitated a moment, then wriggled her fingers under the Virgin's cloak and cowl, slipping her hands under her neck and the small of her back. The fabric felt so clean, so *new* . . . how could this be two thousand years old?

Unsettled, she glanced to her right. What did Dan think? But Dan stood there with his hands under the Virgin's knees and ankles, expressionless, waiting for her signal.

She suddenly realized that things had changed since yesterday afternoon. Until then, Dan had been in charge. Sure, this trip had been her idea, but Dan had made all the flight arrangements, decided where to stay, what car to rent, while she'd done all the research. But here, in this chamber, in the presence of the Virgin, she was in charge.

"All right," she said. "Lift."

And as she lifted, a knifepoint of doubt pierced Carrie for an instant: So light! Almost as if she were hollow. And so stiff.

She brushed the misgivings away. The Virgin was small, and God had preserved her flesh. That was why she was so light and stiff.

Carefully they backed up, cradling the Virgin in their arms, then knelt and gently placed her on the blankets.

"Stiff as a board," Dan said. "You know, Carrie, I really think—"

Carrie knew what he was going to say and she didn't want to hear it.

"Please, Dan. Let's just wrap her up and move her out as we agreed."

He stared at her a moment, then shrugged. "Okay."

Dan seemed to have had a change of heart overnight. Last

night he'd been dead set against her plan to bring the Virgin back to New York, yet this morning he seemed all for it. But not because he'd suddenly become a believer in the authenticity of their discovery. He was still locked into his Doubting Thomas role.

The Virgin's unnatural lightness and rigidity, plus Dan's continuing doubts, only fanned her desire to move the Virgin to a safer hiding place. Even if she fell into the hands of people with the best intentions, they'd want to examine her, test her to verify her authenticity. They'd scan her, take samples of her hair, skin scrapings, biopsy her, maybe even—God forbid—autopsy her.

No way, Carrie thought as she folded the blankets over the Virgin, wrapping her rigid form in multiple flannel layers. *No way.*

Dan helped her tie the blankets in place with the heavy twine they'd bought in En Gedi. They tied her around the shoulders, waist, thighs, and knees. With Carrie leading the way, slipping through the little tunnel first and guiding their precious bundle after her, they moved the Virgin into the front chamber, then through the opening at the top of the cave mouth onto the rock pile.

Squinting in the brightness of the midmorning sun, they carried her to the far edge of the mini-plateau atop the *tav*.

"I didn't realize she was this light," Dan said, "and that gives me an idea on how we can increase our safety factor here."

"Who's safety?"

"Our prize's."

Carrie couldn't get over the change in Dan's attitude.

"I'm all ears," she said.

Dan's voice echoed down from atop the *tav* rock.

"Ready?"

Carrie shielded her eyes with her hand and looked up. Dan was a silhouette against the bright blue of the sky, standing on the *tav*'s overhang thousands of feet directly above, waving to her. She answered with a broad wave of her own.

"Go ahead!"

As Carrie saw the snugly tied-and-wrap over the edge of the lip and start its slow des she became unaccountably afraid. Everyth she'd moved the Explorer under the lip ju suggested, and here she was, ready to guide the vehicle when she was lowered to within r could not escape the feeling that something w wrong.

She should have stayed up top with Dan hands up there were better than one. He'd tie rope to the cords around the Virgin while sh way to the bottom. What if he hadn't tied the k enough? What if the rope slipped out of his har lowering her?

What if he dropped her on purpose, hoping into a thousand pieces to prove that he'd be along?

Carrie reigned in her stampeding thoughts. she even think such a thing? She was sure it h Dan's mind.

Then why had it crossed hers?

Maybe she was losing perspective. It was distance from home, the isolation of the desert the epiphany of standing before the Mother of cradling her remains in her arms.

So much had happened in the past twenty-fo the cumulative effect was . . . overwhelming

She shook herself and concentrated on the descending bundle, twisting and swaying o lengthening tether. Dan was out of sight beyon lifted her arms, waiting. Soon it was just above she had a grip on two of the binding cords. A its descent she swung it around and guided toward the open rear door of the Explorer.

And then it was done. The Virgin was of safely at rest in the back of their car.

Dan must have noticed the sudden slack. Hi down from overhead.

Right where Kesev always turned off.

He gave it a good going over as it passed: black Ford Explorer, dust caked, man driving, woman in the rear seat, Eldan Rent-A-Car sticker on the back bumper. He made a mental note of the license plate.

When he made his usual turnoff and saw the still settling dust trailing west toward the hills, he stopped his Jeep and jotted the license plate number in the notepad he always carried.

Just in case.

Then he gunned the Jeep toward the uplands.

He had a bad feeling about this.

That bad feeling worsened as he spotted patches of rutted earth and tire tracks here and there along the path toward the Resting Place. Never, in all the times he'd been back and forth, had he encountered a single tire track this far into the Wilderness. Not even his own from previous trips. *Sharav*, the incessant desert wind, saw to that, scouring the land clean of all traces of human passage, usually overnight.

Which meant these were fresh tracks. But who'd made them? The couple in that Explorer? Or somebody else— somebody who even now might be desecrating the Resting Place.

Despite the Jeep's efficient air-conditioning, Kesev began to sweat. He upped his speed past the safety limit into the reckless zone. He didn't care. Something was wrong here.

He ground his teeth and cursed himself for not leaving last night.

Finally the *tav* rock hove into view. No other vehicle in sight, but that brought no relief—he was following a double set of tire tracks. Two vehicles? Or a single vehicle arriving and departing?

He swung around the front of the *tav* and let out a low moan as he spotted the lengthy coil of rope tangled under the overhang.

"Lord in Heaven," he whispered, "don't let this be! *Please* don't let this be!"

Fear knotted around his heart as he gunned the Jeep into the canyon and slowed to a halt at the base of the path to the top. Without bothering to turn off the engine, he leapt out and scampered up the ledge as fast as he dared, muttering and crying out as he climbed.

"Never should have left here!" . . . *Please, God! Let her still be there!* . . . "What was I thinking?" . . . *Dear Lord, if she is still there I swear I will never leave this place again. Not even for food!* . . . "Should have moved back after the scroll was stolen, should have foreseen this!" . . . *Please hear me, Lord, and have mercy on a fool!*

The instant Kesev's head cleared the top of the plateau, his eyes darted to the mouth of the Resting Place. At first glance the barricade of rocks appeared undisturbed and he slumped forward onto the ledge, gasping, nearly sobbing in relief. But as he rose to his feet to send up a fervent prayer of thanks, he spotted the dark crescent atop the barricade—an opening into the Resting Place. The sight of it drove a blade of panic into his throat.

"No!"

He broke into a dead run, clambered up the rocks, and all but dived headfirst into the opening. Enough light streamed through the opening to guide his way to the tunnel. He scrambled through to the second chamber. Stygian darkness here. Kesev's heart was a mailed fist pounding against the inner wall of his ribs as he felt his way across the chamber to the niche where the Mother's bier had been set. His fingers found the edge, then hesitated of their own accord, as if afraid to proceed any further, afraid to find the niche empty.

He forced them forward—

Empty!

"No!"

Sobbing, he dropped to his knees and crawled around on the stone floor, running his hands over every inch of its craggy surface, choking in the clouds of dust he raised, all in the futile hope that she might still be here.

But she was not. The Mother was gone. The Resting Place had been vandalized and the Mother stolen.

Tearing at his beard, Kesev staggered to his feet and

screamed as the blackness surrounding him seeped into his
despairing soul.

"NOOOOOOOOOOOOO!!!!!!"

For an eternal moment he stood there, impotent, utterly
lost, devoid of the most tenuous hope, frozen, incapable of
thought . . .

And then he remembered the car he'd seen turning onto
Route 90 earlier . . . the black Explorer.

Maybe it wasn't too late. Maybe there was still a chance.
He had no honor to salvage, and no hope of redemption, but
if he could retrieve the Mother and return her to the Resting
Place, he could continue his task as her guardian.

Hope . . . like a cold spring bubbling up in the heart of
a desert . . . but he dared do little more than wet his lips.

All the way back to the highway, Kesev fixed the image
of the Explorer in his mind, trying to remember whatever
details he could about the driver and passenger. They'd been
shadows, identifiable as male and female and little more.
When he screeched onto Route 90 again, he floored the
accelerator, pushing the Jeep to 150 kilometers an hour in
the open stretches, ready to flash his Shin Bet ID at any
highway cop who tried to slow him down.

He found a public phone on the outskirts of Jerusalem
and learned from information that Eldan had a car rental
office in the Jerusalem Hilton.

Hoped edged a trifle higher.

He located the Eldan desk in the spacious lobby of the
tower portion of the Hilton. The pert brunette there wore a
name tag that said CHAYA in English. Kesev made sure she
was properly impressed by his Shin Bet ID, then he handed
her the sheet from his notepad with the number of the
Explorer's license plate.

"Did you rent a Ford Explorer with this plate out of
here?"

"Explorer, you say?" She tapped a few instructions into
the terminal before her. A few beeps later, Chaya smiled.
"Yes, sir. To an American. Carolyn Ferris. Out of New
York."

What luck! Found them on the first try. Then again, if you were going to explore the area around the Dead Sea, Jerusalem was the ideal base.

"Have they returned the car yet?"

She shook her head. "Not yet."

"When's it due back?"

"Today, I would assume. They took it on a two-day special—unlimited mileage. But there's nothing to say they won't keep it till tomorrow. They have an option for extra days."

Tomorrow—he prayed they wouldn't keep it till then. Especially since he wasn't even sure this Ferris couple were the ones he wanted. The tire tracks around the Resting Place might not be theirs.

But they were the only lead he had.

If only there were some way to involve Shin Bet in this. He could have the tire tracks identified as to their size and brand and from that get a list of what vehicles used them as standard equipment. If a Ford Explorer was on the list, he'd issue an all-points alert for the Ferrises and their vehicle.

But Shin Bet would want to know what crime they'd committed or were suspected of committing. Theft? What did they steal?

Kesev could not answer those basic questions, so Shin Bet had to stay out of it.

He was on his own.

He wrote down his home phone number and handed it to the Eldan clerk.

"I will be close by and will be checking in with you frequently. But if I am not about, call this number immediately should you hear from the Ferrises. Leave your message on my answering machine. Make sure you fill in whoever relieves you."

"Are they dangerous?" Chaya said, a note of anxiety creeping into her voice.

He smiled to reassure her. It wasn't easy. He wanted to grab the front of her blouse and pull her half across the counter and shout that they may have stolen a relic that God Himself had designated as *untouchable* and only God

Himself knew what might happen to Kesev—to the entire *world*—if it was not returned immediately to its designated Resting Place.

Instead he kept his tone low and even.

"Absolutely not. They are just a couple of tourists who may have witnessed something and we may need to question them. The problem is that they don't know we're looking for them and we don't know where to find them. Not yet. But with your help we can clear up this matter swiftly and everyone can go about their business."

Meanwhile, he didn't have to sit idle.

He went to one of the Hilton's house phones and asked the operator to connect him with the Ferris room. He slammed his fist on the counter when she informed him that there was no Ferris registered at the hotel, then glanced around to see if he'd startled anyone. He did not want to attract attention. He forced himself to return the receiver gently to its cradle.

Then he moved to a pay phone and called all the major and some of the minor hotels in Jerusalem, asking to be connected to the Ferris room.

No luck. They weren't registered in Jerusalem. One could almost believe they'd driven to the north end of Route 90, and instead of turning left toward Jerusalem, turned right toward Jordan. Or worse yet, were hijacked by some PLO crazies. . . .

The thought staggered Kesev, weakening his knees.

The Mother . . . in the hands of that rabble!

No. Such a thing was unthinkable, so why torture himself with it?

Kesev found himself a seat in the lobby where he had an unobstructed view of the Eldan desk. He calmed himself with the thought that he had done all that one man could do at the moment. All that was left was the waiting. So he sat and waited. He was good at waiting. An expert.

Sooner or later the Ferris couple would show up to return their car. When they did he would confront them. He'd know if they were hiding something. And if they were, he'd get it out of them. First by intimidating them with his Shin Bet credentials. If that didn't work, there were other ways.

Kesev slipped his left hand into his pocket and gripped the handle of the long folding knife he always carried.

Yes, he thought grimly. He knew other ways, and he was quite ready to use whatever means were necessary to return the Mother to the Resting Place.

14

"It should be right around the next corner to the left," Carrie said, glancing between the street signs and the map on her lap.

"I sure as hell hope so," Dan muttered from the front seat.

Carrie reached forward and gave his shoulder a gentle rub.

Poor Dan. Not a happy camper at the moment. He'd complained most of the trip that her sitting in the back made him feel like a chauffeur. Carrie was sorry about that, but with the way the Explorer had bounced around the hills, she'd been afraid the Virgin would be harmed. She'd folded down part of the rear seat and pulled the Virgin's blanket-swathed form beside her to steady and protect it.

But even after they'd hit paved road she stayed here, her fingers gripping one of the cords that bound the blankets. Carrie felt *good* sitting close to the Virgin. Despite the danger in smuggling her out of the country—Carrie had no idea how the Israeli government felt about smuggling, but she was sure it could cost Dan and her years in jail if they were caught—she felt strangely calm. At peace.

"Damn this traffic!"

Poor Dan. He was anything but at peace. They'd got lost twice already, and now they were sitting in bumper-to-bumper traffic that would give Manhattan's cross-town crawl a run for its money, all of which might have been bearable if the air conditioner had been working. Tel Aviv in the summer . . . almost as hot as the desert they'd left this morning, but suffocatingly humid thanks to the Mediterranean, only blocks away.

"At last!" Dan said as he turned off Ibn Givrol in the northern end of the city.

Carrie saw it too: The Kaplan Gallery. Gold letters on black marble over two large windows filled with paintings and sculpture. A spasm of anxiety tightened her fingers around the cord. She prayed Bernard Kaplan would help them. If not, where else could they go?

Dan had called him from Jerusalem and asked if he could arrange a shipment for them similar to the one he'd arranged for Harold Gold. Dan said Kaplan had been noncommittal on the phone but gave them directions—not very good directions—to his gallery.

Dan double-parked and turned to her.

"Stay with the car. I'll leave the engine running and run inside. Hope this isn't a wasted trip."

Carrie nodded and watched him disappear through the gallery doors. She sat in the heat and fumes, ignoring the glares of annoyed drivers as they inched around the Explorer. As long as they weren't police . . .

Dan seemed to take forever inside the gallery. Finally, when she was almost ready to run in and see what was taking him so long, he emerged with a man in a gray business suit—tall, tanned, silver hair slicked straight back.

Dan introduced him as Bernard Kaplan. He said Mr. Kaplan had called Harold in the interim and Harold had vouched for them.

"He wants to get a look at the size of our, uh, sculpture."

"Ah, yes," Kaplan said with a British accent—or was it Australian?—and flashed a dazzling set of caps as he looked at the bundle. "About life-sized, as you said. I'll have a couple of my men bring it in and we'll—"

"That's okay," Carrie said quickly. "We'll bring it in ourselves."

Kaplan glanced at Dan who nodded and said, "It could be fragile and this way we'll take full responsibility for any damage."

Kaplan shrugged. "Right. Very well, then. I'll have one of my men find a parking spot for your car."

With Carrie taking the shoulders and Dan the legs, they carried the bundled Virgin the length of the gallery to the shipping area at the rear where they placed her on a bench.

Before she could stop him, Kaplan had a knife out and was cutting the cords.

"What are you doing?" Carrie said.

"Going to take a look at this sculpture of yours."

"Must you?"

"Of course. How else can I list it for the manifest?"

She watched anxiously as Kaplan cut the rest of the cords and unwrapped the blankets. He gave a low whistle when he saw the Virgin's face. His diction seemed to regress.

"Well, now, that's bloody somethin', in'it?"

He leaned closer and touched the Virgin's face, running the tip of his index finger over her cheek. Carrie wanted to grab his wrist and yank him away, but restrained herself.

A few more indignities, Mother Mary, then you'll be on your way to safety.

"What is this?" Kaplan said. "Some sort of wax? I've never seen anything like it. The detail is incredible. Where'd you get it?"

Dan glanced at Carrie before he spoke. On the trip from the desert they'd agreed that rather than invent a series of lies, the best course was to give no answers at all.

"We'd prefer to keep our source a secret," Dan said.

Kaplan nodded and straightened. Carrie sighed with relief as he folded the blankets back over the Virgin.

"Very well. But I see no problem shipping this out. We'll simply list it as a wax sculpture—a piece of contemporary art."

An idea flashed in Carrie's mind. She turned to Dan. "Why can't we do that ourselves? Ship it home on the plane with us?"

"You could do that," Kaplan said. "You wouldn't need me for that. But remember, anything going aboard an El Al flight gets a going over like no other place in the world. Direct inspection, dogs, metal scanners, X rays—"

"Never mind," Carrie said quickly as she imagined the Virgin's skeleton lighting up on an inspector's fluoroscopic scanner. "We'll do it your way."

"Very well," Kaplan said. "I can include it with a consignment of our crates I've scheduled for shipment, and have it on a freighter out of Haifa tonight."

"Wonderful!" Carrie said. "When will it get to New York?"

"It's not going to New York," Kaplan said. "At least not on this freighter. The *Greenbriar* will get your shipment to Cork Harbor. After that, we'll have to make other arrangements for the second leg."

"Can't we get a nonstop?" Carrie said.

Kaplan's smile was tolerant. "No, love. We don't want a direct route. Why draw a line straight to your door? Much safer to break up the trip. We ship your crate to a fictitious name in Cork where one of my associates picks it up, holds it a while, then puts in on another ship to New York. Bloody near impossible to trace."

Carrie was uncomfortable with the thought of the Virgin lying in a moldy warehouse in Ireland, but if this sort of route would safeguard her secret . . .

"How do we pay you?" she said.

"Cash, preferably."

She looked at Dan. Cash? Who had cash? All she had was the AmEx card Brad had given her.

"Do you take plastic?"

Kaplan sighed. "I suppose we can work something out."

Jerusalem

Kesev had given up sitting and waiting. Now he was pacing and waiting. He'd explored every nook and cranny of the lobby, browsed all of the shops until he thought he'd explode with frustration. Where were these people, these Ferrises? They had to turn in their rental sooner or later.

Didn't they?

An awful thought struck him. He ran to the Eldan counter. Chaya was still there. She'd just finished with a customer when Kesev arrived.

"How many offices—rental centers—do you have?" he said.

"I'm not sure," she said, furrowing her brow. "Let's see . . . a couple in Tel Aviv, a couple in Haifa, one at Ben Gurion Airport—"

This was worse than he thought. "Can these people, the Ferrises, turn their car in at any of them?"

"It's not a practice we encourage. In fact, there's a drop-off fee that—"

Kesev tried to keep from shouting. "Can they or can't they? A simple yes or no will do."

"Yes."

I am cursed by God, he thought. I have always been cursed.

He wanted to scream, but that would solve nothing.

"I want you to call every Eldan agency in the country."

"But sir—"

"*Every* one of them! It won't take you long. See if the Ferris car has been turned in at any of them. If not, give them this very simple message: The Ferrises rented their car here and you wish to be notified immediately if they turn in their car anywhere else. *Immediately.* Is that clear? Is that simple enough?"

She nodded, cowed by his ferocity.

"Good. Then get to it."

He turned and stalked away from the counter to continue his pacing. And as he paced he was haunted with the possibility that the Ferris couple might have had nothing at all to do with the disappearance of the Mother.

Haifa

Haifa had its beauties and Carrie wished she could spend some time here seeing the sights. Behind them rose Mount Carmel, high, green and beautiful; somewhere on its slopes, near the Stella Maris lighthouse, sat the Mount Carmel monastery, home of the Carmelite order; and in a grotto on the monastery grounds was the cedar and porcelain statue of

Our Lady of Mount Carmel. Carrie would dearly love to climb the mountain to see it.

But she had to be all business now as she and Dan stood in the monolithic shadow of the huge Dagon grain silo and watched the inspector check off the crates on the manifest from the Kaplan Gallery. Her American Express account now carried the purchase price of a piece of "modern sculpture" from the Kaplan Gallery. Carrie had nothing tangible to show for that charge, but the Virgin had been packed up and placed on the gallery's shipping manifest. Carrie scanned the ships anchored in the harbor but couldn't make out their names in the hazy air. One of them was the *Greenbriar*, which would unknowingly start the Virgin on the long first leg of her journey to a new home. Beyond the long breakwater stretched the azure expanse of the Mediterranean, bluer than she'd ever imagined a sea could be.

The creak of nails snapped her attention back to the docks. The inspector was using a pry bar to open one of the crates. She looked more closely.

Good God, it was the Virgin's crate!

She stepped forward but Dan grabbed her arm.

"Easy, Carrie," he whispered. "I told you we shouldn't have come."

True enough. Carrie should have been satisfied that the Virgin was safe after watching Kaplan's staff seal her into that excelsior-filled shipping crate, but she couldn't let her go. Not yet. She'd insisted on accompanying the crate to Haifa. There'd been this overpowering urge to see her off, like a child coming to the docks to wish a beloved parent bon voyage.

And now she was glad she'd come.

"That's *our* crate. Why did he have to pick ours?"

"Kaplan warned us that they do spot checks. Don't worry. She'll pass. Just stay calm."

Carrie held her breath as the inspector lifted the crate top and pushed the excelsior aside. He unfolded the blankets and she saw him freeze for a moment as he stared at the Virgin's face. She watched him lean closer, staring.

Please don't touch her. PLEASE don't!

The inspector looked up from the crate and scanned the area. He had close-cropped gray hair, wore aviator sunglasses, and carried himself like an ex-military man. When he spotted Dan and Carrie, he tucked his clipboard under his arm and approached them.

Beside her, Carrie heard Dan mutter a soft, "Uh-oh."

The inspector thrust his hand at Dan. "Good day. My name is Sidel. You are the owner of that sculpture, I believe?"

"Yes," Carrie said. She noticed that he didn't offer to shake hands with her. "We just acquired it." She emphasized the first word.

"It's most unusual for people to come down to the docks to see off a shipment, but in your case I can understand why. What an extraordinary piece. Who's the artist, if I may ask?"

"Frankly, I don't know," Dan said. "We saw it and just had to have it."

"I can understand," Sidel said, nodding. "I do a little toying with modeling clay myself, so I can appreciate the fantastic detail of this work. You're shipping it to Ireland?"

Carrie felt her heart begin to thump. Why all these questions?

But Dan was cool. "The name's Fitzpatrick, after all."

"Enjoy it," Sidel said, turning away. "I envy you."

Sidel returned to the crate, stared at the Virgin a moment longer, then shook himself and covered her again. Carrie's heart rate began to slow as the crate top was nailed back into place. She sagged against Dan.

"Oh, Lord. That was close. For one very long minute there I thought . . ."

"You and me both," Dan said. "All right. We've seen her off. Time to go."

Reluctantly Carrie had to agree. They'd discussed their options as they'd followed the Kaplan Gallery truck to Haifa. Dan saw two courses: stay in Israel a while longer, then head home, or head directly home tonight. He favored the latter.

Carrie agreed with getting out of Israel as soon as possible. Just as she had at the Resting Place, she felt an urge to keep moving. But she preferred a third route: fly to Ireland and meet the *Greenbriar* in Cork, make sure the Virgin was transferred properly, then fly back to New York and wait for her there.

They'd argued but eventually Carrie had won, as she'd known she would. From the outset she hadn't the slightest intention of doing it any other way but hers.

She called and learned that there was an El Al flight to London tonight. If they hurried, they could make it. From there it was practically a shuttle flight to Shannon.

They wheeled into Ben Gurion Airport with time to spare. But they received a shock when they turned in the Explorer at the Eldan desk.

"Ferris!" said the thin, mustached man behind the counter. "Boy, have you caused a stir."

Carrie saw Dan go pale and felt her own heart kick up its tempo again.

"Really?" Dan said. "What's the problem? Look, I know we rented the car in Jerusalem but I thought we could return it anywhere we—"

"Oh, that's not the problem," he said. "No drop-off fee if you turn it in here. But somebody at the Jerusalem desk has been burning up the wires looking for you two. Something about a Shin Bet fellow who wants to talk to you."

"Shin Bet?" Carrie said.

"Right. Domestic Intelligence. Somewhat akin to your FBI, I believe. But don't worry. You're not in any trouble. Just wants to ask you some questions."

"Well, uh, we'll be glad to cooperate in any way we can," Dan said. "Just, uh, have us paged. We'll be around for a while."

His grip was tight on her arm as he led her toward the El Al ticket counters. Her mouth felt dry. Were they in trouble?

"Dan, what's the matter? Why would this Shin Bet—?"

His voice was tight. "Somebody's on to us. How long before we leave?"

Carrie glanced at her watch. "A little less than an hour."

"Damn!" He stopped. "Look. Before we buy our tickets and check our bags, let's get changed."

"Why? What for?"

"It might give us an edge to be in uniform."

Jerusalem

Kesev had come to the end of his patience. He was about ready to explode with frustration and start breaking some Hilton property when he saw someone gesturing to him from the Eldan desk.

Chaya had gone home. Sharon, a brittle-looking peroxide blonde, had replaced her. She was waving a bony arm over her head.

"We found them!" she said, grinning as he approached.

Kesev's heart leapt. He wanted to take her in his arms and dance her around the lobby. Perhaps God had not deserted him after all. Perhaps this was just a warning.

"When? Where?"

"They turned their rental into one of our Tel Aviv locations just a few moments ago."

"Which one?"

"Ben Gurion."

Kesev went cold. The airport! Merciful God, they're leaving the country!

He wheeled and ran for the door.

"Where are you going?" Sharon called out behind him. "You can call from here. They said they'd be there awhile and you could page them!"

Page them? Kesev groaned as the meaning of her words sank in. The Ben Gurion desk must have blabbered that someone was looking for them. They'd probably be long gone by the time he got there.

Ben Gurion Airport

Kesev was sure he made the fifty kilometers to Ben Gurion in record time. For once luck was on his side. The airport was designated Tel Aviv but actually it was in Lod, just east of the city. If he'd had to fight city traffic, he'd still be in his car. But he wasn't looking for a racing medal. He wanted the Ferrises.

He flashed his ID at the El Al ticket desk and had them run a computer search for a couple by that name. They found a single. Carolyn Ferris. On a one-way to Heathrow. Seat 12C, non-smoking. Boarding now. Gate 17.

A single. He was looking for a couple. But this Carolyn was the only Ferris he had. And if he didn't check her out right now, she'd be gone.

Kesev ran for Gate 17.

He wasn't armed so he had no problem with the metal detectors and his Shin Bet ID got him to the boarding area without a ticket. But along the way he picked up a friend: Sergeant Yussl Kuttner of airport security.

The last thing Kesev wanted at this point was someone looking over his shoulder, but he had no choice. Anything that deviated from normal airport routine was Kuttner's business, and allowing an unticketed man onto an El Al plane, even if he was Shin Bet, was certainly not routine. Kuttner was armed and he wasn't letting Kesev out of his sight.

"Just what is this passenger suspected of, Mr. Kesev?" Kuttner said, puffing as he trotted beside Kesev.

"The home office didn't have time to fill me in on all the details," Kesev said, improvising. "All I know is that an archeological artifact has been stolen and that the thieves will be trying to smuggle it out of the country."

"And Shin Bet believes this passenger in twelve C is involved?"

"We don't know. We do know one of the suspects is named Ferris. That's why I need to speak to her. You really don't have to bother yourself."

"Quite all right. Besides, if you want to remove her from the plane, you'll need me."

Kesev clenched his jaws. This was getting stickier and stickier. If only he'd had more time to set this up.

Kuttner led him down the boarding ramp to the loaded plane and explained the situation to the stewardesses while Kesev moved down the aisle, looking for row 12.

He froze, staring. The right half of row 12 held only one passenger. Seats A and B were empty. Seat C was occupied by a nun. A young, pretty nun. Almost too pretty to be a nun. That gave him heart.

"Excuse me, Sister," he said, leaning forward. "Is your name Ferris?"

"Why, yes," she said, smiling. She had a wonderful smile. And such guileless blue eyes. "Sister Carolyn Ferris. Is something wrong?"

What to say? There was no time to ease into this, so he might as well throw it in her face and see how she reacts.

He flashed his Shin Bet ID and kept his voice low. "You're wanted for questioning in regard to the theft of an archeological treasure that belongs to the Israeli government."

She reacted with a dumbfounded expression.

"What? Are you mad? Just what sort of treasure am I supposed to have stolen?"

"You know exactly what it is, Sister. It doesn't belong to you. Please give it back."

"Does it belong to you?"

The question took Kesev completely by surprise. And she was staring at him, her narrowed eyes boring into his, as if seeing something there.

"No . . . no . . . it belongs to—"

"Who are you?" she said.

"I told you. Kesev, with—"

"No. That's not true." Her eyes widened now, as if she were suddenly afraid of him. "You're not who you say you are. You're someone else. Who are you—really?"

Now it was Kesev's turn to be dumbfounded. How did she know? How *could* she know?

Reflexively he backed away from her. Who was this woman?

"Excuse me, Sister," said another voice. "Is this man bothering you?"

Kesev looked up to see a tall priest rising from an aisle seat a few rows back, glaring down at him as he approached.

"The poor man seems deranged," Sister Carolyn said.

The priest reached above the nun's seat and pressed the call button for the stewardess. "I'll have him removed."

Kesev backed away. "Sorry. My mistake."

The last thing he wanted was a scene. He had no official capacity here and no logical reason he could give his superiors for pulling this woman off the plane.

Besides, he was looking for a man and a woman, not a nun. Especially not that nun. Something about her, something ethereal . . . the way she'd looked at him . . . looked *through* him.

She'd looked at him and she knew. She *knew!*

He staggered forward through a cloud of confusion. What was happening? Everything had been fine until that damn SCUD had crashed near the Resting Place. Since then it had been one thing after another, chipping at the foundations of his carefully reconstructed life, until today's cataclysm.

Kuttner looked at him questioningly as he reached the front of the cabin.

"Not her," Kesev said. "But I want to check the cargo hold."

The head stewardess groaned and Kuttner said, "I don't know about that."

"It will only take a minute or two. The object in question is at least a meter and a half in length. It can't be in a suitcase. I just want to check out the larger parcels."

Kuttner shrugged resignedly. "All right. But let's get to it."

Dan quietly slipped into 12A. His boarding pass had him in 15D—they'd decided it was best not to sit together—but Carrie had this half of row 12 to herself so he joined her. But not too close.

When no one was looking he reached across the empty seat and grabbed her hand. It was cold, sweaty, trembling.

"You were great," he whispered.

She'd been more than great, she'd been wonderful. When he'd seen that little bearded rooster of a Shin Bet man stalk down the aisle, he'd prayed for strength in the imminent confrontation. But he'd stopped at Carrie's seat, not Dan's. And then Dan had cursed himself for not realizing that their pursuer would be looking for someone named Ferris. But

Carrie had stood up to that Shin Bet man, kept her cool, and faced him down. Dan had only stepped in to add the *coup de grace*.

"I don't feel great," she said. "I feel sick."

"What did you say to him at the end?"

"What do you mean?"

"Well, he hadn't seemed too sure of himself in the first place, but—"

Carrie's smile was wan but real. "We can thank your idea of getting into uniform for that."

"Sure, but you said something and all the color went out of him."

"I asked him who he really was. As he was speaking to me I had the strangest feeling about him, that he was an impostor—or maybe that isn't the right word. I think he's truly from their domestic intelligence, whatever it's called, but he's also someone else. And he's hiding that someone else."

"Whatever it is, I'd say you struck a nerve."

"I didn't really have a choice. I just knew right then that I was very afraid of the person he was hiding."

"So am I, though probably not for the same reason. Damn, I wish we'd get moving. What's the holdup?"

Dan looked past Carrie through the window at the lights of the airport and wondered what Mr. Kesev was up to now. He wouldn't feel safe until they were in the air and over the Mediterranean.

"And yet," Carrie said softly, "there's something terribly sad about him. He said something that shocked me."

"What?"

"He said 'please.' He said, 'Please give it back.' Isn't that strange?"

Kesev stood at one of the panoramic windows in the main terminal and watched the plane roar into the sky toward London.

Nothing.

He'd found nothing in the cargo hold or baggage compartment large enough to contain the Mother.

That gave him hope, at least, that the Mother was still in Israel. And if she was still here, he could find her.

But where was she? *Where?*

He trembled at the thought of what might happen if she were not safely returned to the Resting Place.

15

The Greenbriar — *Off Crete*

Second mate Dennis Maguire was rounding the port side of the superstructure amidships when he saw her.

At least it seemed to be a her. He couldn't be sure in the downpour. The figure stood a good fifty feet away in the center of the aft hold's hatch, wrapped head to toe in some sort of blanket, completely unmindful of the driving rain as she stared aftward. He couldn't make out any features in the dimness, but something in his gut knew he was looking at a *she*.

They'd run into the squall shortly after dark the first night out of Haifa. Maguire was running a topside check to make double sure everything was secure. A sturdy little tramp, the *Greenbriar* was, with a 200-foot keel and thirty feet abeam, she could haul good cargo in her two holds, and haul it fast. But any storm, even lightweight Mediterranean squalls like this one, could be trouble if everything wasn't secured the way it was supposed to be. And Captain Liam could be hell on wheels if something went wrong because of carelessness.

So Maguire had learned: Do it right the first time, then double check to make sure you did what you thought you did.

And after he wound up this little tour of the deck, he could retire to his cabin and work on his bottle of Jameson's.

I'm glad I haven't touched that bottle yet, he thought.

Because right now he'd be blaming the whiskey for what he was seeing.

A *woman*? How the hell had a woman got aboard? And why would any woman *want* to be aboard?

She stood facing aft, like some green-gilled landlubber staring homeward.

"Hello?" he said, approaching the hatch.

She turned toward him but the glow from the lights in the superstructure weren't strong enough to light her features through the rain. And then he noticed something: the blanket or cloak or robe or whatever she was wrapped up in wasn't moving or even fluttering in the wind. In fact, it didn't even look *wet*.

He blinked and turned his head as a particularly nasty gust stung his face with needle-sharp droplets, and when he looked again, she was gone.

He ran across the hatch and searched the entire afterdeck but could not find a trace of her. So he ran and told the captain.

Liam Harrity puffed his pipe and stared out at him from the mass of red hair that encircled his face.

"What have we discussed about you hitting the Jameson's while you're on duty, Denny?" he said.

"Captain, I swear, I haven't touched a drop to me lips since last night." Maguire leaned closer. "Here. Smell me breath."

The captain waved him off. "I don't want to be smelling your foul breath! Just get to your bunk and don't be after coming to me with any more stories of women on my ship. Get!"

Dennis Maguire got, but he knew in his heart there'd been someone out there in the storm tonight. And somehow he knew they hadn't seen the last of her.

Paraiso

"Charlie, Charlie, Charlie," the *senador* said, shaking his head sadly.

Emilio Sanchez stood at a respectful distance from the

father and son confrontation. He had moved to leave the great room after delivering Charlie here, but the *senador* had motioned him to stay. Emilio was proud of the *senador*'s show of trust and confidence in him, but it pained him to see so great a man in such distress. So Emilio stepped back against the great fireplace and stared out at the seamless blackness beyond the windows where the clouded night sky merged with the Pacific. And listened.

"I thought we had an understanding, Charlie," the *senador* said. He leaned forward, staring earnestly across the long, free-form redwood coffee table at his son who sat with elbows on knees, head down. "You promised me six months. You promised me you'd stay here and go through therapy . . . learn to pray."

"It's not what you think, Dad," Charlie said softly in a hoarse voice. He sounded exhausted. Defeated.

The fight seemed to have gone out of Charlie. Which didn't jibe at all with his recent flight from Paraiso. If he wasn't bucking his father, why did he run?

Two days ago the *senador* had called Emilio to his home office in a minor panic. Charlie was gone. His room was empty, and he was nowhere in the house or on the grounds. Juanita said she'd passed a taxi coming the other way when she'd arrived early this morning.

Emilio had sighed and nodded. *Here we go again.*

Fortunately Juanita remembered the name of the cab company. From there it was easy to trace that particular fare—the whole damn company was buzzing about picking up a fare at Paraiso that wanted to be taken all the way to Frisco. The driver had dropped his fare off on California Street.

Charlie had run to his favorite rat hole again.

Over the years, during repeated trips in search of Charlie, Emilio had been in and out of so many gay bars in San Francisco that some of the regulars had begun to think he was a *maricon* himself. To counteract that insulting notion, he'd made it a practice to bust the skull anyone who tried to get friendly.

But this time he hadn't found Charlie down in the Tenderloin. Instead, he'd traced him to the Embarcadero. Charlie had taken a room in the Hyatt, of all places.

When Emilio had knocked on his door, Charlie hadn't acted surprised, and he hadn't launched into his usual lame protests. He'd come quietly, barely speaking during the drive back.

That wasn't like Charlie. Something was wrong.

"What *am* I to think, Charlie?" the *senador* was saying. "You promised me. Remember what you said? You said you'd 'give it the old college try.' Remember that?"

"Dad—"

"And you were doing so well! Dr. Thompson said you were very cooperative, really starting to open up to him. And you seemed to be getting into the spirit of the prayer sessions, feeling the presence of the Lord. What happened? Why did you break your promise?"

"I didn't break my promise." He didn't look up. He stared at the table before him, seemingly lost in the redwood whorls. "I was coming back. I needed—"

"You *don't* need that . . . sort of . . . activity," the *senador* said. "By falling back into that sinfulness you've undone all your months of work!"

"I didn't go back for sex," Charlie said.

"Please don't make this worse by lying to me, Charlie."

During the ensuing silence, Emilio realized that normally he too would have thought Charlie was lying, but today he didn't think so.

"It's the truth, Dad."

"How can I believe that, Charlie? Every other time you've disappeared to Sodom-on-the-Bay it's been for sex."

"Not this time. I . . . . I haven't been feeling well enough for sex."

"Oh?"

A premonition shot through Emilio like a bullet. The *senador* should have felt it too, but if he did, his face did not betray it. He was still staring at Charlie with that same hurt earnest expression. Emilio rammed his fist against his thigh. *Bobo!* Charlie's pale, feverish look, his weight loss . . . he should have put it together long before now.

"I've been having night sweats, then I developed this rash. I didn't run off to Frisco to get laid, Dad. I went to a clinic there that knows about . . . these things."

The *senador* said nothing. A tomblike silence descended on the great room. Emilio could hear the susurrant flow through the air-conditioning vents, the subliminal rumble of the ocean beyond the windows, and nothing more. He realized the *senador* must be holding his breath. The light had dawned.

Charlie looked up at his father. "I've got AIDS, Dad."

Madre. Emilio exhaled.

"Wh-what?" The *senador* was suddenly as pale as his son. "That c-can't be t-true!"

He was stuttering. Not once in all his years with him had Emilio heard that man stutter.

Charlie was nodding. "The doctors and the blood tests confirmed what I've guessed for some time. I've just been too frightened to take the final step and hear someone tell me I've got it."

"Th-there's got to be some mistake!"

"No mistake, Dad. This was an AIDS clinic. They're experts. I'm not just HIV positive. I've got AIDS."

"But didn't you use protection? Take precautions?"

Charlie looked down again. "Yeah. Sure. Most of the time."

"Most of the time . . ." The *senador*'s voice sounded hollow, distant. "Charlie . . . what on earth . . . ?"

"It doesn't matter, Dad. I've got it. I'm a dead man."

"No, you're not!" the *senador* cried, new life in his voice as he shot from his seat. "Don't you say that! You're going to live!"

"I don't think so, Dad."

"You will! I won't let you die! I'll get you the best medical care. And we'll pray. You'll see, Charlie. With God's help you'll come through this. You'll be a new man when it's over. You'll pass through the flame and be cleansed, not just of your illness, but of your sinfulness as well. You're about to be born again, Charlie. I can feel it!"

Emilio turned away and softly took the stairs down to his quarters. He fought the urge to run. Emilio did not share the *senador*'s faith in the power of prayer over AIDS. In fact, Emilio could not remember finding prayer useful for much of anything, especially in his line of work. Rather than listen to the *senador* rattle on about it, he wished to wash his hands. He'd touched Charlie today. He'd driven Charlie all the way back from San Francisco today, sitting with him for hours in the same car, breathing his air.

When he reached the bottom floor, he broke into a trot toward his quarters. He wanted more than to wash his hands. He wanted a shower.

The Greenbriar . . . *East of Gibraltar*

"A woman on board," Captain Liam Harrity muttered as he thumbed tobacco into the bowl of his pipe. "What utter foolishness is this? Next they'll be after telling me the ship can fly."

Gibraltar lay three leagues ahead, its massive shadow looming fifteen degrees to starboard against the hazy stars. Lights dotted the shores to either side as the *Greenbriar* prepared to squeeze between two continents and brave the Atlantic beyond. A smooth, quiet, routine trip so far.

Except for this woman talk.

Harrity leaned against the *Greenbriar*'s stern rail and stared at the glowing windows in the superstructure amidships. A good old ship, the *Greenbriar*. A small freighter by almost any standards, but quick. A tramp merchant ship, with no fixed route or schedule, picking up whatever was ready to be moved, from the Eastern Mediterranean to the UK and all points between, no questions asked. Harrity had been in this game a long time, much of it spent on the *Greenbriar*, and this was the first time any of his crew had talked about seeing a woman wandering the decks.

Not that there weren't enough places to hide one, mind you. Small though she might be, the ship had plenty of nooks and crannies for a stowaway.

But in all his years helming the *Greenbriar*, Harrity had never had a stowaway—at least that he knew of—and he wasn't about to start now. Like having a prowler in your house. You simply didn't allow it.

Maguire had started the talk that first night out of Haifa. Harrity's thought at the time was that Dennis had been nipping at the Jameson's a little earlier that usual. He'd let it go and not given it another thought until two nights ago when Clery said he'd seen a woman on the aft deck as they were passing through the Malta Channel.

A temperate man, Clery. Not the sort who'd be after seeing things that weren't there.

So Harrity himself was keeping watch on the aft deck these past two nights. And so far no woman.

He turned his back to the wind and struck a wooden match against the stern rail. As he puffed his pipe to life, relishing the first aromatic lungfuls, a deep serenity stole over him. The phosphorescent flashes churning in the wake, the balmy, briny air, the stars overhead, lighting the surface of the Mediterranean as it stretched long and wide and smooth to the horizon. Life was good.

He sensed movement to his left, turned, and fumbled to catch his pipe as it dropped from his shocked-open mouth.

She was there, beside him, not two feet away. A woman. She stood at the rail, staring into the east, back along the route they'd sailed. She was wearing a loose robe of some sort, pulled up around her head. Her features were hidden by the cowl of the robe. Now he knew why Maguire had thought she'd been wrapped in a blanket.

He shook off the initial shock and stuck his pipe bit between his teeth. He should have been angry—furious, for sure—but he could find no hostility within him. Only wonder at how she'd come up behind him without him hearing her.

"And who would you be now?" he said.

The woman continued her silent stare off the stern.

"What are you after doing on me ship?"

Slowly she turned toward him. He could not make out her features in the shadow of the cowl, but he felt her eyes on him. And the weight of her stare was a gentle hand caressing the surface of his mind, erasing all questions.

She turned and walked away. Or was she walking? She seemed to glide along the deck. Harrity had an urge to follow her but his legs seemed so heavy, his shoes felt riveted to the deck. He could only stand and watch as she followed the rail along the starboard side to the superstructure where she was swallowed by the deeper shadows.

And then she was gone and he could move again. He sucked on his pipe but the bowl was cold. And so was he. Suddenly the deck of the *Greenbriar* was a lonely place to be.

Cashelbanagh, Ireland

Like everyone else, Monsignor Vincenzo Riccio had heard the endless talk about the green of the Irish countryside, but not until he was actually driving along the roads south of Shannon Airport did he realize how firmly based in fact all that talk had been. He gazed through the open rear window at the passing fields. This land was *green*. In all his fifty-six years he could not remember seeing a green like this.

"Your country is most beautiful, Michael," he said. His English was good, but he knew there was no hiding his Neapolitan upbringing.

Michael the driver—the good folk of Cashelbanagh had sent one of their number to fetch the Monsignor from the airport—glanced over his shoulder with a broad, yellow-toothed smile.

"Aye, that it is, Monsignor. But wait till you see Cashelbanagh. The picture-perfect Irish village. As a matter of fact, if you're after looking up 'Irish village' in the dictionary, sure enough it'll be saying Cashelbanagh. Perfect place for a miracle."

"It is much farther?"

"Only a wee bit down the road. And wait till you see the reception committee they'll be having for you."

Vincenzo wished he'd come here sooner. He liked these people and the green of this land enthralled him. But the way things were looking lately, he wouldn't get a chance for a return visit.

And too bad he couldn't stay longer. But this was only a stopover, scheduled at the last minute as he was leaving Rome for New York. He was one of the Vatican's veteran investigators of the miraculous, and the Holy See had asked him to look into what lately had become known as the Weeping Virgin of Cashelbanagh.

The Weeping Virgin had been gathering an increasing amount of press over the past few weeks, first the Irish papers, then the London tabloids, and recently the story had gained international attention. People from all over the world had begun to flock to the little village in County Cork to see the daily miracle of the painting of the Virgin Mary that shed real tears. Healings had been reported—cures, visions, raptures. "A New Lourdes!" screamed tabloid headlines all over the world.

It had been getting out of hand. The Holy See wanted the "miracle" investigated. The Vatican had no quarrel with miracles, as long as they were real. But the faithful should not be led astray by tricks of the light, tricks of nature, and tricks of the calculated human kind.

They chose Vincenzo for the task. Not simply because he'd already had experience investigating a number of miracles that turned out to be anything but miraculous, but because the Vatican had him on a westbound plane this weekend anyway, to Sloan-Kettering Memorial in Manhattan to try an experimental chemotherapy protocol for his liver cancer. He could make a brief stop in Ireland, couldn't he? Take a day or two to look into this weeping painting, then be on his way again. No pain, no strain, just send a full report of his findings back to Rome when he reached New York.

"Tell me, Michael," Vincenzo said. "What do you know of these miracles?"

"I'll be glad to tell you it all, Monsignor, because I was there from the start. Well, not the very start. You see, the painting of the Virgin Mary has been gracing the west wall of Seamus O'Halloran's home for two generations now. His grandfather Danny had painted it there during the year before he died. Finished the last stroke, then took to his bed and never got up again. Can you imagine that? 'Twas almost as if the old fellow was hanging on just so's he could be finishing the painting. Anyways, over the years the weather has faded it, and it's become such a fixture about the village that it faded into the scenery, if you know what I'm sayin'. Much like a tree in someone's yard. You pass that yard half a dozen times a day but you never take no notice of the tree. Unless of course it happens to be spring and it's startin' to bloom, then you might—"

"I understand, Michael."

"Yes. Well, that's the way it was after being until about a month ago when Seamus—that's old Daniel O'Halloran's grandson—was passing the wall and noticed a wet streak glistening on the stucco. He stepped closer, wondering where this bit of water might be trickling from on this dry and sunny day, for contrary to popular myth, it does *not* rain every day in Ireland—least ways not in the summer. I'm afraid I can't say that for the rest of the year. But anyways, when he saw that the track of moisture originated in the eye of his grandfather's painting, he ran straight to Mallow to fetch Father Sullivan. And since then it's been one miracle after another."

Vincenzo let his mind drift from Michael's practiced monologue that told him nothing he hadn't learned from the rushed briefing at the Vatican before his departure. But he did get the feeling that life in the little village had begun to revolve around the celebrity that attended the weeping of their Virgin.

And that would make his job more difficult.

"There she is now, Monsignor," Michael said, pointing

ahead through the windshield. ."Cashelbanagh. Isn't she a sight."

There were crossing a one-car bridge over a gushing stream. As Vincenzo squinted ahead, his first impulse was to ask, Where's the rest of it? But he held his tongue. Two hundred yards down the road lay a cluster of neat little one- and two-story buildings, fewer than a dozen in number, set on either side of the road. One of them was a pub—BLANEY'S, the gold-on-black sign said. As they coasted through the village, Vincenzo spotted a number of local men and women setting up picnic tables on the narrow sward next to the pub.

Up ahead, at the far end of the street, a crowd of people waited before a neat, two-story, stucco-walled house.

"And that would be Seamus O'Halloran's house, I imagine," Vincenzo said.

"That it would, Monsignor. That it would."

There were hands to shake and Father Sullivan to greet, and introductions crowded one on top of the other until the names ran together like watercolors in the rain. The warmest reception he'd ever had, an excited party spirit running through the villagers. The priest from Rome was going to certify the Weeping Virgin as an inexplicable phenomenon of Divine origin, an act of God made manifest to the faithful, a true miracle, a sign that Cashelbanagh had been singled out to be touched by God. There was even a reporter from a Dublin paper to record it. And what a celebration there'd be afterward.

And then Vincenzo was led around to the side of the house to stare at the famous Weeping Virgin of Cashelbanagh on Seamus O'Halloran's wall.

Nothing special about the painting. Rather crude, actually. A very stiff-looking profile of the Blessed Mother in the traditional blue robe and wimple with a halo behind her head.

And yes, there was indeed a gleaming track of moisture running from the painting's eye.

"The tears appear every day, Monsignor," O'Halloran

said, twisting his cloth cap in his bony hands as if there was
moisture to be wrung from it.

"I can confirm that," Father Sullivan said, his ample red
cheeks aglow. "I've been watching the wall for weeks now."

As Vincenzo continued staring at the wall, noting the fine
meshwork of cracks in the stucco finish, the chips here and
there that revealed the stonework beneath, the crowd grew
silent around him.

He stepped closer and touched his finger to the trickle,
then touched the finger to his tongue. Water. A mineral
flavor, but not salty. Not tears.

"Would someone bring me a ladder, please," he said.
"One long enough to reach the roof."

Three men ran off immediately, and five minutes later he
was climbing to the top of the gable over the Weeping
Virgin's wall. He found wet and rotted roof wood at the
point. At his request a pry bar was brought and, with
O'Halloran's permission, he knocked away some of the soft
wood.

Vincenzo's heart sank when he saw it. A cuplike depression in the stones near the top of the gable, half filled with
clear liquid. It didn't take a rocket scientist to deduce that
water collected there on rainy days—rarely was there a
week, even in the summer, without at least one or two rainy
days—and percolated through the stones and grout of the
wall to emerge as a trickle by the painting's eye.

The folk of Cashelbanagh were anything but receptive to
this rational explanation of their miracle.

"There may be water up there," O'Halloran said, his huge
Adam's apple bobbing angrily, "but who's to say that's
where the tears come from? You've no proof. Prove it,
Monsignor. Prove those aren't the tears of the Blessed
Virgin."

He'd hoped it wouldn't turn out like this, but so often it
did. He'd hoped discovery of the puddle would be enough,
but obviously it wasn't. And he couldn't leave these people
to go on making a shrine out of a leaky wall.

"Can someone get me a bottle of red wine?" Vincenzo
said.

"This may be Ireland, Monsignor," Father Sullivan said, "but I hardly think this is time for a drink."

Amid the laughter Vincenzo said, "I'll use it to prove my theory. But it must be red."

While someone ran to Blaney's pub for a bottle, Vincenzo climbed the ladder again and splashed all the water out of the depression. Then he refilled it with the wine.

By evening, when the Virgin's tears turned red, Vincenzo felt no sense of victory. His heart went out to these crestfallen people. He saw his driver standing nearby, looking as dejected as the rest of them.

"Shall I call a taxi, Michael?"

"No, Monsignor." Michael sighed. "That's all right. I'll be taking you back to Shannon whenever you want."

But the airport was not where Vincenzo needed to go. He hadn't figured on this quick a resolution to the question of the Weeping Virgin of Cashelbanagh. His flight out wasn't scheduled until tomorrow night.

"Can you find me a hotel?"

"Sure, Monsignor. There's a lot of good ones in Cork City."

They passed Blaney's pub again on the way out of town. The picnic tables were set and waiting. Empty. The fading sunlight glinted off the polished flatware, the white linen tablecloths flapped gently in the breeze.

If only he could have told them how he shared their disappointment, how deeply he longed for one of these "miracles" he investigated to pan out, how much he needed a miracle for himself.

Cork Harbor, Ireland

Carrie's heart leapt as she recognized the crate on the pallet being lifted from the aft hold of the freighter.

"There it is, Dan!" she whispered, pointing.

"You sure?" he said, squinting through the dusky light. "Looks like any of a couple of dozen other crates that've come out already."

She wondered how Dan could have any doubt. She'd known it the instant it cleared the hold.

"That's the one," she said. "No question about it."

She locked her gaze on the crate and didn't let it out of her sight until Bernard Kaplan's man cleared it through Irish customs and wheeled it over to them on a dolly.

"Are you quite sure you'll be wanting to take it from here yourself?" he said. He was a plump little fellow with curly brown hair, a handlebar mustache, and a Barry Fitzgerald brogue.

Dan glanced at her. "Well . . ."

"Quite sure, Mr. Cassidy," Carrie said, extending her hand. "Thank you for your assistance."

"Not at all, Mrs. Ferris. Just remember, your crate's got to be at Dublin Harbor the morning after tomorrow, six sharp or, believe me youse, she'll miss the loading and then God knows when she'll get to New York."

"We'll be there," Carrie said.

"I hope so, 'cause I'm washing me hands of it now." He glanced at his watch. "You've got turty-four hours. Plenty of time. Just don't you be getting yourself lost along the way."

He waved and walked off.

"Now that we've got her," Dan said, tapping the top of the crate, "what do we do with her? We've got to find a place to store her overnight."

"Store her?" Carrie said. "We're not sticking her in some smelly old warehouse full of rats."

"What do you think crawls around the hold of the *Greenbriar*, my dear?"

There was an edge to his voice. Not sharp enough to cut, but enough for Carrie to notice.

Things hadn't been quite the same between them since finding the Virgin. They'd had some moments of closeness on the plane to Heathrow after outfoxing that Israeli intelligence man, or whoever he was, and some of that had lingered during the whirl of booking the shuttle to Shannon and finding a hotel room in Cork City. But once they were settled in, a distance began to reopen between them.

It's me, she thought. I know it's me.

She couldn't help it. All she could think about since they'd set their bags down in the Drury Hotel was that crate and its precious contents. They'd had days to kill and Dan wanted to see some of the countryside. Carrie had gone along, but she hadn't been much company. One day they drove north through the rocky and forbidding Burren to Galway Bay; on another he took her down to Kinsale, but the quaint little harbor there only made her think about the *Greenbriar* and worry about its voyage. She fought visions of rough seas capsizing her, of her running aground and tearing open her hull, seawater gushing into the cargo hold and submerging the Virgin's crate, the Mediterranean swallowing the *Greenbriar* and everything aboard. She spent every spare minute hovering over the radio, dissecting every weather report from the Mediterranean.

Obsessed.

She knew that. And she knew her obsession was coming between her and Dan. But as much as she valued their love, it had to take a backseat for now. Just for a while. Until they got to New York.

After all, what could be more important than seeing the Blessed Virgin safely to her new Resting Place—wherever that may be?

They hadn't made love since finding the Virgin, and she sensed that was what was really bothering Dan the most. In New York they suffered through much, much longer intervals without so much as touching hands, but that was different. Here they'd been sleeping in the same bed every night and Carrie had put him off again and again. She wasn't sure why.

After they were resettled in New York, Carrie was sure things would get back to normal. At least she hoped they would. She couldn't put her finger on it, but she didn't feel quite the same about Dan. She still loved him fiercely, but she didn't *want* him as she had two weeks ago when they'd left New York for Israel.

Because right now, it just didn't seem . . . right.

"We're taking her back to the hotel with us."

"*What?*" Dan said. She could see his body stiffening with tension. "You can't do that."

"Why not? We're paying for the room and there's nothing that says we can't keep a crate in it. Besides, it's only for two nights."

"You've got to be kidding."

She gave him a long, level look. "I assure you, Dan, I am not kidding."

Dan slipped his arm around her waist from behind and nuzzled her neck. Carrie felt her whole left arm break out in gooseflesh.

"Not now, Dan," she said, pulling free and stepping away from him. She pointed to the crate. Her voice lowered to a whisper of its own accord. "Not with *her* here."

Two bellmen had lugged the Virgin's crate up to their second-floor room and left it on the floor by the window. Beyond the window the River Lee made its sluggish way to the sea.

Dan returned her whisper, Elmer Fudd style. "We'll be vewy, vewy quiet. She'll never know."

Carrie had to laugh. "Oh, Dan. I love you, I do, but please understand. It just wouldn't be right."

He stared at her a moment. Was that hurt in his eyes? But he seemed to understand. She prayed he did.

He sighed. "All right, then, how about we go down to the lounge and see Hal Roach? He's only down from Dublin for one night."

"I don't think so," she said. She wasn't really in the mood for Ireland's answer to Henry Youngman.

"How about we just go for a walk?"

Carrie shook her head. "I think I'd rather just stay here."

Dan's expression tightened. "Watching over her, I suppose."

She nodded. "In a way, yes."

"Don't you think you might be getting just a little carried away with this, Carrie?"

Yes, she thought. Yes, I might. But the Virgin was here, and so here is where Carrie wanted to be. Simple. She'd waited all this time on tenter hooks for the Virgin's arrival from Haifa, and she wasn't about to let her out of her sight until her crate was safely on board the ship in Dublin Harbor.

"I just want to stay here with her, Dan. Is that so bad?"

"Bad?" he said. "No. I can't say it's bad. But I don't think it's healthy."

He stared again, then shrugged resignedly. "All right. This is your show. We'll do it your way." He stepped closer and kissed her forehead. "But I do need to get out of this room . . . stretch my legs . . . maybe cross the river and grab a pint. I'll be back soon."

Before Carrie could think of anything to say, he was out the door and she was alone in the room.

Well, not completely alone. The Virgin was here. She knelt beside the crate and rested her head on its lid. For one shocking, nerve-rattling moment she thought she heard a heartbeat, then she realized it was her own.

"Don't worry, Mother Mary," she whispered to the crate. "I won't leave you alone here. You've given me comfort through the years when I needed it, now I'll stand by you." She patted the lid of the crate. "Till death do us part."

The Judean Wilderness

"*Why?*"

Kesev stood atop the *tav* rock with the thieves' rope knotted around his neck and screamed out at the clear, pitiless night sky. "Why do You torment me like this? When will You be satisfied? Have I not been punished enough?"

But no reply came from on high, just *Sharav*'s ceaseless susurrance, whispering in his ears. Not that he'd expected an answer. All his countless entreaties down through the years had been ignored. Why should this one be any different?

The Lord tormented him. Kesev was not cut out to be a

Job. He was a fighter, not a victim. And so the Lord took extra pains to beleaguer him.

Not that he was without fault in this. If he had been at his post when the errant SCUD had crashed below, he could have chased off the Bedouin boys when they wandered into the canyon, and hidden the scrolls before the government investigative teams arrived.

And then the Mother would still be safely tucked away in the Resting Place instead of . . . where?

Where was she?

Gone. Gone from Israel. Kesev had exhausted all his contacts and what limited use he dared make of his Shin Bet resources, but she had slipped through his fingers. He'd sensed the Mother's slow withdrawal from their homeland. He didn't know how, or in which direction she'd been taken, but he knew in the core of his being that she was gone.

He also knew it was inevitable that soon she would be revealed to the world and made a spectacle of, a sensational object of scientific research and religious controversy. Why else would someone steal her away?

The Lord would not stand for that. The Lord would rain his wrath down upon the earth.

Perhaps that was the meaning behind all this. Perhaps the theft of the Mother was the event that would precipitate the Final Days. Perhaps . . .

Kesev sighed. It didn't matter. He'd failed in his task and now there was no need for him to prolong the agony of this life any longer. Since his usefulness on earth was at an end, surely the Lord would let him end his time on earth as well. He would not see the Final Days, and certainly he did not deserve to see the Second Coming. He did not even deserve to see tomorrow.

He checked once more to make sure the rope was securely tied around the half-sunk boulder about thirty feet back. Then he stepped to the edge of the *tav* and looked down at his Jeep parked below. He'd left plenty of slack, enough to allow him to fall within a dozen feet of the ground. The end would be quick, painless. If he was especially lucky, the force of the final jolt might even decapitate him.

Without a prayer, without a good-bye, without a single regret, Kesev stepped off the edge and into space.

He kept his eyes open and made no sound as he hurtled feet first toward the ground. He had no fear, only grim anticipation and . . . hope.

Cork City, Ireland

Monsignor Vincenzo Riccio wandered through the thick, humid air near Cork City's waterfront. He'd wandered off St. Patrick's Street and was looking for a place to have a drink. His doctors had all warned him against alcohol but right now he didn't care. He'd had a long day of crushing people's hopes and fervor, and he needed something. Something Holy Mother Church could not provide. He needed a different kind of communion.

All the pubs on St. Patrick were crowded and he didn't feel like standing. He wanted a place to rest his feet. He spotted a pair of lighted windows set in dark green wood. JIM CASHMAN'S read the sign, and there was a Guinness harp over the slate where the dinner menu was scrawled in chalk.

Vincenzo peeked inside the open door and saw empty seats.

Bono! He'd found his place.

He made his way to the bar and squeezed into a space between two of the drinkers—a space that would have been too narrow for him just a year ago.

Amazing what cancer can do for the figure.

The bartender was pouring for someone else so Vincenzo took a look around. A small place, this Jim Cashman's— hardwood floor and paneling, a small bar tucked in the corner, half a dozen tables arrayed about the perimeter, a cold fireplace, and two TVs playing the same rugby match.

None of Cashman's dozen or so patrons paid him any attention. And why should they? He wasn't wearing his collar. He'd left that and his cassock back in his hotel room; that left a thin, sallow, balding, gray-haired man in his fifties dressed in a white shirt and black trousers. Nothing at all priestly about him.

He turned to the solitary drinker to his left, a plump, red-faced fellow in a tour bus driver's outfit, sipping from a glass of rich dark liquid.

"May I ask what you're drinking, sir?"

The fellow stared at him a moment, as if to be sure this stranger with the funny accent was really speaking to him, then cleared his throat.

"'Tis stout. Murphy's stout. Made right here in Cork City."

"Oh, yes. I passed the brewery on the way in."

Michael had driven him through the gauntlet of huge gleaming silver tanks towering over both sides of the road on the north end of town, and he remembered wondering who in the world drank all that brew.

Vincenzo said, "I tried a bottle of Guinness once, but didn't care for it very much."

The driver made a face. "What? From a bottle? You've never had stout till you've drunk it straight from the tap as God intended."

"Which would you recommend for a beginner, then?"

"I like Murphy's."

"What about Guinness?"

"It's good, but it's got a bit more bite. Start with a Murph."

Vincenzo slapped his hand on the bar. "Murphy's it is!" He signaled the barkeep. "A pint of Murphy's, if you would be so kind, and another for my adviser here."

When the pints arrived, Vincenzo brushed off the driver's thanks and turned to find a seat.

"Stout's food, you know," the driver called after him as Vincenzo carried his glass to a corner table. "A couple of those and you can skip a meal."

Good, he thought. I can use a little extra nourishment.

He'd lost another two pounds this week. The tumors in his liver must be working overtime.

"Good for what ails you too," the driver added. "Cures all ills."

"Does it now? I'll hold you to that, my good man."

He took a sip of the Murphy's and liked it. Liked it a lot. Rich and malty, with a pleasant aftertaste. Much better than that bottle of Guinness he'd once had in Rome. One could almost believe it might cure all ills.

Vincenzo smiled to himself. Now wouldn't *that* be a miracle.

He looked at the faces around Jim Cashman's and they reminded him of the faces he'd seen in Cashelbanagh, only these weren't stricken with the bitter disappointment and accusation he'd left there.

It's not my fault your miracle was nothing more than a leaky roof.

A young sandy-haired fellow came in and ordered a pint of Smithwick's ale, then sat alone at the table next to Vincenzo's and stared disconsolately at the rugby game. He looked about as cheerful as the people Vincenzo had left at Cashelbanagh.

"Is your team losing?" Vincenzo said.

The man turned and offered a wan smile. "I'm American. Don't know the first thing about rugby." He extended his hand. "Dan Fitzpatrick. And I can guess by your accent that you're about as far from home as I am."

Vincenzo shook it and offered his own name—sans the religious title. No sense in putting the fellow off. "I happen to be on my way to America. I'm leaving for New York tomorrow."

"Really? That's where my . . . home is. Business or pleasure?"

"Neither, really." Vincenzo didn't want to get into his medical history so he shifted the subject. "I guess something other than rugby must be giving you such a long face."

He wanted to kick himself for saying that. It sounded too much like prying. But Dan seemed eager to talk.

"You could say that," he said with a disarming grin. "Woman trouble."

"Ah," Vincenzo said, and left it at that. What did he know about women?

"A unique and wonderful woman," Dan went on, sipping his ale, "with a unique and wonderful problem."

"Oh?" Through decades of hearing confessions, Vincenzo had become the Michelangelo of the monosyllable.

"Yeah. The woman I love is looking for a miracle."

"Aren't we all?" *Myself most of all.*

"Not all of us. Trouble is, mine really thinks she's going to find one, and she seems to be forgetting the real world while she's looking for it."

"And you don't think she'll find it?"

"Miracles are sucker bait."

"As much as I hate to say it"—Vincenzo sighed—"I fear there is some truth in that. Although I prefer to think of the believers not as suckers, but as seekers. I saw a village full of seekers today."

Vincenzo went on to relate an abbreviated version of his stop in Cashelbanagh earlier today. When he finished he found the younger man staring at him in shock.

"You're a *priest*?" Dan said.

"Why, yes. A monsignor, to be exact."

"That's great!" he snapped, quaffing the rest of his ale. "And you're going to New York? Just *great*! That really caps my day! No offense, but I hope we don't run into each other."

Without another word he rose and strode from Jim Cashman's pub, leaving Vincenzo Riccio to wonder what he had said or done to precipitate such a hasty departure.

Perhaps Dan Fitzpatrick was an atheist.

It was after a second pint of Murphy's that Vincenzo decided he'd brooded enough about miracles and unfriendly Americans. He pushed himself to his feet and ambled into the night.

It was cool out on the street. A thick fog had rolled up from the sea along the River Lee, only a block away, and was infiltrating the city. Vincenzo was about to turn toward

St. Patrick Street and make his way back to his hotel when he saw her.

She stood not two dozen feet away, staring at him. At least he thought she was staring at him. He couldn't tell for sure because the cowled robe she wore pulled up around her head cast her face in shadow, but he could feel her eyes upon him.

His first thought was that she might be a prostitute, but he immediately dismissed that because there was nothing the least bit provocative about her manner, and that robe was anything but erotic.

He wanted to turn away but he could not take his eyes off her. And then it was she who turned and began to walk away.

Vincenzo was compelled to follow her through the swirling fog that filled the open plaza leading to the river. Strange . . . the lights that lined the quay silhouetted her figure ahead of him but didn't cast her shadow. Who was she? And how did she move so smoothly? She seemed to glide through the fog . . . toward the river . . . to its edge . . .

Vincenzo shouted out as he saw her step off the bulkhead, but the cry died in his throat when he saw her continue walking with an unbroken stride . . . upon the fog. He stood gaping on the edge as she canted her path to the right and continued walking downstream. He watched until the fog swallowed her, then he lurched about, searching for someone, anybody to confirm what he had just seen.

But the quay was deserted. The only witnesses were the fog and the River Lee.

Vincenzo rubbed his eyes and stumbled back toward the pub. The doctors had told him to stay away from alcohol, that his liver couldn't handle it. He should have listened. He must be drunk. That was the only explanation.

Otherwise he would have sworn he'd just seen the Virgin Mary.

The Judean Wilderness

Kesev sobbed.

He was still alive.

When will this END?

He'd tried numerous times before to kill himself but had not been allowed to die. He'd hoped that this time it would work, that his miserable failure to guard the Resting Place would cause the Lord to finally despair of him and let him die. But that was not to be. So here was yet another failure. One more in a too-long list of failures.

The jolt from the sudden shortening of the rope had knocked him unconscious but had left his vertebrae and spinal cord intact. Its constriction around his throat had failed to strangle him. So now he'd regained consciousness to find himself swinging gently in *Sharav* a dozen feet above the ground.

For a few moments he let tears of frustration run the desert dust that coated his cheeks, then he reached into his pocket for his knife and began sawing at the rope above his head.

Moments later he was slumped on the ground, pounding his fists into the unyielding earth.

"Is it not over, Lord?" he rasped. "Is that what this means? Do You have more plans for me? Do You want me to search out the Mother and return her to the Resting Place? Is that what You wish?"

Kesev struggled to his feet and staggered to his Jeep. He slumped over the hood.

That had to be it. The Lord was not through with him yet. Perhaps He would never be through with him. But clearly He wanted more from him now. He wanted the Mother back where she belonged and was not about to allow Kesev to stop searching for her.

But where else could he look? She'd been smuggled out of Israel and now could be hidden anywhere in the world. There were no clues, no trail to follow . . .

Except the Ferris woman. Who was she? Had that strange, unsettling nun on the plane been her, or someone pretending to be her? And did it matter? All he knew was that the Explorer he'd seen in the desert that day had been rented on her card. There might be no connection at all. The Mother could have been stolen days before then.

He gazed up into the cold, unblinking eye of the night.

"All right, Lord. I'll continue looking. But I search now on *my* terms, *my* way. I'll find the Mother for You and bring her back where she belongs. But you may not like what I do to the ones who've caused me this trouble."

Part III

Miracles

16

Manhattan

Dan finished tightening the last screw in the swivel plate. He flipped the latch back and forth, watching with inordinate satisfaction how easily its slot slipped over the swivel eye. He fitted the shackle of the brand-new combination padlock through the eye.

"We're in business, Carrie."

She didn't answer. She was busy inside the coal room with the Virgin. Or maybe *busy* wasn't the right word. Carrie was engrossed, preoccupied, fascinated, *enraptured* with the Virgin.

The Virgin . . . Dan had heard Carrie refer to the body or statue or whatever it was so often as "the Virgin" that he'd begun thinking of it that way himself. Certainly easier than referring to it as the Whatever.

After an uneventful transAtlantic trip, the Virgin had arrived in New York late last night. He and Carrie were on the docks first thing this morning to pick her up. She breezed through customs and together they spirited her crate through the front door to St. Joe's basement, through the Loaves and Fishes kitchen, and down here to the subcellar. The old coal furnace that used to rule this nether realm had been dismantled and carted off when the diocese switched the church to gas heat. That left a wide open central space and a separate coal room that used to be fed by a chute from the alley. Carrie had chosen the old coal room as the perfect hiding place. It was ten by ten, the chute had been sealed up long ago, and it had a door, although the door had no lock. Until now.

Dan opened the door and stuck his face inside. He experienced an instant of disorientation, as if he were peering into the past, intruding upon an ancient scene from the Roman catacombs. A functioning light fixture was set in the ceiling, but it was off. Instead, flickering candlelight filled the old coal room, casting wavering shadows against the walls and ceiling. Dan had lugged one of the folding tables from the mission down here a couple of days ago and placed it where Carrie had directed, and that had been just about the last he'd seen of her until this morning. She'd spent every spare moment of the interval feverishly dusting, scrubbing, and dressing up the room, draping the table with a blanket, setting up wall sconces for the candles, appropriating flowers left behind in the church after weddings or funerals, making a veritable shrine out of the coal room.

A short while ago they'd opened the crate and he'd helped her place the Virgin's board-stiff body on the table. Carrie had been fussing with her ever since.

"I said, the latch is in place, Carrie. Want to come see?"

She was bending over the body where it rested on the blanket-draped table, straightening her robe. She didn't look up.

"That's all right. I know you did a great job."

"I wouldn't say it's a great job," Dan said, leaning back and surveying his work. "Adequate's more like it. Won't keep out anybody really determined to get in, but it should deter the idly curious."

"That's what we want," she said, straightening. She turned toward him and held out her hand. "Come see."

Dan moved to her side and laid an arm across her shoulders. A warm tingle spread over his skin as he felt her arm slip around his back. This was the closest they'd been since leaving Israel.

"Look at her," she said. "Isn't she beautiful?"

Dan didn't know how to answer that. He saw the waxy body of an old woman with wild hair and mandarin fingernails, surrounded by candles and wilting flowers. He knew Carrie was seeing something else. Her eyes were wide with wonder and devotion, like a young mother gazing at her newborn first child.

"You did a wonderful job with this place. No one would ever know it was once a coal room."

"And no one should ever know otherwise," she said. "This is our little secret, right?"

"Right. Our *little* secret. Our *big* secret is us." Dan turned and wrapped his other arm around her. "And speaking of us . . ."

Carrie slipped from his embrace. "No, Dan. Not now. Not here. Not with . . . her."

Dan tried to hide his hurt. Just being in the same room with Carrie excited him. Touching her drove him crazy. Used to drive her crazy too. What was wrong?

"When then? Where? Is your brother—?"

"Let's talk about it some other time, okay? Right now I've got a lot still left to do."

"Like what?"

"I have to cut those nails, and fix her hair."

"She's not going on display, Carrie."

"I know, but I want to take care of her."

"She's not a—" Dan bit off the rest of the sentence.

"Not a what?"

He'd been about to say Barbie doll but had cut himself off in time.

"Nothing. She did fine in that cave with nobody fussing over her."

"But she's *my* responsibility now," Carrie said, staring at the Virgin.

"Okay," Dan said, repressing a sigh. "Okay. But not your only responsibility. We've still got meals to serve upstairs. I'm sure she wouldn't want you to let the guests down."

"You go ahead," she said. "I'll be up in a few minutes."

"Good." Dan wanted out of here. The low ceiling, the dead flowers . . . the atmosphere was suddenly oppressive. "You remember the lock combination?"

"Twelve, thirty-six, fourteen."

"Right. See you upstairs."

He watched Carrie, waiting for her to look his way, but she had eyes only for the Virgin.

Shaking his head, Dan turned away. This wouldn't last, he told himself. Carrie would come around soon. Once it seeped into her devotion-fogged brain that her Virgin was merely an inert lump, she'd return to her old self.

But there was going to be an aching void in his life until she did.

Carrie listened to Dan's shoes scuff up the stone steps as she pulled the Ziploc bag from her pocket and removed the scissors from it.

Poor Dan, she thought, looking down at the Virgin. He doesn't understand.

Neither did she, really. All she knew was that everything had changed for her. She could look back on her fourteen years in the order—fully half of her life—and understand for the first time what had brought her to the convent, what had prompted her to take a vow of chastity and then willfully break it.

"It was you, Mother," she said, whispering to the Virgin as she began to trim the ragged ends of dry gray hair that protruded from under the wimple. "I came to the order because of you. You are the Eternal Virgin and I wanted to be like you. Yet I could never be like you because my virginity was already gone . . . stolen from me. But you already know the story."

She'd spoken to the Blessed Virgin countless times in her prayers, trying to explain herself. She'd always felt that Mother Mary would understand. Now that they were face to face, she was compelled to tell her once more, out loud, just to be sure she knew.

"I wanted a new start, Mother. I wanted to be born anew with that vow. I wanted to be a spiritual virgin from that day forward. But I couldn't be. No matter how many showers I took and scrubbed myself raw, no matter how many novenas I made and plenary indulgences I received, I still felt *dirty*."

She slipped the hair trimmings into the plastic bag. These

cuttings could not be tossed into a Dumpster or even flushed away. They were sacred. They had to remain here with the Virgin.

"I hope you can understand the way I felt, Mother, because I can't imagine you ever feeling dirty or unworthy. But the dirtiness was not the real problem. It was the hopelessness that came with it—the inescapable certainty that I could never be clean again. That's what did me in, Mother. I knew what your Son promised, that we have but to believe and ask forgiveness and we shall be cleansed. I knew the words, I understood them in my brain, but in my heart was the conviction that His forgiveness was meant for everyone but Carolyn Ferris. Because Carolyn Ferris had done the unspeakable, the unthinkable, the unpardonable."

She kept cutting, tucking the loose trimmed ends back under the Virgin's wimple.

"I've been to enough seminars and read enough self-help books to know that I was sabotaging myself—I didn't feel worthy of being a good nun, so I made damn sure I never could be one. I regret that. Terribly. And even more, I regret dragging Dan down with me. He's a good man and a good priest, but because of me he broke his own vow, and now he's a sinning priest."

Carrie felt tears welling in her eyes. *Damn, I've got a lot to answer for.*

"But all that's changed now," she said, blinking and sniffing. "Finding you is a sign, isn't it? It means I'm not a hopeless case. It means He thinks I can hold to my vows and make myself worthy to guard you and care for you. And if He thinks it, then it must be so."

She trimmed away the last vagrant strands of hair, then sealed them in the Ziploc bag.

"There," she said, stepping back and smiling. "You look better already."

She glanced down at the Virgin's long, curved finger-nails. They were going to need a lot of work, more work than she had time for now.

"I've got to go now," she said. "Got to do my part for the least of His children, but I'll be back. I'll be back every day.

And every day you'll see a new and better me. I'm going to be worthy of you, Mother. That is a promise—one I'll keep."

She just had to find the right way to tell Dan that the old Carrie was gone and he couldn't have the new one. He was a good man. The best. She knew he'd understand and accept the new her . . . eventually. But she had to find a way to tell him without hurting him.

She placed the bag of clippings under the table that constituted the Virgin's bier, then kissed her wimple and blew out the candles. She snapped the combination lock closed and hurried upstairs to help with lunch.

Carrie was adding a double handful of sliced carrots to the last pot of soup when she heard someone calling her name from the Big Room. She walked to the front to see what it was.

Augusta, a stooped, reed-thin, wrinkled volunteer who worked the serving line three days a week, stood at the rear end of the counter with Pilgrim.

"He says he's got a complaint," Augusta said, looking annoyed and defensive.

The guests often complained about Augusta, saying she was stingy with the portions she doled out. Which was true. She treated the soup and bread as if it were her own. Carrie and Dan had been over this with her again and again: The idea here was to serve everything they made, then make more for the next meal. But they couldn't very well tell her she wasn't welcome behind the counter anymore—they needed every helping hand they could find.

Carrie glanced around for Dan, hoping he could field this, but he was standing by the front door, deep in conversation with Dr. Joe.

"Preacher don't want me to say nothin', Sister," Pilgrim said, "but he found this in his mouth while he was eating his soup and I think you would know about it."

He held out his hand and in the center of his dirty palm lay a three-inch hair.

"I'm Preacher's eyes, you know."

"I know that," Carrie said.

Everybody knew that. Mainly because Pilgrim told anyone who would listen whenever he had a chance. Preacher was blind and Pilgrim was his devoted disciple, leading him from park to stoop to street corner, wherever he could find a small gathering that might listen to his message of imminent Armageddon.

"I'm usually pretty good but this one slipped by me. I kinda feel like I let him down."

"Oh, I'm sure Preach doesn't feel that way," Carrie said, plucking the hair from his palm. "But I do apologize for this, and tell him I'll do my best to see that it doesn't happen again."

"Oh, no!" Pilgrim said, agitatedly waving his hands in front of her. "You got me wrong. It ain't your fault." He pointed a finger at Augusta. "It's hers. Look at that gray hair straggling all over the place, and that's a gray hair Preacher found. She's supposed to be wearing a net. I know 'cause I useta work in a diner and we all hadda wear hairnets."

"He has no right to say that, Sister," Augusta snapped.

Just then the basement phone began ringing in the far corner of the kitchen. Hilda Larsen went to get it.

"It's for you, Sister," Hilda called from inside. "Your brother."

Uh-oh, Carrie thought as she hurried back into the kitchen and took the receiver. Brad never called her at Loaves and Fishes. This could only mean that his American Express bill had arrived.

"Hi, Brad," she said. "I can explain all those charges." *Well, most of them, anyway.*

"What charges?"

"On the card. You see—"

"I didn't get the bill yet, Car. And whatever it is, don't give it a second thought."

"I went a bit overboard, Brad."

"Carrie, I've got more money than I know what to do with and no one to spend it on. So let's not mention AmEx charges again. That's not why I called. It's about Dad."

Carrie felt all the residual warmth from her hours with the

Virgin this morning empty out of her like water down a drain.

"What about him?" she said coldly, asking only because it was expected of her. She didn't care a thing about that man. Couldn't. The mere mention of him froze all her emotions into suspended animation.

"He passed out. They had to move him to the hospital. They say it's his heart acting up again."

Carrie said nothing as Brad paused, waiting for her reaction. When the wait stretched to an uncomfortable length, he cleared his throat.

"He's asking for you."

"He's always asking for me."

"Yeah, but this time—"

"This time will be just like the last time. He'll get you all worked up thinking he's going to die, get you and me going at each other, then he'll come out of it and go back to the nursing home."

"He's changed, Carrie."

"He'll always be Walter Ferris. He can't change that."

"You know," Brad said, "I wish you'd take one tiny bit of the care and compassion you heap upon those nobodies down there and transfer it to your own father. Just once."

"These nobodies never did to me what that man did to me. It's because of him that I'm down here with these nobodies. We can both thank him for where we are."

"I've managed to do okay."

"Have you?"

Now it was Brad's turn for silence.

Carrie wanted to ask him why he hadn't been able to sustain a relationship. It seemed every time he got close to a woman he backed off. Why? What was he afraid of? That he was like his father? That a little bit of that man hid within him? And that if he had children of his own he might do what his father did?

But she couldn't say that to Brad. All she could say was, "I love you, brother."

And she meant it.

"I love you too, Carrie."

Suddenly she heard voices rising in the Big Room.

"I've got to go. Call me soon."

"Will do."

As Carrie turned away from the phone, she saw Augusta coming toward her.

"Honestly, Sister. That wasn't my hair. Mine's long and thick. That one Pilgrim gave you is short and fine."

"It's okay, Augusta," she said, brushing past the old woman. "What's going on in the Big Room?"

"Probably another fight," Augusta said. "You know how they are."

But it wasn't a fight. The regulars—Rider, Dandy, Lefty, Dirty Harry, Poppy, Bigfoot, Indian, Stoney, One-Thumb George—and a few of the newer ones were clustered around one of the long tables. She saw Dan standing on the far side of the circle as Dr. Joe bent over Preacher, who sat ramrod straight, holding his hands before his face.

"A miracle!" Pilgrim was screeching, dancing and gyrating among the tables of the Big Room. "I always knew Preacher had the power, and now it's come! It's a miracle! A fucking miracle!"

Carrie pushed closer. Preacher was staring at his hands, muttering. "I can see! Praise God, I can see!"

She stepped back and stared at the short strand of gray hair in her hand. It hadn't come from Augusta. She recognized it now. It was the same length and color as the stray strands Carrie had been trimming from the Virgin a short while ago. It must have stuck to her sleeve downstairs and fallen into the soup as she was adding the ingredients.

A miracle . . .

She wanted to laugh, she wanted to cry, she wanted to grab Pilgrim's hands and join him in a whirling dervish.

Oh, Pilgrim, she thought as she hurried back through the kitchen and down to the subcellar. If only you knew how right you are!

Yes, it was a miracle. And Carrie had a feeling it would not be the last.

• • •

"Preacher can really see again," Dan said for the third or fourth time. Evening had come and they were cleaning up the Big Room after dinner. "Not well, mind you. He can recognize his hand in front of his face and not much more, but at least that's something. He's been totally blind for forty years."

Carrie had decided to hold off telling Dan about the piece of the Virgin's hair in the soup. He'd only go into his Doubting Thomas routine. She'd wait till she had more proof. But she couldn't resist priming him for the final revelation.

She glanced around to make sure they were out of earshot of the volunteers in the kitchen.

"Do you think it's a miracle?" she said softly.

Dan didn't look up as he wiped one of the long tables. "You know what I think about miracles."

"How do you explain it then?"

"José says it might have been hysterical blindness all along, and now he's coming out of it. He's scheduled him for a full eye exam tomorrow."

"Well, far be it from me to disagree with Dr. Joe."

Dan stopped in mid-wipe and stared at her. "Aw, Carrie. Don't tell me you think—"

"Yes!" She said in a fierce whisper. "I think a certain someone has announced her presence."

"Come on, Carrie—"

"You and José believe in your hysterical blindness, if you wish. All I know is that Preacher began to see again within hours of a certain someone's arrival."

Dan opened his mouth, then closed it, paused, then shook his head. "Coincidence, Carrie."

But he didn't sound terribly convincing.

Carrie couldn't repress a smile. "We'll see."

"We'll see what?"

"How many 'coincidences' it takes to convince you."

FRUITLESS VIGIL IN TOMPKINS SQUARE

Approximately 1,000 people gathered last night for a candle-light prayer vigil in Tompkins Square Park. Surrounded by knots of curious homeless, many of whom call the park home, the predominantly female crowd prayed to the Virgin Mary in the hope that she would manifest herself in the park.

Sightings of a lone woman, described as "glowing faintly," and identified as the Blessed Virgin, have been reported with steadily increasing frequency all over the Lower East Side during the past few weeks.

Despite many recitations of the Rosary, no manifestation occurred. Many members of the crowd remained undaunted, however, vowing to return next Sunday evening.

THE NEW YORK POST

17

Manhattan

"Something bothering you, José?"

Dan and Dr. Joe ambled crosstown after splitting a sausage-and-pepper pizza and a pitcher of beer at Nino's on St. Mark's and Avenue A. José had been unusually quiet tonight.

"Bothering me? I don't know. Nothing bad or anything like that, just . . . I don't know."

"That's the first time you've put that many words together in a row all night, and six of them were 'I don't know.' What gives?"

José said, "I don't know," then laughed. "I . . . aw, hell, I guess I can tell you: I think two of my AIDS patients have been cured."

Dan felt an anticipatory tightening in his chest and he wasn't sure why.

"You're sure?"

"It's not just my diagnosis. They were both anemic, both had Kaposi's when I'd seen them in July. They came in last week and their skin had cleared and their hematocrits were normal. I had them admitted to Beekman for a full work up. The results came back today."

"And?"

"They're clear."

"Cured?"

Dan saw José's head nod in the dark. "Yep. They're now HIV neg. Their peripheral smears are normal, their CD four cell counts are normal, their skin lesions are gone. Not a single goddam trace that they were ever exposed to HIV. Hell, they both used to be positive for hepatitis B surface antigen and now even *that's* gone."

José sounded as if he was going to cry.

"But how—?"

"Nothing I did. Just gave them the usual—AZT, didanosine, TP-five—and let me tell you, man, they weren't all that reliable about taking their meds. Fucking miracle, that's what it is. Medical fucking miracle."

Dan's mouth went dry. Talk of miracles did that to him lately. So did talk of seeing the Virgin Mary in his neighborhood.

"Miracle. You mean like . . . Preacher?"

"I can't say much about Preacher. I've got no medical records on him from when he was blind, so I can't say anything about the condition of his retinas when he couldn't see. All I can say is that his vision has improved steadily until it's almost twenty-twenty now. But . . . these two AIDS patients, they were documented cases."

Dan sensed a certain hesitancy in José.

"I wouldn't happen to know these two patients, would I?"

José hesitated, then sighed. "Normally I wouldn't tell you, but they're going to be in all the medical journals soon, and from then on they'll be news-show and talk-show commodities, so I guess it's okay to tell you they're both regulars at your Loaves and Fishes. You'll hear their names soon enough."

Dan stumbled a step.

"Oh my God."

"Well, you knew some of them had to be HIV positive."

Dan tried to remember who hadn't been around lately.

"Dandy and Rider?" he said.

"You guessed it."

"They had it but they're *cured*?"

"Yep. Both with a history of IV drug use, formerly HIV positive, now HIV neg. You figure it out."

Dan was trying to do just that.

He knew Carrie wouldn't have to think twice about an explanation when she heard the news: The Virgin did it.

And how was he supposed to counter that? Damned if he wasn't beginning to think she might be right. First Preacher gets his sight back, then people all over the area start sighting someone they think is the Virgin Mary, and now two of their regular guests at St. Joe's are cured of AIDS.

The accumulated weight of evidence was getting too heavy to brush off as mere coincidence.

He glanced at José and noticed he still looked glum.

"So how come you're not happy?" Dan said.

"Because when I gave Rider and Dandy the news they gave *me* all the credit."

"So?"

"So I didn't do anything. And if they go around blabbing that Dr. Martinez can cure AIDS, it's going to raise a lot of false hopes. And worse, my little clinic is going to be inundated with people looking for a miracle."

A miracle . . . that word again.

Dan clapped him on the shoulder, trying to lighten him up.

"Who knows. Maybe you've got the healing touch."

"Not funny, Dan. I don't have the resources to properly treat the people I'm seeing now. If the clinic starts attracting crowds I don't know what I'll do." Suddenly he grinned. "Maybe I'll direct them all to St. Joe's Loaves and Fishes. If they're looking for a miracle, that's the place to find it."

A knot of dread constricted in Dan's chest, stopping him in his tracks.

"Don't even kid about that!"

"Hey, think about it," José said, laughing. "It all fits. Preacher regained his sight there, and both Dandy and Rider are regulars. Maybe the cure-all can be found at Loaves and Fishes. Maybe Sister Carrie's stirring some special magical ingredient into that soup of hers."

Dan forced a smile. "Maybe. I'll have to ask her."

Carrie held up two Ziplock bags.

"Here they are. The magic ingredients."

When he'd mentioned José's remarks to her this morning, she'd smiled and crooked a finger at him, leading him down to the subcellar. It was the first time he'd been down here since he'd carried in the Virgin. After Carrie lit the candles, Dan saw that the Virgin looked different. Her hair was neater, tucked away under her wimple, and those long, grotesque fingernails had been clipped off. The air was suffused with the sweet scent of the fresh flowers that surrounded the bier.

Carrie then reached under her bier and produced these two clear plastic bags.

Dan took them from her and examined them. One contained an ounce or so of a fine, off-white powder; the other was full of a feather-light gray substance that looked for all the world like finely chopped . . . hair.

He glance back at Carrie and found her smiling, staring at him, her eyes luminous in the candle glow.

"What are these?" he said, hefting the bags.

"Hers."

"I don't get it."

Carrie reached out and gently touched the bag of fine, gray strands. "This one's her hair." She then touched the bag with the powder. "And this is what's left of her fingernails."

"Fingernails?"

"I trimmed her nails and filed the cuttings down to powder."

"Why on earth . . . ?"

Carrie explained about the strand of hair in Preacher's soup, and how he'd begun to see again almost immediately after.

"But that was coincidence," Dan said. "It had to be."

"Are you sure?" she said, trapping him with those eyes.

"No," he said. "I'm not sure. I no longer know what I'm sure of or *not* sure of anymore. I haven't been sure of much for a long time, and now I'm not even sure about the things I've been sure I couldn't be sure of."

Carrie started to laugh.

"Sounds like a country-western song, doesn't it," Dan said, then he too started to laugh.

"Oh, Lord," Carrie said after a moment. "When was the last time we laughed together?"

"Before Israel," Dan said.

Slowly, she sobered. "That seems like so long ago."

"Doesn't it."

Silence hung between them.

"Anyway," Carrie finally said, "I've been dosing the soup with tiny bits of her hair and her ground-up fingernails every day since she arrived."

Dan couldn't help making a face. "Carrie!"

"Don't look at me like that, Dan. If I put in a couple of snippets of hair I mix it with the rosemary. If I use some fingernail, I rub it together with some pepper. Tiny amounts, unnoticeable, completely indistinguishable from the regular spices."

"But they're *not* spices."

"They are indeed! You can't deny that things have changed upstairs since the Virgin arrived."

Dan thought about that and realized he couldn't deny that things had changed. In fact, strange things had been happening at the Loaves and Fishes during the past month or so. Nothing so dramatic as the return of Preacher's sight, but the place had *changed*. Nothing that would be apparent to an outsider, but Dan knew things were different.

First off, the mood had changed. The undercurrent of suspicion and paranoia that had prevailed whenever the guests gathered for a meal was gone. They no longer sat hunched over their meals, one arm hooked around the plate while the free hand shoveled food into the mouth. They ate more slowly now, and they talked. Instead of arguments over who was hogging the salt or who'd got a bigger serving, Dan had actually heard civil conversation along the tables.

Come to think of it, there hadn't been a fight in two weeks—a record. The previously demented, paranoid, and generally psychotic guests seemed calmer, more lucid, almost rational. Fewer of them were coming in drunk or high. Rider had stopped talking about finding his old Harley and had even mentioned checking out a Help Wanted sign he'd seen outside a cycle repair shop.

But the biggest change had been in Carrie.

She'd withdrawn from him. It had always seemed to Dan that Carrie had room in her life for God, her order, St. Joe's Loaves and Fishes, and one other. Dan had been that one other for a while. Now he'd lost her. The Virgin had supplanted him in that remaining spot.

Yet try as he might he could feel no animosity. She was *happy*. He couldn't remember seeing her so radiant. His only regret was that he wasn't the source of that inner light. Part of him wanted to label her as crazy, deranged, psychotic, but then he'd have to find another explanation for the changes upstairs . . . and the cures.

"You think she's responsible," he said, stepping past her to stare down at the prone, waxy figure. She looked so much neater, so much more . . . attractive with her hair fixed and her nails trimmed.

"I *know* she is."

Dan's gaze roamed past the flickering candles to the flower-stuffed vases that rimmed the far side and clustered at the head and foot of the makeshift bier.

"You've done a wonderful job with her. You've turned a coal room into a grotto. It's like a shrine. But how do you keep sneaking off with all these flowers? Aren't you afraid one of these trips somebody in the church is going to catch you and ask you what you're up to?"

"One of what trips? I haven't borrowed any flowers from the church since she arrived."

Dan turned back to the flowers—mums, daffodils, gardenias, gladiolus, their stalks were straight and tall, their blossoms full and unwrinkled—then looked at Carrie again.

"But these are . . ."

"The same ones I brought down the first day." Her smile was blinding. "Isn't it wonderful?"

Dan continued to stare into those bright, wide, guileless eyes, looking for some hint of deception, but he found none.

Suddenly he wished for a chair. His knees felt rubbery. He needed to sit down.

"My God, Carrie."

"No," she said. "Just His Mother."

That wasn't what he needed to hear. Things like this didn't happen in the real world, at least not in Dan's real world. God stayed in his heaven and watched his creations make the best of things down here while priests like Dan acted as go-betweens. There was no part in the script for His Mother—especially not in the subceller of a Lower East Side church.

"Is it her, Carrie? Can it really be *her*?"

"Yes," she said, nodding, beaming, unhindered by the vaguest trace of doubt. "It's her. Can't you feel it?"

The only thing Dan could feel right now was an uneasy chill seeping into his soul.

"What have we done, Carrie? What have we *done*?"

AIDS CURES LINKED TO VIRGIN MARY

A prayer vigil outside St. Joseph's Roman Catholic Church on the Lower East Side last night attracted over two thousand people. Many of those attending proclaimed the recent well-publicized AIDS cures as miracles related to the sightings of the Blessed Virgin Mary in the area during the past month. When asked about the connection, Fr. Daniel Fitzpatrick, associate pastor of St. Joseph's, responded, "The Church has not verified the figure that has been sighted as actually representing the Virgin Mary, and certainly there is no established link between the figure and the AIDS cures. Therefore I would strongly caution anyone with AIDS from abandoning their current therapy and coming down here looking for a miracle cure. You might just find the opposite."

THE DAILY NEWS

CDC to Begin Epidemiological Study on Lower East Side

(Atlanta, AP) The Center for Disease Control has announced it will begin a limited epidemiological study of the five cases of AIDS reported cured of the Lower East Side of Manhattan. Spokesman for the Center . . .

THE NEW YORK TIMES

Paraiso

"Are these all the clippings?" Arthur Crenshaw asked as he reread the *Times* article for the third time.

"The latest batch," Emilio said.

Arthur slipped the rest of the clippings back into the manila envelope but held on to the *Times* and *Daily News* pieces. For a moment he stared through the glass at the Pacific, glistening in the early afternoon sun, then glanced to his right where Charlie lay.

He'd turned the great room into a miniature medical facility: a state-of-the-art AIDS clinic with round-the-clock nursing, a medical consultant with an international reputation in infectious diseases, and a patient census of one.

All to no avail.

Charlie was fading fast. He'd received maximum doses of the standard AIDS medications, including triple therapy, and had even undergone a course of a new and promising drug that was still in the experimental stages. Nothing worked. Apparently he'd picked up a particularly virulent strain of the virus and had ignored the symptoms in the early stages. Only scant vestiges of Charlie's immune system had remained by the time he'd started treatment. On his last visit, Dr. Lamberson would not commit to how much time he thought Charlie had, but he said the prognosis was very grave indeed. Ordinarily Lamberson would laugh at the thought of a house call, but with what Arthur was paying him, he came when called. He'd just brought Charlie through a severe bout of *pneumocystis* pneumonia and said another would certainly kill him.

Charlie was sleeping now. His hospital bed had been wheeled closer to the glass wall so he could read in the sunlight, and he'd dozed off after a few pages. He had no strength, no stamina, and the pounds were melting from his frame like butter. And he was so *pale*. Arthur had begun insisting on colored sheets so that he could look at his son without feeling he was being absorbed into the mattress.

Charlie, Charlie, Arthur thought as he stared at his son. *If only you'd listened! Dear boy, you never meant to hurt anyone. You don't deserve this. Please don't die, not until I can work up the courage to tell you I understand, that for a while I . . . I was like you. Almost like you.*

It had been back in the sixties, in the hedonistic dens behind the Victorian facades of Haight Ashbury. Arthur had been looking for himself, trying anything—drugs, and sex. All kinds of sex. For a year he had lived in a commune where group sex was a nightly ritual. Every combination was tried—men and women together, women with women, and . . . men with men. He had tried it for a while, even enjoyed it for a while, but as time went on, he realized it wasn't for him.

Been there, done that, as the expression went.

But he'd never considered it as a lifestyle. Yet the memories haunted him. What if someone from those days stepped forward with stories of young Artie Crenshaw having sex with other men?

Many a night the possibility dragged him sweating and gasping from his sleep.

Not fair. Those days were long past. An aberration. He'd repented, and he was sure he'd been forgiven. He wanted

Charlie to be forgiven as well. But would learning about his father's past lighten Charlie's burden?

Arthur didn't know. If only he *knew.*

So much he didn't know. Especially about AIDS. Arthur had begun his own research, learning all he could—more than he wished to know—about HIV, ARC, CD4, p24, AZT, TP-5, and all the rest of the alphabet soup that was such an integral part of the AIDS canon. He hired a clipping service to comb the world's newspapers, magazines, and medical journals for anything that pertained to AIDS. The flow of information was staggering, mind-numbing. What he could not comprehend he brought to Dr. Lamberson's attention.

The phone rang. Emilio answered it, said a few harsh words, then hung up.

"Who was it?" Arthur said without looking around.

"That *puta* reporter again. She wants an interview with Charlie."

Arthur closed his eyes. Gloria Weskerna from the *Star*. It still baffled him how she'd got his home number.

Somehow she'd picked up word that Senator Crenshaw's son was sick. Something was wrong with the son of a potential presidential candidate. What could it be? She and others of her tribe had started sniffing around like stray dogs in a garbage dump, hunting for anything ripe and juicy. Emilio had tightened security, carefully screening the nurses, setting up a round-the-clock guard at the front gate, and spiriting Dr. Lamberson and the nurses in and out in the black-glassed limousine.

"Change the phone number, Emilio," he said without looking around.

"Yes, *Senador.* If you wish, I can change this reporter's mind about hounding you."

Arthur turned to face his security man. "Really? How would you do that?"

"She might have a serious accident—a bad fall, perhaps, after which her home could burn and her car could be stolen. She would have so many other things on her mind that she would not have time to bother you."

Emilio said it so casually, as if planning a shopping list for the supermarket. Not a glimmer of amusement lightened his Latin features. Arthur knew he was not being put on. Emilio's sense of humor was about as active as Charlie's immune system.

Arthur trusted Emilio implicitly, but sometimes he was very frightening.

"I don't think so, Emilio. We'll just continue to stonewall. Our position will remain aloof: We admit nothing, we deny nothing. Implicit in our silence is the stance that these rags are not worthy of serious attention. That's the only way to keep the lid on things."

"As you wish, *Senador*."

Arthur realized he could keep the lid on Charlie's illness only so long as he stayed alive. If he died . . . he reminded himself with a pang that it wasn't really an *if*—it was a *when* . . . and soon.

When Charlie died, the shit would hit the fan. He might be able to dissuade the medical examiner from doing an autopsy, but the death certificate was another matter. He could not expect Dr. Lamberson to jeopardize his reputation, his medical license, and his entire career by falsifying a legal document.

He winced as he imagined the headlines.

SENATOR CRENSHAW'S
SON DIES OF AIDS!!

That would be damaging, but he could weather it. He could not be held accountable for his son's actions. In fact, he could turn it around and blame Charlie's death on the moral bankruptcy of modern America. America was on the road to ruin, and who better to turn it around and lead it from the darkness into the light than a man who had been so grievously wounded by the nation's moral turpitude?

Yes, he could survive, perhaps even benefit from public disclosure of the cause of Charlie's death. His only worry was what rats might crawl out of the woodwork when they heard that Charlie had died of AIDS. What vermin from his past might step forward and say, "Like father, like son."

Arthur knew he could weather either one alone, but he would fall before the combination of the two.

Everyone would be properly supportive at first, but he knew it wouldn't be long before the various elements of the coalition he'd been forging began edging away from him. All his Born-Again friends and admirers would begin looking around for someone else to support, someone who's immediate family was not so intimately associated with sodomy.

And then his dream of a renewed America would go down in flames, be reduced to ashes.

He treasured two things most in his life: his son and his dream. Charlie's AIDS was going to steal both.

He looked again at the *Times* and *Daily News* clippings in his lap. Like everyone else who read a paper or watched the network news, he'd heard about the four supposedly cured cases of AIDS in New York. They'd sparked some hope in the growing darkness within him, but after his experience with Olivia he'd learned that cynicism was the only appropriate response to miracle cures. It saved a lot of heartache.

But the *Times* article said the CDC was getting involved . . . budgeting an epidemiological study. If Arthur was correctly reading between the lines, it meant that these cures had been sufficiently verified for the CDC to judge them worth the effort and expense of sending an investigative team to Manhattan.

Interesting . . .

The CDC was headquartered in Atlanta. Arthur had myriad contacts in the Bible Belt. No problem learning what was going on in the CDC, but it might be wise to have his own man on the scene.

"Emilio," he said, "how would you feel about a trip to New York?"

Manhattan

Monsignor Vincenzo Riccio suppressed the urge to vomit as he walked along Catherine Street near the Governor Alfred E. Smith Houses and waited for dark. Dark would not be a safe time to be here, but he did not worry about that. He hadn't shaved for days and was dressed in the shabbiest clothes he'd been able to find at the Vatican Mission uptown. He was not an attractive mugging prospect. But even if he were killed tonight, it would not matter.

The new chemotherapy protocol was not working. It had succeeded only in suppressing his white cell count and making him violently ill. He'd lost more weight. The tumors continued their relentless spread. The end was not far off, so human predators could do nothing to him that the cancer and the chemicals had not already tried. A quick death here might be preferable to the slow death that threatened to linger into the fall, but surely not beyond.

But please, God, not before I see her again.

The Vatican had called today. Since he was already here in Manhattan, would he mind looking into these Blessed Virgin sightings that had become epidemic on the Lower East Side?

He'd agreed, of course. What he did not say was that he'd been investigating for weeks.

He'd read of the sightings and had been struck immediately by the similarity between the witnesses' descriptions of the faintly glowing woman they'd seen down here and the woman he'd seen walking on the fog over the River Lee back in July. He did not resist the yearning to search out this Stateside apparition to see if she was the same.

So far his quest had been as successful as the new chemotherapy.

He scanned the streets around him. He spotted numerous Asian shoppers scurrying home through the fading light, each carrying their purchases in identical red plastic sacks. On his right sat rows of deserted, dilapidated, graffiti-scarred buildings, with empty windows in front and dark, litter-choked alleys on their flanks. All forlorn and forbidding.

She had been spotted twice near here. So like her son to appear down here among the social cast offs. If indeed it *was* her. Perhaps tonight she once more would grace this lowly neighborhood with her presence.

Israel

Kesev could feel the sweat trickle from his armpits as he clutched the ends of his armrests and stared out the window of El Al flight 001. He saw Tel Aviv and the coast of Israel fall away beneath him. Anyone watching him would think he was afraid of flying. He did not like it, true, but that was not what filled him with such anxiety.

Never before in his long life had he left his homeland. The very idea had been unthinkable until now. And even under these extraordinary circumstances, he was uneasy. He had never wanted to be more than a few hours away from the Resting Place. Now there would be a continent and an ocean between him and the site in the Wilderness where he had vowed to spend the rest of his days.

Not that it mattered now. The Mother was gone from the Resting Place. His duty was to follow her to wherever she now lay.

And Kesev had a pretty good idea now where that might be.

New York.

He couldn't be sure, of course. The visions of the Virgin Mary in Manhattan meant nothing by themselves. On any given day someone somewhere thought he or she had been gifted with a vision of the Mother of God, and this was nothing new for New York. Since the 1970s a woman named Veronica in a place called Bayside had claimed to see and speak to the Virgin on a regular basis. And more recently in Queens had been the painting of the Mother that had seeped oil.

Since the Mother's theft Kesev had accumulated a huge collection of reports on these visions. Lately the vast majority seemed to occur in America.

Some were utterly absurd—the image of the Blessed Virgin in the browned areas on a flour tortilla, in a patch of mold on the side of a refrigerator, in a forkful of spaghetti, on the side of a leaking fuel tank—and could be discarded without a second thought.

Others were more traditional apparitions, often repeated on a scheduled basis, such as the first Sunday or first Friday of the month, but although thousands would be in attendance for the occasion, the actual vision was restricted to a single individual. Kesev marked these as possible but most likely the product of one unbalanced mind and fed by the public's yearning for something, anything that might indicate a Divine Presence. Visions had been occurring long before the theft of the Mother and would certainly continue after she was returned to where she belonged.

But these Manhattan visions . . . something about them had sparked a flicker of hope in Kesev. They didn't follow the pattern of the other sightings. They appeared to be random, had been reported by a wide variety of people belonging to a polyglot of races and religions. When Muslims and Buddhists began reporting visions of a softly glowing woman in an ankle-length cowled robe, identical to the image Kesev had seen countless times atop the *tav* rock, he had to give them credence.

And then there was the matter of the cures.

The tabloid press was always touting cures for the incurable, but these cures were linked to no miracle drug or quack therapy. They were spontaneous and random, just like the sightings of the Virgin Mary.

And just like the sightings they all seemed to be clustered in the Lower East Side of Manhattan.

He glanced at his watch. The flight was due to arrive in Kennedy at 5:20 A.M. local time. Shortly after that, Kesev, too, would be in Lower Manhattan.

Searching.

If the Mother was there, Kesev would find her. He *had* to find her. And when he did he would silence the thieves so they could not reveal what they knew. Then he would return the Mother to the Resting Place where she belonged, where she would remain until the Final Days.

Only two questions bothered Kesev. Who were these people who had stolen the Mother away from him? The job was so smoothly and skillfully done, leaving not a trace of a trail, they had to be professionals. If that were so, why was no one trumpeting her discovery? He was overjoyed that there had been no such announcement, for that meant he could still set matters right before irreparable damage was done. But why the silence? Could it be they didn't know what they had? Or were they, perhaps, trying to verify what they had? Whatever the reason, he could not let this opportunity pass.

The second question was more unsettling. Why had the Lord allowed this to happen? Did it mean that the Final Days were imminent? That the End of All Things was at hand?

Part of Kesev hoped so, for he was desperately tired of living. Yet another part of him dreaded facing the Second Coming with this new disgrace to account for.

IN THE PACIFIC

7° N, 155° W

North of the Line Islands, between the trackless rolling swells and the flawless azure sky, a haze forms, quickly thickening into a mist, then a fog, then a raft of clouds, immaculate white at first, but darkening along the underbelly as it fattens outward and reaches upward, casting cooling shadow on the warm water below, which is raised to a gentle chop as the wind begins to blow.

18

Manhattan

"Damn that Pilgrim!" Dan said softly as the door shut behind the two CDC investigators. "Why can't he keep his big mouth shut?"

Poor Dan, Carrie thought as they stood together by the serving counter. She repressed a smile and laid a gentle hand on his arm.

"He doesn't know the trouble he's causing. Preacher's his friend. He was blind and now he can see. He witnessed a miracle and he wants to tell the world about it."

"And he seems to be doing just that—literally."

"Let him."

"Let him? I have no choice. And I wouldn't care, but now he's telling anybody who'll listen that if they're looking for a miracle cure, go to Loaves and Fishes!"

"And what if he does?"

"We just saw the result! Two guys from the CDC asking us about what we're serving the guests! Wanting to know if we're using any 'unusual' recipes! Good God, I thought I was going to have a heart attack!"

Carrie had to laugh now.

"What's so funny?" Dan said.

"You should have seen your face! You started choking while you were reading off the ingredients in my seven-grain bread!"

Dan's reluctant smile broke through. "I did fine until he

asked me about any 'special additives!' *That* was when I almost lost it."

"You were very good. Very calm. The picture of innocence."

"I hope so. We don't need a bunch of epidemiologists sniffing around. I have visions of them doing these in-depth interviews with anyone around here who's been cured of anything in the past few months and entering it all into a computer, then asking the computer to find the common denominator and having it spit out, Loaves and Fishes . . . Loaves and Fishes . . . Loaves and Fishes, over and over again."

"Oh, Dan. Don't worry so much."

"I can't help it, Carrie. At the very least, we have a smuggled artifact in the basement. At the very most, if what you believe is true—"

"What I *know* is true. And you know it's true as well."

Dan blinked, tightened his lips, and gave his head a quick shake. Why wouldn't he let his lips speak what he knew in his heart?

"At the very most," he continued, "we're sitting on something that could shake up all of Christianity and Judaism, and possibly all of Islam as well."

"But no one but you and I will know," Carrie said patiently. How many times did she have to explain this to him? "The Virgin's existence was meant to be kept secret, and we are honoring that secret."

"But just moments ago we had two government investigators here!"

"So? Let's just suppose that when they'd asked you about any 'special additives,' you'd told them, 'Oh, yes. I almost forgot. We've got the Virgin Mary stashed away in the subcellar and we're adding smidges of her finely ground hair and fingernails to the soup.' What do you think they'd put in their report?"

Dan sighed. "Okay. You've got a point. But still . . ."

She reached across the counter and grasped his hand.

"Have faith, Dan. We're not alone in this. Everything's going to work out. Just believe."

Dan looked into her eyes and squeezed her hand in return. "I used to believe in us, and look what happened to that."

Carrie's heart sank. Not this again.

"Dan . . . we've been through this already. Something bigger than you and I has come into our lives and we have to put our wants and desires aside. You said you understood."

"I do. At least partially. But even if I understood fully, I'd still be hurting. I haven't been able to put out the fire so easily."

But you must, she thought, hurting for him. You *must*.

"Don't the miracles make it easier?" she said, hoping to see the pain fade in his eyes. "Don't they make you feel a part of something glorious?"

"The cures are wonderful," he said.

"And they happened because of us! The blind see, the terminally ill are cured, the deranged become lucid. Because we brought her here."

"I just hope those same miracles aren't our downfall. Look what's happening around us. People are seeing the Virgin Mary everywhere, the streets are acrawl with epidemiologists by day and Mary-hunters by night, there's a candlelight vigil on every other corner, and every AIDS patient in the city seems to be trying to move to the Lower East Side. It's getting crazier by the minute out there. It all seems to be building toward something. But what? And if someone puts all the pieces together, we may find ourselves in big trouble, a lot more trouble than we can handle."

Carrie just shook her head. Didn't Dan know? Couldn't he feel it? Everything was going to be fine.

She is here.

Kesev had sensed that the instant his flight had touched down at JFK. Now he sat on a filthy bench in a litter-strewn park named after Sara D. Roosevelt, whoever she was. On the far side of the chain-link fence, across Forsythe Street, stretched a row of dilapidated houses, worse than in the poorest sections of the Arab Quarter in Jerusalem, except for the brightly colored and well kept building on the corner, the only clean structure on the block. Kesev had found it especially interesting because of the six-pointed star of David in the circular window near the top of its front gable. He'd thought it a temple at first, but had been confused by the inscription over the entrance: Templo Adventista del Septimo.

But much closer at hand—directly in front of him—was a hoarse-voiced street preacher. Lacking anything better to do, Kesev listened to his rant.

"Forget not what St. Paul said to the Thessalonians: 'The Day of the Lord so comes as a thief in the night.' The End Times are soon upon us. First there will come the Rapture, then the Tribulation, and then the Son of God will come again. But only those who believe, only those who are saved will be caught up in the Rapture and spared the Tribulation. As Paul said to his church: 'But you, brothers, are not in darkness that that day will overcome you like a thief . . . For God has not appointed us to wrath, but to obtain deliverance by our Lord Jesus Christ!' Heed those words. Repent, believe, be not caught unprepared!"

"Amen, brothers!" cried his helper or disciple or whatever one might call the little man who followed him around like a puppy. "Amen! Preacher should know! Preacher was blind and now he can see! He sees *everything*!"

"First will come war—beware the false peace that surrounds us, for it exists but to lull us into laxity. Then will come plague and famine, followed by worldwide starvation. There will be a great shaking of the earth, the skies will darken, the seas will die, the River Jordan shall run red."

What nonsense is this? Kesev thought irritably. While I suffer the frustration of my fruitless search for the Mother, must I also suffer the words of fools and madmen? If he doesn't shut up I will wring his neck. And that of his prancing disciple as well.

Weeks here and no luck. Roaming these mean, sinister streets at night, hearing of the apparition, rushing to its reported location, always too late to see it. The frustration

was making him ill tempered, building to a murderous rage.
If something didn't break soon . . .

*She must be aware that I am here. Why is she toying with
me?*

"You have four years, brothers and sisters," Preacher said.
"Four years to repent and take Jesus as your Lord. For the
year 2000 is soon upon us. And what more appropriate time
than the end of the second millennium for the End Times?
The setting of the second millennium will be followed by
the dawn of the Second Coming of the Lord!"

The last two sentences shook Kesev. He hadn't realized
the end of the second millennium was indeed upon the
world. The epochal event of its departure dovetailed with
his apprehensions about the meaning of the apocalyptic
events of the summer.

"Listen to him!" the little sidekick said. "*Listen!*"

But the half-dozen people who had paused a moment to
listen to the raggedy man had heard it all before, so they
moved on. And with no audience, the man called Preacher
and his lone disciple moved on as well.

Leaving Kesev and a thin, sickly looking old man sharing
the bench.

Good riddance, Kesev thought.

Monsignor Vincenzo Riccio shifted his weight on the
bench. His wasted buttocks offered no padding against the
hard, rough planked surface. He wanted to get up and
continue his search for the vision, but he didn't know which
way to go in the fading light.

Fading like my body, he thought. Like my life. Slowly,
steadily, inexorably.

He was beginning to think his chance to see the vision
again would never come. He'd been traveling down from
the Vatican mission to the Lower East Side night after night,
hoping, praying, beseeching God and Jesus and Mary
herself to honor him with the vision once more, just once
more before the cancer took him. It had become a contest of
sorts, a race between the tumor and his determination to last
until he saw her again.

He glanced at the bearded man a few feet to his right.

"Do you think he's right?" he said.

The bearded man started, as if surprised that someone would speak to him. Most New Yorkers were shocked initially when a stranger like Vincenzo opened a conversation with them.

"Sorry. Do I think who is right?"

A strange accent. Middle Eastern, certainly, but where? The features framed by the beard and dark hair were Semitic. A Palestinian?

"The Preacher. Do you think we have only four years left until the Second Coming?"

"You mean, will the Second Coming of the Master coincide with the end of the second millennium?"

"Yes. The *fin de millenaire*. He's hardly the first to mention it, but it is an interesting concept, is it not?"

The bearded man nodded slowly. "But if that is true, if the Master is returning with the end of the millennium, then we do not have four years."

Vincenzo wondered at this fellow's use of the term "the Master." Surely he was referring to Christ. Who else could be expected at the Second Coming. But it was such an archaic reference, the way the early church referred to Jesus.

But Vincenzo was even more intrigued by his last statement.

"It's 1996," he said. "Why do you say we don't have four years?"

"Because your calendar is wrong. The Master was not born in the year you have designated one A.D."

Vincenzo realized with a shock that he was right. It was an accepted fact now that the birth year of Christ had been miscalculated by a sixth century monk named Dionysus Exiguus who had been charged by the Church with numbering the years of the Christian era.

"Good Lord, sir, that is true! Jesus Christ is believed to have been born somewhere between four and seven B.C.!"

"Four."

"I beg your pardon?"

"The Master was born in what you now call four B.C."

"I don't think anyone really knows for sure."

"I do."

The man's tone was defiantly authoritative, leaving no room for argument. One would almost think he'd been alive then.

"Yes . . . well," Vincenzo said. "For the sake of discussion we shall accept the year four B.C. That would mean that" . . . a chill rippled up Vincenzo's spine . . . "Heavens, man, that would mean that this very year marks the two-thousandth year since His birth!"

The bearded man nodded slowly. "Yes. Unsettling, no? I just realized that fact myself a moment ago." He shot to his feet. "Good-bye. I must be going."

"Yes," Vincenzo said. "Of course. It was most enlightening talking to you. Perhaps we'll meet some other time."

"I do not think so."

He walked off.

Vincenzo wondered if he was another "Mary-hunter," as one of the local papers had dubbed the hordes of faithful roaming the Lower East Side streets in search of the Blessed Virgin.

Perhaps, perhaps not, Vincenzo thought as he pushed himself to his feet. But certainly something strange about that fellow. Not very friendly, which he supposed was to be expected in New York, but this fellow was almost furtive.

Vincenzo wished he'd had more time to talk to him, though. If he was right, then this year indeed marked the true end of the second millennium. Vincenzo found that more than a little disquieting.

As he crossed Pearl Street a man ran out of an alley, frantically waving his arms in the dusk.

"OhmyGod! OhmyGod! I think I saw her! I think it's *her!*"

Vincenzo's heart leapt. "Where?"

As the fellow pointed toward the black maw of the alley behind him, Vincenzo tried in vain to make out his features in the dusky light.

"Back there! She was just standing there, glowing."

"Show me," Vincenzo said. "Please show me!"

"Sure," the fellow said, waving him to follow. "Come on!"

An alarm clanged faintly in a corner of Vincenzo's brain, but his mind was too suffused with glorious anticipation to pay it proper heed.

The darkness of the alley swallowed him. He saw nothing. "Where?"

He was shoved roughly from behind and fell to his knees on the garbage-strewn pavement. Fear pounded through Vincenzo as he realized he was being mugged. He'd heard about the predators who'd begun stalking the defenseless Mary-hunters. The papers had dubbed them "Holy-rollers." He began shouting for help until a heavy boot slammed into his ribs and drove the wind out of him.

"Shuddup, asshole, an' gimme yer wallet!"

Vincenzo shouted again and was kicked again. The mugger grabbed his wrist and pulled off his watch.

"Where's yer wallet. Gimme yer fuckin' wallet or I cut ya!"

Vincenzo was reaching for his back pocket when he heard a groan above him. He heard scuffling feet, and then a heavy weight slammed onto the pavement next to him.

"Did he stab you? Do you need a hospital?"

Vincenzo recognized the accent—the little bearded fellow who'd been sitting on the bench with him moments ago.

"No. I'm only bruised. Could you help me up, perhaps?"

He raised his hand and felt another grasp it and pull him to his feet.

Immediately the man began to move off.

"Wait. I haven't thanked you. There must be something—"

"You can say nothing of this," the fellow said, stopping and turning. "That will be thanks enough."

"But people should know! You're a hero!"

"That man behind you will be dead before help arrives. I am a stranger in this country. I do not wish to be arrested."

"What did you do to him?"

"My knife did to him what his knife was going to do to you."

"But why?"

"I needed to."

Weak and trembling, Vincenzo leaned against a wall and silently watched the stranger hurry off. The parting words turned over in his mind. *I needed to.* Something about the way he'd said that . . .

Needed to what? Help somebody . . . or stab somebody?

He turned for one final look into the alley that might have been his grave and saw her.

She was only a few feet away, moving closer . . . *flowing* toward him . . . her faint glow a beacon in the black hole of the alley. Her robes were the same as in Cork, only now he was close enough to make out some of her features. The tears in his eyes blurred them but he thought he detected a hint of a smile as she looked at him.

"It's you!" he sobbed, overcome by an unplumbed longing within. "I've been searching for you. I knew I'd find you again!"

She flowed closer without slowing . . . closer . . .

Vincenzo backed up a step but she never slowed her approach. It was as if she didn't see him. When she was within inches he cried, "Stop!" but she continued her irresistible course, pressing against him—but he felt nothing. She had no substance. And then his vision was filled with light that blotted out the alley and the street and the city, light all around, light within him . . .

Within him . . .

The apparition had merged with him. Was he within her or was she within him?

He froze, he sizzled, dazzling spots flashed and swelled and danced before his eyes, he floated, he plummeted . . .

And then the light faded and the city night filled his eyes again. He whirled and saw the apparition directly behind him, flowing away.

She walked . . . right . . . through . . . me!

And then she began to fade. Within seconds Vincenzo was alone again. And then the wonder that filled him also began to fade as the pain began, searing bolts of agony lancing through his chest and abdomen, doubling him over, driving him to his knees.

IN THE PACIFIC

7° N, 150° W

The clouds and wind have organized into a pocket
of turbulence with sharply demarcated borders. The
pocket begins to drift eastward, drawing warm moist
air up from the ocean surface into its high, cool center
where the moisture condenses into droplets. Thunder
rumbles and lightning flashes as rain and wind whip
the churning ocean surface to a froth. The storm swells
as it accelerates its eastward course.

19

"Okay, Monsignor. Another deep breath, and hold this one."

Vincenzo Riccio filled his lungs while Dr. Karras's fingers probed his abdomen under the lower right edge of his rib cage. The young oncologist's normally tanned-looking skin was relatively pale today. The overhead fluorescents of the examining room reflected off the fine sheen of perspiration on his forehead.

"Damn!" he muttered as his fingers probed more deeply under Vincenzo's ribs.

"Something wrong?" Vincenzo said, exhaling at last.

"No. I mean, yes. I mean . . ."

Vincenzo sat up and pulled down his undershirt.

"I don't understand."

"Neither do I," Karras said, running a hand through his short black hair.

"Perhaps you'd better tell me the problem, Doctor. I think I deserve to know."

The examination had started out routinely enough, with Vincenzo arriving at the outpatient cancer clinic, reading in the waiting room until his name was called, and then being examined by Dr. Karras. But after examining him just as he had now, Karras had stepped over to the chart and pulled out yesterday's blood test results. After checking those for what seemed like an unduly long time and shuffling through the sheaf of previous reports, he examined Vincenzo's abdomen again, then sent him for a CT scan of the liver, with comparison to the previous study.

"Stat," he'd said into the phone. "*Double* stat."

So Vincenzo had allowed himself to be swallowed by the metal gullet of the scanner where his liver could be radiographically sliced and diced, and now he was back again on the examining table. He had an inkling as to the nature of Dr. Karras's discomfiture, but he dared not voice it . . . dared not even *think* it.

"The problem is—"

The intercom beeped. "Dr. Weiskopf is here."

"Weiskopf?" Karras said. "From radiology? What's—? Oh, shit. Excuse me." He all but leapt from the examining room door.

A few moments later he was back, trailing in his wake a tall, bearded man whom he introduced as Dr. Weiskopf. He looked about fifty and wore a yarmulke; a large manila X-ray envelope was tucked under his left arm.

"I've never met a walking miracle," Dr. Weiskopf said softly as they shook hands.

Vincenzo suddenly felt weak. "Miracle?"

"What else can you call it? I looked at your scan from today, then called up your initial scan from July, and I said to myself, Moshe, a trick this Karras kid is playing on you, trying to make a fool of you by asking you to compare the very sick liver of one man to the perfectly healthy liver of another. And then I spied an osteophyte—doctorese for a bone spur—on one of the vertebrae of the new scan; much to my shock, there was the very same spur on the old scan. So I had to come and see this man for myself."

Vincenzo looked from Weiskopf to Karras. "What . . . what's he saying?"

"He's saying your liver scan's normal, Monsignor."

"You mean the tumor's shrinking?"

"Shrinking?" Dr. Weiskopf said. "It's gone! *Pfffft*! Like it was never there. On your first scan your liver was, if you'll pardon the term, Swiss-cheesed with tumors—"

"Nodular," Dr. Karras added. "And half again its normal size."

"But now it's perfectly homogeneous. Not even a little fatty degeneration."

"And it's back to normal size," Dr. Karras said. "I can barely feel it anymore."

"Is that what you were doing to me?" Vincenzo said, feeling giddy and dizzy, wanting to laugh or cry or both, wanting to fall to his knees in prayer but struggling to maintain his composure. "For a while there I thought you were trying to feel my spine from the front."

Dr. Karras smiled weakly. "Last week your liver was big and nodular. Your liver enzymes were climbing. Now—"

"Maybe we're onto something with this new protocol," Dr. Weiskopf said.

Dr. Karras was shaking his head, staring at Vincenzo. "No. The protocol's a bust. We haven't seen significant tumor regression with anyone."

"Until now," Dr. Weiskopf said, tapping this X-ray envelope.

"Uh-uh," Dr. Karras said, still shaking his head and staring. "Even if it were the protocol, tumor regression would be gradual. A slow shrinking of the tumors, and even in a best-case scenario we'd be left with a battered and scarred but functioning liver. The Monsignor's CT shows a perfectly healthy liver. Almost as if he'd had a transplant."

"*I* can't explain it," Dr. Weiskopf said.

"Maybe you already did," Vincenzo said. "It's a miracle."

Vincenzo was regaining his inner composure now. He hadn't been totally unprepared for this. After the apparition had passed through him three nights ago, he'd been racked with horrific pain for a few moments, and then it had passed, leaving him weak and sweaty. He'd staggered back to his quarters at the mission where he fell into an exhausted sleep. But when he awakened early the next morning he'd felt better than he had in years. And each passing day brought renewed strength and vigor. A power had touched him outside that alley. He'd been changed inside. He'd wondered how, why. He'd prayed, but he'd dared not hope . . .

Until now.

A miracle . . .

The doctors' smiles were polite but condescending.

"A figure of speech, Monsignor," Dr. Weiskopf said.

Dr. Karras cleared his throat. "I'd like to admit you for a day or two, Monsignor. Do a full, head-to-toe workup to see if we can get a handle on this and—"

Vincenzo shook his head as he slipped off the examining table and reached for his cassock.

"I'm sorry, but I have no time for that."

"Monsignor, something extraordinary has happened here. If we can pin this down, who knows how many other people we can help?"

"You will find nothing useful in examining me," he said as he fastened his Roman collar. "Only confusion."

"You can't say that."

"I wish it were otherwise. But unfortunately what happened to me cannot be applied to your other cases. At least not in a hospital or clinic setting."

"Where then?"

"I do not know. But I'm going to try and find out."

Vincenzo was returning to the Lower East Side. Something was drawing him back.

"Y'soup's goin' cold, guy. Ain't y'gonna eat it?"

Emilio glanced to his right at the scrawny little man next to him—bright eyes crinkled within a wrinkled face framed by a mass of gray hair and beard matted with food and dirt; a gnarled finger with a nail the color of asphalt pointed to the bowl that cooled before him on the table.

"Do you want it?" Emilio said.

This was Emilio's third meal at the church-basement soup kitchen called Loaves and Fishes and so far he'd managed to get through each time without having to eat a thing.

"Well, if you ain't gonna be eatin' it, it'd sure be a sin to waste it."

Emilio switched bowls with the old man, trading his full one for an empty. He placed his slice of bread on the other man's plate as well.

"Ain'tcha hungry?" the old man said, bending over the

fresh bowl and adding his slurps to the chorus of guttural noises around them.

"No. Not really." He'd had a big breakfast in the East Village before walking over to St. Joseph's. "I'm not feeling well lately."

"Yeah?" the old man said. "Well, then, this is the place to be." He leaned closer and spoke out of the side of his mouth. "Miracles happen here."

"So I've heard," Emilio replied.

It was talk of miracles that had brought him to Loaves and Fishes.

Emilio had been in town a week and a half and hadn't uncovered anything. And he didn't expect to. A waste of time as far as he was concerned. But the opinion of Emilio Sanchez did not count in this matter. The *senador* wanted him here, sniffing about, turning over any rocks that the CDC might miss, and so here he was. The *senador* would get copies of the official CDC reports as they were filed. What he wanted from Emilio was the *un*official story, "the view from street level," as the *senador* called it.

To do that, Emilio had rented a room in one of the area's seedy residential hotels, stopped taking showers, and let his beard grow. He'd picked up some thrift-shop clothes and begun wandering the Lower East Side, posing as a local.

And it was as a local that he'd run into someone named Pilgrim who ranted on about this blind friend Preacher who'd begun to see at a place called Loaves and Fishes, and how all the men who'd been cured of AIDS used to come to Loaves and Fishes.

And so now Emilio came to Loaves and Fishes.

Not that he suspected to find anything even vaguely supernatural going on, but there was always the chance that the place might be frequented by someone pedaling a drug or a folk medicine that might have been responsible for the now-famous AIDS cures.

But there was nothing going on here. Just a crowd of hungry losers stuffing their faces with anything edible they could lay their hands on. No fights, which struck Emilio as unusual with this sort of group. Maybe they were just too busy eating. Nothing special about the staff, either. Mostly lonely old biddies filling up their empty days toiling in what they probably thought was service to mankind, plus a beautiful young nun who spent too much of her time in the kitchen.

And a young priest who seemed to be in charge. Emilio had been startled to recognize him as the same priest the *senador* had chewed up and spit out in front of the Waldorf last spring. He doubted the priest would recognize him, but just the same, Emilio kept his head down whenever he came around.

Disgusted, he decided to leave. Nothing here. No miracles of any kind, medical or otherwise. As he rose to his feet, he heard the priest say he was running back to the rectory for something, but instead of leaving through the front of the room, he used a door in the rear of the kitchen.

Emilio wove through the maze of long tables and hurried up the steps to the street. As he ambled along, blinking in the sun's glare and trying to look aimless, he glanced down the alley between the church and the rectory. He stopped. Hadn't he seen the priest go out a door in the kitchen? He'd assumed it led up to street level. But there was no corresponding door in the alley. Where had the priest gone if he hadn't returned to the rectory?

He looked up at the rectory and was startled momentarily to see the priest's blond head pass a window. Emilio smiled. An underground passage. How convenient. He supposed there were all sorts of passages between these old buildings.

He walked on, taking small satisfaction in having cleared up a mystery, no matter how inconsequential. Emilio didn't like mysteries.

Farther along he passed a man wearing a white lab coat and holding an open briefcase before him. The briefcase was lined with rows of three-ounce bottles.

"Hey, buddy!" the guy said. "You got the sickness?"

Emilio looked at him and the guy's eyes lit with sudden recognition. He backed up two steps.

"Oh, shit. Hey, sorry. Never mind."

Emilio walked on without acknowledging him.

How could he learn anything, or even make sense of anything in this carnival atmosphere? The entire area seemed to have gone mad. People were wandering about in droves at night carrying candles and chanting the Rosary and seeing the Virgin Mary everywhere. Hucksters were set up on every corner selling I ♥ MARY-HUNTING badges, OUR LADY OF THE LOWER EAST SIDE T-shirts, Virgin Mary statues, slivers of the True Cross, rosaries, and sundry other religious paraphernalia.

Quick-buck grifters and con artists had moved in too. Emilio had already had run-ins with a few of them, and the guy he'd just passed had been the first. He'd approached Emilio just as he'd started to today, asking him if he had "the sickness"—the local code for AIDS.

Curious, Emilio had said, "What if I do?"

With that the guy had launched into a spiel about his cure-all tonic, claiming his elixir, "Yes, the stuff right in these bottles you see before you here," was the stuff that had cured the AIDS cases everyone was talking about.

Emilio had listened awhile, then pushed him into a corner and knocked him around until he admitted that he hadn't even come to the city until he'd read about the cures.

Emilio had similar run-ins with a number of the snake-oil salesmen he'd come across and under pressure the stories were all the same: charlatans preying on the weak, the sick, and the desperate.

Not that Emilio cared one way or the other, he simply didn't want to bring one of their potions back to Paraiso and look like a fool in the eyes of the *senador*.

This whole trip seemed a fool's errand.

And yet . . .

There was a feeling in the air . . . and in Emilio himself . . . a twinge in his gut, a vague prickling at the back of his neck, a sense that these littered streets, these leaning, tattered buildings, hid a secret. Even the air felt heavy, pregnant with . . . what? Dread? Anticipation? A little of both, maybe?

Emilio shook it off. The *senador* had not sent him here for his *impressions* of the area; he wanted facts. And whatever it was that was raising his gooseflesh, Emilio doubted it would be of any use to the *senador* and Charlie.

But *something* was going on down here.

Vincenzo Riccio stood in the dusk on the sidewalk in front of St. Joseph's church. He did not stare up at its Gothic facade, but at the doorway that led under its granite front steps. People carrying candles were beginning to gather on those front steps. They carried rosaries and clustered around an elderly woman in a wheelchair who was preparing them for a prayer meeting tonight. Vincenzo paid them little heed.

He had wandered the Lower East Side all day, tracing a spiral path from the Con-Ed station by the FDR, following a feeling, an invisible glow that seemed to be centered in the front of his brain, pulling him. Where or why it was drawing him, he could not say, but he gave himself over to the feeling, allowed it to lead him in shrinking concentric circles to this spot.

And now he was here. The invisible glow, the intangible warmth, the only warm spot in the city lay directly before him, somewhere within this church.

In the course of the weeks he had spent down here searching for the vision, Vincenzo had passed St. Joseph's numerous times. He had crossed himself as he'd come even with its sanctuary, and even had stopped in once to say a prayer. But he had not been struck by anything especially important about the place. A stately old church that, like its neighborhood, had seen better days.

Now it seemed like . . . home.

But *what* precisely was it that he had followed here? That the strange sensation was connected to the apparition that had touched him with ecstasy and cleansed him of the malignancy that had been devouring him he had no doubt. Neither did he doubt that the apparition was a visitation of the Blessed Virgin. A *true* visitation. Not a hallucination, not a wish fulfillment, not a publicity stunt. He had seen, he had been touched, he had been healed. This was the real thing. His wish had been granted: He had witnessed a miracle before his death, but as a result of that miracle, his death was no longer imminent. He had been granted extra time. And he'd used some of that extra time to find this place.

Why? What was so special about this St. Joseph's church? What significance could it have for the Virgin Mary? It was built on land that had been an undeveloped marsh until a millennium and a half after the birth of Christianity. Vincenzo did not know of any sacred relics housed here.

And yet . . .

Something was here. The same warm glow that had suffused his entire being a few nights ago seemed to emanate from this building. Not from where he would have expected—from the sanctuary of the church itself—but from its lower level. From the basement which appeared to be some sort of soup kitchen.

What could be here? The remains of some American saint unrecognized by the Church? Was that the reason behind the Blessed Mother's visitations?

Inside . . . it's inside.

Vincenzo was drawn forward. Why shouldn't he go in? After all, he was wearing his cassock and collar. Who would stop a priest from entering a church? Especially a monsignor on a mission from the Holy See. Yes. Hadn't the Vatican itself asked him to investigate the reports of visitations in this parish? That was precisely what he was doing.

As he descended the short flight of stone steps he passed under a hand-painted sign that read LOAVES AND FISHES; he pushed through a battered door and entered a broad room lined with long tables and folding chairs. Toward the rear, a serving counter. And beyond that, a kitchen.

Farther inside . . .

Feeling as if he were in a dream, he skirted the tables and moved toward the kitchen. A growing excitement quivered in his chest. He heard voices, running water, and clinking crockery from the kitchen. He rounded the corner and came upon three women of varying shapes, sizes, and ages busily scrubbing pots, plates, and utensils. The big, red-cheeked one glanced up and saw him.

"Sorry, we're closed until—oh, sorry, Father. I thought you were one of the guests. Are you looking for Father Dan?"

Vincenzo had no idea who Father Dan was.

"Is he the pastor?"

"No. Father Brenner is the pastor. Father Dan is the associate pastor. He went back to the rectory about half an hour ago."

Down . . . it's beneath your feet.

"Is there a basement here?"

"This is the basement, Father," another woman said.

"But there's a furnace room below here," said the thinnest and oldest of the three.

Vincenzo saw a door in the rear corner and moved toward it.

"Not that one," said the old woman. "That leads to the rectory. There's another door on the far side of the refrigerator there."

Vincenzo changed direction, brushing past them, unable to fight the growing urgency within him.

So close . . . so close now.

He pulled the door open. A sweet odor wafted up from the darkness below.

Flowers.

As his eyes adjusted, Vincenzo made out a faint glow from the bottom of the rutted stone steps. He started down, dimly aware of the women's voices behind him speaking of Father Dan and something about a Sister Carrie. Whether they were speaking to him or to each other he neither knew nor cared. He was close now . . . so close.

At the bottom he followed the light to the left and came upon a broad empty space with a single naked bulb glowing from the ceiling.

No . . . this can't be it . . . there's got to be more here than an empty basement.

Off to his left . . . a voice, humming. He followed the sound around a corner and found the door to a smaller room standing open. As he stepped inside, his surroundings became more dreamlike.

I'm here . . . this is the place . . . I've come home . . .

Candlelight flickered off the walls and low ceiling of a room that seemed alive with sweet-smelling blossoms. He saw a woman there, her back was to him and she was humming as she straightened the folds of the robes draped around some sort of statue or sculpture recumbent on—

And then Vincenzo saw the glow. He recognized that glow, *knew* that glow. The same soft, pale luminescence had enveloped the apparition. He could not be mistaken. Hadn't it touched him, been *one* with him for a single glorious instant? How could he forget it? He realized then that this was no statue or sculpture before him. This was a human body laid out on a makeshift bier.

But whose body?

Suddenly Vincenzo knew, and the realization was like a physical blow, staggering him, numbing him, battering his consciousness until it threatened to tear loose from its moorings and . . . simply . . . drift.

This was no holy relic, no unsung, uncanonized saint. This was *her*!

He knew it and yet a part of him stubbornly refused to accept it. Impossible! Tradition held that she was assumed body and soul into heaven. And even if tradition were wrong, even if her body had remained preserved for two thousand years, she would not—*could* not—be here in this church basement in Lower Manhattan. It defied all reason, all belief, all common sense.

Can it be her? Can it truly be her?

As he lurched forward he heard a voice speaking. His own. In his native tongue.

"Puo essere lei? Puo essere veramente lei?"

Carrie cried out in shock and fear at the sound of the strange voice behind her. She turned and saw a man in black silhouetted in the light from the door, staggering toward her. Reflexively she began to dodge aside, but stopped and forced herself to stand firm. Anyone trying to get to the Virgin would have to go through her first.

Then she saw his collar. A priest.

"Father?"

He didn't seem to hear. He continued forward, trembling hands folded before him as if in prayer, eyes fixed on the Virgin as his expression twisted through a strange mixture of confusion, pain, and ecstasy.

"*Puo essere lei?*"

She didn't understand the priest's words, but the devotion in his eyes caused her insides to coil with alarm.

He knows! she thought. Somehow he *knows*!

Sensing he meant no harm, Carrie eased aside and let him approach. Her mind raced as she watched him gaze down at the Virgin. No . . . obviously he meant no harm, but his mere presence was a catastrophe. No matter what his intentions, he was going to ruin everything.

"Who are you?" she said.

He didn't seem to hear, only continued to stare down at the Virgin.

"Who are you, Father?" she repeated and this time touched his arm.

He started and half turned toward her, tearing his eyes away from the Virgin at the last possible second. Carrie hadn't realized how old and thin he looked until now.

"It's her, isn't it," he said in a hoarse, accented English, and Carrie's heart sank as she searched but found no hint of a question in his tone. "It's truly her!"

"Who do you mean, Father?" she said, hoping against hope that he'd give the wrong answer.

But instead of answering in words, he knelt before the Virgin, made the sign of the cross, and bowed his head.

That was more than enough answer for Carrie. She began to shake.

I'm going to lose her, she thought. They're going to take her away from me!

At that moment she heard the scuff of hurried footsteps out in the old furnace room, then Dan dashed in. He skidded to a halt when he saw the figure in black kneeling before the bier, then stared at Carrie, alarmed, confused, breathing hard.

"Hilda called me over . . . said there was a strange priest . . ." He glanced at the newcomer. "Who . . . how?"

Carrie shook her head. "I don't know."

Dan stood in the center of the room, looking indecisive for a moment, then he stepped forward and laid a hand on the other priest's shoulder.

"I'm Father Daniel Fitzpatrick, Father, associate pastor here, and I'm afraid I'll have to ask you to leave."

The older man turned his head to the side, then rose stiffly to his feet. He stared at the Virgin a moment longer, then turned toward Carrie and Dan and drew himself to his full height.

"I am Monsignor Vincenzo Riccio. From Rome. From the Vatican."

Carrie stifled a groan as she heard Dan mutter, "Oh, God. You're the priest from the pub!"

"You must explain this," Msr. Riccio said, gesturing toward the Virgin. "How . . . how is this possible?"

"How is what possible?" Dan said.

"Please," the older priest said. "There is no point in trying to fool me. I was touched by her, *healed* by her. I know this is the Blessed Mother. Do you understand? I do not believe it, think it, or feel it, I *know* it. What I do not know is why she is hidden away in this dingy cellar, and how she came to be here. Will you please explain that to me, Father Fitzpatrick."

Dan held the monsignor's stare for a moment, then turned to Carrie and introduced her as Sister Carolyn Ferris.

"Carrie," he said. "This is your show. What do you want to do? Whatever you decide, I'm with you all the way."

Carrie felt as if she were perched on the edge of a precipice . . . during an earthquake. Her mind was numb with the shock of being discovered. She could see no sense in lying. The monsignor already knew the core truth. Why not tell him the details.

And suddenly hope was alive within her.

Yes! The details. Maybe if he knew how the Virgin had

been hidden away in a cave much like this subcellar room, he'd realize that she had to remain hidden . . . right here.

"It began with a scroll Father Fitzpatrick received as a gift . . ."

"I see," Vincenzo said softly as Sister Carolyn finished her story, closing with the details of the cures and miracles at the soup kitchen one floor above.

He had been too fascinated to interrupt her long monologue more than once or twice for clarifications. He had studied her expression for some hint of insincerity, but had found none, at least none that he could detect in the candlelight. And as she spoke he came to understand something about this beautiful young woman. She was deeply devoted to the Virgin. No hint of personal gain or notoriety had crossed her mind in bringing the Virgin here to her church. It had seemed like the right thing to do, the *only* thing to do, and so she had done it. She was one of the good ones. He sensed a hard knot of darkness deep within her, an old festering wound that would not heal, but otherwise she was all love and generosity. Had she always been like this, or was it the result of prolonged proximity to . . . her?

He turned to stare again at the Virgin.

"An incredible story," he said into the silence.

If I were someone else, he thought, or even if I had happened to stumble upon this little room only last week, before my encounter with the Blessed Mother, I would have said they are both mad. Good-hearted, sincere, and well intentioned, to be sure, but quite utterly mad. But I am not someone else, and I believe every incredible word.

"Then you can see, can't you," Sister Carolyn said, and Vincenzo sensed that she was praying he could and would see, "that she has to remain here? Remain a secret?"

"A secret?" Vincenzo said. "Oh, no. That is the last thing this discovery should be. This is the Mother of God, Sister. She should have a cathedral of gold, she should be exalted as an ideal, a paradigm for a life of faith and purity."

"But, Monsignor, that isn't what the Apostles intended when they brought her to the Resting Place in the desert."

"Who are we to say what the Apostles intended? And besides, these are different, difficult times. True faith, generous and loving, seems to be on the wane, replaced by wild-eyed fundamentalist factions that call themselves Christian, and other violent, non-Christian sects. Think what the physical presence of the Mother of God could mean to the Church, to Christianity, to all of humanity? This could usher in a whole new age of faith."

A new age . . .

The words resonated through his very being as he remembered his conversation with the strange bearded man who saved his life a few nights ago . . .

My life was saved twice that night.

. . . of how the Second Coming might be linked to the end of the second millennium. And of how the second millennium would be ending this year, was perhaps ending even as he stood here speaking to these two good people.

Dear Jesus, it all fit, didn't it. It all made sense now. The discovery of the scroll, the journey of these two people to the Holy Land, finding the remains of the Blessed Virgin, removing her from the desert, the Vatican sending him to Ireland and then New York, the apparitions, his cure, his arrival in the subcellar of this humble old church—these weren't random events. Three times his path and the Virgin's had crossed: in Cork City, on the streets outside, and now in this tiny room. There was a pattern here, a purpose, a plan.

And now Vincenzo saw the outcome of that plan.

The Virgin was to be revealed to the world. And when she was brought to the Vatican, when she joined the Holy Father in Rome, it would herald a new age. Perhaps it would signal the Second Coming.

Philosophers and academics had been speaking of the end of history for years already. What will they say now?

The staggering immensity of the final sequence of events that might be set into motion numbed him for a moment.

The end of history . . . *all* history.

But he couldn't tell these two what he knew. At least not now. He could, however, try to reassure them.

"There is a plan at work," he said. "And we are all playing our parts. You've played your parts, and now I must play mine. And the Vatican must play its own part."

"But what if the Vatican *doesn't* play its part?" she cried. "What if, instead of showing her to the world, they hide her away in one of the Church's deepest vaults where they'll test her and probe her and argue endlessly whether to reveal her or keep her hidden from the world? Don't say it couldn't happen. This may not look like much, but here at least she has some contact with the world. People are benefiting from her presence. Leave her here."

"I can't make that decision."

"Once she gets to Rome, she may disappear forever, as if we never found her."

"That is absurd," Vincenzo said.

But within he wondered if she might not be right. He was more familiar than she with the internecine ways of the Holy See, and realized it was all too possible that the Virgin might be lost in the labyrinth of Vatican politics.

"*Please!*" she cried.

He was wounded by the tears in her eyes. How could he separate her from the Virgin? That seemed almost . . . sinful.

Vincenzo shook himself. His duty was clear.

"I'm sorry," he said, "but I really have no choice. I must report this to Rome at once."

Sister Carolyn began to sob. The sound tore at his heart. He had to leave. Now. Before he changed his mind.

"I'll be back as soon as I have the Vatican's decision."

"Don't be surprised if you find an empty room," Father Fitzpatrick said.

Vincenzo swung toward him. "Please do not do anything so foolish as to move her or try to hide her. I found her here. I can find her anywhere."

He hurried out of the room leaving behind the sobbing nun and the stricken, silent priest.

This is the way it has to be, he told himself. This is the best way, the only way.

Then why did he feel like such a villain?

He would make it up to Sister Carolyn. He would see to it that she was not separated from her beloved Blessed Mother. He would convince the Holy See that Sister Carolyn Ferris must accompany the Virgin to Rome to tell her story.

But first he had to convince the Holy See that the body in the subcellar of this church was indeed the Blessed Virgin. He could do that. They'd believe him. He'd debunked so many reputed visitations in the past that they'd listen when he told them he'd found the real thing. More than a visitation—the greatest find since the dawn of the Christian Era.

And then it would begin.

The Second Coming . . . the end of history . . .

Carrie clenched her teeth and tried to rein in her emotions. What was wrong with her? She'd never cried easily before. Now she couldn't seem to help herself.

She'd just about regain control when Dan stepped up beside her and gently encircled her in his arms. His touch, and the depth of love and warmth in the simple gesture toppled her defenses. She sagged against him and broke down again.

"It'll be all right, Carrie," he said softly. "We'll work something out."

But *what* could they work out? Her worst nightmare had come true.

She straightened and faced him. "They're going to take her, Dan. They're going to take her and seal her away where no one will ever see her again, where no one but a privileged few will even know she exists."

"You don't know that."

"I *do* know that." Anger was beginning to elbow aside the fear and desperate sorrow. "And I know we didn't go to all that trouble to find her and bring her here just so she could be locked up in a Vatican vault!"

"But what the monsignor said about a 'plan' makes sense. Don't you feel it? Don't you sense a hand moving the pieces around a chessboard? We're a couple of the pawns, Carrie. So's the monsignor."

"Maybe," she said, although she knew exactly what Dan was talking about. She'd felt it too. "And maybe the 'plan' isn't meant to play out the way the monsignor sees it. We can't let the Vatican have her."

"How are we going to stop it? You heard what he said about being able to find her if we try to hide her. I don't know how or why, but I believe him."

Carrie believed him too. Maybe it was the cure he claimed the Virgin had performed, maybe it was part of the "plan." Whatever it was, the monsignor seemed to have been sensitized to the Virgin. He was like a smart bomb, targeted on Carrie's dreams.

But there had to be a way to stop him.

And suddenly she knew how.

"All right . . ." she said slowly. "If we can't hide her from the monsignor, we won't hide her at all . . . from anyone."

"I don't—"

"You will."

Excitement and dread blossomed within her as she considered the repercussions of what she was about to do.

She drew Dan to the Virgin's side.

"Will you carry her upstairs for me?"

"Upstairs? Into the kitchen?"

"No. Farther up. Into the church."

Dan stood in the nave of St. Joe's with the Virgin's stiff remains in his arms and tried to catch his breath. The church was locked up tight for the night, silent but for the muffled voices of the latest contingent of Mary-hunters chanting their nightly Rosary outside on the front steps. He wasn't puffing from the exertion of carrying her up from the subcellar—the Virgin was as light as ever—but from anxiety.

What was Carrie up to? She wouldn't explain. Was she afraid he'd balk if she told him? No. He'd do almost anything to keep her from crying again. He'd never heard her cry before. It was a sound he never wanted to hear again.

"Now what?" he said. "Where do I put her?"

She stood in the church's center aisle, turning in a slow circle, as if looking for something. Suddenly she stopped her turn.

"There," she said, pointing to the space past the chancel rail.

"In the sanctuary? There's no place—"

"On the altar."

Dan felt his knees wobble. "No, Carrie. That wouldn't be right."

She turned and faced him, her expression fierce. "Can you think of anyone with more of a right to be up there?"

Dan couldn't.

"All right. But I don't like this."

He passed her and walked down the center aisle, genu-flected, then stepped over the chancel rail and approached the altar, a huge block of Carerra marble. It stood free in the center of the sanctuary so the celebrating priest could say Mass facing his congregation.

This was strange, really strange. What was this going to solve or prove? Carrie didn't expect the Virgin to come alive or anything crazy like that, did she?

The thought rattled Dan as he stood before the altar. His life had been so full of strange occurrences lately that nothing would surprise him.

As he set the Virgin gently upon the gleaming marble surface of the altar, he heard a metallic clank at the far end of the church. He turned in time to see Carrie pushing open the front doors.

"She's here!" he heard her cry to the Mary-hunters gathered outside. "You don't need to look any further. The Blessed Mother is here! Come in! See her! She's waiting for you!"

"Oh, no!" Dan said softly as he saw the Mary-hunters edge through the doors. "Oh, God, Carrie. What are you *doing?*"

They crowded forward, candles in hand, hesitant at first, the curious at the rear pushing those ahead. They were older,

mostly female, with a few younger men and women salted
among them. Plainly dressed for the most part, but they had
an eagerness in common. He saw it in their eyes. They were
searching for something but not quite sure just what.

And when they saw the body stretched out on the altar
they hesitated, but only for a moment, only for a heartbeat.
Then they were moving forward again, surging ahead like
some giant, single-celled organism, filling the center aisle
and splashing against the chancel rail.

Dan listened to the talk within the Mary-hunter amoeba.

"Is it her?" . . . "Do you think that's really her?" . . .
"That's not what I expected her to look like" . . . "Aren't
you forgetting the Assumption? Can't be her" . . . "Right.
She was assumed into heaven, body and soul" . . . "Besides,
she looks too old, all dried up . . ."

And then the crowd was parting like the Red Sea to make
way for a pinch-faced old woman in a wheelchair. She wore
a fur cap despite the heat and was propelled from behind by
a burly orderly in whites.

"Let me through," the woman said, swinging her cane
before her to clear the way. "I'll tell you if it's her or not, but
I can't see from back here."

Her orderly wheeled her up to the brass gates of the
chancel rail and she stared across at the altar.

Over and over Dan hear voices murmur, "What do you
think, Martha?" and "Martha will know," and "What does
she say?"

Apparently this Martha was an authority of some sort
among the Mary-hunters.

"I . . ." she began, then stopped. "This shouldn't be
but . . . Get me closer, Gregory."

Her dutiful orderly unlatched the chancel gates and
pushed them open. Dan didn't want them in the sanctuary
and was stepping forward to stop him when he felt a
restraining hand on his arm.

Carrie was beside him.

"Wait," she said. "Let her look."

Gregory wheeled old Martha through the gates and
parked her next to the altar where she was almost eye level

with the Virgin. She peered closely through her bifocals, then, tentatively, she reached out and brushed the Virgin's cheek with her fingertip.

"Oh!" she cried and threw herself back in her chair as if she'd received a jolt of electricity.

Gregory was standing beside her, hands clasped behind his back, unprepared for the sudden convulsive movement. Martha and her chair went over backward.

For a moment there was mass confusion in St. Joseph's with people shouting and crying out in alarm, and then utter silence as Gregory righted the chair, turned to lift Martha back into it, and froze.

Martha was standing beside him.

Dan couldn't tell who was more surprised—Gregory or Martha.

Martha looked down at her newly functioning legs and screamed. Pandemonium reigned then as the rest of the Mary-hunters added their own screams to hers, surging forward, surrounding the joyfully weeping Martha and the altar with its precious burden.

When a modicum of control was finally restored, the Mary-hunters knelt as one and began to recite the Rosary.

Their hunt was over.

Dan felt Carrie's grip tighten on his arm. He turned and saw her tight grin, the fierce gleam in her eyes.

"Let the Vatican try to keep her a secret *now!*"

MIRACLES IN MANHATTAN

"We've had many healings," Martha Harrington announced to reporters from the front steps of St. Joseph's church on the Lower East Side yesterday.

Mrs. Harrington should know. Three days ago she was wheelchair bound, barely able to stand without the aid of two canes, and even then for only a minute or so. Now she breezes up and down the steps of St. Joseph's like a teenager. She is reportedly the first miracle cure associated with the mummified body on display within the church.

The body, which the faithful proclaim to be the earthly remains of the Virgin Mary, appeared on the altar of St. Joseph's three nights ago during a prayer vigil on the church steps. Since then it has become an object of worldwide devotion and the center of a storm of ecclesiastical controversy. So far, the Archdiocese of New York has had no comment on the healings other than to say that the phenomena are under investigation.

"Not everyone is healed," Mrs. Harrington said. "We can't explain why some are healed and others are not. It would be presumptuous of me to try. 'Many are called but few are chosen,' as the saying goes."

Obviously, Martha Harrington sees herself as one of the chosen.

THE NEW YORK TIMES

IN THE PACIFIC

11° N, 140° W

Now a supercell, the storm increases the whirling velocity of its central winds, growing wider, stretching into the upper atmosphere as it angles northeastward. Its spinning core organizes into a funnel cloud that dips down . . . down . . . down until it brushes the churning surface of the ocean. The funnel latches onto the sea like a celestial leech, whipping the water to a white froth as it draws up a thin stream into its 200-mile-an-hour vortex.

20

Customs Inspector Dov Sidel sat in his office, sipping tea and skimming this morning's *Ha'aretz*. A low-volume day at the port so he was taking his full break. He glanced at an article about inexplicable cures in a New York City church attributed to what was supposedly the remains of the Virgin Mary. After reading half of the first paragraph, he turned the page.

Two heartbeats later he flipped the page back.

A photo was connected to the article, a grainy black-and-white close-up of the face of the miraculous relic in Manhattan. Something familiar about that face . . .

And then he recognized it! The sculpture he'd so admired when it had been shipped through Haifa this summer. When had that been? July? He'd jotted down the name of the Tel Aviv gallery that had shipped it, and on his next trip to the city he'd stopped by the Kaplan Gallery in the hope of seeing more works by the same artist. The owner had told him the Old Woman piece was a one of a kind that he'd bought at auction. He'd had no idea who the sculptor was.

And now Sidel knew why. There *was* no sculptor.

No wonder the owner had seemed so brusque and unhelpful. He'd smuggled out an archeological artifact as a contemporary work of art.

Inspector Sidel dropped the paper, picked up his phone, and dialed his superior at the central Customs Office.

JERUSALEM:
THE LADY IS OURS!

JERUSALEM (AP) The Is-
raeli government has an-
nounced that the mummified
woman on display in St. Joseph's church in Lower Manhattan, currently the object of
hysterical devotion by throngs
of Catholics and Christians of
all denominations, belongs to
them. Spokesman Yishtak
Levin claims his government
has "indisputable evidence
that the remains were
smuggled out of Israel on July
22 of this year." Stating that
"the remains are a historic
national relic and the rightful
property of the Israeli people,"
he demanded its immediate
return.

THE NEW YORK POST

Manhattan

Kesev stood on the front stoop of a crumbling brown-
stone and watched the roiling mass of people that filled the
street in front of the church.

He seemed to be viewing the scene from deep within a
long black tunnel. He had known despair and hopelessness
before, but never like this. Of all the possible outcomes, this
had been his worst-case scenario.

His only hope was the Israeli government's claim to the
Mother. If its demand for her return was honored, he had a
chance. A slim chance, to be sure, but once she was again on

Israeli soil, she was in his domain. As a Shin Bet officer he would be standing by at all times, waiting to leap upon any opportunity to spirit her away.

Certainly he would find no such opportunity here. There was no way in or out of the street, let alone the church where the Mother was on display.

The vulgarity of it drove Kesev into a near frenzy of grief and guilt and rage. He fought the urge to turn and ram his fist through the already cracked glass in the door behind him, then rake his wrist across the razor shards.

But what would that do? What would that prove? It would only draw unwanted attention to him. And the wounds . . . they'd bleed a little, then they would heal up.

And if anyone saw it happen they'd call it another of the Lower East Side miracles. The door might even become a shrine.

He looked over the multitude again, all pressing forward, hoping today would be the day they could get into the church. Some of them had been here for days. They stretched the entire length of the street and into the intersections at both ends. Traffic was snarled throughout the area.

Madness, that was what it was . . .

. . . sheer madness.

Emilio shook his head in disgust as he squeezed between the bumpers of the overheating cars gridlocked on Avenue C. He had always believed the world was full of fools, but this display of gullibility amazed even him.

He checked his watch. Noon. Time for the first of his thrice-daily calls to Paraiso. He found a booth with a functioning phone and leaned close as he tapped in the secure line and calling-card numbers, shielding the buttons from prying eyes. The theft of calling-card numbers had been elevated to an art in this city.

"Yes, Emilio," said the *senador*'s voice as he picked up the line. "I'm glad you're a punctual man. I've been anxiously awaiting your call."

This was not the *senador*'s usual opening. Immediately Emilio was on alert.

"Yes, sir?"

"I know you've been following this thing at St. Joseph's church. Do you still think it's nothing but mass hysteria?"

"All I see around the church are masses of hysterical people, so . . . yes. I do."

"All right, it *is* mass hysteria, but I'm beginning to think it might be something more."

Emilio leaned back and rolled his eyes. *Here we go.* But he kept his voice neutral.

"Really?"

"Yes. I've been in touch with some of my contacts in Manhattan, and the unofficial word—this is being kept from the press for the time being—is that a number of the healings in that little church are genuine. We're not talking psychosomatic reversals here, where someone imagines himself a cripple and can't walk until some phony-baloney healer—and believe me, I saw plenty of those while I was looking for a cure for Olivia—lays hands on him and tells him to walk. They've got bona-fide cases of far-gone osteoarthritis of the hip who now have normal X rays. And Emilio . . ." The *senador* paused here. "Some of those healed have been documented cases of AIDS."

"Do you want me to bring Charlie here?" Emilio said. "To the church? I'll get him inside for you—one way or another." He imagined ramming a truck through the packed throng of Mary-hunters and driving it up the front steps of the church.

"No. He's too weak to travel. He might not survive the trip. And even if he did . . ." The *senador*'s voice trailed off.

Emilio knew what he was thinking: St. Joseph's was ringed with photographers from newspapers all over the world. If someone recognized a sick and wasted Charles Crenshaw in the throng, the tabloids would have a field day.

"Whatever it is you want, *senador*, you simply have to ask and Emilio will see that it is done."

"Thank you, Emilio. I knew I could count on you. But

what I'm about to ask will not be easy. It will be the most difficult task I've ever set for you, and most likely ever will."

Emilio didn't like the sound of this. He waited, holding his breath. What could the *senador* possibly—?

"I want you to bring that relic, or mummy, or whatever it is, here, to Paraiso."

Emilio froze. For a moment he couldn't speak. Then, "*Senador*, did you say you want me to bring it to Paraiso?"

"You can't fail me on this, Emilio. It may be Charlie's only hope."

"You want me to *steal* it? Right out of that church?"

"Not steal—*borrow*. I don't want to own it, I simply wish to make use of it for a few hours, then you can return it."

The Manhattan madness must be highly contagious. The *senador* had caught it all the way out in California.

"Sir . . . how can I steal it when I can't even get close to it?"

"Yes. That is the major problem. I'm working on this end to make that easier for you. But you must be ready to move at a moment's notice."

Emilio's mind raced. The *senador* was asking the impossible, yet he seemed to take it for granted that Emilio could pull it off. Normally Emilio would be buoyed by such absolute confidence, but not this time. He admitted limits to his abilities, even if the *senador* did not.

"I'll . . . I'll need help."

"Decker and Molinari will be on their way on the jet. We'll hangar it at LaGuardia so it will be at your disposal when you secure this relic. You've got the credit card—charge anything you need. And if you require cash, I can wire that within minutes. Spare no expense, Emilio. This is more important to me than anything else in the world. Remember that."

"Yes, *Senador*," Emilio said.

"*Madre!*" he muttered as he hung up. How in the world was he ever going to pull this one off?

He shook himself. Why worry about it? As long as this

thing in the church remained surrounded by a crush of people twenty-four hours a day, there was no possible way the *senador* could expect him or anyone else to steal it.

VATICAN: THE LADY IS OURS!

ROME (AP) The Vatican released a statement today claiming the so-called Manhattan Madonna as property of the Catholic Church.

"The object was discovered on Church property and therefore must be considered Church property unless and until other ownership can be established," contended Cardinal Pasanante, spokesman for the Vatican.

"Too much publicity attends this object already," the statement reads. "It has become the focus of devotion of hysterical proportions. This is of great concern to the Holy Father. The Church intends to investigate the many claims of miracles associated with the object, and to substantiate the object's authenticity, if possible."

When questioned about Israel's prior claim on the Madonna, Cardinal Pasanante replied, "We are disputing that." When asked what the Church would do if the object should be proven to be the remains of the Virgin Mary and if Israel's claim to ownership is upheld, the enigmatic cardinal replied, "There are too many *if*'s in that question."

THE NEW YORK POST

IN THE PACIFIC

15° N, 136° W

Quantas flight 902 out of Sydney encounters a massive storm along its route to Los Angeles. Faced with a raging front of swirling black clouds, the pilot pushes the L-1011 to another 5,000 feet in altitude and angrily radios back to Sydney. He was told there was no weather on this flight path and here he is facing a monster.

The reply comes that radar shows no sign of the slightest storm activity at flight 902's location.

The pilot tells Sydney to get its radar fixed because the mother of all supercells is moving northeast along his course.

21

Manhattan

Carrie turned away from the steaming stove and wiped the perspiration from her face. Hot down here. Already fall, but September was rarely a cool month in New York.

She saw Dan sitting in the corner staring at the floor.

"Why so glum, Father Dan?" she said.

He looked up at her. The usual sparkle was gone from his eyes, replaced by a haunted look.

"I don't know," he said, sighing as he leaned back in the chair. "Don't you get the feeling that everything's spinning out of control?"

"No," she said, and meant it. "Just because we can't see where events are leading doesn't mean they're out of control. We may not be in the driver's seat, but that doesn't mean we're on a runaway bus."

"Is *anybody* in the driver's seat?"

"Always."

"I'll tell you something," he said, jerking his thumb toward the ceiling. "No one's in charge up there in St. Joe's. It's chaos."

"Confused, maybe, but it's not anarchy."

"Talk to Father Brenner about that, why don't you. He's got a slightly different take on the situation."

They'd both received a dressing down for opening the church to the Mary-hunters. They'd expected that. Father Brenner had lost control of his church—he couldn't close it at night, couldn't say Mass for his regular parishioners, couldn't get on with the day-to-day business of the parish. Every square inch of St. Joseph's, from the rear of the sanctuary to the vestibule, down the front steps and into the street, was occupied by a restless, weary mass of humanity in every imaginable state of dress and health.

Father Brenner placed the blame on Dan and Carrie.

Carrie's order had restricted her to the convent until proper disciplinary action could be taken. Carrie refused to submit to what she saw as house arrest and, much to the dismay of Mother Superior, went about her usual duties at Loaves and Fishes. She'd broken the vow of obedience so many times already she couldn't see what difference it made if she kept on breaking it. Besides, she'd made a vow to the Virgin to protect her and always stay near—that vow superseded all others.

"Father Brenner should be honored this is happening in his church. So should you. This is the most wonderful thing that's ever happened to any of us. Or ever will."

Dan shook his head slowly and smiled. "I wish I could look at everything like you do. I wish I could work a room like you do."

"What do you mean?"

"I mean I wish I could get people to respond to me like you do. You move through those people upstairs like an angel. They're hot, tired, sick, irritable, and hurting. Yet you squeeze by, say a few words as you pass, and suddenly they love you."

Carrie felt her cheeks reddening. "Come on . . ."

"I'm serious. I watch you, Carrie. And believe me, you leave a sea of happiness in your wake. Sounds corny, I know, but I see the smiles that follow you. I see the love in their eyes, and they don't even know you. You have that effect on people."

Carrie hesitated, trying to frame a reply, and then the phone rang. Dan picked it up.

"Hello? . . . Hi, Brad. Fine. Yeah, she's right here. Hang on."

He passed the phone over to Carrie, then waved as he took the tunnel back to the rectory.

"Hi, Brad," Carrie said. "What's up?"

"It's Dad."

Carrie groaned. "Now what?"

"He could be on his way out."

I've heard that before. "What is it this time?"

"They were just getting ready to send him back to the nursing home when he had another heart attack. A bad one. They've moved him into the coronary care unit."

Carrie said nothing, felt nothing.

"He's asking for you," Brad said.

"What else is new?"

"The doctors say he's not going to make it this time. He's on a respirator, Car. He looks like hell . . ."

That's where he's going.

". . . and I just wish, before he dies, you could find some way to forgive—"

"How can I forgive what he did to me?" she said in a fierce whisper. "*How?*"

"God forgave—"

"I'm not God!"

"At least give him a chance to say he's sorry."

"Nothing he can say—"

Brad's voice rose. "You're better than he is, Carrie! Act like it!"

And then he hung up.

Carrie stared at the receiver, stunned. Brad had never yelled at her before. Never lost his temper.

She replaced the receiver on the cradle and shoved her hands into her pockets.

Poor Brad. Always the peacemaker—first between that man and Mom, now between that man and her. But how could he think she could ever . . .

Carrie's right hand pressed against the two little Ziploc bags in her pocket. The powdered nail clippings and the ground-up hair . . .

The stuff of miracles.

She decided to make a pilgrimage to the hospital.

• • •

Carrie stood outside the door to C.C.U. and trembled like one of her homeless guests in the throes of DTs.

How bad could this be?

She didn't know. And that was what terrified her. Fourteen years since she'd last seen that man. Half her life. Sixteen years since he'd started sneaking into her bedroom at night . . .

And Brad . . . how much had her older brother known?

He'd never said. They'd never discussed it, never laid it out on the table between them and stared at it. He always referred to it as "the trouble" between her and that man. Brad could have been discussing wrecking the family car or getting sick drunk. "The trouble" . . .

Some trouble.

At first, as a child, Carrie had been afraid Brad would hate her if he found out, hate her as much as she hated herself. And then she'd thought, he *has* to know. How can he *not* know?

And if he knew, why didn't he say something? Why didn't he help her? Why didn't he do something to stop that man?

Carrie was pretty sure Brad had spent the years since she ran away asking himself those same questions. She wondered what answers he came up with. She wondered if he'd ever really faced what that man he called Dad had done to his younger sister. Probably hadn't. Probably had it hidden in some dark corner of his mind, buried under a pile of other childhood and teenage memories where he couldn't see it.

But he could smell it. Carrie knew the stink of those two hideous years had affected the rest of Brad's life. Incessant work . . . a life so filled with deadlines and meetings and shuttling between coasts that there was no room for old memories to surface . . . a life alone, without a wife or even a steady live-in, because a lasting relationship might lead to children and God knows what he might do if he ever fathered a little girl. . . .

Carrie half turned away from the CCU door, ready to

leave, then turned back as Brad's final words echoed through her brain.

You're better than he is, Carrie. Act like it!

She set her jaw, numbed her feelings, and forced herself to push through into the CCU.

White . . . white walls, white curtains between the white-sheeted beds, white-clad nurses gliding from bed to bed, bright white sunlight streaming through the southern windows . . . flashing monitors, hissing respirators, murmuring voices . . .

Carrie turned to flee. She couldn't do this.

"Can I help you, Sister?" said a young nurse with a clipboard.

Carrie mechanically handed her the visitor pass. "W-Walter Ferris?"

A smile. "Bed Two." She pointed to the far end of the unit. "He's stable now, but please limit your visit to no more than ten minutes."

Ten minutes? Might as well say ten eternities.

The air become gelatinous and Carrie had to force her way through it toward Bed Two. She couldn't breathe, her knees wobbled, her hands shook, her intestines knotted, she had to go to the bathroom, but she kept pushing forward. Finally she was standing at the foot of the bed. She compelled her eyes to look down at its occupant.

The room spun about her as she stared at a pale, grizzled, wizened old man with thin white hair and sunken features. His hospital gown seemed to lay flat against the mattress. Wires and tubes ran under that gown, a clear tube ran into his right nostril, a ribbed plastic hose protruded from his mouth and was connected to a respirator that pumped and hissed as it filled and emptied his lungs. His eyes were closed.

He looked dead.

She moved to the side of the bed, opposite of where a nurse was swabbing the inside of his mouth with some sort of giant Q-tip.

"What are you doing?" Carrie asked.

The nurse looked up, another young one, blond. They all

seemed young in here. "Just running a lemon swab over his oral membranes. Keeps them moist. Makes him more comfortable. You must be his daughter. Your brother's mentioned you a lot but he said you couldn't come."

Carrie could only nod.

The nurse dropped the swab into a cup of water on the bedside table. "I'll leave you two alone."

Carrie fought the urge to grab her and hold her here.

No! Please don't leave me alone with him!

But the nurse hurried off. Carrie thanked God he was asleep. She'd do what she came here to do and then leave.

"I forgive you," she said softly.

Who knew what torment he'd been going through during Mom's illness? Perhaps something had snapped within him . . . temporary insanity. There was a good chance he'd never done anything like that before or since. One aberrent period in an entire life . . . true, that period had scarred both his children for the rest of their lives, but now, at the end of his days, it was time for forgiveness. These were words Carrie had thought she'd never say, but her time with the Virgin had brought a change within her, a softening. Humans are frail, and there is no sin that cannot be forgiven.

"I forgive you," she repeated.

And his eyes opened. Watery blue, struggling to focus, they narrowed, then widened. He saw her, he knew her. A trembling hand lifted, grasped her fingers where they clung to the side rail.

Touch . . . he was touching her again!

It took everything Carrie had not to snatch her hand away and run screaming from the CCU. She hung on, quelling the urge to vomit as he squeezed her fingers in his arthritic grasp.

And then he loosened his grip and his finger began to caress the back of her hand. She felt her intestines writhe with revulsion but she kept her hand where it was.

He's half out of his mind, she told herself. Disoriented . . . doesn't know what he's doing.

But then she saw the smile twisting his lips, and the look

in his eyes. No repentance there, no guilt . . . more like fond memories.

Carrie pulled her hand away. She wanted to run but she stood firm. Maybe she was projecting. Wasn't that what they called it when you saw what you expected to see? Maybe he was just glad to see her and she was misinterpreting his responses. After all, she hadn't laid eyes on him in fourteen years . . .

. . . but a day hadn't passed that his memory didn't haunt her.

She couldn't run now. Not after she'd made it this far. Besides, she'd come here on a mission.

To give him a chance.

She glanced around. All the nurses were busy. She pulled out the Ziploc bag filled with the filed nails from the Virgin and dipped a finger into the powder. Originally she'd planned to mix it with a few drops of water and let him drink it, but with all these tubes running in and out of him, she didn't see how that would be possible. But that citrus swab looked perfect.

She pulled it from the plastic cup, transferred the powder from her fingers to the swab, and then leaned over the bed.

He was still looking at her with that . . . that expression in his eyes. She shuddered and concentrated on his mouth, slipping the swab through his open lips and running it across his dry tongue and up and down the inside of his cheeks.

His smile broadened. His hand reached up to grab her wrist but she pulled back in time to avoid him.

"There," she said softly. "I've done my part. The rest is between you and God."

He continued to stare at her, grinning lasciviously. She couldn't stand it anymore. She'd done her duty. No use in torturing herself any longer.

"I'm going to go now," she said. "I never—"

Suddenly his smile vanished and he began to writhe in the bed. Carrie heard the beeps of his cardiac monitor increase their tempo. She glanced up and saw the blips chasing each other across the screen. She smelled something burning, and when she looked down, black, oily smoke was seeping out around the edges of his hospital gown. The skin of his arms began to darken and smoke.

"Nurse!" Carrie cried, not knowing what else to do. "Nurse, what's happening?"

By the time the blond nurse reached the bedside his writhing had progressed to agonized thrashing. Smoke streamed from his now blackened skin and collected in a dark, roiling cloud above the bed as he tore the respirator tube from his throat and belched a steam of black smoke with a hoarse, breathy scream.

The nurse gasped. "Oh, my God!"

At that instant he burst into flame.

The nurse screamed and Carrie reeled away, raising her arm to shield her face from the heat. He was burning! Dear sweet Jesus, the whole bed was engulfed in a mass of flame!

No . . . not the bed. Carrie saw now that the bed wasn't burning. Neither was his hospital gown. Nor the sheets.

Just him.

The CCU dissolved into chaos. Screams, shouts, white-clad bodies darting here and there, shouting into phones, brandishing fire extinguishers, dousing the bed with foam, with white jets of carbon dioxide, but the flames burned on unabated, crisping his skin, boiling his eyes in their sockets, peeling the blackened flesh from his bones, and still he moved and writhed and kicked and thrashed, still alive within the consuming flames.

Still alive . . . still burning . . .

And then when it seemed that there was nothing left of him but his skeleton and a crisp blackened membrane stretched across his bones, he stiffened and arched his back until only his heels and the back of his head touched the mattress. He remained like that for what seemed an eternity, exhaling his last breath in a prolonged, quavering ululation, then he collapsed.

And with his collapse, the flames snuffed out.

All was quiet except for the long high-pitched squeal of his flat-lined cardiac monitor. The nurses and orderlies crowded around the bed, covering their mouths and noses as they gaped at the blackened, immolated thing that had once been Walter Ferris, lying stiff and twisted in his unmarred, unscorched hospital gown.

Sick with the horror of it, Carrie staggered back, fighting to maintain her grip on consciousness. She turned and stumbled toward the swinging doors, the voices of the CCU staff echoing above the howl of the monitor . . .

"Christ, what happened?" . . . "An oxygen fire?" . . . "Naw, look at the bed—not even scorched!" . . . "What happened to the smoke alarms? How come they never went off?" . . . "Damnedest thing I ever seen!" . . .

Out in the hall Carrie stepped aside to let the hospital's emergency crew pass. She leaned against the wall and retched.

She'd come here to forgive him . . . she *had* forgiven him.

Apparently someone else had not.

ARCHDIOCESE TO CLOSE ST. JOE'S

John Cardinal O'Connor has announced that the Archdiocese of New York will temporarily close St. Joseph's Church until the Diocese and Vatican officials have time to evaluate the phenomena surrounding the relic displayed on the altar of the Lower Manhattan church.

"Let's just call it a cooling-off period," the Cardinal declared at a news conference yesterday. "In the present climate of crowds, hysteria, and conflicting claims of right of ownership, clear, reasoned, dispassionate judgment is quite nearly impossible."

St. Joseph's parishioners will be instructed to attend services at St. Mark's-in-the-Bowery until their own church is reopened.

The city has announced it will clear the area around St. Joseph's in order to allow Church investigative teams to do their work without interference.

THE NEW YORK POST

Emilio stood back and watched the police herd the Mary-hunters from the street in front of St. Joseph's. The hordes of the faithful were reluctant to go and protested vociferously. Some protested with more than their voices, crying they had driven thousands of miles to be healed and weren't about to be turned away now.

But they were indeed turned away. And some of those who would not leave voluntarily were either dragged away or driven away in the backs of paddy wagons.

By whatever means necessary, the entire block was cleared by nightfall. The church doors were locked and a police cordon was set up across each end of the street.

Emilio shook his head in admiration. He didn't know how he had done it, but he saw the *senador*'s hand in all this. There were still roadblocks before him, but the *senador* had cleared the major obstacle between Emilio and the relic.

The rest was up to him.

Already he had a plan.

IN THE PACIFIC

20° N, 128° W

The storm continues to gain in size and strength as it races along its northeasterly course. It now stretches one hundred and fifty miles across as its cumulonimbus crown reaches to forty thousand feet.

The spinning core of its heart increases its speed, and the entire storm moves with it. The swirling mass of violent weather is aimed toward northern Mexico.

22

Decker honked and yelled and edged the D'Agostino's truck through the crowd until it nosed up against one of the light blue "Police Line" horses that blocked access to the street ahead. Beyond the barrier the pavement stretched dark and empty in front of St. Joseph's, illuminated in patches by the street lamps. An island of calm in a sea of frustrated Mary-hunters.

"You know what to say?" Emilio said.

Decker nodded. "Got it memorized."

He jammed some gum into his mouth and slid out from behind the wheel as one of the cops approached.

Emilio watched from his spot in the middle of the front seat. Molinari slouched to his right, trying to look casual with his elbow protruding from the open passenger window. Emilio was keeping a decidedly low profile at this point in their little mission. Decker and Mol sported extra facial hair, glasses, and nostril dilators to distort their appearances, but Emilio had gone to the greatest length to disguise himself. He'd added a thick black beard to augment his mustache, a shaggy wig, and a navy-blue knitted watch cap pulled low over his forehead, almost to his eyebrows. He was often caught in the background when the *senador* was photographed leaving his office or his car, and he didn't want the slightest risk of being identified later.

"Street's closed, buddy," the cop said. "You gotta go down to—"

"Gotta delivery here," Decker said, chewing noisily on the gum as he fished a slip of paper from his pocket. "The rect'ry."

"Yeah? Nobody told me about that."

"We deliver alla time, man. Youse guys maya shut down da choich, but dem priests still gotta eat, know'm sayin'?"

As the cop stared at Decker, Emilio winced and closed his eyes. He hard Mol groan softly. Decker was laying it on thick. Maybe *too* thick.

The cop pulled a flashlight from his belt. "Let's have a look at what you're deliverin'," he said. "You wouldn't be the first Mary-hunters tried to sneak by us tonight."

Emilio nodded as Mol nudged him. They'd done this right. This was no fake D'Agostino's truck. This was the real thing. They'd hijacked it just as it left the store. The driver was bound, gagged and unconscious in the trunk of a car Mol had stolen this afternoon. The back of the panel truck was loaded with grocery bags, all scheduled for delivery elsewhere, but Emilio had changed the addresses on half a dozen bags; they now read "St. Joseph's rectory."

Emilio heard the rear doors open, heard the rustle of paper as a few of the bags were inspected, then heard the door slam closed.

Seconds later Decker was slipping back behind the wheel as the cop slid the barrier aside and waved them through.

" 'Choich?' " Mol said, leaning forward and staring at Decker. " '*Choich?* ' "

Decker shrugged, grinning. "What can I say? I'm a Method actor."

Mol laughed and grabbed his crotch. "Method this!"

Emilio let them blow off a little steam. They were in—past the guardhouse, so to speak—but they still had a long way to go.

Decker gave a friendly wave to the cop standing on the sidewalk in front of the church as he drove past, then backed the truck into the alley on the far side of the rectory. Mol and Emilio got out, opened the rear of the trunk, grabbed some bags, and left the doors open as they approached the rectory's side door with loaded arms.

A middle-aged woman opened the door.

"A gift for Father Dan from one of his parishioners," Emilio said. "Is he in?"

Emilio knew he was in—he'd confirmed that with a phone call thirty minutes ago.

"Why, yes," the woman said. She let them into the foyer, then turned and called up the stairs behind her. "Father Dan! Someone here to see you!"

By the time she turned back again, Mol had put his grocery bags down and had a pistol pointing at her face.

"Not a word," he said, "or we'll shoot Father Dan. Understand?"

Eyes wide, jaw trembling, utterly terrified, she nodded.

"Anyone else in the house besides Father Dan?" Mol said.

She shook her head.

"Good." Mol smiled. "Now, let's find a nice little closet so we can lock you up where you won't get hurt."

Emilio had his own automatic—a silenced Llama compact 9mm—ready and waiting for Father Dan when he came down the stairs.

"Hello," the priest said. "What—"

And then he saw the pistol.

"Let's go to church, shall we, Father?" Emilio said.

The young priest looked bewildered. "But there are police all over—"

"The tunnel, Father Dan. We'll use the tunnel."

The priest shook his head. "Tunnel? I don't know what you're—"

Emilio jabbed the silencer tip against his ribs. "I'll shoot your housekeeper in the face."

"All right!" Father Dan said, blanching. "All right. It's this way."

"That's better," Emilio said, following close behind.

Mol rejoined them then and gave Emilio a thumbs-up sign. The housekeeper was safely locked away. She'd keep quiet to protect her precious priest from being shot while the priest was leading them to the church in order to keep his housekeeper from being shot.

Weren't guns wonderful?

But repeated reminders never hurt. Emilio had worked this one out and memorized it: "No heroics, please, Father. We're not here to hurt anyone, but we're quite willing to do so without hesitation if the need arises. Remember that."

Why are all these things happening, Mother?

Carrie sat in the front pew, staring at the Virgin where she lay upon the altar.

She could not get the sight of her father—now that he was dead, had died so horribly, it seemed all right to call him that—out of her head. The flames, the oily smoke, the smell, the obscene sizzle of burning human flesh, haunted her dreams and her waking hours, stealing her appetite, chasing her sleep. That had been no ordinary fire. Only the man had burned, nothing else.

Did I do that, Mother? Did you? Or was that the work of Someone Else's hand?

And now the church was closed, the sick and lame turned away, the building sealed, the street blocked off. What next? Tomorrow these aisles would be crowded with investigators from the Archdiocese and the Vatican, trailed by nosy, disrespectful bureaucrats from City Hall and Albany, from Washington and Israel, all poking, prodding, examining.

They'll be interrogating me about how you got here. I won't tell them a thing. It's not me I'm worried about, Mother. It's you. They'll treat you like a thing. An it. They may even decide you belong back in Israel. What'll I do then, Mother?

Carrie felt tears begin to well in her eyes. She willed them away.

There's a plan, isn't there, Mother. There has to be. I just have to have faith and—

She heard a noise in the vestibule and turned. She smiled when she saw Dan leading two other strange-looking men up the aisle, but he did not return her smile. He looked pale and grim.

And then she saw the pistols.

"Dan?" she said, rising. "What's going on?"

"I don't know." His voice was as tight as his features. "They came into the rectory and—"

"What we want is very simple," the bigger, bearded one said. He stopped a dozen feet or so down the aisle from Carrie and let Dan continue toward her. He gestured toward the altar with his pistol. "We want the lady."

Carrie was stunned for a few seconds, unable, *unwilling* to believe what she'd just heard.

"Want her for what?" she managed to say.

"No time for chatter, Sister. Here's how we'll do this. You two will carry her back through the tunnel to the rectory, and we'll take her from there. No tricks, no games, no heroics, and no one gets hurt." He gestured with his pistol at Dan. "You take the head and she'll take the feet. Let's move."

"No!" Carrie said.

The bearded man snapped his head back in surprise. Obviously he hadn't expected that.

Neither had Carrie. The word had erupted from her with little or no forethought, propelled by fear, by anger, by outrage that anyone could even *think* of stealing the Virgin from the sanctuary of a church.

She rose and faced him defiantly.

"Get out of here."

He stared at her for a heartbeat or two, then pointed his gun at Dan.

"You cause me any trouble and I'll shoot your priest friend."

"No, you won't. There's a cop outside that door. All I have to do is scream once and he'll be in here, and that will be the end of you. Get out now. I'll give you a chance to run, then I'm going to open the front doors and call the police inside."

"I'm not kidding, lady," the big one said through his teeth. "Get up there and do what you're told."

"Carrie, please," she heard Dan say from her left. "It's okay. They can't get past the cops with her anyway. So just do as he says."

Dan might be right, but Carrie wasn't going to let these creeps get their filthy hands on the Virgin for even a few seconds.

"Get out now or I scream."

The shorter one looked about nervously, as if he wanted to take her up on the offer, but the bearded one stood firm. His eyes narrowed as he raised his pistol and aimed it at her chest. His voice was low and menacing.

"*No me jodas.*"

He wouldn't dare, she thought. He's got to be bluffing.

"All right," she said. "I gave you your chance."

Still they didn't move, so she filled her lungs and—

She saw the flash at the tip of the silencer, saw the pistol buck in his hand, heard a sound like *phut!*, felt an impact against her chest, tried to start her scream but she was punched backward and didn't seem to have any air to scream with. And then she was falling. Darkness rimmed her vision as a distant roaring surged closer, filling her ears, bringing with it more darkness, an all-encompassing darkness. . . .

Emilio stood frozen with his automatic still pointed at where she had been standing as he watched her fall and lay twitching on the marble floor, the red of her life soaking through the front of her habit and pooling around her.

"Christ, Emilio!" Mol gasped beside him.

"Carrie!" the priest cried, dropping to his knees beside her and gripping her limp shoulders. "Oh, God, *Carrie!*"

I'm sorry, Emilio thought. I'm so sorry!

And that shocked him. Because he'd killed before without the slightest shred of guilt. Anyone who threatened him or stood between him and what he wanted didn't deserve to live. It had always been that simple. But here, now, in this place, before that old woman's body on the altar, a new emotion, as unpleasant as it was unfamiliar, was seeping through him.

Guilt.

The priest looked up at him, tear-filled eyes wild, rage and grief distorting his features almost beyond recognition. With a low, animal-like growl he hurtled himself at Emilio.

A bullet in the head would have been the simplest, most efficient response. But Emilio couldn't bring himself to pull the trigger. Not again, not here, with . . . *her* here. Instead he dodged aside and slammed the Llama's butt and trigger guard hard against the priest's skull, staggering him. Before the man could shake off the blow, Emilio hit him again, harder this time, knocking him to the floor where he lay still with a trickle of red oozing from his scalp.

Mol had already started back down the center aisle.

"Where are you going?"

Mol turned and looked at her, fear in his eyes. "I—"

"Shut up and stand still. Listen!"

Emilio strained his ears through the silence. And as he'd hoped, it remained just that: silence. None of the noise in here had penetrated the heavy oak front doors; the cop outside had no idea there was anything going on inside.

"All right," Emilio said, gesturing toward the altar. "Let's get moving."

Mol hesitated, glanced once more at the front doors, then shrugged and hurried toward the altar. Emilio directed him toward the head of the body while he took the other end.

But as he reached to take hold of the feet, he hesitated. He hadn't believed in this church-priest-God-religion bullshit since he'd been a little boy in Camino Verde and watched his older sister screw the neighborhood men in the back corner of their one-room shack. Any guilt he'd felt a moment ago had been a leftover from the times his grandmother would drag him off to church before he was big enough to tell her to go to hell. And yet . . . a deep part of him was afraid to touch this mummified old woman, afraid a lightning bolt would crash through the ceiling of the church and fry him on the spot.

"Bullshit!" he whispered and gripped the body's ankles. Nothing happened.

Angry with himself for feeling relieved, he nodded to Mol, who had her by the shoulders, and together they lifted her off the altar.

Surprisingly light. They each got a comfortable grip on her, then hurried down the center aisle, Emilio leading, carrying her feet first. Through the vestibule, down the steps into the locked-up soup kitchen in the cellar, through the tunnel, and back up into the rectory. All still quiet there. Decker would have been inside if anyone had come in. They eased the body out the side door, slipped her into the back atop the grocery bags, and locked the doors.

Emilio climbed into the cab next to Decker and slapped the dashboard. "Let's go."

"Any trouble?" Decker said as he nosed the truck into the street.

"Not really," Emilio said.

Mol snorted. "Like hell!"

"What happened?" Decker said.

"I'll tell you later," Emilio said. "Just drive."

He wanted Decker cool and calm for the drive back past the police and through the crowd, but he needn't have worried. The police waved them by, and even made a path for them through the horde of Mary-hunters.

Once they were free of the crowd and rolling toward the FDR Drive, Emilio allowed himself to breathe a little more easily. And he'd breathe even more easily when they ditched this rig and switched the body to the Avis panel truck he'd rented earlier. But he knew he wouldn't be able to relax fully until they had it aboard the *senador*'s waiting jet and were airborne over LaGuardia.

She is gone!

Kesev violently elbowed his way through the crowd near St. Joseph's, leaving a trail of sore and angry Mary-hunters in his wake. Let them shout at him, wave their fists at him, he didn't care. He had to reach the church, had to know if his suspicion was true.

During the past hour he had felt a dwindling of the Mother's presence, and then suddenly it was gone.

Finally he reached the front of the crowd, but as he squeezed under the barricade, two blue-uniformed policemen, one white, one black, confronted him.

"Back on the other side, buddy," the white one said.

"You don't understand," Kesev told him. "She's gone. They've stolen her."

He heard the crowd behind him begin to mutter and murmur with concern.

"Now don't go starting trouble, mister," the black one said. "The lady's fine. We've been out here all night and nobody's been in or out of that church."

"She's gone, I tell you!" Kesev turned to the crowd and shouted, "They've stolen the Mother right out from under your noses!"

"You shut up!" the white policeman hissed in his ear.

But Kesev wrenched free and began running toward the front of the church.

"Come!" he shouted to the crowd. "Come see if I'm not telling you the truth!"

That was all the crowd needed. With a roar they knocked over the police line horses and surged onto the street, engulfing any cop who tried to stop them.

The lone policeman stationed in front of the church backed up to the front doors but decided to get out of the way as Kesev charged up the steps with the mob close behind him. A few good heaves from dozens of shoulders and the doors gave way and they flowed through the vestibule and into the nave.

And stopped with cries of shock that rapidly dwindled, finally fading into horrified silence.

The altar was bare. And near the end of the center aisle two figures huddled on the floor. Kesev recognized them immediately—the nun and the priest from the El Al plane back in July.

The priest was kneeling in a pool of red, weeping, his deep, racking sobs reverberating through the church as blood from a scalp wound trickled down his forehead to mingle with his tears. In his arms lay the limp, blood-soaked form of the nun.

Kesev, too, wept. But for another reason.

CHUCK SCARBOROUGH: "This just in: the object in St. Joseph's church in Lower Manhattan, believed by many to be the remains of the Virgin Mary, has been stolen. Sister Carolyn Ferris, beloved by the thousands who have visited the church since the object first appeared there, was killed during the robbery, apparently while trying to prevent the theft. The devotees of the object, known as Mary-hunters, have gone on a rampage in the area around the church, demanding immediate capture of the killers and the return of what has come to be known as the Manhattan Madonna.

A camera crew is on the way to the scene and we will bring you live coverage as soon as it is available.

To repeat . . ."

NewsCenter 4

"Do you remember me?"

Dan forced his eyes open. He was cold, he was sick, he was emotionally drained and numb; his head was pounding like a cathedral gong, and his scalp throbbed and pulled where it had been stitched up. But the greatest pain was deep inside where no doctor could see or touch, in the black void left by Carrie's death and the brutal, awful, finality of her dying.

He looked up from his seat in the Emergency Room of Beekman Downtown Hospital. For a rage-blinded instant he thought the black-bearded man with the accented voice standing over him was the bastard who'd shot Carrie. He tensed to launch himself at him, then realized this was someone else. Just as intense, but much too short. He'd seen this man before but his grief-fogged brain couldn't recall where or when.

"No," he said. *And I don't care to.*

"At Tel Aviv airport last summer . . . I was questioning your nun friend and you—"

Now Dan recognized him. "The man from the Shin . . ." He fumbled for the word.

"Shin Bet. The name is Kesev. But I'm here unofficially now."

"I wish we'd never gone to Israel," he said, feeling a sob growing in his chest. "I wish you'd arrested us and jailed us. At least then Carrie would still be alive."

Carrie . . . dead. Dan still couldn't believe it. This had to be a dream, the worst nightmare imaginable. A dream. That was the only logical explanation for all these fantastic, unexplainable events, the most unbelievable of which was Carrie's death. Life without Carrie . . . a Carrie-less world . . . unthinkable.

But it had seemed so real when he'd held her limp, cold, blood-drenched body in his arms back there in St. Joe's.

So *real!*

"So do I," Kesev said. "For more than her sake alone. There are other matters to consider."

"Yeah? Like what?"

Dan heard the belligerence creeping into his tone, into his mood. What right did this Israeli bastard have to come up to him here in the depths of his grief and start bothering him about Carrie? What did anything matter now that Carrie was dead?

"We must find the Mother."

"*You* find her! She's brought me nothing but grief."

He started to rise but Kesev restrained him with a surprisingly strong hand on his shoulder.

"If we find the Mother, we find the killers."

Dan leaned back into the chair. Find the killers . . . wouldn't that be nice? To wrap his fingers around that big bearded bastard's throat and squeeze and squeeze, and keep on squeezing until—

"Father Fitzpatrick?"

Dan looked up. One of the homicide detectives who'd questioned him before was approaching—Detective Sergeant Gardner. He carried a black plastic bag in his hand.

What did he want now? He'd told him everything, given descriptions of the killers, the sound of their voices, anything he could think of. He was tapped out.

He noticed Kesev slipping away as the detective neared.

"They're shipping her body uptown," Detective Gardner said.

Dan lurched to his feet. "Why? Where?"

"S.O.P. To the morgue. They're going to autopsy her right away."

"So soon?" Hadn't Carrie been through enough? "I'd've thought—"

"The pressure's on, Father. We've got a big, mean, unruly crowd outside your church, and from what I hear, the commish has already heard from the Cardinal, the mayor, Albany, even the Israeli embassy. Everybody but everybody wants these guys caught and that relic returned. The commish wants a full forensic report on his desk by six A.M., so they're going to do her right away."

"Can I see her before—"

Gardner shook his head. "Sorry. She's gone. Saw her off myself." He held out the black plastic bag. "But here's her personal effects. You want to return them to the convent? If not . . ."

"No, that's all right," Dan said. "I'll take them."

Detective Gardner handed the bag over and stood before him, awkward, silent. Finally he said, "We'll get them, Father."

Dan could only nod.   •

As the detective hurried away, Dan sat down and opened the bag. Not much there: a wallet, a rosary, and Carrie's Ziploc bags of the Virgin's clippings and nail filings.

For an insane moment Dan thought of cabbing up to the morgue—it was up in the Bellevue complex, wasn't it? . . . First Avenue and Thirtieth . . . he could be there in a couple of minutes. He'd sneak into the autopsy room. He'd sprinkle the entire contents of both bags over Carrie's body and . . .

And what? Bring her back to life?

Who am I kidding? he thought. That's Stephen King stuff. Carrie's gone . . . forever.

Without warning, he broke into deep racking sobs. He hadn't even felt them coming. Suddenly they were there, convulsing his chest as they ripped free.

A hand touched his shoulder. He fought for control and looked up. The man called Kesev had returned.

"Come, Father Fitzpatrick. I'll take you home. There are things we must discuss."

Dan nodded absently. Home . . . where was that? The rectory? That wasn't home. Where was home now that Carrie was dead? He didn't care where he went now, he just knew he didn't want to stay in this hospital any longer.

He bunched up the neck of the plastic bag and followed Kesev toward the exit.

Dr. Darryl Chin, second assistant medical examiner for New York City, yawned as he pulled on a pair of examination gloves. This is what you get, he supposed, when you're down-line in the pecking order and you live in the East Village: They need somebody quick, they call you.

"Could be a lot worse," he muttered.

He looked down at the naked female cadaver supine before him on the stainless steel autopsy table, dead-pale skin, breasts caked with blood, dark hair tangled in disarray, jaw slack, dull blue eyes staring lifelessly at the overhead fluorescents. The murdered nun he'd heard about on the news tonight. Young, pretty, and fresh. The fresh part was important. Only a few hours cold. He might get some useful information out of her. Better than some stinking, macerated, crab-nibbled corpse they'd dragged out of the Hudson. And this was a neat chest wound, not some messy gut shot. They'd be through with this one in no time.

If they ever got started.

Where the hell was Lou Ann? She was supposed to assist him tonight. She lived in Queens and had a longer ride, but she should have been here by now. Probably had to put on her face before she came in. Joe had never seen her without two tons of eye liner and mascara.

Vanity, woman be thy name.

No use in wasting time. He could get started without her. Open and drain the thorax at least. These chest wounds always left the cavity filled with blood.

He probed the entry wound with his little finger. Looked like the work of a 9mm slug. Good shot. Right into the heart. Poor girl probably never knew what hit her.

He reached up and adjusted the voice-activated mike that hung over the table. He gave the date and read off the name of the subject and presumed cause of death from the ID card, then reached for his scalpel.

Time to open her up. Get the major incisions out of the way, drain and measure the volume of blood in the thoracic cavity, and by then Lou Ann would be here and they could start in on the individual organs.

He poked his index finger into the suprasternal notch atop the breast bone, laid the point of the blade against the skin just below the notch, and leaned over the table to make the first long incision down the center of the sternum.

"Please don't do that."

A woman's voice. He looked around. *Who—?*

Then he looked down. The cadaver's blue eyes were no longer dull and unfocused. They were bright and moving in their sockets, looking at him.

The scalpel clattered on the metal table as he jumped back.

"Jesus *Christ!*"

"Please don't take His name in vain," the nun said, staring at him as she levered up to a sitting position on the table.

Darryl felt his heart hammering in his chest, heard a roaring in his ears as he backed away.

She's dead! She's dead but she's talking, moving!

She swung her legs over the side of the table and slipped to the floor. Still backing away, Joe dumbly watched her naked form cross the room like a sleepwalker and pull a white lab coat from a hook on the wall.

Darryl's heel caught against something on the floor and he fell backward, his arms pinwheeling for balance. He grabbed the edge of a table but his fingers slipped off the shiny surface and he landed on his buttocks. His head snapped back and struck the painted concrete block of the wall.

Darryl tried to call out but found he had no voice. He tried to hold onto consciousness but it was a losing battle. The last thing he saw before darkness closed in was the dead woman slipping into the lab coat and walking out the door, leaving it open behind her.

IN THE PACIFIC

24° N, 120° W

Reconnaissance flight 705 out of San Diego is buffeted by tornadic winds and blinding torrents as it fights its way toward the center of the huge, mysterious Pacific storm that shows up on satellite photos but not radar. An unclassifiable, logic-defying storm with the combined properties of an Atlantic hurricane, a Pacific typhoon, and a Midwestern supercell. All that can be said of it from orbit photos and fly-by observation is that a towering colossus of violent weather topping out at fifty-thousand feet is crossing the Pacific in the general direction of northern Mexico.

Reconnaissance 705's mission is to classify it, but right now, hemmed in by roiling clouds and radar that shows clear, calm, open sea ahead of them, they are truly flying blind. The pilot, Captain Harry Densmore, has never experienced anything like this. The barometric readings are in the mid-twenties as he approaches what should be the center of the storm. He wants to turn back but he needs to know what's at the heart of this monstrosity. There's no eye visible from orbit, but all indications point to an organized center. One look, one reading, and he'll turn tail and run. This monster hasn't killed anybody yet but he's afraid he and his crew might change all that. He'll count himself lucky if he sees San Diego again.

Just a little farther . . .

Suddenly the plane is buffeted by a gust that knocks it forty-five degrees off line. Metal shrieks in Densmore's ears and he's sure she's going to come apart when suddenly they're in still air.

"It's got an eye!" he shouts. "We're through the eye wall!"

But an eye should be clear. And in an eye this huge, blue sky should be visible above. Not here. It's dark in this eye. Very dark. And raining.

Maybe it'll clear up ahead.

The copilot calls out the barometric reading: Twenty-three.

"Twenty-*three*? Check that again. That's got to be wrong!"

Then lightning flashes and Densmore sees something through the rain ahead. Something huge. Something dark. The far side of the eye wall? Maybe this eye isn't as big as he thought. Maybe—

"Oh, Christ!"

He turns the wheel and kicks the rudder hard, all but standing the plane on its wing-tip as he banks sharply to the left. The shouts of alarm and surprise from his copilot and navigator choke off as they see it too.

He finishes the turn and levels off on a circular course around the center of the eye, catching lightning-strobed glimpses of the cyclopean thing in the heart of the storm. His copilot's and navigator's hushed, awed voices fill the cabin.

"What in God's name *is* that?"

"I don't know."

They are at 20,000 feet and whatever it is reaches from the ocean below and disappears into the clouds miles above them.

Densmore realizes that what he sees before him is impossible. He knows his physics, and something that big breaks all natural laws. Just like the storm itself.

Which means something else is driving this storm that breaks all the rules and defies the world's most sophisticated radar tracking system.

And God help whoever is in its way when it makes landfall.

Suddenly he wants to be as far away as possible from this unnatural phenomenon.

"Take some pictures so people won't think we're all crazy, and let's get the hell out of here."

Moments later reconnaissance flight 705 reenters the eye wall but instead of flying through, it is tossed back by the hellish fury of the tornadic winds. Densmore tries again and again to pierce the eye wall but each time his craft is rejected like an unwanted toy.

The storm won't let them leave. They're trapped . . . in the eye . . . with that thing . . .

Densmore resumes a circular path along the eye wall, staying as far as possible from its center. They're safe here in the relative calm of the eye—safe at least from the winds—as long as their fuel holds out.

But they've only got a few hours' worth left.

Part IV

Assumptions

23

HURRICANE WATCH

THE NATIONAL WEATHER SERVICE HAS
ISSUED A HURRICANE WATCH FOR SANTA
BARBARA, VENTURA, LOS ANGELES,
ORANGE AND SAN DIEGO COUNTIES.
BRING IN LOOSE OUTDOOR OBJECTS,
FILL UP YOUR CAR WITH GAS, AND STAY
TUNED FOR FURTHER DEVELOPMENTS.

THE WEATHER CHANNEL

Manhattan

Neither Father Brenner nor Mr. Kesev of the Shin Bet
wanted a drink, but Dan didn't let that stop him. Monsignor
Riccio had come by to offer his condolences. He seemed to
know Kesev—apparently they'd met on the street awhile
back.

The Monsignor didn't say, "This is what you get for
recklessly going public with the Virgin," but Dan guessed
he was thinking it. He was gracious, however, and sincerely
wished for the speedy capture of the killers, then he left.
Father Brenner had sat up with him awhile, then he went to
bed. Now it was just Kesev and Dan, sitting in silence.

"Sure you won't have one?" Dan said, crossing the front
room of the rectory to pour himself a third Dewar's.

"No," Kesev said, "and I do wish you would not drink too
much."

Dan stopped in mid-pour. Kesev was right. This wouldn't do him any good. Wouldn't ease the pain, even a little. The wound was too wide, too deep, too fresh.

"This is my last. But what's it to you? What do you care about me or how much I drink?"

"I'm sorry for you and for that poor dead woman. But I'm concerned for my own sake as well. You see . . . for many years I have been the Mother's guardian."

"'The Mother,'" Dan said softly. "The Virgin. How Carrie loved her." Then the rest of Kesev's words sank in. "Guardian? We had a fake scroll supposedly written by the Virgin's guardian back in the first century."

The memory of Carrie's girlish excitement over that scroll punched a new ache through his chest.

Carrie, Carrie . . . why couldn't you have just let them take her?

"Yours was a forgery, a copy of another, but the words were true, as you discovered."

"Any idea who wrote it?" Dan said.

"I did."

Dan stared at him. "You must know your first century, Mr. Kesev. That was a pretty convincing scroll. Where'd you learn all that?"

Kesev shrugged. "From life."

"You mean from the guardians before you, passing it down. Who are these guardians anyway? Members of some sect?"

"No. Only one guardian."

This conversation was getting strange.

"You mean just one at a time . . . one guardian from each successive generation, right?"

Kesev shook his head. "No. Just one guardian. Ever. From the beginning. Me."

"But that would make you a couple of thousand . . ."

Kesev nodded slowly, but he wasn't smiling.

"No . . ." Dan said. "No, that would be—"

"Impossible?"

Dan was about to say yes when it occurred to him: Was anything impossible anymore?

And then he heard the rectory's side door open. He stood up and started to cross the room. *Now* who was it?

Paraiso

"So this is what all the excitement is about."

Arthur Crenshaw stared down at the mummified body where it rested before him on the glass coffee table.

Paraiso was empty except for him and Charlie and Emilio. Decker and Molinari had returned to their respective homes directly from the airport. Arthur had sent all the help—domestic as well as nursing—home for the night. The fewer who knew about his "borrowing" of the relic, the better. Beyond the floor-to-ceiling windows of the great room lay the unrelieved gloom of the night and the ocean. No starlight broke through the restless mantle of cloud that stretched above the Pacific like a shroud. The only sound in the great room was the swoosh of the wind against the glass and Charlie's labored breathing.

He walked around the table, examining the body from all sides. Not very impressive. Hardly lifelike at all. You could tell it was somebody old and female, but that was about all. Could this be the actual remains of the Virgin Mary? Didn't seem possible. All right, possible, yes, but highly improbable. You'd think there'd be some sort of glow or aura about it if it was really Mary. So maybe it was just the nicely preserved remains of an early saint.

Whatever it was, could it save Charlie?

Arthur sighed. Apparently it had healed others—many others—back in New York. No reason why it shouldn't do the same here.

But whatever it did, it had better do it quickly. Charlie was fading away before his eyes. The latest try at a new experimental therapy had failed. Charlie's CD-4 count was lower than ever. He didn't have much time. This relic was his last chance at a cure.

But how to go about it?

Charlie was running one of his fevers again, semicomatose most of the time, and when he was responsive he was delirious—no idea of who he was or where he was or even that he was sick. He couldn't pray to this object, couldn't ask it or anyone else for help.

So that left it up to Arthur to do the praying.

Maybe Charlie and the object should be closer. And since it was such a major task to move Charlie's setup with its IVs and oxygen tank, Arthur figured the easiest way to get the two together was to move the body.

If Mohammed can't come to the mountain . . .

He turned to Emilio. "Let's move her over by Charlie, table and all."

Emilio held back a moment. He'd seemed to be keeping his distance from the body. Strange . . . Arthur had always thought of Emilio as the least superstitious man he'd ever met. When he finally approached, they each took an end of the coffee table and, carrying it like a stretcher, moved the table and its burden around the couch and set it down next to Charlie's hospital bed.

Arthur then said a prayer, asking the Lord to forgive Charlie for his past and to allow the healing powers in this relic—be it the remains of His earthly Mother or some other holy person—to drive the infection from his son's wasted body so that he might continue his life and have an opportunity to make up for the evil ways of his past.

As he finished the prayer with a heartfelt recital of the "Our Father," Arthur slipped Charlie's painfully thin, limp, clammy arm through the guardrail and guided it toward the body on the table. He pressed the back of Charlie's hand against its dry cheek and held it there.

Arthur wasn't sure what he'd expected, but he was hoping for more than what he got, which was nothing.

He swallowed his disappointment. He had to keep in mind that there'd been no pyrotechnics associated with the Manhattan healings, so the lack of them here didn't mean that nothing had happened.

He held Charlie's hand against the skin for a good fifteen minutes, all the while praying for mercy for his son, then he replaced the arm under the bedsheet.

He noticed Emilio standing off to the side, staring out at the darkness. He seemed preoccupied.

"Well," Arthur said, "all we can do now is watch and wait."

Emilio nodded but said nothing.

Arthur shrugged and turned on the TV to check out the latest on the big Pacific storm. The Weather Channel said it was still headed for the southern part of the state. Paraiso would get only the fringe winds.

Good. In the morning he'd have some blood drawn on Charlie for a stat CD-4 count. If this relic had done its work, the count would be up and Charlie's fever would break.

Please, God. Not for me . . . for Charlie.

He switched to CNN in the middle of a story about the theft of a religious object from a Manhattan church. Film showed close-ups of enraged faces and crowds tipping over police cars and smashing store windows.

Arthur's stomach lurched and he glanced back at the body on the table next to Charlie's bed. That was the only object they could be talking about. But why such coverage—on CNN of all places? He hadn't expected this kind of commotion. He'd have to have Emilio drop it off someplace where it could be "discovered" tomorrow.

And then the screen showed the newswoman at a desk with the face of a young nun superimposed over her shoulder. Arthur leaned forward, straining his ears because what she was saying could not be true. The young nun had been *murdered* during the theft of the object.

Murdered!

Arthur swiveled in his seat and tried to rise to his feet but his legs wouldn't support him.

"Emilio?" he gasped. "You didn't . . . you couldn't have . . ."

But the look in Emilio's eyes told him more than any words could say.

"Dear God, Emilio! Dear *God!*"

Manhattan

As Dan watched, a pale, dark-haired woman in a long white coat stepped inside the rectory side door.

Dan dropped his drink. His knees buckled and he

clutched the back of a chair to keep from falling. He opened his mouth to speak but his voice wasn't there.

Carrie!

"I have to go to California, Dan," she said evenly as she entered the front room.

He stumbled forward and threw his arms around her.

"Carrie!" he croaked. "You're alive! Thank God, you're—"

She stood stiff and unresponsive in his embrace; her skin was cold against his cheek. Her chill transmitted to him. Spicules of ice formed in his blood as she spoke again.

"No, Dan. I'm not."

Dan released her and backed away. She was staring at him with her bright blue eyes, but they were her only lively feature; the rest of her face was slack, and her voice . . . hollow. Not movie-zombie dead and robotic. It had timbre and tone, but there was something missing. Emotion. She was like some of the guests at Loaves and Fishes who came in stoned on downers.

An inane question popped out of his reeling mind: "How did you get here?"

"I walked."

He noticed Kesev had risen and was standing beside him.

"Carrie . . ." Dan said, his mind whirling, refusing to accept what he was seeing. "I . . . you . . . the doctors said you were dead."

She reached forward and took his hand—her touch was so *cold*. She freed his index finger from the others and pulled the front to her lab coat open. She pressed the tip of Dan's finger into the small round hole along the inner border of her left breast.

"He killed me, Dan."

Dan cried out in anguish and revulsion as he tore his hand free. The room dipped and veered to the left, then the right. The Scotch, the concussion, seeing Carrie murdered, getting her back but not getting her back because she wasn't really back . . . it was all too much. Unable to stand any longer, he sank to his knees before her.

"Oh, God, Carrie! What is this? What does it *mean*?"

"I have to go to California, Dan. Please help me get there."

"Calif—?"

Kesev stepped forward. "Why California? Is that where the Mother is?"

Carrie turned and stared at Kesev as if seeing him for the first time. She took a step backward and something twitched in her expression. Dan tried to decipher it: Surprise? Wonder? Fear?

"You . . . I know who you are."

"The Mother?" Kesev said quickly. "She's in California now?"

"Yes. I have to be with her."

"Can you take us to her?"

"I need help. We have to hurry. We have to fly."

"Yes, yes!" Kesev said excitedly. "We will leave immediately!"

"Now just a damn minute!" Dan said, struggling back to his feet. "We're not going anywhere until I know—"

"The Mother is there!" Kesev said, eyes bright as he leaned into Dan's face. "The sister will lead us to her."

"No! This is crazy! I'll call the police. Detective Garner—"

As Dan turned to reach for the phone, Kesev grabbed his arm. His fingers cut into him like steel cables.

"She came to *us*, Father Fitzpatrick. Was *sent* to us. Not to the police. *Us!* That means that *we* are meant to go with her. It is not our place to involve the police. Do you understand what I am saying?"

Dan nodded. He was beginning to understand—at least as much as someone could understand something like this. He realized Kesev had his own agenda here. He wanted the Virgin back. If what he'd said was true, he'd been guarding the Virgin for two thousand years and wasn't about to quit now. In the face of Carrie's reanimated corpse standing here before him, Dan found that relatively easy to accept.

But who *was* Kesev?

Carrie was the other mystery. Had she been brought back from death for a purpose, or had her desire to be with the Virgin overcome death itself?

Dan could find little comfort in either alternative.

But it didn't matter. Carrie was here, asking for his help. Dan would do everything in his power to give her that help.

"All right," he said. "Let's call the airlines."

IN THE PACIFIC

30° N, 122° W

As its fringe winds begin to brush the coast of southern California, the storm veers sharply north.

Captain Harry Densmore stares bleary-eyed through the windshield and adjusts 705's circular course along the eye wall. They should have been out of fuel long ago, but the needle on the gauge hasn't budged since they entered the eye. So they keep on flying. They've *got* to keep on flying.

But what are the engines running on?

24

HURRICANE WARNING

THE NATIONAL WEATHER SERVICE HAS
ISSUED A HURRICANE WARNING FOR
SANTA CRUZ, MONTEREY, AND SAN LUIS
OBISPO COUNTIES. HURRICANE LAND-
FALL IS EXPECTED BY 9:00 A.M. EVACUA-
TION OF OCEANFRONT AND LOW-LYING
AREAS SHOULD BEGIN IMMEDIATELY.

THE WEATHER CHANNEL

Paraiso

Emilio fought through the horizontal sheets of rain
assaulting the ambulance as he wound up the road through
the woods to Paraiso. Bolts of lightning lanced the sky,
clearing the way for the ground-shaking thunder, but the
heavy vehicle hugged the road.

When the storm changed course and it became clear that
it would strike Monterey County, the *senador* had sent him
to find an ambulance for Charlie, to take him inland out of
harm's way.

But there was no ambulances to be had. The city had
placed every available ambulance, public and private, on
standby alert. Emilio had stopped by a few services personally, contacted many more by phone. No matter how much
he offered, they would not risk their licenses by hiring out
for a private run during the emergency.

Call the county Civil Defense, they said. All you've got to do is tell them it's an emergency, that you need an ambulance immediately to remove an invalid from an evacuation area, and they'll okay it. No problem.

No problem? Not quite. Emilio could hardly get Monterey County officialdom involved in moving an AIDS patient who happened to be Senator Arthur Crenshaw's son. The word would spread like the wind from this storm. He couldn't even allow a private ambulance company to know who it was transporting. He wanted to rent a fully-equipped rig and drive it himself. The answer everywhere was the same: Nothing doing.

After the last call, Emilio had torn the pay telephone off the wall in a blind rage. He could not let the *senador* down on this. He'd already suffered the withering fury of his anger after he'd learned about the nun. The *senador* had been quiet at first, then he'd exploded, calling Emilio a murderous fool, a ham-handed incompetent, a dolt who had jeopardized a lifetime of effort. The *senador* had turned away in disgust, telling him to see if he could do something as simple as hiring an ambulance without screwing that up.

Hurt, humiliated, Emilio had vowed never to fail the *senador* again, but events continued to conspire against him. He *had* to get an ambulance. To return to Paraiso without one was unthinkable.

So Emilio stole one.

Quite easy, actually. He'd parked his own car at an indoor garage, then walked two blocks to the lot of one of the ambulance services. Amid the tumult of the storm, they never heard him jump start the engine and drive away.

A particularly violent blast of wind buffeted the ambulance as it crossed the one-car bridge over the ravine. The top-heavy vehicle lurched and for an instant—just an instant—Emilio lost control as it seemed to roll along on only two wheels. It slewed and skidded and veered toward the guardrail, but before he could panic there came a thump and it rocked back onto all four wheels again.

And then a deafening *pop* and a sizzle as a blinding bolt of lightning wide as a man arced into the base of a huge ponderosa pine on the far side of the ravine. There was no pause between the flash and the thunder. The ambulance, the bridge, the entire ravine shook with the deafening crash.

Emilio slowed as he blinked away the purple after-image of the flash. Through the blur he saw flames licking at the blackened trunk of the pine. The whole tree was swaying wildly in the wind . . . seemed to be moving toward him.

He blinked again and cried out in terror as he saw the huge pine toppling toward him. He floored the accelerator, swerving the ambulance ahead on the bridge. The right rear fender screeched against the metal side rail. Emilio bared his clenched teeth and let loose a long, low howl as he kept the pedal welded to the floor. Had to move, had to get this huge, filthy *puerco* going and keep it going, couldn't go back, couldn't even *look* back, straight ahead was the only way, even if it looked like he was driving into the face of certain death, his only hope was to get off this bridge and onto the solid ground straight ahead on the far side of the ravine. Because this bridge was a goner.

Branches slashed, crashed, smashed against the roof and windshield, spiderwebbing the glass in half a dozen places. It held, though, and Emilio kept accelerating. He heard the flashers and sirens tear off the roof as he slipped the ambulance under the falling trunk with only inches to spare. But he wasn't home yet. He heard and felt the huge pine's impact directly behind him. The ambulance lurched sideways as the planked surface of the span canted right and tilted upward ahead of him. He fought to keep control, keep moving, keep accelerating, because he knew without looking that the bridge was going down behind him. The wet tires spun and slipped on the rapidly increasing incline and Emilio filled the cabin with an open-throated scream of mortal fear and defiant rage.

Emilio Sanchez refused to die here, smashed on the rocks

a hundred feet below. His destiny was not to meet his end as a storm victim, a mere statistic.

The tires caught again, the ambulance lunged forward, its big V-8 Cadillac engine roaring, pushing the vehicle up the tilting incline and onto the glistening asphalt and solid ground.

Emilio slammed on the brakes and sagged against the steering wheel, panting. When he'd caught his breath, he held his hands before his face and watched them shake like a palsied old man's. Then he stepped out into the wind and rain and looked back.

The bridge was down. The giant pine had broken its back, crashing through the center of its span and dragging the rest of it to the floor of the ravine.

Emilio began to laugh. He'd stolen an ambulance and now he couldn't use it. No one could use it. And no one would be leaving Paraiso, not Emilio, not the *senador*, and certainly not Charlie.

Prisoners in Paradise.

His laughter died away as he remembered the fourth occupant of Paraiso. That ancient body. He'd have to do something about that. It was evidence against him. He had to find a way to dispose of it. Permanently.

"Turn here."

Dan sat behind the wheel of their rented Taurus and stared at the electric security gate that stood open before them. Through the wind-whipped downpour he made out identical red-and-white signs on the each of the stone gateposts:

PRIVATE PROPERTY
NO TRESPASSING
VIOLATORS WILL BE
PROSECUTED

"Are you sure?" Dan said. "This is a private road."

"Turn here," the voice from the backseat repeated.

Dan glanced at Kesev in the front passenger seat.

The bearded man nodded agreement that they should proceed through the gate.

"Yes. The feeling is strong. The Mother is near."

Dan then turned to look at Carrie where she sat in the back seat, staring up the private road.

She wore one of Dan's faded plaid flannel shirts over his oldest pair of jeans, and a pair of dirty white sneakers they'd found in the housekeeper's closet. She looked like a refugee from a Seattle grunge band.

Once again Brad's AmEx card had come in handy for the tickets and the rental car agency. They'd drive south from San Francisco, following Carrie's directions as she took them deeper and deeper into increasingly severe weather. Now they were somewhere near the coast in Monterey County.

Dan faced front and did as he was told.

He was on autopilot now. His head throbbed continually, but it had been aching so long now he barely noticed anymore. The post-concussion dizziness and nausea were what plagued him physically. Emotionally and intellectually . . . he was numb.

With no sleep for thirty-six hours, with the woman he loved murdered but sitting in the backseat giving him directions toward the corporal remains of the Virgin Mary, what else was there to do but shut down his emotions, turn off his rational faculties, and become some sort of servo-mechanism?

Go through the motions, follow instructions to get to where you're going, do, do, do, but don't think, don't question, and for God's sake, don't feel.

Because mixed with the guilty joy of having Carrie back was the horrific realization that she wasn't really back . . . not really back at all. And Dan knew if he unlocked his emotions he'd go mad, leap from the car, and run screaming through the trees.

So he kept everything under lock and key, turned the car onto the narrow asphalt path, and kept his eyes on the road.

Water sluiced down the incline toward the Taurus but the front-wheel drive kept them moving steadily. Pine needles, pine cones, leaves, and fallen branches littered the roadway. Dan drove over them, letting them snap and thud against the underbelly of the car. He didn't care. Didn't care if they punctured the oil pan or the gas tank. All he wanted was to get where he was going. Somewhere ahead was the Virgin, and with her maybe the man who shot Carrie.

And then what will I do? he wondered.

Whatever he did or didn't do, Dan sensed that he was on his way toward a rendezvous with destiny . . . or something very much like it. Whatever it was that lay ahead, he wanted to confront it and have done with it. Things had to change. *Something* had to give.

Because he couldn't go on like this much longer.

The trees thinned as they came to the top of a rise. It looked open ahead. And then Dan saw why it was open: a deep ravine lay before them.

"Keep going?" Dan said.

"Straight ahead," Carrie said.

"I see a bridge," Kesev said, pointing.

Dan gunned the engine. The car accelerated.

"And so, *Senador*," Emilio said, spreading his hands expressively, "I'm afraid we are stuck here."

Arthur Crenshaw nodded slowly, amazed at his own serenity. Here he was, trapped in a house that was little more than a giant bay window set in a cliff overhanging the ocean, looking down the barrel at the most powerful Pacific storm on record. He'd watched the front steamroll in, the lightning-slashed clouds sweep past, blotting out the rest of the world as the storm launched its assault on the coast—his *coast*. And every time he'd thought he'd seen the peak of the storm, it got worse. The ocean below churned and frothed like an enormous Jacuzzi; thirty-foot waves lashed at the rocks, hurling foam a hundred feet in the air; wind and rain battered the huge windows, warping and rattling the glass, and yet he was not afraid.

That amazed him.

Perhaps he was too drained to be afraid.

Charlie was worse.

Arthur didn't need a CD-4 count to know that. Instead of falling, Charlie's fever had risen through the night. He was now in a coma.

His son was dying.

Arthur moved to Charlie's side, passing the so-called miraculous relic as he did. He was tempted to boot the piece of junk off the table, even drew his foot back to do so, but for some reason changed his mind at the last moment. Why bother? Just another in a long line of fakes. And to think a young woman had been killed in order to bring it here.

And then it occurred to Arthur that perhaps that was why Charlie had not been healed. An innocent life had been snuffed out in order to save Charlie's, and so Charlie could not be saved. Because a life had been taken on one end of the country, another life would be allowed to burn out on the other. A balancing of the scales.

Rage flared. Damn Emilio!

But he'd only been following orders. Arthur remembered his own words: *Bring me that body—no matter what the cost.*

But he'd meant money and effort and expense—not life. Hadn't he?

Not that it mattered now. The inescapable reality of Charlie's impending death was truly hitting home for the first time.

"He's going to die, Emilio," he said, staring at Charlie's slack features. "Charlie . . . my son . . . flesh of my flesh and Olivia's . . . the last surviving part of Olivia . . . is going to be gone. Why didn't I appreciate him while he was here, Emilio? When did I stop thinking of him of a son and start seeing him as a liability? That never would have happened if Olivia were still here. She was my heart, Emilio. My soul. When I lost her, something went out of me . . . something good. Charlie was harmless but I came

to loathe him. My own *son!* And that loathing infected
Charlie, causing him to loathe himself. That's when he
stopped being harmless, Emilio. That's when he started
becoming harmful to himself. His self-loathing made him
sick so he'd end up here in this pathetic miniature intensive
care unit in the big gaudy showplace of a home where he
was never really welcome when he was well."

Arthur bit back a sob.

"I've got so much to answer for!"

And unbidden, unwelcome, another thought slithered out
of the darkest corner of his mind, whispering how if Paraiso
were damaged by the storm . . . if, say, some of the windows were smashed and Charlie's terminally ill body were
washed out into the Pacific, he'd be listed as a storm victim
instead of an AIDS victim, wouldn't he?

Arthur shook off the thought—though, despairingly, not
without effort—and shoved it back down the dank hole it
had crawled out of.

Is this what I've come to?

He backed away from the windows as the wind doubled
its fury, battering those floor-to-ceiling panes until he was
certain one of them was going to give.

Emilio watched the *senador* retreat from the storm, but
he stood firm. He felt no fear of wind and rain. What were
they but air and water? And even if he were afraid, he would
not show it. He feared nothing . . . except perhaps that
body he'd brought back from New York. He had to get rid
of that.

An idea formed . . . put the body in the back of the
ambulance . . . send them both over the edge of the cliffs
into the wild, pounding surf far below . . .

And as the plan took shape . . .

The storm stopped.

The thunder faded, the wind died, the rain ebbed to a
drizzle. Suddenly there was only swirling fog beyond the
windows.

"*Senador*?" Emilio said. He rested his hands against the

now still windows and stared out at the featureless gray. "It is over?"

"Not yet," the *senador* said, his voice hushed. "I've read about this type of thing. I believe this is what they call the eye of the storm, the calm at its center. It won't last long. But why don't you hurry up topside and take a look around, see how much damage we've got up there. Don't get too far from the door. As soon as the wind starts to blow again, get back inside, because the back end is going to be just as bad as the front, maybe worse."

Emilio nodded. "Of course."

He hurried up the stairs and stepped outside into a dead calm.

The still, warm air hung heavy with moisture. Fog drifted lazily around him, insinuating through his clothes, clinging to his skin. So strange to have no wind. Emilio could not remember a time when a breeze wasn't blowing across the cliff tops.

And silent . . . so eerily silent. Like cotton wadding, the fog muffled everything, even the sound of the surf below. No birds, no insects, no rustling grass . . . silence.

No, wait. Emilio's ears picked up a hum, somewhere down the driveway, growing louder. It sounded almost like . . .

A car.

Emilio gasped and took a hesitant step toward the noise. He glanced at the carport. The *senador*'s limousine and the ambulance were where he'd left them. And still the sound grew louder.

No! This is not possible!

Instinctively he reached for his pistol before he remembered that he'd left it downstairs in the great room when he went into town. He hadn't retrieved it because what need for a pistol with the bridge out and Paraiso isolated from the outside world?

The bridge was *out!* He'd seen it fall. He'd almost gone down with it. How could—?

Emilio stood frozen as a Ford sedan rounded the final curve in the rain-soaked, debris-littered approach road and pulled to a stop not a hundred feet in front of him. Normally Emilio would have rushed forward to confront any trespassers, but this was different. Something was *wrong* about this car.

A short, bearded man stepped out of the passenger side and glanced around before staring at Emilio.

"The Mother," he said in an unfamiliar accent. "She is here. She *has* to be here. Where is the Mother?"

The Mother? Emilio wondered. What is he—? He was jolted by a sudden thought: Can he be talking about the ancient body below in the house?

But Emilio had questions of his own.

"How did you get here?"

"In the car," the man said with ill-concealed impatience. "We drove up the road."

"But the bridge—!"

"Yes, we came over the bridge."

"The bridge is *out!* Down!"

The bearded man looked at him as if he were crazy. "The bridge is intact. We just drove over it."

No! This couldn't be! This—

The driver door opened then and out stepped a familiar figure. Emilio steeled himself not to react, to hide the sudden mad thumping of his heart against the inner walls of his chest.

The priest! Father Daniel Fitzpatrick!

The priest looked Emilio square in the face but there was no recognition there. Without the hat, the mirrored glasses, and the phony beard he'd worn that night in the church, Emilio was a different person.

But if he hadn't come looking for Emilio, if he hadn't brought the police to arrest him for the murder of the nun, why was he here?

"Where are we?" the priest asked.

Emilio was about to answer, to tell them both to get back into their car and get off the *senador*'s private property, when the rear door opened and out stepped a dead woman. He knew she was dead because he'd killed her himself.

"You," she said softly, staring at him levelly. "I know you. You murdered me. Why? You didn't have to kill me. Why did you do that?"

Something snapped within Emilio. He could stand no more. He turned and fled back inside, slamming the door behind him. As he turned the deadbolt, he leaned against the door, panting and sweating.

This was *loco*! A car carrying a walking, talking dead woman drives across a bridge that is no longer there. He was going *loco*.

He turned and shut off the power to the elevator.

Good. If they were real, they now were locked outside and would be at the mercy of the second half of the storm. If they were not real, what did it matter?

Emilio pulled himself together, took a deep breath, and descended to the great room.

"All is well topside, *Senador*."

But the *senador* did not seem to hear. He stood by Charlie's bed, staring out through the windows, a mix of awe and terror distorting his features.

Emilio followed his gaze and cringed against the stairway when he saw what was taking shape out over the Pacific and racing toward them.

"*Madre!*"

Everything had happened so fast.

You murdered me.

Dan had been momentarily stunned by Carrie's words. His mind whirled, adding a beard, hat, and glasses to the mustachioed face staring at Carrie in horrified disbelief, comparing this voice to the one he'd heard in the church, and then he was sure: This was the motherless scum who had put a bullet in her heart.

Before he'd been able to react, the man had turned and dashed back to the hemi-dome behind him and vanished through a doorway. And then a Navy reconnaissance plane had swooshed overhead. He'd just started wondering what sort of idiot would be flying in this hellish storm when another sound captured his attention.

A dull roaring filled Dan's ears. At first he assumed it was enraged blood shooting through his battered brain, then he glanced beyond the hemi-dome and saw something impossibly tall, incalculably huge looming out of the foggy distance and hurtling toward them.

"Oh, my *God!*"

Nearly a half a mile wide and God knew how tall, it stretched—swirling, twisting, writhing—from the dim, misty heights to the sea where it terminated in an eruption of foam on the wave-racked surface of the Pacific. Water . . . an angry towering column of spinning water . . . all water . . . yet bright lights flashed within it.

To call this thing a waterspout was to call Mount Rushmore a piece of sculpture.

And it was coming here, zeroed in on this spot.

Dan spun around, looking for a place to hide, but saw none. The car—no . . . too vulnerable. The door in the hemi-dome—it had to lead below, to safety.

He ran to it, pulling Carrie with him, and tugged on the handle. The handle wouldn't turn, the door wouldn't budge. Kesev stood back, strangely detached as he watched death's irresistible approach.

"Locked!" Dan shouted, and began pounding and kicking at the unyielding surface. "Let us in, damn you! Open up!"

And all around him the roaring of the approaching waterspout grew to a deafening crescendo.

This is it, he thought. We're going to die right here. In a few minutes it'll all be over. But God, I'm not ready to go yet!

And then Carrie laid a hand on his shoulder, reached past him and turned the knob.

The door swung open.

Dan swallowed his shock—he had no time to wonder how the door had become unlocked—and propelled Carrie through ahead of him. Kesev followed at a more leisurely pace, closing the door behind him.

Stairs ahead, leading downward toward light. Dan went to squeeze past Carrie but she'd already begun her descent.

He followed her down the curved stairway into a huge, luxuriously furnished room. His hope of surviving this storm rose as he saw that it was carved out of the living rock of the cliff itself, and then that hope was dashed when he saw the huge glass front overhanging the ocean. The monstrous waterspout was out there, still headed directly for them, and no glass on earth would stop that thing.

He noticed two—no, three—other people in the room: a new face, unconscious in a hospital bed, the man who had shot Carrie, and . . . Senator Arthur Crenshaw. The killer and the senator stood transfixed before the onrushing doom.

And supine beside the bed . . . the Virgin.

Carrie must have spotted her, too, for she began moving toward the body . . .

Just as the windows exploded.

With a deafening crash every pane shattered into countless tiny daggers. Dan leaped upon Carrie to shield her—she was already dead, he remembered as he pushed her to the floor and covered her, yet his instincts still propelled him to protect her. Instead of slashing everyone and everything in the room to ribbons, the glass shards blew outward, sucked into the swirl of the storm outside.

A thundering roar filled the room as warm sea water splashed against his back, soaking him. Dan squeezed his eyes shut, encircled Carrie with his arms, and held her cold body tight against him . . . one last embrace . . .

Any second now . . .

But nothing happened. The water continued to splatter him but the roar of the waterspout remained level. Dan lifted his head and risked a peek.

It had backed off to a quarter mile or so, but still it was out there in the mist, dominating the panoramic view, lit by flashes within and around it, swirling, twisting, a thousand yards wide, snaking from the sea to the sky, but moving no closer.

Dan rose and studied it. For no reason he could explain, it occurred to Dan that it seemed to be . . . waiting.

Ahead of him, the senator and the murderer were strug-

gling to their feet and staring at it through the empty
windowframes.

"What *is* that?" Senator Crenshaw cried.

"Not 'what,'" Carrie said as she rose to her feet behind
Dan. "*Who.*"

The senator turned and stared at her a moment. He
seemed about to ask her who *she* was, then decided that
wasn't important now.

"'Who?'" He glanced back at the looming tower. "All
right, then . . . *who* is it?"

"It's Him," Carrie said, beaming. She pointed to the
Virgin. "He's come for His Mother."

The senator glanced at the Virgin, gasped, and gripped
the edge of the hospital bed for support. Dan looked to see
what was wrong.

The Virgin was changing.

The sea water from the spout that had soaked into her
robes, into her skin and hair, was having a rejuvenating
effect. The blue of the fabric deepened, her hair darkened
and thickened, and her face . . . the cheeks were filling
out, the wrinkles fading as color surged into her skin.

The murderer cringed back and murmured something in
Spanish as the senator leaned more heavily against the bed.
Carrie moved closer and dropped to her knees. Dan glanced
to his right and saw that Kesev, even the imperturbable
Kesev, was gaping in awe.

And then the Virgin moved.

Moving so smoothly it seemed like a single motion, she
sat up, then stood and faced them.

Dan saw Kesev drop to his knees not far from Carrie, but
Dan remained standing, too overwhelmed to move.

She was small framed, almost petite. Olive skin, deep,
dark hair, Semitic features, not attractive by Dan's tastes,
but he sensed an inner beauty, and there was no denying the
strength that radiated from her sharp brown eyes.

And those eyes were moving, finally fixing on Carrie,
kneeling before her. Smiling like a mother gazing upon a
beloved child, she reached out and touched Carrie's head.

"Dear one," the Virgin said softly. Her voice was gentle, soothing. "We're almost through here."

Her smile faded as she turned to Senator Crenshaw.

"Arthur," she said. "The prayermaker."

Crenshaw held her gaze, but with obvious difficulty.

"Emilio," she said, frowning at the murderer. "The killer."

He turned away.

Then it was Dan's turn.

A tiny smile curved her lips as she trapped his eyes with her own.

"Daniel. The hunger-feeder."

Dan felt lifted, exalted. He sensed her approval and basked in it.

Finally she turned away and Dan felt the breath rush out of him. He hadn't realized he'd been holding it. She could have called him vow-breaker, fornicator, doubter . . . so many things. But hunger-feeder . . . he'd take that any day.

Her expression was neutral as she faced Kesev.

"So, Iscariot . . . you broke another trust."

Iscariot! Dan's mind reeled. No . . . it couldn't be!

"Mother, events conspired against me. I beg your forgiveness."

"It is not my place to forgive."

"Perhaps it is *I* who should forgive!" Iscariot said, rising to his feet. "Once again I have been used! *Used!*"

"You are not alone in that," the Virgin said pointedly.

Iscariot's head snapped back, as if he been struck, but he recovered quickly.

"Perhaps not. But it is I who have been reviled throughout the Christian Era. And yet without me, there would *be* no Christian Era—no crucifixion, no resurrection."

"You wish to be celebrated for betraying Him?"

"No. Just understood. I believed in Him more than the others—I was led to believe He was divine. I thought He would destroy the Romans—all of them—as soon as they dared to lay a hand on Him. But he didn't! He allowed them to torture and kill him! *I* was the one who was betrayed!

And I've spent nearly two thousand years paying for it, most of them alone, all of them miserable. Haven't I suffered enough?"

Her expression softened into sympathy. "I decide nothing, Judas. You know that."

Judas Iscariot! Of course! It all fit.

The scroll's author had mentioned being educated as a Pharisee, and of being an anti-Roman assassin, using a knife—they were called *iscarii*. Judas Iscariot had been all those things. And *Kesev* was Hebrew for . . . *silver*!

"But you hung yourself!" Dan blurted.

The man he'd known as Kesev looked at him and nodded slowly. "Yes. Many times. But I was not allowed to die."

"W-why are you here?" Crenshaw said.

The Virgin turned to him and pointed to Emilio.

"Because you told him to bring me here."

"Yes-yes," Crenshaw said quickly, "and I'm terribly sorry about that. Grievously sorry." He pointed at the waterspout still roaring outside the empty window frames. "But why is He here?"

Again the Virgin pointed to Emilio.

"Because you told him to bring me here."

"*No!*" Emilio screamed. He had a pistol—no silencer this time—and was holding it in a two-handed grip. The wavering barrel was pointed at the Virgin. A wild look filled his eyes; he crouched like a cornered animal as he let loose a rapid-fire stream of Spanish that Dan had difficulty following. Something about all this being a *treta*, a trick, and he'd show them all.

Then he began pulling the trigger and firing at the Virgin.

The reports sounded sharp and rather pitiful against the towering roar from outside. Dan didn't know where the bullets went. Emilio was firing madly, the empty brass casings flying through the air and bouncing along the floor, but the Virgin didn't even flinch. No holes appeared in her robes, and Dan saw no breakage in the area behind her. The bullets just seemed to disappear after they left the muzzle.

Finally the hammer clinked on an empty chamber. Emilio

lowered the pistol and stood staring at his untouched target. With a a feral whine he cocked his arm to throw it at her.

That was when the light went out.

Not the electricity—the light. An instant blackness, darker than a tomb, darker than the back end of a cave in the deepest crevasse of the Marianas Trench. Such an absolute absence of light that for an instant Dan panicked, unsure of up or down.

And then a scream—Emilio's voice, filled with unbearable agony as it rose to a soul-tearing crescendo, and then faded slowly, as if he were falling away through space.

The blackness, too, faded, allowing meager cloud-filtered daylight to reenter the room. And when Dan could once again make out the details of the room, he saw that Emilio was gone. His pistol lay on the rug, but there was no trace of the man who owned it.

Dan staggered back and slumped against a support column. He leaned there, feeling weak. So fast . . . one moment a man in frenzied motion, the next he was gone, swallowed screaming by impenetrable blackness.

But gone where?

"Oh, please!" the senator cried, dropping to his knees and thrusting his clasped hands toward the Virgin. "*Please!* I meant you no harm, I meant no one any harm in bringing you here. I only wanted to help my son. You can understand that, can't you? You had a son yourself. I'd give anything to make mine well again."

"Anything."

"Absolutely *any*thing."

"Then you must give up *every*thing," she told him. "All your possessions—money, property—and all your power and ambitions. Give everything away to whomever you wish, but give it up, all of it, get it out of your life, out of your control, and your son will live."

"Charlie will live?" he said in a hushed voice as he struggled to his feet.

"Only if you do what I have said."

"I will," Senator Crenshaw said. "I swear I will!"

"We shall see," the Virgin said.

Dan had gathered enough of his wits and strength to dare to address her.

"Why are you here?" he said, then glanced at Carrie. "Is it our fault? Did we cause all this?"

"It was time," the Virgin said. "Time for Him to return and speak to His children. And what I say now shall be heard by all His children."

25

Kiryat Bialik, Israel

Customs Inspector Dov Sidel sat before the TV in his apartment sipping tea while his wife Chaya did the dishes. He was half dozing, half watching a special on the Holocaust when the picture dissolved into the face of a woman.

Dov stared at her and she stared back. Something familiar about her face. He felt he knew her, and yet he couldn't quite place her.

Oh, well . . .

He reached forward and turned the channel knob. The same face. He turned again and again and it was the same on every channel, even the unused frequencies. This woman's face, in perfect reception.

And then it struck him. That relic, that body that had been slipped past him as a sculpture, the one he'd reported as being on display in New York. This woman resembled a younger version of that mummified body. In fact, the longer he stared at her the more convinced he became.

He was reaching for the phone when Chaya screamed from the kitchen.

Manhattan

Monsignor Vincenzo Riccio was just finishing his lunch alone in the dining room of the Vatican Mission when he heard a scream from the kitchen, followed by the crash of breaking china. Then another scream. He set down his coffee cup and hurried along the hall to see what was wrong.

The cook was standing by the sink, her hands pressed against her tear-streaked cheeks as she stared at the soapy water. She was praying in her native Italian.

"Gina?" Vincenzo said, approaching. "What's wrong?"

She looked up at him, her eyes filled with fear and wonder, and pointed to the water.

"Maria!"

Vincenzo stepped closer and saw a woman's face reflected in the surface of the water. Not Gina's face. Another's. And immediately he knew who she was. He felt lighthearted, giddy. He swung around, looking for someone, anyone to tell, to call over and share this wondrous moment. But then he saw the same face in the gleaming surface of Gina's stainless steel mixing bowl, in the shiny side of the pots stacked next to the sink.

She was everywhere, in every reflective surface in the kitchen.

He ran back to the dining room and there was her face again, this time in the mirror over the hutch, and in the silver side of the coffee service.

He ran into the next room where two of his fellow priests crouched before the television, pressing the channel button on the remote, but on every channel, broadcast and cable, was the same face.

Vincenzo shakily lowered himself to the edge of a chair, and sat and waited.

Cashelbanagh, Ireland

Seamus O'Halloran paused on his front stoop and sniffed the clean coolness of the early evening air. He looked about his empty yard. After word spread that the monsignor from the Vatican had found a perfectly natural explanation for the tears, the crowds of faithful no longer flocked to Cashelbanagh to see the Weeping Virgin. In some ways he missed the throngs on his side lawn waiting breathlessly for the next tear, and in other ways he did not. It was nice to be able to work around the yard without clusters of strangers watching over your shoulder. And he no longer had those reporter folks asking him the same questions over and over again.

Life was back to normal again. Which meant it was time for him to head down to Blaney's for a pint. But first he decided he'd take a look at the side lawn and see how it was coming along. He strolled around the corner of the house and admired the grass. Without the constant trampling of the crowds, it was filling in smooth and green again. As he turned to go, he glanced up at his grandfather Danny's painting of the Blessed Mother and froze.

The painting was changing. He watched, rooted to the ground by terror, as her skin tones darkened while her features ran and rearranged themselves into a different face.

When she smiled at him, Seamus uprooted himself and ran shouting for his wife.

Everywhere . . .

In the streets of Manhattan there is gridlock. The ever-swirling schools of cars, trucks, taxies, and buses screech to a halt as a face appears in their side- and rearview mirrors. It is seen dimly on the surface of every windowpane and brightly in every puddle. It is the same across the country, in the towns, in the cities, in the fields, in schools, barrooms, and on the computer screens of corporate offices.

And across the world, in Sydney, Beijing, Luzon, New Delhi, Baghdad, Tunis, Johannesburg, Bosnia, Quito, and Rome, it is the same. Every surface capable of reflecting an image is filled with the same face.

For a moment a fascinated world stops, gathers together, and watches.

As she begins to speak, the billions of watchers, even the deaf, hear her words and understand.

"I bring you word from our Creator. The words I say are His, not mine, and He wishes all of you to listen. I shall call Him 'He' simply because that is how we traditionally think of the Creator, but He is neither 'He' nor 'She.' What can those words mean when there is only one? And He is the One.

"I was one of you, and for a short time, He was part of me. We have touched, and for that reason I am allowed to be His voice. Listen:

"Today marks the end of the two-thousandth year since the Creator allowed an infinitesimal fragment of Himself to gestate in my womb and become human. He dwelt among a subjugated people who believed in a single God and He planted his message of kinship among all humans there.

"I feel your shock and puzzlement as you wonder about Christmas, about December twenty-fifth, still months away. Your dating of the Coming is wrong, wrong as to the year as well as the month, wrong as are so many things in your Gospels and traditions.

"One thing is true: He said He would return and now He has, but He is not pleased with the way His message has been distorted and manipulated and prostituted and profiteered during the intervening millennia. You all have the same Parent, therefore you are all kin. He did not create you so you could divide up into warring factions. Yet you have done just that.

"You, His children, who have so recently come through a century-long crisis of nations that threatened your continued existence, now have a chance for a glorious future if you can but learn to see past the walls that divide you. There is peace between many nations now, and a chance for peace between all nations soon. But after that there must be peace between people. One to one. You must learn to recognize the walls that divide you and break them down. One by one.

"Tear down your walls, children, and find Harmony.

"You have become masters of your world. You have struggled to the apex of your corner of Creation. You rule it now. But with mastery comes obligation. The rulers of Creation become responsible for it.

"Remember this: every living thing, animal, reptile, vegetable, contains a spark of the Creator. You hold within yourselves the brightest spark, but not the only spark. It is arrogant of you to think that all other living things were put here merely to be disposed of at your whim. They were not. A balance must be struck. It is a law of Creation that one thing must die that another may live, a law that holds true for all things, for the plants as well as the animals. But you fail in your responsibility when you wantonly lay waste to the land. You dim the spark within when you kill for sport and not for sustenance, when you kill for mere vanity to steal another creature's beauty to wear as your own, or cause a creature pain to test the paints and scents you daub on your bodies. All life has value. Yes, there is a hierarchy in that value, but nothing that lives is without it.

"And if you must respect the place of the lower life-forms in the world around you, certainly you must cherish the life-right of your fellow humans a thousand-fold more. You must not diminish, must not damage, must not shorten the lives around you, for in doing so you also smother His spark within yourself. And nothing dims that spark, nothing hardens the human heart to the value of human life more than the ghastly slaughter of war. You must halt all war, children, especially the unseen war: Never shall there be true peace around you while you wage war on the unborn lives within you.

"Respect *all* life, children, and find Harmony.

"Abolish your ceremonies, your communions, your sacrifices, real and symbolic; discard your dietary laws, cast off your clerical vestments, disband your sects, cease calling yourselves Catholic or Christian or Jew or Muslim or Buddhist, for these customs, these identifications, these sects, these labels serve only to set you apart from your kin.

"Silence your prayers. He will not answer because He will not listen while you call out from within walls that separate you from your kin. Cease your worship, your kneeling, your bowing, your prostrating, your fasts, self-denials, and self-inflicted injuries. You demean not only yourselves but your Creator when you believe that such obeisances please Him. Harmony is the only prayer He heeds.

"Abandon your rituals, children, and find Harmony.

"Do not look to Him for guidance or relief; look instead to each other.

"Close your churches, your temples, your mosques, for these are the most tangible and obvious walls between you. Gather instead in the streets and parks and squares where there are no walls. Try to reach Him by reaching each other.

"Discard your Bible, your Koran, your Torah, for each is only partly true, and they lead you into the belief that you have found the One True Path to God, or the One True Voice that will catch His ear. You have not. And that delusion raises another wall, a wall of exclusivity. He did not create you to be divided.

"Forsake your beliefs, children, and find Harmony.

"I say again, use your own lives well, and respect each life around you. You are all kin. Touch one another. You are all living this life together. And so you must all work together toward creating Heaven. It is possible. You have the power. You need only find it and use it.

"If you do not, if you continue along the same path you have trod these thousands of years, you will create a hell for yourselves and your children.

"Look not for a Third Coming. And act not in fear of eternal reward or punishment. Your reward or punishment is here. This is your world, these are your lives. He has given them to you. Use them well, make the most of them, make them *mean* something, make them *count*. For *this* is your Heaven or Hell. You have the power to make it either. The choice is yours.

"Do not wait for the Rapture of the faithful, or for the Tribulation of the unbeliever. They will not come from on high. Your rapture arises from each other, as do all your tribulations. Heaven or hell will be of your own making. You have but to choose.

"This then is the whole of the law:

"Find Harmony, children, and you will find Love."

26

Paraiso

Dan had listened raptly. She'd been speaking to the world, he knew, to all of humankind, but he'd felt as if she were speaking only to him. For what she'd said reflected exactly his innermost thoughts and feelings. Because of his vows, his membership in the priesthood, he'd been afraid to vocalize them, even to himself. But now that *she* had said them, he could acknowledge what he'd sensed, *known* all along.

He wondered if that was why he was here, in this house, in her presence — in *His* presence — why he'd been with her all along.

As the Virgin finished speaking she touched Carrie's bowed head and said, "Come, my devoted one."

Carrie rose to her feet. The Virgin held out her hand and Carrie took it.

The Virgin said, "Our time here is done."

Our time is done. What did she mean by that?

Dan swallowed and addressed her again.

"Wait . . . please. Can't you . . . bring her back? Make her live again? You can do that, can't you?"

The Virgin shook her head. "Her time here is through. She is coming with me."

"With you? You're taking her away? Where?" Dan felt a sob building in his chest. He still hadn't come to terms with Carrie's death. "Oh, please. I've only just begun to know her. You can't take her away from me now."

"I haven't taken her away. One of your brothers did that."

And then Carrie and the Virgin began to rise.

When they were floating half a dozen feet above the floor, they began to drift toward the ruined windows, toward the sea, toward the towering column of water that waited for them.

"Wait!" cried another voice. It was the man who called himself Kesev, whom the Mother called Iscariot. "Mother, please wait!"

Their seaward drift slowed.

"Yes, Judas?"

"What of me?"

"What of you, Judas?"

"Am I to be left here alone? Haven't I suffered enough? Two thousand years, Mother! Haven't I earned forgiveness?"

"Forgiveness does not come from me, Judas. You know that."

"Then intercede for me, Mother. He listens to you. Don't leave me here alone. Everyone I've ever known has left me. Please . . . I do not deserve this anymore."

The Virgin paused, as if listening, then extended her free hand toward Judas.

"Come."

Judas rushed forward, leaped to catch her hand, and when their fingers touched, he floated up to join her, clutching her hand in both of his.

Dan saw tears in Judas's eyes, and felt them well up in his own. Carrie . . . Carrie was leaving.

He fought the urge to call her back, knowing she wouldn't, couldn't respond. He'd lost her—not now, not today, but yesterday, when Emilio had put a 9mm hole in her heart.

The three of them drifted through the ruined window frames, out into the storm, toward the gargantuan swirling, roaring column of water that loomed outside.

Dan ran to the frames, clung to one, leaning over the precipice that fell away to the pounding surf below. He sobbed unashamedly and let the tears flow down his cheeks.

He watched longingly as their progress accelerated and their retreating forms shrank.

Soon they were lost in the mist.

Moments later, the cyclopean waterspout began to retreat, shrinking as it moved off into the Pacific. Gradually it thinned from a thousand yards across to a slender tornado-like funnel, and then it was gone.

The storm, too, was gone. Magically, the encircling winds died, the fog melted away, the clouds dispersed. Midday sunlight burst free and flooded the sky, warming Dan's face and spirit.

He clung there a few moments longer, wiping his eyes, gathering his wits, girding himself to face a world without Carrie. Finally, when he turned away, he saw Senator Crenshaw leaning over the hospital bed, whispering to his unconscious son.

"Did you hear that, Charlie? You're going to be well again. All I've got to do is give away everything I own. But that's no problem, Charlie. I'll set up trusts for everything, even for Paraiso. That way all my assets will be out of my control, but we can still live here. And I'll put my nomination bid on hold. I won't do anything until you're better, Charlie. After that, you'll see the god*damndest* campaign you ever saw in your life. You just wait and see, Charlie."

As Dan walked past he couldn't resist saying, "You just don't get it, do you."

"What?" Crenshaw said, straightening. "What do you mean?"

"Weren't you listening?"

"Of course, I—"

"Then think about what you heard, fool."

Dan could spare not any more time here. There was a new world outside. He could feel it.

He hurried up the stairs and burst out into the new fresh air. He had no idea what he'd find when he got back to civilization, but he knew the events of the past few moments had changed it forever.

For better or for worse? And for how long? He would see.

He dearly wished Carrie were here to explore it with him. And maybe she was. She'd touched his life so deeply, he knew he'd always carry a part of her with him.

He thrust his hands into his pockets and realized that Carrie was still with him in a more tangible way. He pulled out her Ziploc of powder and clippings and stared at them. Whatever he found out there in the new world, he was sure now that the new age of miracles was not over yet.

Perhaps it had just begun.

Find Harmony, children.
And you will find Love.